"You look hungry."

He was, indeed.

Sunny blushed, her face turning an exquisite crimson. Quickly she snatched up the picnic basket and spread a blanket beneath the overhead rocks.

Bar could see that she was nervous about being alone with him this long. He wanted to reassure her, but to do so would only lead to trouble. He wanted to touch her hand. His heart leapt every time he thought about it.

Just touch her, he told himself.

Sunflower
Sky

SAMANTHA HARTE

HarperPaperbacks
A Division of HarperCollinsPublishers

HarperPaperbacks *A Division of* HarperCollins*Publishers*
10 East 53rd Street, New York, N.Y. 10022

Copyright © 1994 by Sandra L. Hart
All rights reserved. No part of this book may be used or reproduced in any manner whatsoever without written permission of the publisher, except in the case of brief quotations embodied in critical articles and reviews. For information address HarperCollins*Publishers*,
10 East 53rd Street, New York, N.Y. 10022.

Cover illustration by R.A. Maguire

First printing: September 1994

Printed in the United States of America

HarperPaperbacks, HarperMonogram, and colophon are trademarks of HarperCollins*Publishers*

❖ 10 9 8 7 6 5 4 3 2 1

DEDICATED TO

Laura and Joe
for taking a chance on love

Bob
for taking a chance on life even after
reading Revelations

Erica
for taking a chance on Bob

Kathy
for taking a chance on God

David
for taking a chance on yourself

and

Justen
for being you

. . . Long time coming . . . to the sweet, sweet water,
Land of my heart
Where primroses bloom
And my love smiles down . . . from a sunflower sky.

. . . I've traveled so far . . . from the sweet, sweet water,
Land of my heart
Where the grass grows green
And my love smiles down . . . from a sunflower sky.

Sunflower Sky

1

Crystal Springs, Colorado 1881

A chilling wind swept up High Street, warning Susanna Summerlin to hurry. The looming Rockies, still blue shadowed with snow in the recesses, looked forbidding under a ceiling of black rain clouds. Lightning flickered, and thunder followed, growling like a hungry mongrel in the distance.

Clutching her percale sunbonnet in place, Susanna ducked into Tilsy's Mercantile. The big display window shook as a gust of wind slammed the door against the wall. The brass bell at the top of the door jangled wildly.

"Whoa!" Frank Tilsy called. "That window came all the way from St. Louie." He climbed down the ladder that leaned against the uppermost shelf on the far wall. Reaching the floor, he saw Susanna and softened his startled expression. "Oh, it's you, Sunny. Mornin', dear. Looks like a washer comin'."

Pressing the heavy door closed, Sunny steadied herself. This day had been long in coming. She needn't rush about like a nervous ninny on account of a little rain. Drawing a deep breath, she gave Frank her best smile. "I forgot my umbrella."

The narrow interior of Frank's store delighted Sunny as much now as when she had first seen it as a child of eight. Frank displayed five of everything from neatly arranged tins of peaches to brown bottles of snakeroot oil on the shelves along each side wall. Fringed reticules and nickel-plated hair combs lay in rows on the top shelf of the glass-fronted mahogany case near the door. Storm lanterns, kid gloves, and factory-made hats hung from the joists overhead.

Sunny pressed her calico skirts against her legs to move between iron-bound barrels and rough berry crates crowding the floor without disturbing anything. She hugged Frank, her mother's longtime beau, and kissed his cheek. He looked solid and reliable in his collarless blue shirt, plain web suspenders, and brown flannel trousers, all much in need of a woman's attention, she noted with scheming affection.

"I'm ready to pick up the wallpaper I ordered," she said, still breathless. "This is going to be the best birthday surprise Ma ever had. When you get done hanging the paper for me, she's going to think you're awfully clever, matching that pattern of yellow roses."

Frank had a fleshy face that creased up nicely when he smiled, but he wasn't smiling now. He smoothed his thinning gray hair with a big, pale hand. "The freight wagon threw a wheel coming up the pass yesterday. It'll be days before the goods get here."

"And my wallpaper?"

"It was on that wagon."

"Wouldn't you just know it," Sunny said. Then she smiled quickly. She didn't want to distress Frank. He was a workhorse of a man who would have gotten her anything she wanted if he could have.

"I did so want Ma to have something nice this year. You know how she is, never thinking of herself. Her room looks as plain as a paper bag."

With his brow knit, Frank polished his oval spectacles. Another rumble of thunder shook the window glass. Hooking the spectacles over his ears, he squinted at the darkening sky beyond. "I could take the train to Denver. There's sure to be more paper like the pattern you ordered."

Sunny's heart lifted. "You'd do that for me? You're a dear." She gave him another hearty squeeze that left him blushing. "That would be so good of you."

"I want your ma to be pleased on her birthday, too," he said.

"If I have anything to say about it, she's going to say yes to you. And soon. Oh, look how dark it's getting. I'd better hurry." Sunny patted the bulging buckskin pouch under her arm. "I've sold enough liniment to pay off the loan six months early. Can you believe it, after all these years? Ma's going to be doubly surprised on her birthday."

Frank broke into a grin. "I told you that recipe was worth more'n two bits a bottle. Got any more? I'm sold out again."

"I'll bring a new batch in a few days." She hurried to the window and looked out. Another silver zigzag of lightning leapt between the foothills and churning clouds.

"Don't be late Friday," she said as she jerked the

door open. "At least we'll *have* the paper, even if we won't have time to put it up."

She ducked outside and dragged the door closed. Ten years had passed since her beloved father had died. Abel Summerlin's debts had forced her mother to turn their sprawling home on Pine Ridge Road into a boardinghouse. The two women had worked long hours every day since to pay off the debts and the loan they had needed to buy linens and supplies for their first year.

Sunny missed her father with all her heart, but with their loan about to be paid, it was time for her mother to send the boarders packing and marry Frank. Sunny longed for a life of her own. She couldn't think about that until she had Ma settled and happy.

As Sunny stepped down from the boardwalk, big raindrops hit the broad, dusty street in front of her. Making an unladylike display of her calfskin boots and the petticoats and long drawers beneath her blue calico skirts, Sunny sprinted between two loaded ranch wagons to the stone bank.

How the town had changed since she was a child, Sunny thought, pausing on the boardwalk to gawk at the new hotel on the corner. Rain pelted her sunbonnet, causing it to wilt as she admired three stories of yet-to-be-painted pine clapboard and more glinting St. Louis-made windows. The structure dwarfed every false-fronted building on the street, but compared to the massive backdrop of Granite Pass and the surrounding rocky ranges, the Crystal Springs Congress Hotel looked like a miniature.

The town still had a few shadowed side streets lined with saloons, but generally Crystal Springs was peaceful now, a decent place where a young woman like Sunny could spin dreams of a husband and family someday. On this eventful morning the key to Sunny's dreams was about to unlock her future. All she had to do was turn loose of every dime she had saved over the past four years, she thought.

Squaring her shoulders, she stepped through the bank's iron-reinforced doorway into a hushed interior cool enough to be a cave. Her heart began to pound.

To the left stood the nervous young teller behind his oak-spindled grille. Catching Sunny's eye and nodding, he went on carefully counting a patron's deposit.

A low fence separated banker Ethridge Foote's desk from the common area where six more unsmiling customers stood in line. The scrawny man seated behind the desk in his threadbare brown suit was waiting for Sunny.

Sunny untied her bonnet and bared her neatly coiled chestnut hair. Brushing raindrops from her jacket, she approached the swinging gate in the presumptuous little fence like a queen entering her court.

Ethridge Foote's expression seemed especially disapproving that morning, Sunny thought. Perhaps she was late, but then again, she had never seen the man smile and shuddered to think what he might look like if he did.

Sunny knew the old bachelor far better than she wished to, because he had lived at their boardinghouse for six years. At fifty-some years he could scarcely manage the trek to the Summerlin house each evening. He couldn't drink hot coffee or chew beef steak because his teeth were bad. Inside his shoes was enough darning wool to have knit him a whole new pair of socks. Sunny knew because she'd darned his socks herself a dozen times. He wore his shirts until the cotton fabric disintegrated against her mother's washboard. His shoes only sported new soles when the old ones fell off.

Because he was such a frail-looking, cautious little man, and carried the keys to the bank's big front door in his right-hand trouser pocket, he had a little self-cocking pistol tucked in his vest. He didn't frighten Sunny, though. No, sir. All he could do was shoot the cones from a defenseless pine tree, or perhaps his elbow. He was a dyed-in-the-wool miser, about as pleasant to deal with as a skinned knee. She didn't like him, and would never trust him.

"Good morning, Mr. Foote. How are you on this fine morning?" Sunny forced a toothy smile that she knew he considered forward.

Glancing nervously toward the door Sunny had left open, Ol' Foote, as everyone secretly called him, watched from the corner of his eye as she sat down on the edge of the worn chair facing his desk. Since her eighteenth birthday Sunny had been making the payments for her mother, insisting that the unpleasant chore was part of a modern young lady's responsibility.

In truth, Sunny had taken over the duty because Ol' Fart, as *she* secretly called the parsimonious banker, could shred her mother's composure with a glance. Sunny had grown tired of seeing her mother return from the bank each month in tears, and vowed to protect her.

About that same time when she took over the books, Sunny began brewing Pa's secret recipe for horse liniment. Frank sold it at his store. She felt the price he charged was exorbitant, but Frank insisted she must make a profit. She'd been saving ever since, aiming for this very special day and this unexpected gift for her mother's fortieth birthday. Today she had a surprise for the nasty, bad-breathed Mr. Ethridge Fart. He was their lord and master no more. She and Ma would finally be free.

Before Sunny could announce her intent to pay off the loan, Foote cleared his throat. "My *dear* Miss Summerlin," he said, his voice a disapproving rasp, "I have a great number of accounts to go over before closing for the afternoon. I'm expecting a sizable cash deposit in a few minutes. Save your impudent smile and make your payment."

He withdrew his thick black ledger from the center drawer of his desk and, with an expression that made Sunny feel indignant and delinquent instead of happily victorious, he opened it to the lengthy Summerlin account.

Upside down, Sunny read the last entry. Then she looked sternly at the man. "I do hate to point out *once again,* Mr. Foote, that you've forgotten to subtract your monthly board from the balance. I believe Ma and I give you superior service. Was there a problem with the meals or laundry last month . . . sir?"

Oh, how she did hate this little ritual, she thought, returning his frigid stare. He did the same thing each month. She knew that he hoped she wouldn't notice his "oversight." If Ol' Fart had his way, she'd pay forever and he'd live at their house until he withered and blew away.

The banker scowled at the entries. He made calculations, consulted the calendar, and then with great exasperation and a surprisingly uncertain hand, subtracted ten dollars from the balance. That left a total owing of one hundred forty-three dollars and fifty-seven cents. His expression would have caused her mother to wilt, but it only made Sunny prickle with increased resentment.

Sunny dumped coins and paper bills from her pouch and slowly counted the amount due to the last penny. Her hands trembled, too, as she pushed so much money toward him.

"Paid in full," she said, her heart dancing. "Please don't mention this to Ma. It's a surprise for her birthday Friday. Next month you'll be paying *me,* unless you'd care to move into town. It's such a steep walk to our place, I know."

Looking alarmed, he counted the money three times and frowned at her as if to ask where she'd come by so much.

Her tiny smile said she had no intention of explaining. He complained constantly that her liniment stank and stayed as far as possible from the shed where she brewed it. But folks around Cassidy County swore by the gooey black syrup for horses and humans alike. Nothing relieved the swelling of joints like Summerlin Salts. Nothing cleared the sinuses like it, either.

"My cash receipt, if you please," Sunny reminded him, smiling broadly just to gall him.

He scrawled one for her.

"And the note . . . indicating payment in full, if you would be so kind." Her face ached with the effort to keep smiling.

Foote scraped his chair back, and slunk to his imposing steel safe in the rear corner. He positioned his body so that no one might chance to see him spinning the combination lock on the three-foot-high black box.

With snakelike speed, he extracted the promissory note and slammed the door. Returning to his desk, he sat heavily and took a ragged breath. Finally he lifted his pen from the holder, dipped, tapped a drop of excess black ink from the tip, and wrote "Paid in full" at the bottom of the yellowed paper. He glanced at the door and then back to Sunny. He had difficulty releasing the note to her eager grasp.

Rising, she bowed her head slightly. "Thank you, Mr. Foote, for lending us the money when we so desperately needed it to get the house in order for boarders."

He gave an indignant huff. "Your father should have thought to provide for his widow and daughter a bit more adequately."

He looked positively hateful and Sunny could not fathom why.

"He should have managed his affairs more wisely," he added.

Go, she admonished herself, *before he spoils it.* He looked angry, she thought. Hastily, she pushed her way through the swinging gate in the little fence. Why would he be unhappy to receive all the money she and her mother owed? Did he fear losing his hold over them? Did he think they'd make him move out? There was a thought.

She made the door just as Ol' Fart said, "Supper promptly at six, if you please, Miss Summerlin. I won't tolerate another late meal."

Several people standing in line turned to look.

Sunny paused in the doorway. When had they ever served late? she wondered, instantly furious. *Don't say anything. You're not a thoughtless fifteen-year-old any longer. You won't cause a scene.*

Nevertheless, she turned around. She knew her smile didn't reach her eyes. "Six *sharp,* Mr. Foote. And please do remember that Friday is my mother's birthday. It's her only day off during the year. We won't be serving supper at all. The other boarders are eating in town. I hope you've remembered to make arrangements. I wouldn't want you to go hungry."

There, she thought. Now folks knew how hard Ma worked. For all she cared, Ol' Fart could starve.

Shaking with anger, Sunny went out into the rain. "Petty little man," she muttered, her triumph tarnished. For six years he had watched her and her mother as if waiting for them to do God-knows-what. She wanted to fling the promissory note on the ground and stomp on it, but instead, she pulled the door partly closed and let the gusting wind fling it open again.

Standing on the boardwalk, Sunny let her anger cool. She had no money left. All her morning's errands were now complete. It was time to go back to her chores at home and the boredom of her daily life. She should have felt wonderful, but didn't. As she puzzled over this unexpected reaction, an old buggy with a badly cracked leather quarter top rolled to a stop at the hitching rail nearby.

A woman dressed in widow's black took great pains to secure the worn harness lines but didn't get out of the buggy.

"May I assist you down, ma'am?" Sunny asked, wondering who the woman was. "Señora," she corrected herself, noting that the woman wore a Mexican-style black lace mantilla over her head that completely obscured her face.

The woman shook her head.

Lightning split the sky. An immediate, jolting thunderclap gave Sunny a start of alarm. She ducked beneath the awning of the nearest boardwalk.

Coming down the street, taking their half out of the middle, was a ranch wagon flanked by two riders on Appaloosas. That had to be May Sue McKidrict on the seat, Sunny thought. No other girl in Cassidy County had a red wool mantle like that. Halfheartedly, Sunny waved, unsure if she was up to an encounter with the troublesome McKidrict clan that morning.

Sitting beside May Sue on the wagon seat was her father, easily the tallest, heftiest man in the county, and the most disliked, most would say.

Sunny felt hard-pressed to decide which man was more disagreeable, bony little Ethridge Foote or big, arrogant Luck McKidrict. While Ethridge Foote wielded his power with a thick ledger and scratchy steel-tipped pen, Luck McKidrict wielded his with bloody-knuckled fists and expensive guns.

Luck McKidrict had gained his nickname, some said, because he was lucky he was still alive after thirteen years in Cassidy County. The Mexicans hated him. Most whites did, too.

At last count, Luck, his two sons, and their assorted rowdy ranch hands had driven six Mexican squatter families from his range with unnecessary and excessive force. And not a white girl between the ages of twelve and forty felt safe from the McKidrict boys' crude advances.

Sporting a soggy Stetson and rain-stained duster, Lyford McKidrict, the elder son, had a dull and shiftless look about him as he rode past. Cale McKidrict was younger, about twenty-three and, drunk or sober,

thought himself irresistible. Sunny tugged her sunbonnet over her hair and hurried on before the irre-
pressible Cale might chance to see her.

She would never forget the day the three
McKidrict children had invaded Crystal Springs's
schoolhouse and crowded onto the bench behind her.
The following day, wielding a huge horn-handled
pocketknife, Cale McKidrict deftly sliced ten inches
from each of Sunny's long chestnut braids. Eight-
year-old May Sue with her long blond corkscrew curls
had wanted to have the longest hair in the county.
Thanks to her brother, Cale, thereafter she did.
Sunny's hair grew back but it still wasn't as long as
May Sue's.

The McKidricts' wagon came to a stop at the bank,
facing the Mexican woman seated in the black quarter-top buggy. Luck McKidrict in his fringed buckskin coat made a great show of getting his arrogant
bulk down from the seat. He hoisted an iron-studded
wooden strongbox to his shoulder and lugged it into
the bank as if it were filled with gold bars. For all
Sunny knew, it might be. Theirs was the largest ranch
in two counties.

Left on the seat, May Sue carried on until Cale
remembered himself, dismounted the Appaloosa, and
handed her down. More thunder rumbled and they
looked around, their expressions tired and sour.

May Sue cussed softly as she scraped mud from
her boots at the edge of the boardwalk. Then she
smacked her brothers for eyeing the nearest saloon.
"Pa said to stay sober!"

"Morning, May Sue," Sunny said as the young
woman hurried past her, still grumbling.

"Oh, how-do, Sunny. Gull-danged wind!" May Sue

clutched a shabby bow-trimmed green bonnet to her disheveled blond curls. Beneath the flapping red mantle was a puce-colored satin dress once elegant but now badly mended and stained. "And the rain. We come through a mess of it. Plumb soaked me to the bone. Maria only *thinks* she's done with the laundry. She's been at it all morning, and now I'll be bringing her more.

"Crystal Creek's all muddied up. Pa's fit to chew ten penny nails. How you be, Sunny? You ain't come to see me in an awful long while. Ain't I good enough to visit no more?"

Caught off-guard, Sunny fell into step beside her former schoolmate. "The work's never-ending with four boarders to do for, what with all the cleaning," she said, her standard excuse.

"Tell me, do. All I got is menfolks to gall me." Nervously, she glanced at Sunny and then looked away.

May Sue's cheeks were streaked as if she'd been crying, but Sunny assumed she'd gotten dusty during the long ride from their ranch that morning, and then drenched in the rain. Yet May Sue always looked smudged and shabby.

"How's Helen these days?" May Sue asked of Sunny's mother, pushing open the door to the druggist's shop.

Sunny was about to go in after May Sue and answer when she felt someone grab her elbow. She tottered backward and came shoulder to shoulder with Cale McKidrict, grinning down at her, his left cheek bulging with a wad of chewing tobacco.

As hard as she tried, Sunny couldn't bring herself to be more than civil to the overgrown boy. Cale was handsome; all the McKidricts were. But "handsome is as handsome does," as Ma always said.

"Hey, there, Ornery," Cale said with a wink. "I ain't seen you in an *awful* long time." Scratching his belly through his dingy plaid shirt, he let his gaze travel boldly down her body as if at one time he had indeed seen what was covered by her jacket and skirt.

Embarrassed, Sunny extracted her arm from his grasp. She edged back toward the shop door. She couldn't see May Sue inside, but she could hear her.

"I got to have it," May Sue was saying to the druggist.

When Sunny didn't respond to Cale's remarks, his grin wilted to a pout. He spat into the street and wiped brown drool from the corner of his mouth. "I don't know what the hell ails you, Ornery. I'm always polite to you. I've 'pologized for cuttin' off your braids more'n a thousand times now."

"I have errands to run, if you please, Cale," Sunny said, always just a bit frightened of this unwelcome admirer. "Nice to see you again."

He mimicked her words and then made a grab at her that she eluded.

"Hey, now, Ornery, I intend to call on you some fine evening. You and me, we belong together. I've always knowed it ever since the first day I seen you at the schoolhouse all decked out in them blue hair bows and white stockings. Still got them white stockings on that I like so much?" He toed her hem up several inches.

"Cale!" She whirled around. "You haven't seen me in months. You won't see me again for many more. You've gotten on just fine, and you always will. My name is not Ornery, and whether or not I wear white stockings is *none* of your business."

"What have I ever done to—"

They both could hear May Sue pleading with the druggist inside, but before Sunny could go in to explain about the freight wagon delayed down the pass, several people dashed out of the nearby bank.

"Holdup!" one of them shouted, ducking for cover on the far side of a parked delivery wagon. "She's packin' a gun!"

Seconds later, two shots sounded inside the stone building. Two more shots, and then another followed in quick succession. People on the boardwalks scattered.

Sunny didn't know what to do.

Cale froze. His grimy right hand closed on the Colt he wore holstered at his hip.

"What is it?" May Sue demanded from the druggist's doorway. Knocking Sunny aside, she stomped outside to stand beside her brother on the edge of the boardwalk, her hands on her hips. "What the hell's goin' on out here?"

The old quarter-top buggy rattled by, hellbent for leather. Standing as she drove, the Mexican woman lashed her horse, her black mantilla plastered against her face by the wind. Luck McKidrict's strongbox bounced on the seat behind her. Rounding the curve in the street, she clattered out of sight in the direction of the pass.

Frank Tilsy came to the doorway of his mercantile, a double-barreled shotgun clutched in his hands. Several more shopkeepers crept from their stores. The sheriff and his deputy came running, guns drawn.

"She shot him!" one of the patrons who had fled the bank cried, "Killed him dead."

Not Ol' Fart? Sunny thought in disbelief.

Rain began falling again as May Sue stumbled off the boardwalk into the rutted street. She looked first in the direction of the fleeing buggy and then back toward the bank. *"Pa?"*

Luck McKidrict? Sunny was incredulous. Who would have the nerve to shoot him?

The sheriff stuck his head out of the bank's doorway and waved a blood-smeared paper. "He didn't sign it. Is Doc still gone? McKidrict's taken one dead in the chest."

Holding her shabby skirts high, showing her bare legs and muddy oversized boots, May Sue ran up the street. She pushed aside the sheriff and looked inside the bank. Then her shriek split the air.

Sunny folded her arms across her stomach and turned away. She couldn't remember the last time such a thing had happened in Crystal Springs. Less than ten minutes before she had been in that bank herself. She might have been robbed or killed.

Peeking back, Sunny watched Foote emerge from the bank on unsteady legs. No one paid him the slightest heed as he staggered and finally found a seat on the edge of the boardwalk. In seconds he was drenched, looking for all the world like a drowned rat.

" . . . undertaker . . ." someone called, splashing through the mud past the hotel toward the furniture store.

Cale couldn't seem to move. His hand remained on the holster, his face registering shock. Sunny felt sick to look at him.

Still clutching her own paid promissory note in her trembling fist, Sunny sank to the bench in front of the druggist shop. Why had the Mexican woman robbed the bank and killed the meanest rancher in two counties? Now all sorts of riffraff would come to Crystal Springs, seeking the bounty Ol' Fart would surely offer for the return of that stolen strongbox.

2

Belching black smoke two hundred feet into the air, the locomotive inched toward Resurrection Pass on the Colorado side of the New Mexico Territory border. Watching from the open window for wheels slipping on the narrow iron rails, brakeman Juan Arquilla braced himself for the hairpin curve ahead. Then his attention strayed to the man sitting in the last seat of the coach car.

The man had reversed his seat to face the wall. Beside him in the unoccupied seat lay an open case lined with black velvet. For the entire fifty miles up from Novaocha in the New Mexico Territory the man had been lifting piece after machined piece from the case, painstakingly polishing, oiling, and assembling what appeared to be one of the deadliest looking long-barreled handguns Juan had ever seen.

The stranger had thick black hair curling down to his coat collar.

On Juan's last pass through the coach car he noted that he wore black merino woolen trousers, well made and new looking. His frock coat, recently brushed, was of the same material, expertly tailored to fit his broad shoulders. His boots were made of unadorned black snakeskin. Even his shirt studs were made of jet.

Save for a bit of gun oil that had crept under his fingernails, the stranger's hands were clean. He handled the parts of his gun with a concentration Juan associated with priests preparing the host.

Iron wheels screeching now, the train rounded a curve and began the treacherous descent into Bull Valley just south of the divide. At the window, Juan watched a collection of weathered adobe houses beyond an aspen stand near the rail bed. As the train's whistle whooped, his sister Tomasina and her boy came out of their house and waved.

"Crystal Springs, Colorado. Fifteen minutes," Juan called, turning from the window to see if the man in black would look up.

Except for steadying the case, the stranger never faltered in the final assembly of his ebony-handled gun. Juan saw no notches on the gleaming handgrip and supposed such a man had no need to display his reputation.

Juan hadn't heard of a bounty being offered yet for the person who had robbed the Crystal Springs Bank and shot Luck McKidrict three days before. Few in the county gave a damn about McKidrict's death, but everyone was itching to know who had dressed up like McKidrict's Mexican cook, who was Juan's own mother, and killed the rancher who so many agreed needed killing.

If Maria Arquilla hadn't been up to her elbows in laundry suds when the sheriff rode out to the McKidrict ranch after the robbery, she might have been arrested. Juan took it as a personal affront that anyone should have considered his long-suffering mother guilty even for a moment.

Juan ambled to the end of the car, tugging his boxy blue uniform coat around his hips. He glanced down to see the black-clad stranger sliding his weapon into the tooled leather folds of a custom-fitted holster lashed low on his right thigh. Juan licked his dry lips and said, "That is a very fine piece of workmanship, señor."

"Yes, it is," the stranger said.

Looking something less than thirty years, the stranger was arrestingly handsome, Juan thought. His cheeks were smoothly shaven and unlined. His eyes were a midnight blue, almost black. Juan saw no evil in them, no malice, not even hostility. The man's eyes were untroubled holes in his face.

In less time than it would take to spread the word of this bounty hunter's arrival, the man would have his quarry, Juan thought with satisfaction. Once again Cassidy County would be a serene mountain valley where decent folks could enjoy clean air, clean water, and clean living.

After the train wheezed to a stop, the bounty hunter made his way back to the horse car. Buttoning his black frock coat, Barnabas Landry led his gleaming black gelding down the ramp. He lashed his gun case to the saddle and adjusted his gun belt around his hips.

You don't have to do this, Bar reminded himself as Sundown sank to his fetlocks in the rich red mud of

Crystal Springs's depot yard. Bar's head pounded with pain so intense that his vision became blurred. The beginning of a hunt had never troubled him like this before.

His headache had started early that morning when he boarded the train. He'd hesitated then, wanting to talk himself out of the trip, but he'd heard about the robbery. A man was dead. Bar had to go.

You almost died last time, Bar reminded himself as he leaned briefly against Sundown. *That outlaw wasn't worth your life. Neither is this one.*

For a moment Bar thought he might get back on the train. Eyes burning, he squinted at the adobe depot with its crumbling pink stucco walls and weathered shutters. He could turn around.

Weeds grew knee-high everywhere. A nervous wind rattled the dry stems. The weeds looked like those which had grown around the depot back in Hickory Creek, Missouri, Bar thought, surprised to be reminded of his hometown a thousand miles away. His breath went out in a long, sad sigh.

As an imaginative lad of fourteen, he had crouched in weeds like those, playing adventuresome games of King Arthur while his father sorted mail inside the depot.

Bar remembered his father teaching him to pitch horseshoes in the town's square, too, and whiling away hours fishing along the creek, but his favorite memory was of the man's beaming smile when Bar brought home his diploma from grammar school, first in his class.

The years following the war when his father had been recovering from the amputation of his left leg had been the best of Bar's life. Together they had studied everything from Greek classics to English poetry. Bar's father had wanted Bar to be a lawyer, and Bar had sworn that he would try.

But Bar would never forget the day that gentle man fell headlong into the weeds, dead, his crutch snapping beneath him. The sound of a single gunshot rang in Bar's ears as if it had been fired just seconds ago by a reckless train robber instead of twelve years before.

Straightening his shoulders, lifting his face to the bracing chill of mountain air, Bar drew in a breath as sharp and cold as the mindless craving now driving him through the mud to the rutted street ahead.

Six months had passed since Bar had last brought in an outlaw. It had been six months since he'd felt that exquisite surge of satisfaction in his gut as he cornered his quarry and fired. Six months had been necessary to get over the devastating realization of what he'd done, and of what he feared he would be driven to do again and again.

Each time, Bar swore that he would never seek another bounty.

Since his last hunt Bar had tried harder than ever to stay clear of newspapers and general-store porch fronts where gossips gathered. He kept out of sight and out of touch, working on an isolated ranch, living a life of rigorous self-discipline.

He had tried not to think about the outlaws he'd brought to justice, all dead instead of alive. He had tried not to think of the outlaws still roaming free across the West, all needing justice meted out to them with the same swiftness and finality that had cut down his father so long ago.

Then, two days earlier, Bar had been in a Novaocha livery, when he overheard the story of Luck McKidrict, gunned down in a two-bit bank by somebody posing as a Mexican señora.

Since that moment Bar hadn't been able to forget about the two surviving McKidrict sons, or the daughter. Bar imagined two bewildered little boys and a girl, weeping beside a grave. He had to help them.

This time he'd stay in control, Bar assured himself. He would check everything out carefully. He would determine where to look for the coward who had dressed as a woman in order to rob a bank. He would follow the trail and bring back *this* outlaw alive. Swift and simple.

You will kill before you can think, a voice inside reminded him. *You won't remember pulling the trigger.*

Behind him, the locomotive chuffed impatiently. The steam whistle bleated once, loudly enough to echo across the valley.

Bar wished he could go all the way back to Missouri, to start over, but the memory of his father, lying face down in those weeds, prevented rational thought. Inside Bar there was a wound running as red with grief as the blood on the back of his father's blue shirt.

Impatiently, Sundown stamped his hoof. Red mud splattered against Bar's black woolen pant leg and Bar was brought back to reality. "Easy, boy," he said softly, stroking Sundown's flank. "I'll be careful."

Along Crystal Springs's broad, muddy streets the false-fronted stores huddled together in the usual assortment, brick against frame, two-storied clapboard buildings next to squat log cabins.

Wagon traffic was light for a Tuesday afternoon. The sky was overcast. Bar wondered if it was going to rain some more.

Because the main street curved at a slight upward grade toward the west, Bar walked a full block before seeing the small stone bank. It looked as solid and secure as any bank ought to look. He had pictured something less sturdy.

Pausing, he let a young lady cross the street ahead of him who was dragging a stubborn, child-sized wooden wagon through the thick mud. The wagon was filled with clattering brown glass bottles. As she went by, Bar got a sharp whiff of turpentine and tar strong enough to make his eyes water.

At the mercantile she called out the name Frank. A stocky middle-aged man came out to help her lift the mud-spattered wagon onto the boardwalk, and a lad in an apron came out to unload the bottles and carry them inside.

As the merchant untied his own apron and donned a coat, the pretty young woman talked and gestured, touching the merchant's arm now and again for emphasis. Then both of them looked in the direction of the depot. The train's steam whistle whooped three times. Last boarding call. She gave the merchant a dazzling sunshine-after-a-storm smile. Bar had never seen a smile more beautiful.

"Hurry back!" she called as the middle-aged man started toward the depot.

She was perhaps twenty-two, Bar thought, lithe and graceful, with flowing blue calico skirts and a short brown jacket. Bar felt surprised to think that he was noticing a young woman at all, much less the color of her hair and clothes. Then he realized his headache had vanished. He could breathe deeply and smell the bracing morning air.

Like a mischievous sprite, a gust of wind snatched

the sunbonnet from the young woman's head and blew it into the street. As it rolled toward Bar, she gave a half-cry, half-laugh, and gathered up her skirts to chase after it. The merchant turned back, but she waved him on. "You'll miss the train!"

The man went on toward the depot.

As she scrambled after the bonnet, almost catching it twice, her hair began to come loose from its pins. She tried to hold it, but it began cascading down past her shoulders, fanning into the wind like a fall of glistening chestnut silk. Bar had never seen hair more alive.

When the bonnet reached him, Bar bent and retrieved it. The young woman stood ten yards away now. Her brown eyes were lively with intelligence. Their dark beauty struck him full in the chest like a blow.

A tingling sensation went through his limbs. He felt his hands, hanging like deadweights from the ends of his arms, begin to itch with warmth. His heart began beating too fast and his breathing became shallow. Every nerve in his body began to awaken as if from a long dark sleep.

As he held out the muddy sunbonnet to her, he felt as if he were hanging from the edge of a cliff, reaching in a dream toward something he would never be able to touch. What Bar wanted from this young woman, he was not capable of putting into words. He felt cold, and she was all that was warm. He felt dead, and she was all that was alive.

"Oh, look at it, the ol' thing," she said, taking the bonnet by one muddy tie and letting it dangle in front of her. "I needed an excuse for a new one."

Her smile reached up to him. Her eyes danced. Her

teeth were straight and pretty and white. Her cheeks were rosy from the wind, and as smooth as satin. She was everything he pictured the beautiful Guinevere to be, or the great Helen of Troy in his father's books.

Standing only a few inches shorter than he, with her shoulders small and square, she smiled confidently at him as if expecting him to speak. He wanted to say something gallant but so many years had passed since Bar had allowed himself the company of a young lady, he could only look down at her, an empty shell of a man. Like sunlight and forgiveness, she was out of reach to him, a hardened bounty hunter.

He tried, at least, to smile. He felt foolish for having to work at something that had once come so naturally. His face remained immobile, as hard as his glacial heart.

Her expression wilted. With one sweep of those keen brown eyes, she took note of his black coat and trousers. Her gaze fixed on his holstered gun. She looked back into his eyes with the obvious realization that he was a dangerous-looking stranger.

He expected her to become frightened and flee. Instead, she frowned fiercely, as if she couldn't comprehend his presence in her world. Maybe she feared he was an outlaw.

It didn't matter what she thought, Bar realized, because he would never know her. He watched her step back.

"Thank you," she said curtly, starting away as if pulling herself back from the edge of a precipice.

She glanced back at him once and then moved away even more rapidly. In moments she had her empty wagon in tow and was jerking it hastily after her, up the street and out of sight.

The man looked like something out of a nightmare, Sunny thought, shivering as she hurried away. He was dressed like some kind of dandy. How could he stand in the middle of the street looking like that, with that unforgettable face and those incredible shoulders, and wear such a huge, ugly gun?

Sunny marched up Cassidy Street toward home so quickly her heart felt ready to burst. Three times she looked back, afraid the stranger in black was following her. He wasn't. He just stood in the middle of the street, watching her like the grim reaper.

Throwing the muddy sunbonnet into the empty wagon, Sunny ran her hand through her loose hair. She probably looked as untidy as May Sue McKidrict, and about as . . .

Sunny shook herself. What possible difference did her appearance matter to a man like that? It was just as she feared. The first of the riffraff had arrived.

She hurried on. She didn't want to think about the robbery or the funeral for May Sue McKidrict's father this morning. The thought of a funeral brought back painful memories of her own father's death. She didn't want to think about the day she came home from school ten years before to find her father laid out on his office cot, kicked in the head by a horse. Oh, mercy, life could take such unpredictable turns sometimes.

Most certainly Sunny didn't want to think about the stranger in black. She had never seen cheekbones molded in quite that way. Nor had she ever seen a jaw quite so firm, or eyes so empty looking. When would she ever see another man like that one? She resisted looking back. Of all the maladies she had ever known, muddled thinking was the worst.

At the rutted road that turned up toward her mother's boardinghouse, Sunny had to pause to compose herself. She'd almost been running. Her heart was still galloping.

One man with a gun didn't mean the town was going to rack and ruin, she told herself. As yet, there was no bounty, so he'd have no reason to stay. If he did, the sheriff would run him off. She took a deep breath and resolved not to trouble her mother with this news.

In the distance came the faint whoop of the departing train as it crossed the road heading toward Durango three miles up the track. It was carrying Frank to Denver. Feeling strangely forlorn, Sunny watched black smoke dissipating over the pines like her troubled thoughts. Frank would bring more wallpaper. There might even be enough, once the rest arrived, to do her own room, too.

There, Sunny thought, she felt better already. But she couldn't remember when the appearance of a stranger had left her feeling so weak and lightheaded. Cale had once given her pause until she realized he was only interested in what was beneath her skirts rather than what was inside her head or heart. Luck McKidrict had frightened her, too, but in an unpleasant way.

This handsome stranger, with a bearing and presence that made her reluctantly turn back to catch one final glimpse of him, seemed different. He didn't look mean, and he didn't look rough, low class or cold hearted.

As if in pain, he was now walking his big black horse toward the weathered church at the far end of town. With each step he moved more slowly. She wondered if he was ill. A lone ranch wagon was parked next to the undertaker's glass-sided hearse and the preacher's buggy. Maybe he was just a friend of the McKidricts, she thought.

A half hour later Sunny hurried, panting, into the sloped, muddy dooryard of her mother's sprawling boardinghouse. Chickens scattered in all directions as she turned over her mud-clotted wagon to their handyman, Homer, and walked up the pink flagstone walk into the kitchen in the original log portion of the Summerlin home.

"Ma, you will *not* believe the man I just saw in town, dressed all in black, with a big black horse and . . ." Sunny stopped and tried to breathe.

She felt dizzy and had to sit down. So much for not mentioning him, she thought, more than a bit undone by her preoccupation with the stranger.

Helen Summerlin didn't turn from the tin-topped pie table but went on thumping the wooden rolling pin over a pale circle of dough. "The door, Sunny."

Sunny elbowed it closed before their half dozen dogs could race inside from all corners of the yard. "Give me a minute to change my clothes," she said, "and we can get started for the funeral. The bell began ringing as I was coming in. It sounded so sad. May Sue must be beside herself. Poor girl. I see that Homer's got the buckboard ready."

Yanking off her muddy boots, Sunny resisted the temptation to peek out the door again. She felt like a schoolgirl. The stranger in black filled her mind's eye as if he were standing before her in the flesh. A prickling of confusion washed through her. She wanted to forget him, but could not.

Brushing a stray curl from her temple and leaving a

smudge of flour in her hair, Helen turned to look solemnly at Sunny. Her face glowed gold from the leaping fire in the pink flagstone hearth. Her eyes were full of words, but she said nothing.

"I saw the McKidricts' wagon parked at the church," Sunny prattled on, thinking she was hiding her agitation. "There weren't any other wagons. You don't suppose no one's going?"

At the thought of May Sue and her brothers being snubbed in their hour of mourning, Sunny jumped to her stocking feet and rushed toward the door leading to the main part of the house where her bedroom was located.

"Frank had to go to Denver unexpectedly, so he won't be there. Ma—" Sunny stopped long enough to look closely at her mother's workaday attire. "You're not dressed for the funeral yet."

Her mother's voice sounded hushed but firm. "I've got supper to cook for the boarders, same as always. I'm not going."

"Have you been crying?" Sunny's whirling thoughts about the handsome stranger finally stilled as she noticed her mother's reddened eyes.

"Goodness, no." Helen turned away to slip the pie dough expertly into the baking tin. "Good riddance to the man."

Sunny watched her mother crimp the edge of the crust. She was so surprised by her mother's expression, she couldn't think of what to say.

"I suppose it brought your pa to mind," Helen added, squirming beneath Sunny's stare.

Sunny touched her mother's shoulder. "I've always wondered what was between you and the McKidricts."

Helen didn't reply.

"I used to think . . ." Sunny stopped herself. Even as a child she had felt uneasy visiting the ranch house with its fine furniture, dirty carpets, and that lonely Alabama belle who served tears with her afternoon tea. "We used to go so often. Why did we stop?"

Helen beat another handful of dough into a submissive circle. "I married your pa at sixteen," Helen said to the rhythm of the rolling pin's usually forceful strokes. "I'd been the Finleys' maid since I was twelve, lucky to have a place, they always said. Abel apprenticed Mr. Finley's veterinary practice. After we married, I went on working. We were fortunate they let us stay on. No sooner were you born and your pa went away to war."

"What has this got to do with—"

"I was so afraid for Abel," Helen went on as if talking about those years long past made perfect sense even though they had been discussing Julia McKidrict. "I suppose you heard me crying in the night."

"Yes, I did, Ma," Sunny said softly.

Helen's cheeks reddened. "I loved your pa. I didn't want to come west, but finally I did." She paused to patch a thin place in the circle of dough. "There was so much work once we got here. I was lonely. So we called on Julia McKidrict. It was only neighborly. In those days we were the only two white women for twenty-five miles. That's where I met Luck McKidrict, and I *never* liked him. He was a beast in every sense, and he never changed a hair. I'm *glad* he's dead."

"Is that why we stopped visiting May Sue and her mother?" Sunny asked. "Every time I see her I don't know what to say. Now we're going to be late to the funeral. I'll never hear the end of it."

"I'm *not* going," Helen said. "Luck McKidrict used

to beat Julia. You should have seen her when she tried to . . . But she wouldn't save herself."

"She came here one night, didn't she, Ma? I think I heard her."

Helen nodded. "Luck had tried to kill her. We gave Julia money to go away. I suppose Luck would have hunted her down if she had taken the children. Lord only knows what became of her. It's been ten years. Can you imagine how I feel when *I* see May Sue? She carries on about her ma deserting her, and here I am the one who helped Julia go. I didn't dare visit May Sue after that, not with Luck around. I've never wanted *you* going out to that godforsaken ranch by yourself. May Sue should have moved to town and cleaned up decent. Sometimes it's best to let things go, honey."

Startled by her mother's candor, Sunny hung her head. "It's not that I *want* to go to the funeral. I just don't know how I'll explain if I don't."

"May Sue turned out just like Julia, blaming the world for her misfortunes. Have we sat around bemoaning our fate since your pa died? No, we haven't. We've worked. Another year or two and our debt will be paid. We'll be able to hold our heads high. If no one goes to Luck's funeral, I won't be surprised." Dabbing at her eyes with the hem of her apron, Helen marched resolutely to the kitchen door and called out sharply, "Homer, unhitch that buckboard. We're not going after all."

When Helen didn't come away from the door, but went on staring across the dooryard in the direction of the road up from town, Sunny tiptoed uneasily to her side.

Mounted on his glossy black horse, the black-clad

stranger whom Sunny had seen in town was watching them from the shadows of the big blue spruce tree at the corner of their property. Rain was falling again.

A tremor went down Sunny's spine. Her heart began to patter, with excitement or alarm, she wasn't sure. "That's the man I told you about," Sunny whispered. "But don't you worry, Ma. I'll get rid of him."

3

Bar gazed upon the ramshackle house nestled among pines. The place looked as though it had been built by unskilled hands in three sections. The newest was two stories of weathered blue clapboard with tall, narrow windows set in a bit crookedly. A porch wrapped to the left, meeting a small stone-walled annex. The faded sign by the hitching post identified the separate entrance as the office of Abel M. Summerlin, veterinarian.

Two women stood in the doorway of the original log portion. Between the logs and clapboard was an adobe section with a ready-made window in the front that must have been shipped from the East.

Beyond a stand of pines on the far side of the house stood a small weathered barn with a rail corral. A bearded man in overalls was unhitching a horse from a buckboard there. He watched Bar with a noticeably alarmed expression.

Rhode Island Reds ran loose all over. Dogs of several mixed breeds came from every corner of the yard to bark and prowl about Bar. Cats of all colors sat beneath the porch.

Bar tried to straighten in the saddle but his renewed headache stabbed again. He hadn't made it to the church; the tolling bell had summoned unbearable memories of his pa lying cold and still in his casket.

Deciding to take a room in order to rest, Bar had guided Sundown as far as a side-street saloon with extra rooms to rent, but he couldn't stand the stale smell of alcohol and tobacco. He'd considered the hotel but suddenly couldn't find the energy to dismount and climb the sweep of steps to the porch.

A man had come by. "If you're looking for the doctor, friend, he's gone to Chambersville. Big fire there last week."

"I need . . . a quiet room," Bar had managed to say, knowing anyone who chanced to see him would see that he was ill.

"There's a boardinghouse yonder, but . . ."

The man had pointed in the same direction the lovely young woman in the blue skirt had taken when she hurried away. Bar had followed. Now he found himself looking at her again, wanting something from her that he couldn't name.

Looking furious, she marched straight toward him, then stopped a distance away. She shielded her eyes from the rain with her hand and scowled up at him. "What are you—" She stopped and began again, trying to soften her tone. "This road goes no farther. Have you lost your way?"

He tried to concentrate. "Someone said . . . you have rooms." His voice came out strained.

The young woman shook her head. "This is a long-term boardinghouse. There's no place for *you* here."

The older woman started across the puddled dooryard. Bar concluded she was the young lady's mother. They had the same worried frowns.

Ma, he thought, with all the strength leaving his arms. He slid sideways into nothingness.

Sunny gave a cry of alarm. Seeing the man pitch toward her from his saddle, she threw out her arms to catch him.

"He'll break his neck!" her mother cried, rushing to help.

His body fell against them both. Digging her stockinged feet into the mud, Sunny braced herself. "What's the matter with him?"

Her mother tried to keep his boot from snagging in the stirrup, but as his leg came down, he fell into the mud. "Let's get him inside, honey."

"No, Ma!" Sunny exclaimed, struggling to hold one of his sleeves. "He looks like an outlaw. Homer! Ride for the sheriff!"

Helen laid her hand on his forehead. "He's burning up. We can't leave him out here. Lift his shoulders."

"Just what we need, a sick gunslinger in our house," Sunny muttered to herself. "I'll ride for the sheriff myself."

Helen straightened and scowled. "A pistol on his belt doesn't make him an outlaw. Your pa wore a gun for all the years he lived around here. Until Doc gets back, we have to help him. Homer?" Helen called. She glanced back at Sunny. "With another renter, we might get that loan paid this year."

"You can't mean he should *stay?*" Sunny cried, her heart constricting with dismay.

Sunny was about to confess that she'd already paid off the loan, but Helen silenced her with a look. Like a recalcitrant child, Sunny gave a silent pout and glared at the unconscious stranger.

As the handyman approached, his permanently misshapen face, damaged by a beating years before, looked apprehensive as always.

"Help me with his legs, Homer." Helen motioned for him to come closer.

Shaking his head, Homer scurried back to the barn.

"I forgot how frightened he is by guns," Helen said.

Sunny closed her eyes. She wanted to drop the stranger and run, too.

Helen struggled to keep the man's long legs under her arms. "We'll put him on the cot in the office. Until we know what's wrong with him, I don't think we should tell the boarders he's here. No need for a fuss. I don't need Howard putting this in his newspaper. And I sure don't want Ol' Foote sticking his beak into my business, telling me what I can or cannot do in my own place."

"*Mother,*" Sunny said, refusing to move. "We are *not* taking this stranger into Pa's office. Homer can hitch the buckboard. We'll drive him into town."

"Who would take him in, Sunny? When they brought Homer here all stoved in, your pa didn't hesitate to help. Neither shall we."

Ashamed for feeling so hard-hearted, Sunny stuck her arms beneath the stranger's armpits and lifted. His weight made her stagger. As his head lolled back, she saw the beautiful way his brows curved. She leaned close enough to smell his fevered skin, wet

with rain. They were close enough that she could
have kissed him.

Her heart skittered with unbidden agitation.
Setting her jaw, Sunny lugged him toward the office.
The cold mud beneath her stocking feet made her slip
and slide.

"I always suspected one of the McKidrict boys beat
up Homer," Helen remarked as they stumbled toward
the office door.

"You couldn't have been very certain of it," Sunny
replied, panting. She almost lost her hold. "I'd
remember if you had spoken to the sheriff about it."

"It doesn't do to falsely accuse a McKidrict," Helen
said.

"If Luck McKidrict was as bad as everyone claims,
why didn't the sheriff just run him out of town years
ago?"

"No one . . ." Helen grunted as she stopped to
unlock the door from one of the keys on the ring in
her skirt pocket, ". . . ever . . . caught them at anything."

They jockeyed the unconscious man through the
doorway. Sunny's clothes were soaked by then and
she was shivering. She and her mother lifted the
stranger and arranged him on the cot. Then Sunny
straightened, teeth chattering, and pushed dripping
hair from her face.

Her mother's cheeks looked flushed. "Where did I
put the whiskey?"

"Ma, stop and look at me," Sunny said. She edged
away from the man's arm, which was hanging over
the edge of the cot as if reaching for her.

"Change out of those wet clothes, honey," Helen
said absently.

"Ma, you're acting very peculiar. For all we know, this could be a long-lost McKidrict. I don't want one of them here."

Helen Summerlin's eyes sparkled in a way that Sunny hadn't seen in a long while. "He looks nothing like a McKidrict. If supper's late I'll have to listen to Ol' Foote's threats to foreclose. Now hush your foolishness and help me. Where's your Christian charity?"

Sunny scowled as her mother unlocked the door leading to the hall and the main part of the house. Her mother wasn't thinking of the extra rent. She was simply doing what came naturally to her, helping someone in need.

Contrite, Sunny inched toward her father's wallmounted gun case next to the desk. It held three shotguns locked behind glass doors. Rattling the doors, Sunny didn't feel as reassured as she would have liked that the stranger wouldn't be able to get the doors open if he wanted.

Sunny heard her mother calling to Homer from the kitchen doorway. "Get that gelding into the barn, Homer. Bring in the saddlebags 'fore they get soaked through."

Sunny pulled the chair from the kneehole in her father's desk and dropped into it. Cold dribbles of water traced chills down her neck. Tucking her damp hands into her armpits, and wiggling her toes inside her mud-caked stockings, Sunny glowered at the black-clad figure on the cot.

She refused to admit to herself that this was the most excitement she had known in years. Even so, they couldn't keep him here. He was just too . . . too.

He lay there, with his graceful hand dangling, a puddle forming on the floor beneath his fingertips.

He had an unhealthy pallor, and his breathing was shallow and rapid.

Heaving a sigh, Sunny went to his side and stood over him, noting the fine stitching on his coat. The muddied gun stuck up crookedly from the tooled leather holster against his hip.

Gingerly, Sunny tugged the weapon free, laid it on the dusty table across the room, and wiped her hands. Feeling like a thief, she decided to unload the gun and dropped the cartridges into her skirt pocket.

Then she pulled his arm up by the sleeve and laid his hand across his chest. His fingers were long, his nails pared. His face was smooth shaven, his nose straight and well formed, his eyelids were faintly purpled. His lips looked a soft dusky rose color, parted slightly. A strange fluttery feeling went through Sunny's stomach. She had to turn away.

Helen soon returned, wearing dry clothes and carrying a kettle of steaming water. She filled the tin basin on the washstand. "It's time to lay the table," she said. "The boarders will be up from town any minute. Tell Homer to bring more kindling. This fireplace hasn't been used since . . ."

Since Pa died, Sunny thought as her mother's voice trailed off.

She frowned at the streaks her muddy hem had made across the floor and tried not to think of the day Abel Summerlin lay in his casket in the dining room, the house filled with mourners.

Helen caught Sunny's unhappy expression and gave her a motherly pat. "If this man's an outlaw, we'll send him packing. If he's . . . well, look at him, Susanna. He's no drifter."

Sunny did not reply, but hurried from the office

and shut herself into her bedroom two doors away. She was not in control of her feelings and that annoyed her.

She couldn't allow herself thoughts of this man, or of any man. Her sole concern was helping her mother to marry Frank. Only then could she entertain fancies of how a man's lips looked, or how his hair curled against his collar, or how his hand might feel on her. . . .

A blossoming of warmth spread through Sunny's body. She clamped her eyes shut. He was the finest-looking man she had ever seen. If only he hadn't been wearing that gun.

Battling her unruly thoughts, Sunny stripped off her wet clothes and washed hurriedly at the basin without looking at herself in the mirror. As on any other late afternoon, she laid the supper table. Homer delivered the firewood to the back door, refusing to come inside as always. Sunny carried some of the wood into the office.

Helen was sponging mud out of the stranger's hair from when he fell from his horse. "He's awfully sick, honey," Helen said softly, never taking her eyes from his face.

Nodding silently, Sunny crept away. By the time the four boarders had arrived, she was serving supper with both hands and wondering if her secret stranger on the cot had yet awakened.

"Has there been any word about that fire in Chambersville, Mr. Ivery?" Sunny asked. "Is Doc Hamilton back yet? Were many folks hurt?"

Howard Ivery, the local newspaper reporter, frowned at her. "Didn't you read the paper this week? He's due back tomorrow."

"I couldn't bear to be reminded of the robbery. I've had nightmares every night," she said.

Howard seated his lanky frame on the bench and filled his plate. "Not a soul went to the funeral today. Any more of them biscuits, Miss Susanna? How come you and your ma didn't go? Butter, please, Grodie. I seen them McKidrict boys ride back up the pass afterwards. They looked like statues."

"Miss May Sue cried all the way, I'll bet," Grodie put in.

Howard pinned Foote with a shrewd newspaperman's eye. "It's hard to believe, McKidrict opening the strongbox, you gettin' the note from the safe, and before McKidrict can sign, the money gets stole. I reckon the McKidrict place is yours now, Foote. I ain't seen Lyford or Cale makin' any effort to pay off the debts since the robbery. You goin' to sell it to that Texan? When'd you say he's comin' to town?"

Ethridge Foote didn't look at any of his fellow boarders. "Humph," was all he said, but his hand shook as he picked up his fork.

"I was busy painting the sign for the hotel all day," Willis Tate, the sign painter, said. His face was still flushed from hurrying up the road in the rain. "So *I* couldn't go to the funeral. Didn't think it mattered if I did. Never painted a sign for that bunch. Didn't think they could read 'em anyhow." He laughed nervously.

Grodie Meahan, the barber who had to stand on a stool to cut hair, finally spoke as he reached for seconds. "I expected a big crowd . . . big crowd for the occasion. Must've swept the barbershop twenty times if I did it once today. Twenty times. Not a haircut or shave for anybody all day. Seems like nobody gave a tinker's damn—" He paused, glancing with embarrassment toward Sunny. "S'cuse me, Miss Susanna."

Too distracted to notice Grodie's inadvertent oath, Sunny opened the butter crock and watched the men gouge out pale yellow hunks for their biscuits.

"Hey, Sunny girl," Grodie went on, apparently excused for his language. "Where *is* your ma this evenin'? You asked after Doc. Is she ailin'?"

"Ma's fine."

"That's good, 'cause I'm fixin' to bring in a heap of trout come Saturday night. They'll be running thick in Crystal Creek after all this rain we've had. I want her to fry 'em up good like she always does. I'll be mighty hungry after missin' supper here Friday."

Sunny didn't smile. Her mother was little better than their slave.

"And for her birthday I had the dressmaker stitch up a real nice apron. Wrapped it myself." Grodie beamed. "All by myself."

Sunny felt like screaming. "I think I'll go check on Ma. Can I get you gentlemen anything more?"

"Mustard pickles," Willis said.

"Greens," Grodie said.

Ol' Foote wrapped his lips around his fork and glared at the stew. He didn't look himself, she thought. She supposed it was rather upsetting for the old miser to have his precious bank robbed.

She studied the assortment of men seated at the table and wondered suddenly how she and her mother had borne them this long. By the time Sunny had brought more pickles, and jelly, and biscuits, and cider, and corn relish, and greens, her anxiety had reached fever pitch. For all she knew, the stranger was holding her mother at gunpoint. Then she remembered that she had taken the cartridges and felt silly.

As soon as possible, however, she escaped the men and hurried down the dark hall to the office where she used to visit with her father in the evenings. The stone addition had been new then, the fireplace always blazing, some recovering furry critter always tethered to the desk leg.

Now the room was cast in flickering orange firelight. Her mother sat next to the stranger, chafing his long-fingered hands to warm them.

"I got his wet clothes off," Helen said. She indicated the black frock coat, trousers, and dark gray cambric shirt hanging from the edges of the nearby table. "Hand tailored in St. Louis. He isn't poor."

"I shouldn't wonder," Sunny muttered, her opinion of gunfighters extremely low.

The man's snakeskin boots propped against the hearth had already been scraped clean. His hat hung on the hook where Sunny's father's hat had hung long ago. Helen had evidently brushed it. Sunny wanted to throw everything, including the unconscious stranger, out the door.

He lay bare chested now, wearing only the bottoms of long underwear still smelling musty from the storage trunk standing open in the far corner.

Now Helen worried the mourning brooch pinned to her collar. "It bothers me that he won't wake up."

"How did you get his clothes . . ."

Sunny decided she didn't want to know how her mother had managed to strip and re-dress a man that size. Had her ma taken a shine to this stranger? Sunny wondered with genuine alarm. He was younger than thirty. She supposed he did resemble her pa in his youth somewhat, if she closed her eyes and pretended with a lot of license.

That was it, Sunny concluded with a twist of her heart. Her poor ma. That awful day ten years before had likely been just like this one, ordinary in the extreme until somebody had brought Abel Summerlin home, a gash in his caved-in head bleeding from the hoof of a McKidrict horse.

Her mother had been thinking of Abel earlier, Sunny thought. She'd talked about him while her fingers caressed that brooch. Now an ailing man lay on the cot in the office, giving Helen a way to cope with emotions roused by Luck McKidrict's funeral.

Sunny tiptoed to her mother's side. "I'll sit with him, Ma. The boys are asking after you. Somebody saw this man get off the train. Now they're all wondering where he went. I didn't let on that he's here, sick. I put on more water to boil. Do you think he'll want some broth if he wakes?"

Helen pulled the blanket up to his chin. "Did you find the whiskey?"

Sunny heaved a sigh. "Ma, I wouldn't know where to look. This is *supposed* to be a dry boardinghouse. Doc's due back tomorrow. I'll ride for him in the morning."

Standing and tottering wearily, Helen finally met Sunny's eyes. "Sensible folks *always* have a touch of medicinal whiskey tucked away. I suppose we could lose business because he's here. Folks will talk. I just . . ."

"It's all right, Ma," Sunny said softly, hugging her mother's slim shoulders. "I understand how you're feeling."

Helen left the room with one worried backward glance.

At the thought of having to sponge a fevered man's half-naked body, Sunny shivered. Bringing the lamp nearer, she sank onto the chair beside the cot. Her hand stole to the side of his neck where his blood throbbed, hot and furious, through his body.

She remembered a time, long ago, when she had been ill, too. She'd been in her parents' big bed, feeling limp and frightened. Her father had put his cheek to hers and said with perfect confidence, "You will be just fine, Sunflower."

She had believed that she would be, and she had been.

Her throat thickened. Dear heaven, how she missed her father. Ordinarily she didn't let herself think of it. She loved Frank and would welcome him as Ma's new husband, *but Papa, oh, Papa,* she thought. *I'm frightened. I don't know what to do about these feelings I'm having for this stranger.*

As if he were feeling the same helpless, anguished confusion as she, the stranger's face contorted. With his brows tilted and his eyelids moving with dreaming eyes beneath, he looked younger suddenly.

His breathing became ragged. His legs twitched, as if he were running in a nightmare. Then he reared up as if he were going to leap off the cot and run out the door.

Sunny caught a glimpse of his chest, swirled with silky hair, as she caught the full weight of him in her arms. The chair slid from beneath her. She wrapped her arms around his chest to keep him from pitching face first onto the floor.

He was strong in his anguish, his midnight blue eyes wide but unseeing, staring in horror at something over her shoulder that she couldn't imagine.

They tumbled together onto the floor. Whimpering in his deep, husky voice he called out a ragged, "Pa-a-a!" and began sobbing in a way that Sunny had only heard once before when her mother gave way to grief. Sunny had never allowed herself such heartache. It was too painful to be borne. She blocked it out, just as she had for ten years, focusing her attention instead upon the overturned chair.

The stranger couldn't be a monster if he suffered like this for his father. Mustering all her strength, Sunny pushed him back onto the cot. His shoulders were beautifully broad and round with muscles.

Grabbing the blanket and pressing it tightly beneath his chin, Sunny laid her cheek next to his hot one. A faint rasp of stubble chafed her skin. "You will be all right," she said in her father's confident voice.

Almost at once the stranger relaxed back into the pillow just as she had done in her sickbed so long ago, with relief and trust.

Standing back, Sunny wrapped her arms about herself and studied him. Finally, taking firm hold of the chair, she righted it, planting it three feet from the cot where she would not have to sit and hear the soft, even rhythm of the stranger's breathing, or smell the heat of his fevered skin as he began to dream again.

When her mother came in to sit with him at nine, Sunny got up and went to the door.

"What did I have that time when I was sick and Papa sat by my side day and night? I was in your bed. Remember, Ma? It was before the main house was built, back when everything was in the kitchen. I remember staring at the hearth fire for hours."

Helen wrung out a cold cloth. She draped it over

the man's forehead. "Diphtheria, honey. You were nine years old and dying. Abel brought you back."

A chill went through Sunny.

Her mother gazed thoughtfully at her. "This man is *not* going to die, honey. I won't let him."

"I'll relieve you at midnight," Sunny said, kissing her mother good-night with more feeling that usual.

Lying stiff and fully dressed beneath her covers moments later, Sunny listened to the boarders plod one by one up the creaking stairs to their respective rooms. The floorboards groaned under their weight, and then the beds. In time she heard faint snores.

She listened to the rain fall steadily for over two hours. When it stopped, she listened to the stillness of the cold, dripping night.

Sunny pondered the fact that her father had once saved her life. Her parents had never let on that she had been so sick. And now her father was gone, ten long years. She needed Frank Tilsy to take his place because she was lonely for a deep voice to comfort her and a big hand to hold hers when she felt small and afraid.

Then she realized that when Frank Tilsy came to live with them as her mother's new husband, Helen would be the one to hear Frank's deep voice in the night and hold his warm hand.

Sunny would still be alone.

4

Feeling his way through swirling fog, Bar believed something safe waited ahead if he could just find it. He tried to run, but his legs wouldn't move. When he finally drifted close, the object he sought slid cunningly out of reach. Falling suddenly, he swung his arms to protect himself.

Trying to keep the blanket pulled over the unconscious man, Sunny ducked just in time to avoid being hit by his wild swing. He knocked his forearm against the washstand's corner, which was only inches from the head of the cot, and seemed about to regain consciousness. Then suddenly all tension drained from his body.

The clock in the kitchen tolled a distant and forlorn two in the morning. Holding her palm against his blazing forehead, Sunny was surprised to discover his fever was down a bit. She wished it was her mother's turn to sit with him instead of hers, but her mother needed rest if she was to have breakfast on the table for the boarders at the usual time.

Sunny could understand why her mother didn't want this man's presence in their house known. If he had one of the dread diseases, she, her mother, and their four boarders would probably be quarantined together, a prospect Sunny didn't relish.

Sponging his brow some more, Sunny wondered if she would soon be tossing and turning in her own bed, suffering this fever. When he was sleeping peacefully at last, she rose and stoked the fire, hoping the heat searing her face would burn away whatever danger he might spread to her.

Bar found himself falling toward a tunnel where a locomotive, belching black smoke, had disappeared. He followed, emerging into a pleasant summertime scene, the depot where his father had once worked. Like that day twelve years before, there were several horses tethered in the timber along the tracks. Six strange men, crouching nearby, were pulling kerchiefs over their faces.

Seeing their drawn guns, Bar ran to Front Street to sound the alarm just as he had done when he was fourteen. His father was hobbling out of the depot's office, his crutch under one armpit, looking as if he intended to prevent the robbery himself.

Unexpectedly, one of the outlaws fired at him.

Bar cried, "No!" and threw out his hand as if he could catch the bullet. He tried to fling his body between the outlaw's gun and his father, but the man he loved most in the whole world fell dead without a sound.

The scene played again in Bar's fevered mind, and then again. Each time it was the same. Each time he saw the train robbers and ran to sound the alarm. Each time his father went down, but Bar could not catch the bullet.

He was wrenched suddenly from the scene by water cutting cold rivers of pain, like tears, down his hot cheeks. He couldn't move to stop the pain or the grief.

Sunny was sponging his face and chest, but he still didn't wake. Exhausted, she settled back in the chair and fell asleep almost at once to troubled dreams of her own.

When Bar finally woke briefly a while later, he felt groggy and disoriented. He didn't recognize the young woman slumped on the chair nearby, dozing with her chin on her chest. Her thick chestnut waves were hanging on either side of her face, obscuring her features.

He couldn't speak to her because of his parched throat, but felt better somehow, knowing she was watching over him. He fell back onto the sweat-soaked pillow and spiraled once again into the fog of his dreams.

At dawn, realizing the stranger was scarcely breathing, Helen, who had just sent Sunny off to fetch the doctor, slapped his flushed cheek. "Come back!" she commanded him. "Don't give up. The doctor will be here soon."

What was she to do, Helen wondered, getting up and pacing. He couldn't die nameless. Finally she took his saddlebags, which Homer had brought in hours before, and dumped everything onto the floor.

Noting a text on law and the novel *The Man in the Iron Mask* among the man's personal belongings, Helen found a leather wallet containing cash and personal papers. "Barnabas," she said at last, relieved to find the man's name scrawled on a bill of sale from a gunsmith in St. Louis.

She went to him and dropped onto her knees to whisper in his ear. "Barnabas! You want to live!"

Bar was fishing along the creek with his father, relishing the feel of the sun warm on his young back, unconcerned with his bleak future among the living. His father spoke then in his deep, soft voice. "Go home, son, before it's too late."

Bar opened his eyes. He could feel breath going in and out of his lungs. His head was cradled on a pillow. His back was pressed against a sagging but not uncomfortable surface.

He wiggled his toes, flexed his aching fingers, and blinked hard enough to feel his dry, taut skin stretch across his cheeks. Yes, he thought, he was back.

A fire crackled nearby. He smelled the comforting aroma of pine wood smoke and wool drying. Then he smelled beef broth, and his mouth watered.

A woman sat in the chair beside him, but she looked older. Seeing that he was conscious, she smiled and leaned closer, about to speak.

He grasped her hand. "Ma," he said, his voice little more than a gasp. "I'm sorry, but I had to do it. I had to go."

Helen didn't understand what Barnabas was talking about. She was just glad to see him awake. "There's not a thing wrong with you, Barnabas. I've found no wound on you, no snakebite, rash, or blister. Your eyes are clear. Your throat's not red."

Shaking his head ever so slightly, he let his eyes close and he was gone again.

"Oh, Barnabas," Helen said with a sigh. "I can see that you're a stubborn one."

Helen rose to look out the window. On Friday she would turn forty, she thought. She had expected to feel older and wiser, but after such a night she felt strangely alert as if realizing for the first time in a long while how quickly life could pass a body by.

With clouds hanging low over the valley, the day promised to be bleak. Homer was already up, chopping kindling, the steady whack of his ax echoing against the mountain. Looking back at Barnabas, Helen marveled that he had survived this long. He was shivering now, mumbling words she couldn't make out. Apparently his fever hadn't yet broken.

So many years had passed since Abel slipped from her grasp in this room, she thought, fingering the mourning brooch pinned to her collar. She unpinned in and went to sit at her late husband's desk where he'd spent so many hours trying to balance their accounts. Opening the brooch's thick silver cover, she gazed sadly at the lock of glossy brown hair inside, his hair, clipped from his head on the day he was buried.

She had buried him behind the house on the grassy rise where they buried strays and orphaned wildlife that didn't survive. Folks had thought it queer for her to bury her husband among animals instead of people, but Helen had known that Abel would have wanted it that way. Why was it so difficult for her to imagine how Abel might feel if she chose to marry Frank?

Helen gazed at the stranger lying on her husband's cot. Everything she knew to be true about people, and particularly men, told her that this Barnabas Landry with his custom-made gun and menacing black clothing was nothing more than a stray in need of care.

He was not a bad man, she knew, for bad men did not suffer their heartaches in dreams, thrashing about the way he had all night long. They suffered them not at all. When he woke she was certain that he would tell them he was a lawyer.

Giving herself up to the strange emotions of the night past, Helen wondered how much longer she would make Frank wait for her answer. He loved her. She loved him. At this very moment she might be sewing that dear, gentle man a shirt, or stirring his favorite stew, or anticipating a warm and wonderful night alone with him.

Surely Abel would have wanted that kind of happiness for her. Even their precious Susanna said she wanted that for Helen. Life was meant for the living, Helen reminded herself.

She had only just begun to love Abel deeply, in spite of their hardships, and in spite of their disagreements. She'd only just begun to value him for his kindness, generosity, and courage when he was abruptly taken from her.

It had taken a rough man like Luck McKidrict to remind her how fortunate she had been to have had Abel in her life. All Luck had had to do was dirty her lips that one time with his whiskeyed mouth and Helen had known to the very depths of her soul how much more a man Abel Summerlin was.

Abel had been dead so long that Helen found his face difficult to recall. She could remember the rumble of his voice and the feel of his chest beneath her stroking hand. His kindly eyes, his endearing smile seemed so very dim in her memory now. What was she to do? Thank God, Luck McKidrict was dead. She was so glad, she hung her head in shame.

If she married Frank at last, Luck would not be around to bother her and pick fights with Frank. That, more than anything, had kept her from responding to Frank Tilsy these past five years when he had tentatively courted her. She had been protecting Frank. She had been afraid of losing him. It was no wonder Sunny wouldn't look at a man, Helen thought. She hadn't learned to live because Helen hadn't had the courage to teach her how.

Helen dashed away tears. To accept Frank after resisting for so long . . . Was there any hope that he might still want to marry her after all the times she had turned away?

Helen rushed from the office into the biting chill of the morning. The sight of the doctor's black buggy, pulling to a stop in front of her house, filled her heart with relief.

"He's still unconscious," Helen cried.

Dr. Joshua Hamilton climbed down and handed the lines to Homer as the handyman came from the woodyard to help. The doctor was a tall, husky man, with a big gut, big hands, and lots of unruly white hair still laced with soot.

He gave off an air of calm that was terribly welcome to Helen at that moment. His clothes were covered with black char as well. He looked exhausted.

Helen grasped his arm. "You haven't rested, have you, Joshua?"

"Your daughter looked mighty upset when she

came to find me this morning, dear," he said, plodding ahead into the office. "I figured I was just as much good to you dead tired as half rested."

Sunny rode in moments later and slid to the ground. "He told me the fire in Chambersville was terrible, Ma. The whole town is gone. I felt awful the way Doc looked when he returned and found me on his porch, waiting."

"We'll fix him lunch. The moment he's done with Barnabas, we'll make him lie down. I'll tidy my room." Helen hurried into the office where the doctor was bent over the sick man.

"Barnabas?" Sunny repeated, following her mother inside with a yawn. "That's not much of a name for a gunslinger."

"The door," Helen said automatically.

Noting the items scattered on the floor, Sunny elbowed the door closed. "You went through his saddlebags?"

"I think he's a lawyer," Helen said, although she couldn't be sure. A law text didn't make a man a lawyer any more than a gun made a man a gunman.

The doctor rubbed his eyes and sighed. "I can't tell what the hell's wrong with him, Helen. You say he's had a killing fever since last night?"

"Worst I've ever seen," Helen replied.

"Then I got no choice but to quarantine you ladies." He dropped heavily into the chair beside the cot. "I could dig out a bullet or set a leg, but figure out what kind of fever he's got. . . . no, ma'am. I've got to have me some sleep before I can think, or at least some food."

"This way, Doc," Helen said. "Sunny will bring you a plate of leftovers from breakfast."

The doctor hoisted his bulk from the chair and followed Helen as if the real reason he'd come so far
was her cooking. "Susanna," he said, "send word
back to town that I'm here. I'll explain to your boarders this afternoon. They won't be able to stay here for
a week or so."

"Where will they go?" Helen asked, half worried,
half elated to think that she and Sunny might have a
rest.

"They'll figure something out. Men always do
when they have to," the doctor said.

Helen ushered him into her bedroom. "Thank you
for coming when you were so tired, Joshua."

With an acknowledging grunt, the doctor rolled
across Helen's bed. She caught his muddied boots
with her apron to prevent them from dropping onto
her spotless pieced coverlet. Awkwardly she bent and
untied her apron strings, letting the doctor's legs sink
into the tick, his boots wrapped in her apron.

By the time Sunny brought his plate, he was asleep.
"You think he's a *lawyer?*" she whispered. "Ma, really.
I suppose next you're going to tell me that he's the
man in the iron mask like that book in his bag. You
look so tired, Ma. Why don't you lie down on my bed.
I'll look in on Barnabas while I tidy the kitchen."

"Just think of it," Helen said, deciding she did
deserve a nap. "Peace and quiet for a week."

"I'm thinking that without those four fussbudgets
to protect us, Homer will be all we have standing
between us and a stranger crazed with fever."

Chuckling, Helen went into her daughter's room.
She hadn't liked Abel Summerlin the first time she
saw him either.

5

Sunny bustled from one corner of the
kitchen to the other, scrubbing, sweeping, putting
things to rights on the shelves and in the cupboards.
Due to a fever of unknown type, they were quarantined. She gave a shudder of anxiety. But a week
without their four boarders to order her about, what
a treat!

She built up the fire and automatically began two
pies for supper, realizing too late that they wouldn't
be needed. She slid them into the hearth oven anyway
and went to check on Barnabas. The name did not
suit that gunslinger lying on her father's cot, not at
all, she thought.

Hearing the doctor stirring in her mother's room,
Sunny paused to peek in the doorway. "Can I get you
anything, Doc?" she asked.

"The aroma woke me," he said, mouth half full,
pointing the fork at the plate of cold food on the night-

stand. "I forgot to check the patient for ticks." He stopped chewing long enough to frown at the apron swaddling his muddy boots. Then he smiled. "Help me get these off."

"I'm sure Ma would have noticed a tick," Sunny said, assisting the doctor with his boots. "She changed his clothes. He was soaked through when we carried him inside last evening."

"I wouldn't want to overlook spotted fever," he cautioned, shoveling the last bite of cold fried potatoes, steak, and eggs into his mouth. He flopped back on the bed. "Wish your ma had a room for me here. She can cook better'n any woman I know. Wake me about an hour before you expect the boarders back. They won't be happy with the news, so you and your ma shouldn't have to break it to 'em. I'll look in on our patient then and write my report. Just to ease your mind, Susanna, I don't think it's serious, whatever he's got. Call the quarantine an early birthday present for your ma."

"Thank you, and we do appreciate it. I'll have supper ready by the time you're rested," Sunny said, smiling.

He closed his eyes and began to snore.

Was every man in town in love with her ma? Sunny wondered, pulling the door closed.

She tiptoed down the hall, past where her mother lay napping on her bed. In the office, it was warm, dim, and cozy. Barnabas Landry lay on the cot as she had left him, flat on his back, looking dead. She edged closer, worried he would wake and startle her.

His breathing was so shallow she had to lean close to hear him. He was pale now, looking nothing like the sinister character she'd encountered in the street. Had it only been yesterday afternoon?

She laid another log on the fire, and shook out his coat and trousers. Her mother had piled the contents of his saddlebags on the desk.

The man in the iron mask indeed, Sunny thought, thumbing through the novel. There was also a shirt, and a change of socks and long drawers that must have been wet, otherwise her mother would not have put Abel Summerlin's drawers on him. Sunny wondered why he was carrying two battered old spoons in his bag.

She let her gaze skim over the muscular body of the stranger. His hair had dried in tousled ringlets. His jaw was rough with stubble now. She fingered the worn shaving brush and tin of shaving soap next to his socks.

His belly looked a bit hollow because he probably hadn't eaten anything since early the day before. She checked the iron pot of beef broth positioned near the fire on the hearth and found it still warm. Then, she stole another look at the man.

Returning to his side, she tucked the blanket around his feet. Not a man in town left her feeling as breathless as this stranger did.

It didn't mean a thing, she reminded herself. Anyone would be nervous with a stranger like this around. But this was no ordinary stranger. He was gorgeous. There was no other word to describe the way he looked. His brows were tilted up just a bit, making him look perplexed. And the curve of his lips . . . Oh, my, they were the lips of a thoughtful, sensitive man. Sunny wondered what his kiss might feel like.

For the moment she forgot the eyes she had seen in that same face the afternoon before, eyes looking blank and empty, almost dead. After this life-threatening illness, she told herself, he would be different.

His hands were smooth and graceful looking, not battered or rough. That meant he didn't work at manual labor, and he didn't fight. His arms were muscled, his body just about the finest she'd ever seen, and . . . and . . .

Sunny turned in breathless circles. If he woke and saw her staring like this, he'd know what she was thinking!

She waited for the telltale heat to drain from her cheeks. She was acting like a child, she thought. She had never been one to peek through privy knotholes like May Sue McKidrict used to do.

"I must be losing my mind," Sunny whispered, turning from the crackling fire to gaze back at the stranger.

She returned to his side and pulled back the blanket. Barnabas, she said the name to herself. He wasn't just a stranger. He wasn't just a man. He was someone called Barnabas. When the air touched his bare chest, his dusky nipples tightened.

She felt a burst of something warm go off deep inside.

"I've got to be certain you haven't been bitten by a tick," she whispered, as if to explain why she was standing so near. "A tick bite could make you mighty sick."

Placing her hand on his shoulder, she shook him slightly. Barnabas didn't stir. She could tell by the feel of his skin that his fever wasn't as high as it had been during the night.

Holding her breath, she ran her hands down behind both his arms, feeling for the small lump of a brown wood tick attached to the skin. When she felt nothing but sinewy muscles, she pushed him onto his side and examined his back.

She supposed she might feel a tick if she ran her hands over his backside and down along his legs with his long underwear still on but wild horses couldn't make her do it.

Sinking back onto the chair, Sunny shut her eyes. What she really wanted to do was simply too indecent to think about. She would just have to wait until she was married, which seemed a distant and uncertain possibility. If she was to look at this man while he was unconscious, simply to satisfy her unladylike curiosity, she'd never be able to face him once he was awake. Her mother wasn't the only woman in this household who needed a husband, she thought.

When Helen came in to check on the patient an hour later, she found Sunny asleep in the chair by the cot. Barnabas hadn't moved but his fever was down.

Rousing Sunny, Helen sent her off for a nap. Deciding that Barnabas would be all right alone for a while, Helen started supper and took the pies outside to cool.

The sky had cleared. Most of the frost had melted except for some lying in the shadows of the house. The air was crisp and bracing. Helen could hear Homer whistling in the barn. A basket of fresh eggs lay at the door along with several pails of water and more kindling. Homer was more than willing to work, Helen thought, but he still trusted no one.

She started up the hill behind the house. It had been a bleak October day when she buried Abel there, she thought, crouching to clear away some grass that had matted on her husband's grave. Settling on a boulder nearby, Helen gazed at the vista they had so often enjoyed from the dining room window that last year before he died.

Abel had built the adobe addition to the cabin as a bedroom for them the year after she and Sunny followed him to Crystal Springs. At the time the addition had only a small window which barely admitted light.

"What's the use of being on the side of a mountain if we can't see anything?" Helen had complained to her husband.

That summer he knocked out the addition's front wall and inserted the window hauled by wagon from Denver. Helen had loved him for trying so hard to please her.

The following year the room became the dining room as Abel secured a mortgage from the new banker in town, good Ol' Foote, and added two stories, a porch, and his office. Business had been picking up, and they had hoped for more children.

"Well, dear," Helen said softly to Abel's weather-worn headstone, "I've gotten the rest I've been praying for. There's a strange man in the house. He's very sick."

Wind answered from the tops of the pines in a comforting rush. The sun felt hot on her cheeks, blazing now from a peaceful turquoise sky.

"We've had a lot of rain since the first thaw. It's my birthday Friday. Sunny was planning a party for me. I guess we won't be having it now. I invited Frank, but with the quarantine . . ."

Taking the brooch from her pocket, Helen remembered how solemnly she had pinned it to her collar the day Abel was buried. She'd sworn she would never take it off.

"I loved you, Abel," Helen whispered, feeling foolish for being so sentimental over a brooch. "I was happy with you. I really was."

She heard the faraway cry of a hawk, and finally located it circling in the distant sky. "Sunny keeps to herself too much these days. Since she finished school she's been stuck here with me, working. She should be married, having babies, not serving four boarders. For that matter, *I* shouldn't spend the rest of my life waiting on them either. The debts are almost paid. Another year maybe.

"You remember Frank Tilsy and his store? He was the one whose wife divorced him and disappeared with their little girl. He's a kind man, Abel. He'd do anything for Sunny and me. It doesn't make sense for us to be alone and lonely when we could be together. Would it trouble you greatly if I remarried?" Helen asked, her throat closing.

Helen expected to feel awful, having this conversation with her dead husband, but instead she felt a bit impatient with herself. What was she waiting for?

She straightened and drew in a deep, cleansing breath. "You'll always be a part of me, Abel Summerlin. I'll never forget you. But I don't want to see another birthday pass with so little to show for my life."

Only the rushing wind replied. Helen studied the spring grass poking up from the dried grass around Abel's grave. She had loved him, and mourned him, but now her heart yearned for more than just memories.

She placed the brooch at the base of the headstone and got to her feet. Other women remarried. Did it pain them to turn from the past where the memories were sad but secure? Did other women feel this anxiety, facing the uncertainties and dread possibilities of the future?

Well, she hadn't wanted to come west with an

eight-year-old child in tow, but she had found this lovely valley and new friends. Abel had died much too soon, but Frank was healthy and sensible. Nothing would happen to Frank simply because she decided to admit that she loved him. She didn't have to fear losing him, too.

It was strange how illness brought things into perspective, Helen thought, returning to the house. On Friday she was *not* going to be older. She was going to start her life anew. If Frank couldn't come for her birthday, if he'd given up on her, well, she'd just have to see about that.

Sunny handed the doctor his coat. He and her mother started for the door. The first of their boarders was arriving from town, rounding the bend in the road by the spruce.

"I won't say anything about him," the doctor said of Barnabas. "It'll cause less of a stir if folks think you've got a touch of the grippe or something."

"You'll stop back soon?" Helen asked.

"I'll come by tomorrow. If you need anything, send Homer with a note. Take the rest, Helen. You deserve it."

"You'll tell Frank I'm all right?"

The doctor cast her a knowing smile. "Helen, as soon as he gets back, I'll do my darnedest to ease his mind. Don't worry." He signaled Homer to bring his buggy around and then started across the yard. "Willis, my boy," he called to the sign painter. "You'll have to stay in town for a couple of nights. I've quarantined the Summerlin place. Can't have fever spreading this late in the season. Sunny will send some of your clothes to town in the morning. . . . Ah, Grodie. Would you like to bunk with Willis at the hotel?"

The doctor's explanation grew too distant for Sunny to hear. She watched from the window as her mother closed the door.

"Ol' Foote will want a refund or credit on account of this," Helen muttered, turning back to her chores. "I wonder if that loan is ever going to be paid. Two steps forward, one step back."

Three of the boarders were standing at the far end of the yard, looking bewildered and concerned as Foote trudged up behind them. The little man took the news with his usual sullen silence.

The doctor climbed into his buggy and drove away. The boarders, told to go back to town immediately, turned away. When Ol' Foote marched out of sight, Sunny breathed a sigh of relief.

"I'll sit with Barnabas until midnight," Helen said. "I can't imagine why he hasn't woken up by now. It seems strange, don't you think, honey?"

Sunny cast her mother an exasperated look.

"I know, I know," Helen said with a smile tugging at her lips. "I shouldn't get carried away by someone we know nothing about."

"Just be careful, Ma," Sunny said. "Now we can't visit May Sue and . . ."

"She'll hear about the quarantine, and she'll just have to understand. I'm only sorry we won't be having my birthday party. Oh, I forgot. It was supposed to be a surprise." Helen smiled.

For a moment Sunny wondered if her mother knew about the other surprise she had planned, like the paid note, but Helen said nothing more. Two steps

forward, one step back, she had said. "We'll be celebrating, even if it's just you and me," Sunny said,
hugging her.

"And Barnabas," Helen put in.

"Ma, do you really think he'll be here that long?
Just because he's under quarantine, what's to stop
him from riding away once he wakes?"

"You have a point," her mother said, sounding as
if she thought Barnabas Landry had become a permanent addition to their household and would never
think to leave once he had found two such wonderful
women.

As on the night before, Sunny lay fully clothed
beneath her covers. In case she had to leap out of bed
to assist her mother in the night, she didn't want to
do so in her nightdress.

But sleep was long in coming. When it did come,
Sunny's dreams eventually woke her and left her
breathlessly listening for unfamiliar sounds. What if
he never woke? What if he remained unconscious forever?

She got up, and warmed water for tea, then turned
back her mother's bed, which the woman had already
remade since the doctor had slept on it.

In the office, Sunny noted the damp floorboards
where her mother had scrubbed away the muddy
streaks from her skirt. She should have done that herself, Sunny thought. She stood a long moment looking at her mother who was quietly reading the Bible
by firelight.

Barnabas Landry was curled on his side and snoring
softly. He looked young and harmless.

Glancing up, Helen sighed and laid the Bible aside. "His fever broke a while ago."

"I'm glad of that," Sunny murmured.

After Helen retired to bed, Sunny settled into the chair and let her mind wander.

She thought of the long, hard trip west and her first impression of the lonely-looking log cabin where her father had been living for a year. A coyote howled, reminding her of those first wide-eyed nights she had spent sleeping between her parents in the big rope-slung bed. In time she had grown to love their new home. She couldn't imagine leaving it.

Sunny dozed and woke and dozed again until a dim lavender dawn showed outside the office window. Straightening and stretching in the chair, Sunny ran her fingers through her loosened hair. Their quarantine wouldn't prove to be much of a rest if she and her mother had to sit in this chair half of each night.

Then Sunny felt his gaze on her.

In the dim light, with fire little more than orange coals in the hearth, she could barely make out his features. But he was awake. Those midnight blue eyes were finally open, focused, cognizant.

He was still lying on his side, facing the room. The blanket had slipped from his shoulder to reveal the sleek muscular breadth of one arm. He was keeping very still, breathing regularly, blinking slowly as he watched her. For a moment Sunny wondered if he was sleeping with his eyes open. No, he was looking at her, studying her.

She ducked her head and squinted. He followed her movement. Was he all right? Was he in possession of his senses? He looked so relaxed, so calm, so content just to lie there gazing at her.

"Good morning," she whispered, her voice husky. She cleared her throat. "Are you finally with us?"

He took a while answering. "Are there two of you?"

"My mother and myself," Sunny said, uncertain what she should do. "Are you thirsty? Hungry?"

He licked his lips. "Where am I?"

"This is a boardinghouse that my mother and I keep. You've been sick with a high fever. How are you feeling now?"

"Weak."

"I shouldn't wonder. You've had nightmares. It's been two nights. . . . Do you have any idea what ails you? The doctor wasn't sure, so he quarantined us." She forced herself to stop prattling nervously. "We know your name is Barnabas Landry. We . . . we went through your things. I hope you're not angry about that. If we had had to bury you . . . Why are you here in Crystal Springs?"

He looked at her so long she felt the heat of her curiosity the previous afternoon flooding her face again.

"To find you," he said softly.

6

Bar couldn't remember when he had last felt so peaceful. He snuggled into the pillow, gazing at the beautiful young woman with the chestnut hair.

Although his body ached from his scalp to his toes, his headache was gone. His frenzied thoughts had finally been stilled.

"Who are you?" he asked, his few words a great effort.

"My name is Susanna Summerlin. My mother is Helen. She's sleeping just now. We've been up with you two nights. This is a boardinghouse located outside of Crystal Springs. Do you remember coming here . . . and why?"

"The train," he said, his eyes drooping as fragments of a disturbing dream flickered through his mind and then disappeared. "I don't know what ails me."

"What have you been dreaming about?" she asked.

He paused and struggled to recall. "I can't remember."

"You must be thirsty. I'll fetch fresh water."

The moment she disappeared through the doorway, Bar pushed off the blanket and attempted to swing his legs over the side of the cot. His feet hit the cold floorboards like deadweights.

Struggling to sit, he found that the energy necessary just to keep from pitching face first onto the floor was all he could manage. His heart was racing, his head spinning.

The rustic stone and log-walled room was a comfortable size. The rolltop desk in the corner was rather more tidy than his desk had been at the Lasiter ranch. There was a broad window in the rear of the room near a coatrack, gun case, and bookcase.

A washstand stood beside his cot and an open trunk with some clothing spilling out was at the foot of the cot. A small window in the front wall next to the plank door admitted cheerful morning light. Across from him was a table equipped with straps. On the wall above the table hung an anatomical chart of a horse.

Susanna, what a beautiful name, Bar thought, marveling to think he was in her house after seeing her in the middle of the street in town. Fate, he thought, with a smile. Blessed fate.

She hurried back into the room and seemed surprised to see him sitting up. "Oh, do be careful, Mr. Landry. Let me set this down." Her voice trembled as she set the loaded breakfast tray on the desk. She had tied back her hair.

Bar looked up at her with what he hoped was a reassuring smile. It certainly felt like a smile. "I don't think I'm going anywhere on these legs. That smells good. What is it?"

"A special willow bark tea, fresh wheat bread, and elderberry pie. I'll bring coffee later, but I think you should sleep as much as you can. We make our coffee strong here. It would keep you awake for hours. The doctor may be by later." She paused. "W-why are you looking at me like that?"

Her dark brown eyes were large and luminous, her words frank and refreshing. She smelled like mountain air and sunshine, like clean laundry and summer days.

"I'm wondering what this room is used for. That's no ordinary table."

"My father was a veterinarian. That table was made for small surgeries. The straps kept an injured animal from moving. This was his office."

Bar recalled the sign outside.

He accepted the cup of tea from her and saw that her hands were trembling. Was she afraid of him? He didn't know what to do or say to put her at ease. He was unsteady, too, but not from weakness. He felt . . . alive.

"Thanks," he said, and took a sip. "I don't think I've ever tasted anything this good."

She caught the cup as he swayed. "Lie back now." Her alarmed tone softened. "You nearly died, Mr. Landry. I'm awfully glad you didn't."

"So am I," he said.

He believed that he wasn't really ill, not physically, anyway. His heart had been sick, and his soul, but now he felt cleansed, as if during the fever he had been reborn.

"Don't you want to lie back and rest?"

"I really should tend to myself," he said, touching his stubbled jaw with a suddenly chilled hand. It had been two days? He longed for a bath, but a wave of exhaustion swept over him. For a moment he was afraid that he would faint.

"There's a privy out back, but it's a long walk. It's too cold for you to be traipsing out there in your condition," she said matter-of-factly. "You'll have a hard enough time getting your boots on. They were soaked through and have curled a bit while drying. I'm sorry. There's a chamber pot. If you can't . . . I could . . ."

He looked deeply into her eyes and suddenly couldn't help but grin. "I don't think I'm that weak, Miss Summerlin."

A red blush stained her face from her hairline to her throat. She looked away, and suddenly she was giggling like a schoolgirl. What could she possibly be thinking? he wondered, fascinated by her beauty.

"Do what you can, Mr. Landry," she said, holding a hand in front of her unbidden smile. "I'll excuse myself now, and if I hear you fall over onto your face I'll just . . ." She let herself meet his eyes, laughed, and then shook her head. "Oh dear." She hurried away.

What a peculiar feeling it was to laugh again, Bar thought, wondering if he should have sent Susanna away. Assistance in this delicate matter was, perhaps, more needed than he realized.

Warmth flared in his neglected lower regions. He couldn't remember the last time he had felt interest for a woman. He had no use for sporting girls. Decent young women usually avoided him, which made for a mighty lonely existence for an otherwise healthy man.

His cheeks felt tight, his lips chapped. His whole body seemed as light as air. He was actually smiling. No, he was more than smiling. He was grinning like a fool.

Planting both feet on the floor and pushing, he got himself in a somewhat upright position. In time he managed what proved to be quite an endeavor of balance and coordination. Relieving himself had never been such a chore until now when he could scarcely hold his head up much less aim at a small white porcelain pot and hit it.

Edging the chamber pot out of sight beneath the cot then, Bar staggered to the front window and peered out into glorious morning light spilling across a rutted dooryard edged with pines.

He remembered the spruce at the corner. The view to the valley beyond was the most beautiful he could remember seeing in all his life. Thin wisps of clouds—mare's tails his father had always called them—swept across the sky. Rugged mountains still glistened white with snow on the peaks. Dark green pines spread below timberline like a thick skirt.

Bar's eyes, and his fingertips which were gripping the sill, and his thudding heart, ached with awareness. Time seemed to stand still so that he could drink in everything as if for the first time in his life.

He could feel the breath going in and out of his nose, and then down into his chest. He could feel his heart thundering in his ears, and feel the warmth of the fire flooding across the room to caress his bare back.

His feet were wonderfully cold, his hands flexing with renewed life, his belly growling with hunger.

Glancing at the items from his saddlebags piled neatly on the desk alongside his gun—it was covered with mud!—he had to wonder if he had been sleepwalking for the last several years.

For the life of him, he couldn't remember anything he had been doing in all that time. Drifting . . . working here and there . . .

He shook his head. He didn't want to think about the past. That deathlike existence and the things he had found himself doing, as if he had no control over himself, were over and done with.

Then his knees began buckling.

"Miss . . . Summerlin . . ."

He clutched the windowsill and turned, comprehending finally the depth of his weariness. He *had* nearly died.

But his time had not yet come. There was something yet to be done that Barnabas Landry had been spared long enough to do. And that, Bar was certain as he fought to maintain consciousness, was atonement. He needed to make amends for all he had done that had been so useless, and wrong.

He staggered back to the cot and dropped so heavily upon it that he nearly overturned the cot and washstand next to it. Susanna was back instantly, her expression of alarm a very welcome sight to him.

"Are you feeling any better? No, obviously not. Lie back now." She covered him with the blanket and felt his forehead. "How about a little of this bread."

"Sundown?" he murmured.

"What?"

She lifted her brows so beautifully, he thought. "My horse?"

"He's in the barn. Homer is taking care of him.

What happened to your pa?" she asked, "you kept calling his name."

Bar waited for the pain to start. He waited for his head to slice open in agony and for his emotions to hide behind defenses as thick as prison walls. But nothing more than the words, "He died," came from his lips. They were simple words bearing no misery for him. His father was dead. His father was dead.

"My pa died, too," she said, meeting Bar's questioning gaze.

They both turned as Helen Summerlin bustled into the room. "Mr. Landry! You've come back to the land of the living. How are you feeling?"

Bar watched the older woman with fascination. "I would have guessed you two were sisters," he said.

Helen laughed. "You *are* feeling better." She brought him a bowl of stew. "Thanks to you, Sunny and I are having a vacation. She told you about the quarantine, I trust. Our boarders are staying in town. I can't remember the last time I slept this late."

"Last year, on your birthday," Sunny remarked.

"Usually this ol' body wakes at the same time every morning, but having been up half of the last two nights . . . not that we minded tending you, Mr. Landry. You needed us, and we were glad to oblige."

"There's enough money in my saddlebags to compensate," Bar said.

Helen brushed the subject aside. "We'll take care of that when you're feeling better." From the trunk at the foot of the cot she pulled out a man's shirt. "This should fit you. Now that your fever's down, you shouldn't allow yourself to get chilled."

Sunny stoked the fire.

"I'm grateful, ma'am," Bar said, liking Helen at

once. "I'd be a lot more comfortable if you'd just call me Bar." He almost added that his friends called him that before recalling that he had none left.

"And what is it that you do for a living that brings you to Crystal Springs?" Helen asked in a light tone that didn't fool him for an instant. With a confident smile, she lifted his law book from the table. "Are you a lawyer?"

Concluding that she had every right to know the truth, Bar answered, "I was studying law when I came west about six years ago. I've had a lot of jobs since then, but in general I'm a bounty hunter."

Bar listened to the discouraging silence that followed.

Sunny looked up from her crouched position at the hearth. That same dark, fierce expression that Bar remembered from their first meeting in the street an eternity ago had returned to her face. His heart sank. Truth could be so tiresome.

Helen drew a breath, lifted her chin as if she had just received news that she hadn't wanted to hear, and forced a smile. There was no light in her eyes. The bitter wind of his lonely existence had returned.

"I see," Helen said, replacing the law book. "You're here in regard to that robbery. As far as I have heard, Mr. Landry, no bounty has been offered."

Bar frowned. "I see."

She laid the shirt she'd taken from the trunk across Bar's legs and started for the door. Bar could see her struggling to find the right words to say. Part of him didn't want to be rejected by the only warmth and comfort he had found in years, but another part of him braced for the inevitable.

Sunny swept the hearth with a small broom and then straightened. "You must have a reason for choosing that sort of endeavor over the practice of law, Mr. Landry."

His hope flared. He had reached Sunny Summerlin, Bar thought, startled. That bit of laughter they had shared moments ago had left its impression upon her.

"It seemed the right thing to do at the time," he said, unwilling to explain further.

He found his heart pounding. He wasn't well enough to ride away yet, but if there was no bounty . . . He started to sit back up. "If you want me to go . . ."

Sunny and Helen looked at each other as if they had already discussed this possibility. They hadn't known who or what he was when he arrived, he realized, and yet they had helped him. Now they were quarantined with him, not knowing what they might catch from him.

Sunny came forward and pressed him back onto the pillow. "You're not going anywhere so long as you're sick. We'll talk about this later. Ma and I have chores. Just call if you need either of us."

Helen slipped out.

Sunny stood there for a long moment, looking at him from the doorway. "What sort of bounty did you expect, Mr. Landry?" she asked.

"Bar," he reminded her.

Her expression was anything but friendly, and yet he sensed she wasn't ready to send him packing. "Bar," she said at length.

"It's not the money," he said. He chose his words with care. "I don't enjoy the work, although I'm told I'm good at it. I'm not proud to be a bounty hunter. Folks think bounty hunters are mighty low characters and fear me, but I don't want to be feared."

"Then why do it?" Her question was sharp, impatient.

"I couldn't go on reading law. I was working as an accountant and secretary for a rancher in New Mexico. When I heard about this robbery, I couldn't get the picture of those children out of my mind. I have to do something for them. I'll give them the bounty, as I have done in the past."

"What children?"

"The McKidrict children, left orphans by the bank robber who killed their father."

Sunny looked astonished. "Lyford and Cale McKidrict are grown men, more than capable of avenging their own father's murder. May Sue McKidrict is my age. Are you always so well informed when you take it upon yourself to seek a bounty?"

"Not children?" he said. He gave a bitter laugh. "I guess that makes me a fool, Miss Summerlin."

"Call me Sunny. If anyone is going after that outlaw, Mr. Landry—Bar—it'll be Lyford and Cale. They love to fight. To my knowledge, however, they've been drunk at one saloon or another since Saturday night. Everyone hated Luck McKidrict. I doubt very seriously if anyone cares who killed the man, even his sons. The only one to have any concern in the matter might be the banker who was expecting the money in Luck McKidrict's strongbox."

Uncomfortable beneath the harsh light in Sunny's accusing eyes, Bar averted his gaze. When he made no reply, Sunny sighed softly and left him to his thoughts, pulling the door closed behind her.

He had no right to smile at a young woman like Sunny, Bar chided himself. He had been correct to remind himself that such a young woman was out of reach for a man like him. If he had had the strength to leave, he would have done so right then.

7

"*It won't be much* of a rest for us," Sunny said, sitting at the kitchen table with the new spring seed catalogue open to the annuals, "if we spend it cleaning every room from top to bottom."

Helen paused scrubbing the hearth stones. "I realize now that you were right, Sunny. We should never have taken Barnabas in."

"Oh, Ma."

Sunny struggled with her own misgivings. She had been afraid of Bar Landry at first, but she wasn't now. Even knowing that he was a bounty hunter didn't erase the impression Sunny had gotten when she looked into his midnight blue eyes those first moments he was awake.

He'd been so happy to be alive then. She had wanted to know everything about him and could have talked to him for hours.

The moment her mother came into the office with

her questions and her expectations, however, Sunny had seen the happy light leave Bar's eyes.

Tracking outlaws for a reward couldn't be such an awful thing to do, Sunny tried to tell herself. It meant Bar had a strong sense of justice. It meant he cared enough about people . . . and about orphaned children . . . to give away his reward.

She had wanted him to go, yet she wanted him to stay, too. That glowing light in Bar's eyes had changed him from the frightening stranger she'd seen on the street two days before into the fascinating man she'd seen awaken in her late father's office.

"I don't understand, Ma," she said at length. "Why are you suddenly against him? Yesterday and the day before you were willing to do anything for him. I was the one being unfair."

Leaving the hearth stones only partially cleaned, Helen hung up her apron. Her hand stole to her throat, and it was then that Sunny noticed the mourning brooch was missing.

Sunny's heart leapt. Was the brooch lost, or had her mother taken it off? Sunny was about to ask, but the quarrelsome look on her mother's face made her swallow her questions.

"We could still go on that picnic we planned, Ma," Sunny said gently, thinking that if it weren't for the quarantine, Frank would have come this afternoon to paper her mother's walls. "I think we need to get out for a while."

Helen shook her head. "Not with that bounty hunter here . . . needing us." She rubbed her eyes. "I think I imagined our Mr. Landry as being something like Abel," Helen said after a pause. "When he was unconscious I could make him out to be whatever I liked.

"I really did believe he was a lawyer. I wanted him to be one, for you, Sunny. When he told us he was a bounty hunter, as you suspected, I was so disappointed. Isn't that silly? Even so, a man who can hunt other men isn't the kind of man I want for you. I was playing at matchmaking. Now we can't send him away."

Sunny dared not respond to her mother's revelation. She was thinking of Bar Landry in just such imaginative ways herself, and knowing that her interest in him could only be fantasy. "Do you really want him to go, Ma?"

Her mother stalked to the back door. "Can I ever know for certain what I really want?" she said, looking more distressed than the conversation warranted. "I'm going for a walk."

Sunny sat there for several minutes, staring thoughtfully at the door where her mother had gone out. She hadn't seen her mother so emotional in years. Usually the two of them were too busy to think beyond preparations for the next meal. Barnabas Landry's presence was having a disturbing effect on both of them.

She dipped fresh water into a pitcher and went through the sunlit dining room and down the dim, narrow hall toward the office. She heard a pained grunt and paused outside the door, wondering if Bar was all right.

When she pushed it open a little, she saw him standing near the surgery table, shaking out his own long underwear, which had gotten damp in his saddlebags. They were dry now. He had already removed the underwear that her mother had taken from the trunk and put on him while he was unconscious.

Seeing him naked, Sunny's heart took off in a gallop. She ducked back out of sight.

Hard-pressed to know which part of him was more wonderful, she peeked back in, taking in his broad muscular shoulders, his tapered waist, his firm, rounded backside and his strong-looking legs. For just a moment he turned enough for her to see what May Sue used to giggle about.

But Sunny didn't giggle. A flashfire of warmth spread through her body. As he stepped into his drawers, she saw just how a man was formed, and she wanted him. He was beautiful, all of him. Sunny was certain he had a good heart, too. All he needed was someone to understand him, to encourage him, to help him give up the profession that had made him a self-proclaimed outcast.

Since sitting up with him two nights and sharing his suffering, Sunny felt she knew him. Seeing him without his clothes didn't seem so very different from seeing him in the grips of his fever, weeping against her breast as he had that first evening.

Sunny held her breath until her heart slowed. After a count of ten, she called softly, "Mr. Landry, how are you feeling?" Then she walked loudly to the door and went into the office as if she had not just witnessed the delicious display of his body. "What are you doing?" she cried in genuine surprise to see him pulling up his trousers now.

His eyes were no longer glowing with the joy of being awake and alive. "I'm leaving before I cause you and your mother any more distress." He buttoned his trousers and winced. "Damned headache's back."

"That's not a good sign, Bar," Sunny said softly, going to him.

Her heart pulsed in her throat and her body tensed as she drew closer. Gingerly she laid her hand on his forearm and felt a spark of excitement leap from him to her fingertips. "Your fever's returned, too. Where would you go, even if you could?"

He swayed and then leaned against her.

She received the weight of him eagerly and smiled with a warmth she was certain he could see. He looked so sad that it tore her heart.

"I apologize for being harsh with you earlier," she said, eager to make his smile return. "You're welcome here as long as you need to stay. I mean that. And Ma wants you here as well. She and I were just disappointed, I think. She had a picture of you in her mind, a picture that you were like . . . my father, perhaps. And I had opinions about strangers that were . . . unfavorable. Later, when you're stronger, I'd like to know more about why you do this sort of work."

His face was pale. He looked as if he truly did want to be convinced to stay on.

"Lie back on the cot, please," Sunny whispered, guiding him toward it. "I think you need us, Bar. Tomorrow is my mother's birthday. After supper, if you feel up to it, I'd like you to join us for cake. Until then, you need a lot of rest."

Sunlight spilled in yellow splendor from a turquoise sky the following afternoon as Frank Tilsy went into Doc Hamilton's office. His boots thudded across the floorboards.

Frank pulled off his traveling hat that was dusted with soot. His spectacles slipped down his nose.

"What's this I hear about a quarantine up at Helen Summerlin's place?"

Seated at his desk, Joshua Hamilton glanced up from the thick medical text open before him. "Well, how-do, Frank. How was Denver?"

"Crowded." He perched on the edge of the nearest chair, rubbed his spectacles, and then sprang up again. "What's she got? She isn't goin' to die, is she?"

"Don't get in a lather. It's just a precaution. I'd been up to Chambersville three days and nights. I couldn't think except that Helen was having a birthday today and deserved more than one day off. As for that man's fever, I don't know what the hell is causing it. A quarantine was a perfect excuse to clear out that passel of boarders who run her ragged."

"Homer's got a fever?" Frank drew a deep breath, nearly passing out with relief. "Soon as I stepped off the train, folks were asking me if I knew what Helen had up there. I nearly lost my mind with worry. I couldn't get here fast enough."

The doctor shook his head. "It's not the handyman. And Helen's fine. So's Sunny. It's the stranger who's sick. Got a touch of melancholy, I think. Nice-looking man, up from Novaocha, he tells me. A bounty hunter."

"At Helen's place?"

Joshua chuckled. "You look like your face hurts, Frank. I don't mean to laugh at a lovestruck ol' fool like you, so go see for yourself that Helen's all right. But if you do, you'll have to stay until I lift the quarantine. I ought to come up with something by Sunday." The doctor thumped the text.

"I'll have to stay?"

"And she'll feed you. Now's your chance. Ol'

Foote's holed up at the hotel, complaining that he can't be in his own bed at night. Grodie, Willis, and Howard, they're all in town. Word's leaked out and folks are asking how come there's a bounty hunter in town when there's no bounty.

"And for that matter, they're asking how come there ain't no bounty being offered. I tell you, Frank, I'm a tired man. I've talked to the sheriff, but there's no good reason to run Landry off. Sheriff says he has quite a reputation. Brought in four or five outlaws, according to the reports."

In a daze, Frank stumbled from the doctor's office. If all of Helen's boarders were staying in town, that meant she was alone with Sunny and that addled excuse for a handyman as their only protection.

And some no-good bounty hunter, with a fever . . .

Without another thought, Frank turned up Pine Ridge Road. Grippe. Scarlet fever. Diphtheria. Smallpox. Cholera. Frank didn't care if the bounty hunter had galloping Black Death. Frank was going to Helen's birthday party. And because of the quarantine, she'd have to put him up for the night.

"My father grew up on the farm," Bar explained in the dining room as Sunny lit four small white candles stuck into the dark, glossy frosting of her mother's chocolate birthday cake. "I loved the same places he did, the meadow, the river, the stony ford. Best fishing in the world there, he used to say."

"Sounds lovely," Helen said, having warmed to Bar again, if only a little.

"After the war, Pa couldn't farm. Lost most of his right leg at Shiloh. Ma had been gone for years. My stepmother had people in Hickory Creek, so we moved there."

Sunny nodded. She was so darned pretty, Bar could scarcely think.

"Pa wanted to work on the train, but he had to settle for the depot. Said he liked to pretend he was going places." A smile came to his lips. "This is the first time I can remember talking about Pa without feeling sick and it's been twelve years."

Sunny smiled across the table at him. Her face was gold with candlelight. He wanted to touch her cheek.

"A body heals, talking about the good times, and the bad," she said.

Bar wondered what Sunny would think if he talked about his first trip west. His smile faded. What was the use, trying to be different from what he'd become? he asked himself. Helen Summerlin was right. He was a disappointment.

Outside in the late afternoon shadows, the dogs began barking. Helen rose from her seat at the end of the dining table. "I'll see what's bothering them."

Noting the look of puzzlement crossing the woman's face, Bar came to his feet. Automatically his hand went to his hip where his holster was usually lashed. Without it he felt naked and defenseless.

"Do you get many visitors this late in the afternoon, ma'am?" He remembered that he hadn't cleaned his gun since it fell in the mud his first night here.

"Please stay at the table, Mr. Landry. Sunny and I have lived here for ten years. Yes, we occasionally have visitors at unexpected hours, and all are welcome."

Bar sank back down. In his weakened condition he could have afforded them precious little protection in any case. What troubled him, he thought, staring into the four candles' flames, was that at the sound of someone's approach he had expected trouble. She had not.

He and the Summerlins were worlds apart, he thought. He glanced at Sunny and watched her force a smile. She had noted his automatic response to an unexpected visitor, too.

"Your mother's a generous woman, Susanna," he said. "I wonder where I'd be now if she hadn't welcomed *me* the other evening."

"Don't take her tone too much to heart, Bar," Sunny said softly as excited voices came from the kitchen. "It sounds like Frank!" she dashed from the room.

Bar sat back and listened to the happy reunion in the kitchen.

"What are you doing here?" Sunny exclaimed from the other room. "Don't you know we're quarantined?"

Feeling suddenly tired and out of place, Bar watched the candles dribble more and more wax onto the dark frosting. Sunny Summerlin had urged him to stay out of politeness, he told himself. There was no spark between them.

He had been about to depart the boardinghouse earlier that day because he didn't want to cause Sunny and her mother further distress. It occurred to Bar now that he should leave at once to protect himself . . . from their kindness.

Helen came into the dining room with the merchant whom Bar recognized from his first day in Crystal Springs. "This is Frank Tilsy," she said, hugging the man's arm. "Frank, this is our patient with the mysterious malady, Barnabas Landry. Bar has already told us that he is a—a bounty hunter." Helen gave Bar a pointed look. "Frank was concerned."

"I remember you," Frank Tilsy said, raking Bar with suspicious eyes. Finally he reached out his hand. "Interesting to know you, Mr. Landry. I haven't been back in town long enough to hear for certain, but as far as I know, there's no bounty being offered."

Bar was struck by the man's obvious effort to treat him fairly.

"Ol' Foote's a tightwad," Sunny remarked, taking up a knife to slice the cake into wedges, "but surely he'd want the contents of that strongbox recovered."

"Not really," Frank said. "With the McKidrict debts unpaid, the money missing, and the unsigned notes still in Foote's possession, the ranch belongs to him now. Find the money, pay the debts, and Foote loses the ranch."

"Let's not talk about the robbery, all right?" Sunny said. "Did you have a good trip to Denver? Please, sit down beside Ma. Have some cake."

Frank looked at Sunny and his mouth dropped open. "I clean forgot, Susanna."

Realizing the man had arrived empty-handed, Sunny's expectant expression fell, too.

Grinning sheepishly down at Helen, Frank patted her hand. "Sunny ordered wallpaper with yellow roses for you, dear, but it didn't come. I brought more from Denver, had it boxed up real nice so it wouldn't get dirty on the train. Soon as I stepped off the coach, Lardy Miller comes up and asks if I knew you folks were quarantined. I left the box with him and lit out for the doctor's office."

Sunny smiled at her mother. "He was supposed to have hung the paper yesterday afternoon while we were picnicking, Ma. I wanted to surprise you."

Helen looked touched and pleased. "Now, honey,

you don't need to be buying things for me with your hard-earned liniment money."

Sunny pointed to the cake. "The candles, Ma, before they go out."

Helen looked down at the four flickering stubs in the frosting and chuckled. "Thanks, honey. We'll hang the paper in the summer after I've had time to clean my room. No use hanging new paper in a dingy room. It would make everything look shabby by comparison. Why, I'd need new curtains and a new rug. I'd have to piece a new quilt. . . ."

Helen blew out the candles, laughed like a girl, and babbled happily on about all she'd have to replace in her room if she had new paper on the walls.

Bar savored the conversation like a starving man.

In time, however, the subject returned to him. "Tell us more about your family, Barnabas," Helen said, trying to sound cordial when all she was really thinking about was Frank. Even Sunny noticed the intensity of her mother's gaze as she looked at Frank. Helen acted as if she hadn't seen him in years.

"Not much more to tell, really," Bar said. "After Pa died, my stepmother remarried. I stayed with her until I finished school and began reading law."

"How did your father die?" Frank asked, working on a second slice of cake.

Bar tried to find words to tell them but the silence grew lengthy.

Finally Sunny spoke. "It's a painful subject, I'm sure. Tell Bar about when we first got to Crystal Springs, Ma."

Helen laid down her fork.

"Frank had just opened his store. He was kind

enough to advance Abel and me quite a lot of credit," she said, looking gratefully into the merchant's eyes. "We had virtually nothing but the clothes on our backs. No pots. No flour. We came by stagecoach, Sunny and I. Abel had come the year before and was just putting the roof on the cabin." She indicated the adjoining kitchen, and then fell silent.

This appeared to be an inopportune time to be thinking of Abel Summerlin, Bar concluded, seeing Sunny's wistful expression.

Pushing aside his plate, Frank groaned with satisfaction. "Well, I have to tell you, Sunny, this is just possibly the best chocolate cake I ever had. You should enter it at the county fair baking contest on Independence Day."

"Maybe I will," Sunny said with forced cheer.

"It was supposed to have been my gift to hang the wallpaper, Helen," Frank went on, pushing back his chair. "But while on the train I got the idea to come back with something more than good intentions."

Helen blushed. "You needn't bring me a thing but your most welcome company, Frank," she said. "After all, we're under quarantine. By coming here, you've taken your life into your hands."

"And my heart," he said softly, glancing self-consciously at Sunny, and then at Bar.

As Frank withdrew a small jewelers' box from his trouser pocket, Helen's hand went nervously to her unadorned collar.

"For you, dear, on the occasion of your birthday." Frank's face reddened. "May you have many more as beautiful."

Helen lifted a gold-rimmed white cameo brooch from the box. "It's lovely," she said, her eyes widening and beginning to glisten with tears. Immediately she pinned it on. "How does it look?"

Frank stared as she did so. Sunny appeared amazed to see Helen adjust her large oval pin and then rise to admire herself in the mirrored sideboard.

"It's wonderful, Ma."

"Oh, yes, very lovely, Frank. Thank you." Helen turned, smiling.

Frank swallowed with difficulty.

"I haven't told you about *my* gift," Sunny announced then, her tone strained, her eyes glistening, too. "My surprise."

Bar felt the excitement building and marveled at the love so openly exhibited in this family.

"I thought the wallpaper . . ."

"That was just something you needed and deserved," Sunny said, taking on the flushed excitement of a girl. "In any case, I still can't believe Ol' Foote didn't spill the beans."

"What on earth are you talking about, Susanna?" her mother asked, sitting down next to Frank and taking his arm again.

"I've paid off our loan." Sunny produced the promissory note with "Paid in full" scrawled at the bottom. She presented it to her mother with a flourish.

Taking the paper, Helen looked at it a full minute, her brow furrowing. "But how?"

As Sunny explained the extra hours brewing liniment, the increasing demand for the little brown bottles of brew at Frank's store, Helen's face took on an expression that brought a tightness to Bar's throat.

Frank looked earnestly into Helen's wide brown eyes. "Without the loan to pay off, Helen, you won't need to take in boarders anymore. Your working days are over, dear. You already grow most of all the food you need to survive here, just the two of you. Sunny's liniment sales are steady. It would be enough to—" Frank paused.

It was apparent to Bar that much remained unsaid due to his presence. He edged his chair back. "The doctor told me he'll lift the quarantine Sunday if I don't show further signs of fever. I should get some rest. I'd like to be on my way as soon as possible."

Helen blinked as if trying to rouse herself from a dream. She looked at Bar and said, "I don't have to run a boardinghouse any longer." When she realized she was speaking to a stranger her gaze shifted to Sunny.

Sunny beamed. "Just think of it, Ma. You've been cooking and cleaning for folks almost all your life. Now it's time for you to start doing the things you enjoy. Happy birthday."

Helen dabbed her eyes. "That old grouch can't threaten to take my house ever again."

With great ceremony, Frank stood. "Well, now. Mr. Landry looks tuckered out. So do you, Sunny. Helen, would you do me the honor of walking with me in the moonlight? It's cool, but I did a heap of thinking while on that train. I'd like to talk to you, in private."

Sunny dashed for her mother's jacket and mittens. In moments the couple had gone out, leaving Bar alone with Sunny, who couldn't resist peeking out the window into the darkness.

"Where does your handyman sleep?" Bar asked in an effort to turn the conversation away from the emotional scene he had just witnessed.

"The handyman? He has a room in the barn. He's

afraid of people because he got beat up one time. Almost died. You've probably heard him chopping wood or playing with our dogs." Sunny came away from the window wearing a pensive smile. "Homer's very loyal, but he keeps to himself."

"He doesn't eat in here with you and your ma and the boarders?"

"He won't come inside. We leave him a tray on the back step. I know it sounds odd, but so long as we don't force him to do something he doesn't want to do, he works very hard for us. He tends all the stock, and my summer garden. He makes all the repairs around the place, and believe me, there are plenty. Sometimes he helps me stir the liniment. It makes my eyes water but the smell doesn't bother him. Ma thinks his nose was damaged in the beating."

"Who did it?"

"We've never known for certain. It happened outside a saloon more than ten years ago. Doc Hamilton hadn't come to town yet, so they brought him to Papa. I think it was Lyford McKidrict who did it. He has quite a temper when he's drunk. It could've been Cale. They're a family of no-accounts even if they do have the biggest ranch in two counties. Ma's convinced it was Luck McKidrict himself."

"Luck McKidrict, the man shot during the robbery?" Bar asked, starting for the office and the blessed comfort of the cot.

"Yes, the man you thought . . . I shouldn't attempt to imagine what you were thinking when you came here, Mr. Landry. It must feel awkward for you now, knowing you came all this way for nothing."

"Call me Bar, please, Sunny, if you will."

She looked up into his eyes.

Bar wanted to look away and avoid the penetration of her questioning gaze, but he went on staring back at her. He wanted to memorize her face.

"You apparently have little faith in the system of law and justice since you quit studying law to hunt outlaws. And you say you always give the bounty away?"

Bar nodded. "I work, too, at whatever I can find, as I said. I'm not much of a cowboy, but I make a tolerable bank clerk."

"Have you brought in many men?"

"It doesn't seem like it to me, but some tend to think I'm a fast gun."

Sunny seemed to be growing more tolerant of his occupation, Bar observed. Apparently she didn't understand it fully.

"And what becomes of the men you hunt? Do they go to prison and learn the error of their ways?"

Bar searched Sunny's dark brown eyes. Didn't she know what kind of world was out there, a world where men were beaten outside saloons, where fallen women degraded themselves inside them, where greed, crime, and hatred reigned from one end of the country to the other? Was all she knew right here in this safe, secluded valley?

He wanted to make her understand but that would mean telling her the truth, that sometimes when a man tried to do the right thing, he did the worst possible deed instead.

"Nothing became of them," Bar finally said. "I gave them no opportunity to learn the error of their ways. I shot them before they could get away and do more harm."

He let silence reign for a long time before continuing.

"Evil men don't learn, Susanna. They just die. And so do good men, sometimes. It all depends on who's doing the shooting. I decided I was going to be the one to even things out." He was breathing deeply, passionately, feeling an icy calm settling over his heart. His eyes were locked with hers. "I do it for justice."

Her eyes widened as his words sank into her imagination and she saw him killing again and again in the name of justice. He saw horror dawn and darken those eyes he so wanted to make dance and twinkle instead.

"But 'Vengeance is mine, saith the Lord,'" Sunny whispered in a quiet voice.

"What vengeance did the Lord seek for my father?" Bar demanded. The question chilled his own heart and caused Sunny to back away.

"Your father was murdered?" she asked.

"He was an innocent bystander, killed during a train holdup."

"Oh my, I'm sorry. Nothing was ever done about it?"

He didn't answer. He didn't have to. The answer was evident in all that he had been driven to do since.

Sunny shook her head. "You can't become a self-appointed avenging angel of God. That just makes you an outlaw with the name bounty hunter. If you've killed someone, Bar, I wonder how you sleep at night." Clapping her hand over her mouth, she left him at the doorway to the office and hurried away.

8

"*What did you think* about on the train, Frank?" Helen asked, hugging his arm as they strolled away from the house.

"I thought about you." He smiled. "And Sunny. I knew that she paid off the loan last Saturday, just before the robbery. She might have been in the bank when it happened. I thought about that."

"Oh, Lord," Helen said, shivering. "She's the dearest girl. I can hardly believe we're out of debt. I—I've kept her from having a normal life, working here with me for so long. It's time things changed."

Frank looked a bit taken aback. "Sunny's the most well-liked young lady in Crystal Springs. You should be proud."

"But she has no beaux."

"Ain't a man in town worthy of her."

"I don't know what came over me the evening that bounty hunter showed up. I took him in without a thought. It's true I was overwrought, thinking of things best left forgotten. I fancied the handsome young stranger was . . . well, I wanted him to be right for Sunny. Come to find out he's a man-hunter. I can't reconcile the truth with my fantasy. Isn't that silly?"

"Not at all." After a pause, Frank looked deeply into Helen's eyes and said softly, "Has it occurred to you, dear, that I can't go back to town tonight?"

Helen's heart fluttered with excitement. She looked away. It was time for her to start living, too, she reminded herself. Now that she was alone with Frank, she felt giddy.

He stopped in the night shadow of the big spruce. "I'm not mentioning that in an improper way, you understand," he said, clearing his throat and shifting nervously. "It's my way of pointing out that we've been lollygagging around this subject for darn near five years. I'm not about to compromise you tonight, Helen, much as I want to."

"Oh, Frank," Helen whispered. "I—I don't know what to say."

His hand stole to her cheek and he tilted her chin. Helen forced herself to meet his eyes. They were so unreadable in the moonlit darkness. But she heard his words. She felt his excitement in his tender touch.

"Do you still want me to come around? Now that you don't have to work anymore—" He took his hand away and rubbed it anxiously against his side.

"You're making it sound as if the boarders are never coming back, Frank. They'll be back Sunday night, probably. And they've paid through the end of the month." Helen began to wonder if she'd kept the boarders all these years as an excuse to avoid Frank's affection. "What I mean is, they'll need time to get used to the idea . . . of moving into town for good. I've spoiled them."

"I want you to start spoiling me, dear. And yourself. I know you're scared. So am I." Frank edged close again. "You're afraid I might die. I worry about losing you. I wake up in the night wondering where the hell my little girl is after all these years, and she's Sunny's age now. All I can do is trust that the good Lord's looking after her, wherever she is, since I can't."

Helen took his hand. The poor man. If he could let go with such faith, why was it so difficult for her to do the same? "You're such a good man, Frank."

He ducked his head and grinned. "You're the only woman I've given thought to since Aggie left me. Your Sunny's been like my own daughter. I want to know if I can come courting you proper now. I want to build a fire under all this. You're forty today, Helen. Well, I'm pushing fifty. I—I want to hold you and say foolish things and not worry that you'll laugh."

"I've never laughed at you, Frank!" Helen cried.

"No, ma'am, and you haven't hardly smiled either. Give me some encouragement, woman. I love you."

Helen giggled like a girl, her heart swelling with long-repressed emotion. Frank's arms slipped around her tenderly, engulfing her in warmth. She met his eyes and saw the love that she had known was there, protecting her from afar all these years. It was hers for the taking now.

"I haven't kissed a man since Abel died," she whispered. Her eyes stung with unshed tears. "I don't remember what it feels like."

Helen watched Frank bend closer. She saw his eyes close, and she almost sobbed in the joy of being loved by him. His soft warm lips pressed gently against her mouth. Then he backed off, grinning broadly.

"Wasn't so bad, was it?" he asked. "I'm no expert."

Helen couldn't find the words to express what it felt like to step forward into her new life. "I don't know why I've waited so long."

"Well, I had my doubts, too. I swore I'd never trust another woman with my heart. But you took it, Helen, before I even had a chance to think things over."

Throwing her arms around Frank's neck, she showed him just what she remembered about kissing. And Frank held her with a reverent passion that promised them both happiness.

Alone in the office, with the taste of chocolate cake still on his lips, Bar massaged the back of his aching neck. Then he pulled on his coat and went outside into the darkness. The cold snap had ended. The spring night felt dry and cool. The black sky spread overhead with a fine dusting of stars.

Pale moonlight illuminated the dooryard well enough for Bar to find his way back to the privy. By the time he came out, a half dozen dogs were prowling about him, ready to make friends. He stooped to pet them, and his troubled thoughts eased. The Summerlins' boardinghouse was indeed a wonderful place.

In the dim moonlight, Bar saw Frank and Helen coming back up the road. He heard the soft exchange of their voices and felt a stab of loneliness. Still massaging his neck, he sank to the flagstone step and waited for them to notice him. When Helen did, Bar pulled himself to his feet and stood as if at attention.

"Mrs. Summerlin, I can't stay if . . ." For a moment Bar couldn't go on. He didn't want to leave. "I can't stay if you feel that my presence is threatening."

"Let's not go over this again," Helen said in a soft tone he hadn't expected. She gave him a conciliatory smile. "You can't go. Even if you could, I wouldn't want you to. Go inside before the fever returns."

"I'd like to offer my cot to Mr. Tilsy," Bar said, feeling confused. She looked apologetic, but *he* was trying to apologize to *her*. "Since he has to stay now, on my account, I want him to be comfortable. I saw no other room available. I assume you aren't at liberty to offer him one of the boarders' rooms."

Frank responded to Helen's perplexed look. "The washhouse is fine for me, dear."

"I can't let you sleep in there, Frank."

Bar laid his hand on Frank's shoulder. "I'll sleep in the washhouse, sir, if you will allow. Mrs. Summerlin and her daughter have pointed out that I haven't much cause to be in Crystal Springs without a bounty to pursue. They're right. As long as you don't mind using the cot after a sick man, I see no reason why I should inconvenience anyone further."

"Very well," Helen said, looking bewildered and contrite. "It's true, I can't put anyone in my boarders' rooms. You'll be lonely in the washhouse, Barnabas, but I venture you've been by yourself before. There's a good heating stove in there, and a bench to sleep on. Sunny will fetch some blankets for you."

"I apologize for all the trouble I've already caused you. The moment I can be certain I'm not contagious,

I'll be gone. I would feel better, too, if you would write a bill of services rendered so that I can pay you before I leave. You've been more help than you'll ever know."

Feeling better for having cleared the air with Helen, Bar watched her smile and nod as she took Frank into the house. Bar looked forward to the two remaining nights of solitude. He could be there near them all, but apart, and safe.

By the time he had gathered his belongings into his saddlebags, Sunny was standing in the office doorway once again, a load of blankets in her arms. Her hair was down, and she was trying to keep a shawl wrapped tightly around her shoulders. Boots peeped from beneath the hem of her wrapper and nightgown. She looked utterly appealing.

"Ma tells me you'll be sleeping in the washhouse tonight," she said, looking worried. "Are you sure about this?"

"You know as well as I that it's better this way," Bar said.

"I'd rather you didn't tell me what I know. I *don't* know that it's better this way. I'm beginning to understand that you're a stubborn, single-minded man."

With a toss of her head, she led the way out into the chilled night.

"I don't like this idea one bit, if you would like to know what I really think," Sunny went on. "I sat up too many hours with you in a very hard and uncomfortable chair to see you catch your death out here after all. But since Ma thinks this is what *you* want, I'll show you how to light the stove. Then I'll leave you to yourself. The washhouse is better than the shed where I brew the liniment.

Summerlin Salts have an eye-watering smell." She gave him a smile that looked more challenging than playful.

Bar didn't want to tell Sunny that he needed to be apart from her and her mother in order to sort out his thoughts. After all they had done for him, it would surely sound insulting. Now he could think about where he intended to go without a beautiful, spirited young woman watching him from the partially opened doorway. She had no idea how aroused he felt, knowing she had seen him naked.

Sunny led him up a path behind the house along a series of stone-terraced levels to a large shed with no window. The spring gurgled just behind it. She went inside and lit a candle. As she began stuffing kindling into a potbellied stove, he followed her in.

It was a serviceable place with clotheslines, wash-tubs and supplies. Along the near wall a bench stood about a foot off the slatted floor.

A swiveling trough protruded from the back wall. "Homer invented this," Sunny said, showing him how it moved to catch water from the spring outside to fill the washtubs or bathing tub.

Bar dropped his saddlebags in the corner. Taking the blankets from her, he was about to say good-night when the look in her eyes stopped his heart. Every muscle in his body tensed with the desire to gather her into his arms. He held himself rigid, his gaze locked with hers.

"Do you think you'd feel well enough to go walking with me tomorrow?" she asked. "I could show you the Indian cave and the old gold mine where I used to play make-believe."

Her lashes were thick and dark, her eyes beautiful

and hypnotic. She smiled self-consciously as a flush spread across her smooth cheeks.

He found her face so captivating that it blotted every care from his mind. With Sunny Summerlin in his life he might actually be able to quit pursuing the outlaws who haunted his nightmares.

"I—I suppose it might be too difficult a climb for you just now, considering how sick you've been," she added when he didn't reply.

"Sick only at heart, Sunny."

"We could talk."

Bar felt that surge of energy again that had filled him when he woke from his fever. He felt young, alive, and full of hope. Looking at her made him feel that way.

"Did you play there alone when you played make-believe?" he asked in a husky tone. He imagined a young Sunny Summerlin in a smudged pinafore, playing with the imaginative boy he had once been. What mischief they would have made!

"Back then, the only girl my own age was May Sue McKidrict. She lives on the far side of the valley. Ma and I used to visit May Sue and her mother Julia. After May Sue's mother disappeared, and then my father died, Ma and I were too busy to visit. I played alone when I had the time. My childhood seems like a long time ago."

Bar nodded. "So does mine."

"What were you like as a boy?" Sunny asked, turning away abruptly to arrange a pallet for him on the bench.

"Quite naive, I'm afraid," Bar said. "That must be hard for you to imagine."

"I might be willing to believe a number of things

about you, Bar," she said. She smoothed the blankets to her satisfaction and then sat next to them on the bench. "Tell me about the first time you . . . uh . . . hunted an outlaw." Her expression was politely curious. She had no idea what she was asking.

A memory, so painful that it made him squint, came rushing into Bar's mind. The last thing he wanted to talk about was that first time he had tapped the rage in his heart.

"I mean, if you would, please," Sunny added softly, noting his strained expression. She got up to stoke the fire in the stove. Poking in several more splits of kindling, she added, "It's warmer in here already." Then she shivered as if realizing what unpleasantness she had started with her question.

Taking a place on the bench, Bar searched his mind for a way to begin. He had never explained to anyone how it had all begun. No one but newspaper reporters had ever asked and they were notorious for embellishing the truth. From the day he brought in those first outlaws, decent people had kept a healthy distance from him and his avenging gun.

Sunny turned from the stove.

Bar couldn't seem to remember the exact sequence of events that had made him walk away from everything he'd worked toward for so many years.

"I was twenty-one," he finally said, letting the words hang until silence closed in again.

She tried to smile. "So young."

To buy time and arrange his thoughts, Bar rummaged in his saddlebags until he found his two silver spoons. Putting them together, he tapped them lightly against his palm.

"I was tall and raw-boned. The world's ills troubled

my sleep. Some said I would be too sensitive to take up lawyering, but I was bound to try, for Pa." He tried to chuckle but the sound he made was more like a cough.

Tentatively, Bar began tapping the two spoons against his knee. Sunny folded her arms and tried to keep her expression open and receptive. Bar could tell she was sorry that she had asked.

The nervous clackety-clackety-clack of the two silver spoons began to sound irritating to him, too. If he could just make her understand . . .

In a husky drawl different from his usual speaking voice, Bar began singing. "Come nigh, li'l Johnny, for to tell you a story. . . ."

He had to clear his throat and then interrupted himself to explain.

"I met a shoeshine man on the street corner near where I used to walk to my library each day. His name was Cajah, and he was born a slave. He had come north after the war, looking for work. I thought he gave the best shine in town. He called me Marsy, which was an affectionate name for a young master where he once lived, he told me. 'Marsy,' he'd say. 'Step up here. Git them boots happy.'" Bar chuckled as pleasant memories filled his mind.

"Go on," Sunny prompted.

"He borrowed tunes and made up his own songs which he sang while he shined my shoes." Bar tapped his spoons. ". . . 'bout a man I knew long, long ago . . . wasn't much a farmer, couldn't shoot straight or whistle, but let me tell you what he meant to me. . . ."

Finally looking up, Bar smiled.

Sunny's face was outlined by the glow of the fire

shining through the grate. She was so beautiful. He didn't want to tell her this story. He didn't *have* to tell her.

"Go on," she urged softly.

For the longest moment his eyes caressed her lips. Then Bar realized he couldn't remember what a sweet kiss tasted like. He had tried easy women a few times, but the aftertaste was always far too bitter to be borne. He didn't know what the intimate touch of a decent woman's body felt like and feared he never would.

"'Twas the kindest living soul 'neath the stars and moon, my Johnny. An' he's done gone away from you and from me. . . ."

He stopped singing and debated whether to continue. It was an insult not to honor the memory of a man he had come to respect by singing his music, but the pain in Bar's heart threatened to choke him.

"These spoons remind me of Cajah. He taught me to play," Bar said. "When I play I feel as if my pa is back home working at the depot. I can pretend Cajah is on that corner still, buffing my boots."

"What happened to Cajah?" Sunny's cautious tone implied she had already guessed.

Bar sighed. "Cain't get to where he's gone to, little Johnny. Come nigh, boy. Let me tell you. . . ."

After a moment he said, "Cajah shined shoes outside a bank where the businessmen went by. They could afford a good shine and a sizable tip. Cajah died in the cross fire of a robbery one day. I wasn't there. I heard about it afterwards."

"How awful."

"At his funeral I met Cajah's wife and eight children. Half those children were already working. His wife took in laundry. She gave me Cajah's spoons.

After that, when I went by and Cajah wasn't there, I wondered what had become of his family. I expected something would be done for them."

"But nothing was?" Sunny asked.

"I read about them in the newspaper three months later. Cajah's wife and children had been turned out into the street. But a reward was being offered for the stolen money, a bounty. I was so angry I went to the bank, asking questions. It took me three days to learn what I needed to know. Then I bought a gun. Hundreds of miles away, in a saloon, I found the suspect and two of his friends."

Sunny's eyes widened.

"We had whiskey. We played poker. I lost all I had, except my gun. When they got drunk enough to babble, they laughed about shooting the shoeshine man just because he was there. I . . . I was going to force them to come back with me to stand trial. I can't quite remember. . . . "

Bar saw it clearly in his mind. He had felt the surge of power explode in his veins. A gun had gone off. Once. Twice. Three times. The circular in his pocket had said, *"Wanted:* Dead or Alive." Since those men hadn't been willing to come along with him and submit to arrest and a trial, Bar had taken them, all three of them, dead.

Bar was on his feet then, drawing an invisible gun from his waistband and pointing his hand at Sunny as if it were a weapon.

Sunny pressed herself against the wall next to the stove, a shocked expression on her face. "Bar? Bar!" she said with alarm.

Just telling the story of his first hunt produced this mindless response in him, Bar thought. The power of his obsession was stunning. If he couldn't control his hand reaching for an imaginary weapon during a story, how would he control himself when he faced the outlaw who had robbed the Crystal Springs Bank?

Edging back to the bench, he sank down and swallowed hard. He had thought the impulse to deal out justice with this gun gone with his mysterious fever, but nothing had changed. Nothing had changed!

"I gave Cajah's wife the bounty," Bar muttered.

He looked up. Sunny was staring at him as if she were just beginning to comprehend who and what he really was.

"I—I think the fire's going well enough in the stove now," Sunny said in a small voice, "and I think I understand what it's like for you . . . Bar. If you'll excuse me . . . Good-night."

She slipped out and pressed the washhouse's flimsy door tightly closed.

Hating himself, and angry with her for making him tell the story when he hadn't wanted to spoil the budding friendship between them, Bar began tapping the spoons again rapidly, trying to summon back the soothing memory of his friend. He began a different tune. "Back where the grass grows tall, where the sky is yellow, I see you smile, and I am. . . ."

Throwing the spoons aside, Bar lay back on the bench until the side of his body nearest the stove felt seared with heat and his far side felt numb to the bone.

He wished he understood why he had awakened from his two-day fever feeling so refreshed and alive, and he wished he could get the feeling back again.

What he did as a bounty hunter couldn't be right if

afterward he tried for six months to forget about it, Bar told himself. It couldn't be right to kill even an outlaw if he promised himself over and over that he would never do it again.

A normal man wouldn't hide in out-of-the-way jobs, trying to avoid contact with the world, determined to avoid triggering the impulse he knew he couldn't control. A normal man would leave justice to the courts and God. Bar closed his eyes. The temptation to disappear forever into the night came upon him.

Outside, Sunny stood shivering, listening to Bar's sad song. When she heard the spoons clatter to the washhouse floor, she almost went back inside. She wanted to help, to change him into the kind of man he was meant to be, but that expression on his face, that blazing, mindless look of hate and vengeance in his eyes overwhelmed her. Barnabas Landry was capable of terrifying her. She had to stop thinking he was a part of her life, and stop immediately.

9

The next morning, Sunny abruptly sat up in bed, marveling that she had been able to sleep after tossing and turning half the night, worrying about Bar.

It was later than usual, so she dressed quickly. Was there any hope of convincing Bar to give up bounty hunting? she wondered, knotting her hair and pinching her cheeks. That was what she had to do. But should she allow herself to be alone with him if they went for a walk today?

The smell of coffee, sizzling fatback, and freshly baked biscuits drew Sunny to the kitchen where Helen was serving Frank her best peach preserves on her Sunday china. She was wearing her favorite ruffled Christmas apron over her best dress.

"Good morning, sleepy head," Helen said, looking younger and prettier than Sunny had seen her mother in years.

"This is so strange, having the boarders gone. What'll we do with ourselves when they've moved out?" she asked.

Sunny saw her mother give Frank a little smile. What would they do, indeed! she thought. Just as Sunny had hoped, her mother was going to say yes to Frank, and soon. Sunny wondered how long it would take for Frank to propose to her mother. Weeks? Months?

"I, uh, asked Bar to go for a walk later," she said as a chorus of barking started outside. "Have you checked on him?"

One of their dogs ran past the back window, cutting across the laundry yard.

"Not yet," Helen said, with her thoughts obviously elsewhere.

Sunny got up and went to see what the ruckus was. The washhouse door hung open. Her heart stopped at the thought that Bar might have left in the night. She'd left him in a terrible frame of mind.

The dog raced past again, and it was then Sunny saw that the old mutt was chasing a thrown stick.

"I think I'll go out," she said, snatching a shawl that was hanging from a peg by the door.

In her bare feet Sunny stepped onto the broad flagstone that served as a rear porch. The morning air was brisk and sweet.

"Good morning," she called to Bar who was standing near the barn.

"Just checking on Sundown," Bar called back, whipping another stick to his left, across the front dooryard. Three dogs went after it that time. He grinned. "This is quite a menagerie you have here."

"More every year. Looks like you weathered the

night all right in the washhouse," Sunny said, thinking of how her father used to enjoy playing with animals. Bar was also wearing her pa's old brown plaid shirt, which looked odd compared to his expensive black trousers.

She saw Homer emerge from the barn and was about to call a warning to Bar to be cautious and gentle with the handyman when the timid man went right up to Bar and tugged his shirtsleeve. Sunny was astonished at how comfortable Homer seemed with Bar already.

Bar waved to Sunny and followed Homer back into the barn. Moments later Sunny heard Bar's clacking spoons tapping out a lively rhythm.

"Ma, you won't believe this," Sunny whispered as if afraid her words would end the magical moment. Quickly she ducked back inside to pull on her boots.

"You're not going out without a proper breakfast," Helen warned.

Sunny giggled. "You haven't used that tone with me since I was twelve years old. Bar's in the barn with Homer."

Helen put down the bowl of hash browns she'd been offering Frank. "Oh, no," she said, hurrying toward the back door where Sunny was motioning for her to come and look. "Homer's going to pitch a fit," Helen said.

"Listen." Sunny hissed.

Sunny could hear Bar tapping out "Dixie," accompanying his singing with the spoons. After a brief silence, Sunny and Helen heard the clumsy efforts of their handyman giving the song a try.

Frank came up behind Helen and Sunny. "That poor fella doesn't even take to me all that much, and

I've known him for years. I reckon Homer knows something about your bounty hunter that we don't."

As Sunny dashed out to join Bar and Homer, she called back to her mother. "Pack us a lunch, would you please, Ma? If I can talk Bar into staying on . . . awhile . . . would you mind? Please, Ma?" Sunny realized she hadn't begged like that since she was twelve, either.

Sunny didn't wait for a reply. She was certain her mother wouldn't object. She wouldn't allow her to.

Coming up short at the barn door, Sunny stood squinting until her eyes adjusted to the dusty gloom within.

Homer sat on a crate, and Bar was crouched beside him, helping the handyman get the spoons arranged between his fingers. Homer grinned lopsidedly and went on grinning even after he glanced up and found Sunny standing in the doorway, watching. Ordinarily he would have been upset at being caught unawares and would have run off to hide.

As Homer tapped happily, Bar straightened and ruffled the handyman's hair as if he were a boy instead of a fully grown man.

"Sundown's never been tended this well," Bar said, going to the stall where his black gelding stood curried to perfection. "I've been trying to thank your handyman for his help. I just about scared him out of his wits this morning when I happened in. I was afraid he was going to tear me to pieces, but I think he heard me playing the spoons last night. He took me up to the washhouse and . . . well, it was hard figuring out what he wanted from me until we found the spoons under the washtub. I, uh, dropped them. I've been his best pal ever since. Isn't that right, ol' buddy? What's his name, Sunny?"

"Homer," Sunny answered. "That's all we know. He's never been able to tell us where he was from, or the rest of his name."

Sunny was moved. Not a man in Crystal Springs would have given Homer the time of day, much less given him two silver spoons that held such sentimental value. Most folks just made fun of Homer. He was a freak and a misfit, folks said, and should not be left alone with two women all day long, but Helen and Sunny knew he was harmless.

"Are you hungry?" Sunny asked, quivering with excitement. "I hope Homer will allow you to walk with me. He's taken quite a shine to you, it looks like. I never would have believed it possible. Thank you for . . . being so generous."

As Bar moved closer, Sunny's heart began thundering in her chest.

"I'm sorry about last night," he said. "I didn't mean to frighten you."

Shrugging, Sunny led Bar into the morning sunlight. "You startled me, is all. I'm concerned that Homer won't return your spoons when you want them back."

"If they make him happy, he's welcome to them."

Sunny looked up into Bar's face. His expression was wistful—not smiling, but not too sad, either. He'd shaved, and his black hair was still a bit damp. She couldn't get over how gentle he looked, how thoughtful, and yes, sensitive. It was that sensitivity that drove him, she concluded, reminded of his story about Cajah, the shoeshine man.

"You know, Bar, there's really no reason for you to pursue . . . What I mean to say is, our town has a perfectly competent sheriff who is looking into the bank robbery. He'll find the person who did it. You needn't . . ."

"Interfere?"

"Well, yes. All you need to do is trust that . . . I mean, Cajah was a black man and so it was unfortunate that justice wasn't served."

"The next victim I avenged was a clerk, a young white man, killed accidentally when a random gunshot went through the front window of the store where he'd been working about a week. No one cared about that, either. He left a mother and sister destitute. The bounty I gave them enabled them to go back east to relatives. The next was an elderly rancher killed for the cash in a quart jar that he had buried in his barn. Senseless. Do you want me to go on?"

She shook her head. The last thing she wanted to do was anger him.

"I can't bring back the outlaws I killed, even if I wanted to, which I don't. I am a bounty hunter now, Sunny. I'm scarred by what I've done. To be rather melodramatic about it, I believe that I am damned."

"Forgive yourself and you'll be forgiven. Turn over a new leaf. Since May Sue and her brothers won't need any bounty, let it end here."

His jaw hardened stubbornly. Was there any use? she wondered.

"Let's forget it for today, Sunny," Bar said, tentatively touching her sleeve. "Tomorrow I'll be gone in any case. You said something about a walk. . . ."

"But you could . . . stay on in Crystal Springs. And work." She made a face that was intended to tell Bar that she knew she was acting foolishly. "Isn't there something else you could do to make a living? I mean, you're not always stalking some outlaw, are you? What were you doing before you got on the train Tuesday morning?"

"Counting cows," he said, smiling. "Keeping books for a rich rancher who is very annoyed that I left on such short notice. He had me writing letters to senators and congressmen about the new range laws. He's very ambitious. There's a lot I can do. I suppose I could even go back aast and get my degree." His expression darkened. "I'll consider the idea."

They went inside to the rich aromas of breakfast, but Sunny didn't feel reassured.

Sunny was still trying to think of ways to convince Bar to give up bounty hunting when they set out for their walk later that morning.

"Tell me if you get tired," she said, leading the way up behind the house.

She kept the pace slow, so slow in fact that by the time they reached the ridge she'd forgotten her cares. She felt like a girl again, seeking adventure. Bar never let on that he was tired. A man couldn't be as ill as he had been and recover completely in a day. She supposed she was being selfish, wanting to be alone with him a while.

"There, see the rocky hollow?" she asked.

He came alongside her and followed her pointing finger. Sunny suddenly couldn't catch her breath.

"Can you make it?" She panted, pretending that the climb had winded her, and not his glance into her eyes.

"I would gladly follow you anywhere, m'lady," he said in a gallant tone. "Lead on."

Sunny darted ahead, scrambling along the narrow deer trail until she had reached her favorite place in all the world.

"Here it is," she called loudly, pausing to listen for her echo.

Huffing from the exertion, Bar finally joined her and placed the picnic basket on the ground. He turned to survey the valley stretching out for miles. The sky was high and pale, ablaze with eye-stinging sunlight.

Sunny's heart shivered. "Isn't it beautiful up here?"

"I can see why you like it," he said, spreading his arms and drawing in a deep chestful of the bracing air.

"See the smudges here?" Sunny said, indicating the roof of the stone hollow where they stood, darkened by the smoke of ancient campfires. "Ute Indians used to camp here. One day I played here for so long Ma was afraid I'd been carried off."

She turned, feeling as young and carefree as she had that year before her father had died. The way Bar was looking at her made her realize that for all the minor flaws she was likely to see in herself on any given day, on this particular day, in this special place, Barnabas Landry thought she was perfectly beautiful.

"You don't hate Indians like most folks," Bar said, his eyes fixed on her every movement.

She found a seat on a boulder. "I don't know," she said, feeling self-conscious. "I hate to hear about their attacks on settlers. Ma was right to worry back then. Utes still lived in these mountains. I wouldn't say we're entirely safe, even today. Why must it be like that, the strong vanquishing the weak?"

Bar looked back over the valley. "That would depend on your opinion of evolution, Miss Summerlin."

His tone was teasing, as if he were introducing a controversial subject in a formal drawing-room atmosphere. Behind his words, however, she heard the seriousness of his tone.

They chattered on for what seemed like hours, their subjects ranging from brands of coffee to the newly elected president. In time, Sunny could see that Bar was tiring. He fell silent and seemed content to watch her as she went on, happily filling the silence, trying to stretch the day and make it last.

As Bar leaned back on his elbow, he tried to memorize every part of her.

Her hair was the most glorious chestnut color, dark and rich with glinting red highlights. He longed to bury his face in those cool, glistening waves as he held her close. Her eyes flashed and twinkled, sometimes pinning him with the truth, often coaxing him with innate kindness. He felt warm when she smiled. He felt safe. He felt free.

She liked to wave her arms about when she talked, indicating this place or that. Her stories were innocent, wholesome. He tried to control his more carnal desire for her, which he could only contain by reminding himself of what he had become, a man hunter, someone Sunny instinctively feared. And rightly so. Even he could not predict what he would do with the rest of his life once this day ended.

If only it did not have to end. Touch me, Sunny Summerlin. Draw me into your world, Bar thought.

The wind blew the calico snug along her thighs. She was wearing the brown jacket that fit snugly over her torso, outlining her full young bosom. He wanted to see all of her, possess her in every way.

Finally, when he had not made so much as a grunt of a reply in a long while, she let the silence fall over them. She looked at him, concerned, and gave a tender smile.

"You look hungry."

He was, indeed.

Almost at once, Sunny blushed, her face turning an exquisite crimson. Quickly she snatched up the picnic basket and spread a blanket beneath the sooty overhead rocks. "I talk too much."

He could see that she was nervous, being alone with him this long. He wanted to reassure her, but to do so would only lead to trouble. He wanted to touch her hand. His heart leapt every time he thought about it. *Just touch her,* he told himself, never moving an inch closer. *A touch won't hurt,* he told himself. But he felt frozen.

"Come and sit," she said, arranging herself on the blanket and folding her legs beneath her skirt Indian style.

Bar summoned the strength to join her. They ate thick slices of bread spread with sweet apple butter. The cider she brought along was so strong it made his eyes water.

"Where's that gold mine you were telling me about?" he asked when he was finished eating.

Jumping up, she brushed crumbs from her skirt. "It's not far. I'll race you." Then she was off, clambering up between boulders, scrambling around bushes and laughing like a girl.

He was falling in love with her, Bar thought, watching her disappear along the faint deer trail. He let the feeling spread through his body, marveling at the sweet intoxication of it.

He didn't have to prove anything to himself, he thought, closing his eyes and trying to keep his thinking straight. He could just stay in this out-of-the-way mountain town with Sunny and . . .

He scrambled to his feet. He wanted to roar with frustration.

If he didn't test his resolve by hunting the bank robber and bringing him back alive, he would never be able to trust himself. He would never know what he might do if those old feelings of vengeance were triggered again. It would be better to swear off thoughts of Sunny now rather than risk loving her and hurting her later.

"Bar?" she called down the trail. "You didn't fall off the mountain, did you?"

"Coming," he said, shaking off his self-doubts.

When he caught up with her, she was standing alongside some huge gray boulders the size of the washhouse. He wanted to sweep her into his arms and promise that he would never kill again. He'd show her. He'd vanquish the demons in his heart. He'd be whole again. With her.

But he didn't sweep her into his arms. He just looked at her with the certain knowledge that if he loved her, as he did at that moment, he had to be whole. He could only be whole by his own doing.

Behind Sunny, between the huge boulders, was a dark, ominous-looking opening that was the entrance to the abandoned gold mine. Bar's heart went cold to see it.

She grinned and said, "Come on. It doesn't go in very far, but it slopes downward. There's one big step down over some rocks. I fell the first time I went in and skinned my knees. Be careful. It's dark."

With a toss of her head, she disappeared inside.

Bar couldn't move.

His heart began to thud. His stomach knotted around the tart cider. He could hear her faint voice and wanted to shout for her to come out before she became trapped. Trapped by what, he wondered.

"Well, are you coming?" She stuck her head back out. "Scaredy-cat." Her cheeks were flushed as if she were forcing herself to be a bit more daring than usual. "Bar?"

"My dream . . ." was all he could manage to say.

The wind moaned through the tops of the surrounding pines and the brilliance of the morning dimmed.

Sunny stood a full minute staring at him, watching his face drain to a ghastly white. He looked ill suddenly. Her heart sank as she realized their afternoon was not going to end as she had hoped, in strong and mutual friendship.

Drawing a quick breath, she sighed as if not noticing his pallor. "It's awfully dark in there," she said, dusting her skirts. "I don't really like it. I feel like the mountain is going to swallow me. I think I need to sit down."

Pretending to be faint, she came out into the glaring sunlight, which seemed harsh now instead of beautiful. Most men would take that as an invitation to assist her.

But Bar didn't respond. He didn't seem to hear her.

Alarmed, Sunny forced herself to lean casually back against one of the boulders, hoping to regain the levity she'd felt moments before. "I guess I'm not as brave as I used to be," she said.

Still Bar didn't seem to hear. He was apparently thinking of something ugly that twisted his face and deadened his eyes. *Oh, mercy,* she thought, how she feared him when he looked like that.

All morning she'd been trying to pretend that she hadn't seen a murderous rage in his eyes the night before. But she couldn't keep lying to herself. This was a man capable of killing. His victims had been outlaws, true, but he had killed just the same.

He might be handsome, and he might be good with her dogs and with Homer, but pretending that he was well, and normal, was not a good idea.

"Bar," she said, dropping the lighthearted tone. "What's wrong?"

Although he finally looked at her, she couldn't be certain that he was seeing her.

"I can see you don't want to go into the mine," she said. "That's fine. It's not important to me that we do. I was just . . . trying to have a little fun. Honestly, Bar. You're acting so strange. Have you lost your senses?"

Suddenly she felt impatient and reckless.

"What would you do if an outlaw was in a place like this? Could you follow him in or would you wait until—" She clapped her hand to her mouth. "I can't believe I said such a thing," she whispered, recalling how she had challenged him the night before, too.

Provoking a bounty hunter was not wise. Was she trying to punish Bar for being something she couldn't abide?

Still Bar gave no reaction.

"Forgive me, Bar. Do you feel faint?"

She went to him and took hold of his rigid arm. She ran her hand up over his shoulder, thrilled just to touch him. Then she settled her palm on his forehead. His skin was damp and clammy.

Blinking, he looked down at her hand, which was clutching his arm, steadying him. He took hold of her other wrist and removed her palm from his forehead.

His eyes began to soften, and Sunny's heart danced with relief. He was back.

"I don't know what came over me." His brow furrowed, and sweat beaded in the creases of his forehead.

She helped him find a seat on a fallen pine trunk. "What were you thinking?"

"When I was sick," he began, "I dreamed about a tunnel."

"You remember now?"

He shook his head.

"You dreamed about your pa, Bar. You screamed his name. You must've dreamed about the train robbery you told me about."

Bar looked into her eyes with such intensity, Sunny could almost feel him touch her soul. He was having difficulty getting the words out.

She watched his lips twist.

"He got in the way."

She tightened her grasp on his arm. "Your father got caught in the cross fire? Before, or after Cajah was killed?"

"I was fourteen."

The words sank into her. A mere boy. "Oh, Bar. Were you there?"

The cords in his neck began to strain. She'd never seen a grown man suffer so. She didn't want to see it now, not in this man who could look so malicious at times and so tender at other times.

"You *saw* him die?" she asked, probing his pain. "And nothing was ever done." *Of course not,* she thought.

He stared at her silently, his midnight blue eyes almost black with anguish.

"Don't you see what you've been doing?" she asked, her heart hammering. It was so clear to her. She watched puzzlement replace the intensity in Bar's eyes.

"You're not hunting outlaws for the justice of it." She put her hand around his shoulder. "You're killing the man who killed your father, over and over again. It's got to stop, Bar. It won't bring your pa back."

10

All Sunny had wanted to do, she thought, trudging down the trail ahead of Bar, was to make him see the uselessness of trying to avenge his father's death. Instead of freeing him from grief, however, she seemed to have plunged him back into it. In the last hour, he hadn't spoken a word.

As they emerged at the stand of pines near where her father was buried, behind the sprawling boarding-house, Sunny could see that Bar's thoughts were a thousand miles away.

Unable to bear looking at her father's grave with-out touching a similarly sore spot in her own heart, she started toward the back door to the kitchen, thinking Bar would follow.

"I'm going to rest awhile," Bar said, veering off toward the washhouse without looking at her.

"I'll wake you when supper's . . ."

Her words trailed off as he went inside the small structure and quietly closed the door.

She could have kicked herself. Couldn't she learn to leave well enough alone? They'd been having a wonderful time.

But what did it matter? He'd be gone in another day. He seemed to have little interest in staying on, and who would want to, relegated to the hard narrow slats of a washhouse bench?

Suddenly she felt angry with Frank for being there, not only because he was taking the cot from Bar but also because he was distracting her mother. Sunny needed to talk to her. She needed to get her thoughts clear.

Inside, Sunny found the kitchen deserted and untidy. Frowning at dishes piled in the dry sink and the bread left uncovered on the cutting board, she hurried into the dining room to find more silence. Where were her mother and Frank? An absurd possibility popped into her mind as she peeked into her mother's bedroom, but she found it empty as well. Mentally, she shook herself for thinking such unlikely thoughts.

Then she heard voices, hushed and intimate sounding, coming from the parlor, which they kept closed off except for evenings and Sunday afternoons. She found her mother sitting on the divan, showing Frank their collection of stereopticon slides, holding the viewer up to his eyes and giving him little kisses on his cheek while he marveled at the seven wonders of the world.

Sunny cleared her throat. "We're back, Ma. I . . . I don't think Bar's feeling well again."

Her mother edged back from Frank and smiled like a shy schoolgirl. "Did you have a nice walk, honey?"

"I think I took him too far," Sunny said. "Do you want me to tidy up and start supper?"

Helen looked distracted. "We're not hungry."

Confused, Sunny excused herself and spent the next two hours in the kitchen. Her mother was behaving like a love-struck girl, Sunny thought with a pang of jealousy. It was such an abrupt change, Sunny found it difficult to accept. At this rate her mother and Frank would be married before the end of the year!

Where did that leave her? Sunny wondered, laying the table for dinner and feeling a wave of exhaustion overtake her. It left her exactly where she wanted to be, she told herself. After her mother was married, she would work alongside her at the daily chores, the same as always. There just wouldn't be any boarders. There would be Frank.

Appalled at her own unanticipated resentment, Sunny scolded herself for begrudging her mother the very thing she had so long prayed for, happiness. If she was feeling left out, Sunny told herself, it was her own fault. It was high time she gave thought to her own future. She needn't be an old maid forever.

Taking a moment to rest in her room, Sunny couldn't stop wondering if Bar was all right. She kept getting up from her bed and going to the window to see if he was up and about. Homer was carrying loads of kindling to the kitchen door, looking as if he wondered where Bar was, as well.

She was being silly, Sunny told herself. She had no hold on Bar. He was a virtual stranger. Even if he might prove to be someone special in her life, it would take months, perhaps years to get to know him, to trust him, to welcome him as Helen was now welcoming the courtship of a man she'd called friend for a very long time.

Was it possible that Sunny was so starved for a man's attentions that she wanted to interfere with the first one to come along, and mold him into her ideal? Could she really want a man so much and yet be unaware of it, the way Bar was unaware of his true motivations for being a bounty hunter?

Sunny was still stewing when she went out to the washhouse at dusk to wake him for supper.

She tapped lightly on the door and stepped in to find him seated on the bench, a lighted lantern close at hand.

Whatever she had been about to say next evaporated at the sight before her. The pieces of his ebony-handled gun lay neatly in the recesses of an open velvet-lined case. He was cleaning them one by one, polishing away every speck of mud that had gotten on it when he fell off his horse into her arms. The expression on his face was dark and forbidding.

A chill went up her spine. "Supper's on . . . if you're hungry," she said in a small voice.

As he glanced up at her, she noticed a distant look in his eyes. She had indeed overstepped her bounds that afternoon, she thought miserably. He had closed himself off from her now. He was a bounty hunter again. She could see that he was growing harder and colder as the memory of his feverish dream receded.

"Thank you," he said, not coldly, but more formally than she would have liked. "I'll be along in a moment. Don't wait on my account."

"A-are you all right, Bar?"

He studied her face and briefly his eyes softened.

"I'm much better, thank you. What time will the doctor be coming tomorrow?"

"Noon, most likely, after church lets out. You won't have to go right away, will you? Frank will probably go back to town, so you can have the cot again. If I know our boarders, they'll want to talk to you. I—I'm sorry, Bar, if I said something I shouldn't have."

Bar looked thoughtful. "I've been going over what you said, about me trying to kill the man who killed my father. I think there's more to what I'm doing than that, Sunny. If it was that simple . . ."

"Simple?" she said. "It's not simple at all. You haven't grieved for your father."

His expression told her she couldn't begin to fathom his feelings on the matter and should stop trying. Suddenly she was ashamed for thinking she had any right or even the ability to judge his reasons for hunting outlaws.

"Supper will get cold," she said, wishing instantly that she could snatch back even those words once they were said. She sounded like a mother prodding a reluctant child.

Wanting to apologize but not knowing how, she finally slipped out the door.

She was still scolding herself as she took her place at the supper table a few minutes later. When Bar joined them, looking subdued, she couldn't stop herself from stealing looks at him every so often, hoping against hope that he would yet come around.

How desperately she missed that warm, relaxed look in his eyes when he first woke. Thinking back to that morning, Sunny began to wonder if he'd actually been himself at that time. Maybe his gentle gaze and playful smile had been some kind of reaction to that terrible delirium he'd been in. Maybe he would never be like that again.

Helen and Frank talked about Frank's trip to Denver and all the sights to be seen there. Helen looked ready to go see them. Sunny only nodded or gave an occasional remark.

Bar remained quiet throughout the meal, giving replies only when addressed. His appetite was off, and he seemed apathetic.

Helen caught Sunny's eye only once, silently asking what was wrong. Sunny could only shrug.

Sunny insisted that Helen and Frank take another moonlit walk after supper and met with little resistance. By the time she had finished cleaning up after the meal, she found Bar on the porch, staring into the valley's velvety darkness.

She stood there a long time, wondering if she should attempt another serious conversation with him or just give up.

"Did Homer bring you enough firewood for the night?" she asked when the silence threatened to madden her. She wanted to talk to Bar. She wanted him to confide in her.

"I'm fine in there, Sunny," he said.

She took a seat on the step nearby and huddled within her shawl. It took every ounce of her self-control to resist reaching out to touch him. If she had, she would have encountered his knee, and that was completely inappropriate.

"If I spoke out of turn this afternoon," she finally said, unable to feign a casual attitude, "it's only because I'd like to help."

She heard him sigh, but she didn't care. She had to keep trying.

"You're more than welcome to board here with us for as long as you like. That's what I'm trying to tell you, that you're welcome and wanted. I can't imagine that Ma will actually send our boarders packing at the end of the month. Her heart's too soft for that. You watch. Tomorrow when they return she'll cater to them as if they were petty kings."

"Tell me more about your ma's boarders," Bar said as if trying to distract her from her original intent.

Sunny was willing to go along in hopes of lifting his mood. "Grodie's an adorable little man, a barber so short he stands on a stool to cut hair. He loves to talk, and if that isn't enough, we also have the newspaper reporter living with us, so Ma and I know everything there is to know about what goes on in Cassidy County. There's a jolly man who letters signs. He's really quite good at lettering. It would also be nice if he could spell, but most folks don't mind that he can't. He proposed to me a week after he arrived in town."

"But you declined?" Bar asked, his voice softening.

"When I accept a proposal of marriage, it'll be because the man wants *me* and not just my abilities in the kitchen."

"In other words, you want love," he said.

She broke out in goose bumps. "Yes, I do."

"I can see that your mother's very much in love with Mr. Tilsy."

"My, yes. I knew she was fond of him, but these past two days, she's outdone herself. I can't think what changed things in her mind unless it was her birthday."

"Perhaps it was Mr. Tilsy's daring," Bar said. "He braved the quarantine to be with her. I admire him for that."

"Frank's a dear," Sunny said. The gesture *had* been remarkable, she thought. She realized that she was finally adjusting to the idea of the man being around permanently. "For years he's been like a father to me. Bar, where will you go, if you go tomorrow?"

She heard him chuckle softly in the darkness.

"You are a determined young woman, Miss Summerlin." He sounded amused. "What is it you want from me? Repentance?"

"Don't be silly. I—I just felt we somehow became friends during those hours together when you were unconscious. This has had a disturbing effect on me."

"What has?"

"This . . . this change in our routine, a stranger in the house who needed our help . . . your dream . . . the way you looked at me the morning you first woke. I can't say you are the same man now as you were that morning." Her heart drummed with the audacity of her words. Never had she spoken so frankly with a man before.

"I'm not the same man," he said, his tone deeper. "I think it was just . . . I don't know, either. I was glad to be alive, I guess. Everything smelled so good. Colors seemed brighter. Food tasted better for some reason. I felt . . . awake in a deeper sense. It's not like that now. I feel like I'm walking through fog, hardly able to lift my feet, much less my spirits."

"You're weak yet. That's why I want you to stay."

"I sense that you're trying to help me, Sunny, and I'm grateful. I truly am, but I'm not the kind of person you want around. I have business to attend to, if not here, then somewhere else."

"More bounty hunting?"

"That depends. I came all this way. I should look

into things before leaving. I'll go to the hotel if my investigation troubles you."

"I don't understand why—"

"I told you. There's more to what I do than killing a substitute for the outlaw who killed my pa. If I knew what it was that drove me, perhaps I could explain it. All I know is, something has to be done about this senseless violence. Who, better than me, to take up the task?"

Sunny looked at him and could tell that he believed his own reasoning. Did she have any hope in the face of that?

11

Bar woke, flailing his arms. Twisting as if trying to catch something, he tumbled from the narrow bench to the floor, striking his head on the bathing tub nearby.

Then he remembered where he was. He sagged back against the washhouse bench and groaned.

His forehead was cold with sweat. His inner struggle had returned, he thought with a sinking heart. He was what he had made of himself, and now he couldn't change back.

Bar struggled to his feet. In a few hours the doctor would pronounce him well. He'd be gone from Crystal Springs before any more damage could be done to the beautiful young woman who had tried to help him. Bar couldn't risk staying near Sunny another day. If he did, she'd have him making promises he couldn't keep.

But after stoking the fire in the stove and lying

back on the bench, Bar couldn't sleep. He couldn't recall his dream no matter how hard he tried. And he couldn't get the thought of Sunny Summerlin out of his mind.

How he would have liked to live up to her expectations, but he couldn't pluck back the bullets he had fired into those men. Because of him, they had found a swift and permanent justice. He was a killer, and a killer didn't deserve love.

At dawn he felt exhausted. Even if the doctor ordered him to stay, he would have to leave. He couldn't go on living with his own torment and his feelings for Sunny, too.

To Bar's surprise, however, he woke what seemed like seconds later to find Homer bending over him, a looming shadow surrounded by glare.

By the sunlight slanting through the open doorway, Bar could tell it was now nearly nine o'clock. "Good morning, Homer," he said softly, trying in spite of his headache to smile for the handyman. "I didn't think I'd sleep again. What's wrong?" He sat up and groaned over his sore muscles and aching back.

Homer revealed the two silver spoons. The handles were bent. He shrank back when Bar took them.

"How'd this happen, huh? Must've been a humdinger of a tune you were playing, ol' buddy," Bar said. He wondered if Homer had a temper. "Did you get angry because you couldn't play them?"

Homer just watched Bar warily, as if expecting punishment.

Bar tried to straighten the handles but couldn't.

"Well, never mind," he said. "Maybe Mrs. Summerlin has a couple old ones to spare. These were too heavy for you."

Homer couldn't take his eyes from Bar's gentle smile as Bar stood and stretched. Bar wondered what went on inside that battered head of Homer's. He had to admire Sunny and her mother for giving someone like that a place and a purpose.

"It's all right, ol' buddy," Bar said. "I know about frustration. They were only spoons, after all."

Bar paused long enough to ponder his own words. He shook off the disquieting possibility that perhaps he should be turning his own uncontrollable emotions to less harmful outlets.

After running a comb through his hair and changing into his own gray shirt in anticipation of the doctor's arrival, Bar took Homer down to the kitchen. The morning was brisk, swaddled in early morning mist. As usual, Homer refused to go inside the house. Bar ruffled his hair and left him cringing on the doorstep.

"You look a little tired this morning, Barnabas," Helen said when Bar walked in. "Good morning to you." She gave Bar her full attention for the first time since Friday evening.

Bar couldn't help but smile. "You've been very kind, Mrs. Summerlin. I don't suppose you've written out my bill yet."

"No, and I don't intend to so long as you look like a sick calf."

Grinning, he took a seat at the table as if he'd lived at the Summerlins' for years. The place was already so familiar and comfortable. "Could I trouble you for two old spoons to give to Homer? The ones I gave him aren't working now."

"Teaspoons or tablespoons?"

"Whatever you can spare. Put the cost on my bill,

of course. It would do Homer good to have a pair of his own."

"Of course, I'll see what I can find. Do they have to match?"

"No, ma'am," Bar said, amused. "They just need to fit."

After breakfast, Helen offered Bar two rather nice-looking spoons which he took out to Homer. Bar left the handyman in the barn, happily tapping on his knee once again.

When Bar came back to the kitchen, Helen was off with Sunny, airing the parlor for the coming afternoon, leaving Bar to drink his coffee while Frank contemplated him from across the table.

"Sunny tells me you're bound to go as soon as the quarantine is lifted," Frank said.

Bar nodded. It was time, he knew, for the future man of the house to exert his authority over the interloper.

"Where will you go?"

"Don't know," Bar said. "I don't call any one place home."

"Do you need money, son? Is that why you're after another bounty? I could offer you a job. Helen and Susanna have taken a shine to you."

Meeting the merchant's eyes, Bar was startled by the sympathetic sincerity in them. He wanted to tell Frank Tilsy to mind his own business, but it had been so long since anyone, much less three people, had taken an interest in him, he couldn't be rude.

"No, thanks, sir. As I've told Sunny, it's never been the money I sought, except for what it could do to ease another's grief. I've never forgotten that year after my pa was killed. My stepmother was alone, with me and my sisters to look after. I worked after school but that wasn't enough. I always wondered if she married her next husband out of necessity."

Frank didn't press for details, but Bar added a brief account of his father's death. As he spoke of the tragedy again, it seemed to pain him a little less. Was it possible that he might get over his grief merely by speaking of it to people he could trust? Bar wondered if healing could ever be that easy.

"Tell me something about Luck McKidrict," Bar said, changing the subject. "Why isn't there a bounty?"

"Ol' Foote would be crazy to turn loose of that ranch now that he's gotten it so easily by default," Frank said. "If you were to go out and find that strongbox with McKidrict's money still in it, most folks would consider the debts paid. The ranch would belong to the heirs after all."

"Chances of finding the strongbox are small, don't you think?" Bar said. "The money is surely gone, but for decency's sake, someone should offer a bounty to bring in the killer. He could come back, you know. He might see Crystal Springs as an easy target."

Frank pondered that. "Back when McKidrict first came to Crystal Springs folks speculated that he had been a jayhawker during the war. He damn well acted like a renegade sometimes. We couldn't figure how he came by his ranch. The deed was signed in Denver, but I knew he couldn't read worth a lick."

"A lot of ranchers can't," Bar put in.

"True, excepting that the signature on that deed looked like the man who signed it could. McKidrict had himself a Southern belle of a wife. Planter's daughter, she claimed. Why would she take up with the likes of McKidrict and give him three children? She ran off ten years ago. Nobody was surprised, excepting that she didn't take her children." Frank frowned.

With sentiment running against McKidrict all the years that he had lived in Cassidy County, Bar figured that more than one of the local residents might have wished him dead.

Frank went on. "Them McKidricts brought in fine furniture one year, a whole house full of it," he said. "Their everyday clothes were more fit for a Sunday sociable. But they never joined in. Never invited nobody out. Strange people. I never trusted 'em."

"McKidrict did well in cattle, though?"

Frank shook his head. "Didn't know a damn thing about running cattle at first. I swear, he stole half of what he ran, and rustled the rest. But he had money when he got here. Yankee gold. He was always gambling, drinking, carrying on with the girls on the line. Crystal Springs was a wild place in the gold days. We've tamed her considerably."

"So it's true that last Saturday was the first time McKidrict ever set foot in a bank, in thirteen years," Bar said. "Sounds like someone knew he'd be there."

"Hell, yes," Frank said, straightening excitedly. "The whole town knew. Most of us was afraid to call in our debts. Luck was known for his violent temper when he was drunk. I can't recall seeing him sober more than once or twice, so a body could count on him being violent nearly all the time.

"One day at a town meeting we realized McKidrict owed all over town. Feed and grain. Livery stable. Gunsmith. Harness maker. Dressmaker. Smithy. You name it. Liquor wholesaler." He shook his head. "I'd let him run a tab, too. It was easier than see his boys run roughshod through my store. My glass case cost me dearly.

"Then about a month ago Ol' Ettie Foote wishes out loud that he could buy up all McKidrict's debts, call 'em in, and when McKidrict couldn't pay, seize his ranch, run him off, and sell the whole sheebang to some investor fella from Texas who had just written him, asking about buying land hereabouts.

"I was all for it. Together we all figured we could finally get rid of McKidrict. The sheriff took six deputies out to the ranch to serve the legal papers. Thirty days to pay up or get out, they said. McKidrict didn't bat an eyelash. Said he'd be in town Saturday, ten-thirty sharp. And sure enough he was. He carried that strongbox into the bank. Then before you know it, he's dead. We had a town meeting about it that night."

"The person who robbed the bank wanted to prevent McKidrict from paying the debts so that the banker could seize the ranch," Bar said. "He decided to kill McKidrict to be sure."

"Hell, I don't know," Frank said. "A couple of other folks thought he was killed outright, too, but I say plain confusion took over. I don't think whoever it was ever meant to kill Luck. That's the irony of it, don't you see? Everybody hates the bastard's guts, and he gets killed accidentally. I say that's prime justice."

Bar studied Frank's animated expression. Accidental justice? Was there such a thing?

"What did the witnesses say?" Bar couldn't resist asking.

"Foote's an odd fella," Frank said. "Can't say I ever liked him. He's sitting there, dealing with McKidrict, he says, showing him the total owed. In walks this person dressed up, with a face covered by that black lace thing so nobody can tell who it is.

"Foote's interrupted, and he don't like that. She's holding a big gun, aiming it at the patrons. They run out. Foote says he's pretty sure McKidrict drew first to defend the strongbox, but next thing Foote knows, bullets are flying. She's running out with the strongbox. McKidrict's dead on the floor. I don't think it was a woman. No woman could run with a heavy strongbox. Probably some outlaw heard about the deal and decided to take advantage, but in disguise."

"How much money do they figure she, he . . . the robber . . . made off with?" Bar asked.

"No telling. I don't recall Foote's final tally, but it was enough to lay claim to the ranch in place of cash payment of the debt. I wonder if anybody's gone out to the ranch since McKidrict died. If the sheriff needs deputies, I won't be one of 'em. Bought me a little something extra while I was in Denver."

Frank withdrew another box from his trouser pocket and lifted the lid to reveal a gold filigree engagement ring with a real diamond chip.

"When I feel the moment is ripe, I'll be picking me a peach of a woman." Frank grinned from ear to ear. "Waited five years for this, so I couldn't care less who killed McKidrict."

Bar rose and shook Frank's hand. "Congratulations in advance, Mr. Tilsy. I hope you and Mrs. Summerlin will be very happy together. Thanks for the information."

Bar was about to excuse himself when the sound of a buggy arriving out front made his stomach knot. The time to leave was almost upon him.

Sunny and Helen appeared as if on cue and let the doctor in the kitchen door. In with the big man came a gust of fresh spring wind and the clean aroma of pine.

"Well, well, well," he boomed, thumping across the floor and focusing his attention upon Bar. "You look a sight better, Landry. It's this Summerlin food, I'll wager." He shook Bar's hand until Bar's shoulder ached.

"Thanks for coming, Doctor," Bar said.

"Miss a chance at Sunday dinner here? Not likely. You take a pale second to that, son. Hello, Helen, dear," he said, greeting the woman and chucking Sunny under her chin as if she were a child. "Behaving yourself, little lady?"

Sunny blushed and pretended to be annoyed.

The doctor shrugged out of his coat and Sunny carried it away.

"Let's get this examination over with. I hesitate to tell you ladies about the four aggravating ol' hounds who have been dogging my heels since I put the quarantine on this place. A worser idea I've never had. They camped on my porch, pepperin' me with questions." He gave a belly laugh. "Mornin', Frank. Feeling all right? Thought so. The boys are waiting at the bend right now, chafing to get up here. Helen, if you ever close this place, I won't wonder when those men take to violence and drink."

Helen looked genuinely alarmed.

The doctor chuckled and winked to indicate that

he was teasing. He ushered Bar back to the chilly office vacated by Frank earlier that morning.

Bar wondered if the doctor knew Helen was now debt free and might actually send her boarders packing. He almost wished he'd be around to see it.

"Now, Landry," the doctor said the moment he slammed the door to the office, "you ain't got nothin' I can find in a medical text. I busted my britches trying to figure if you had some rare affliction that warranted all this commotion."

"I'm fine now," Bar said.

"I'll be the judge of that, thanks. Sit down. Say ah. Eatin' right, are you? I'll bet you are. Open up your shirt there so I can listen to your ticker. Got pain anywhere?" He peered into Bar's eyes, listened, grumbled, probed, and thumped.

Bar bore it all with amused patience.

"Ain't a damn thing wrong with you, son, that a decent bed each night and decent job to do each day wouldn't cure. Now, why the hell do you want to come to a little town like this and cause such a stir? I can't see that you'd hunt humans for the thrill like some kinda jackass gunslinger."

Bar felt ready to explode with frustration. "I have my reasons, sir. With no bounty, I'll be on my way in about an hour."

"That's just the trouble, son. Ethridge Foote's changed his mind. Now he's offering two hundred dollars for the capture of the person who robbed him, and information about the strongbox. Says he don't want the McKidrict boys stalking him for not making the effort."

"That puts a new light on things," Bar said with surprise.

"Sure does, excepting that outlaw's probably in Californee by now. After a week, you won't find no trail. It rained like a son of a bitch that day. What I'm wondering is how the fella drove that rig through ankle-deep mud."

Bar heaved a sigh. He could still leave, but his curiosity was piqued.

"Landry, you're free to go. Or stay. Or do whatever comes to mind. Just don't do nothin' that'll get some innocent bystander hurt in the process."

"You can be certain of that, sir."

The doctor lumbered out, and Bar heard him announce the end of the quarantine at the top of his voice. Moments later the man bellowed out the kitchen door, "Come on up, boys! It's as safe as it's ever goin' to get around these two beautiful gals."

The first man to pass the office window was the barber in his black derby. The sign painter in his overalls and misshapen sugarloaf cap was next, and the newspaper man followed close behind.

Another smallish man in an outdated brown suit went by more cautiously. So the banker was also one of the boarders! Sunny had neglected to tell him this tidbit, Bar thought, eager to question the man.

Behind the boarders came a throng of people, riding in wagons fresh from church services, carrying baskets and hampers. Bar warmed to hear all the shouts of "Happy birthday, Helen!" and loud, friendly calls of "Howdy!" that filled the house.

A few minutes later the newspaperman burst into the office.

"M-Mr. Landry!" The man thrust out his trembling hand. "I'm Howard Ivery of the Crystal Springs *Gazette*, at your s-service. No doubt you've heard that our banker, Mr. Ethridge Foote, has decided to place a bounty on the party who stole a strongbox from his bank last Saturday morning about ten-thirty-five. What are your thoughts on the m-matter? In your . . . uh . . . expert opinion, who do you think did it, and why?"

The little barber squeezed past Howard Ivery and eyed Bar. "I'd consider it an honor to cut the hair of the famous Bar Landry, sir," he said.

Behind the two of them came the sign painter and a tall man with a crooked tin star on his vest proclaiming him the sheriff. He immediately took charge.

"Howard, Grodie, Willis," he said, after officiously clearing his throat, "you'll have your turn at Mr. Landry. I got to have a word with him first. Clear out."

The others reluctantly backed out of the office. The sheriff fixed his experienced eyes on Bar and then spat into the nearest corner, apparently heedless that there was no spittoon for his convenience. "Sheriff Brummer here," he said.

"My pleasure, sir." Bar rose and firmly shook the man's callused hand.

"I've seen some characters in my time, Landry, but you ain't what I expected. I thought you'd be older, meaner looking. Juan said you looked like some heathen killer when he first seen you on the train. What you got to say for yourself? Do I run you out of town to save trouble now or later?"

In the kitchen, Sunny had plenty to keep her busy as folks from town swarmed into the house. Soon baskets and hampers covered the kitchen table, and more had to be placed in the dining room.

The kitchen rang with loud, excited talk that didn't abate even after the hampers were opened and the delicious contents displayed. If Sunny hadn't been so worried about Bar and what he planned to do, with the quarantine being over, she would have thrilled to the attention being heaped upon her mother on the occasion of her belated birthday celebration.

Except for the McKidrict offspring, every one of the Summerlins' friends from town and from the surrounding county ranches was there. May Sue and her brothers probably didn't even know about the quarantine, Sunny thought irritably, rushing to and fro to get cups and plates for everyone. And it would likely be Sunny who would have to go apologizing to them in due time.

Grodie and Howard stood off to one side of the kitchen, arguing as usual as to which of them had first acquired a bit of information and whether or not it was publishable.

"I tell you, Howard, he told me he seen her dancing on the grave. There was no mistaking who it was. I'm thinking it's just possible she really did do it. Up and shot him for all he done to her family over the years. Maybe the strongbox wasn't so heavy after all. Maybe she saw him load it and knew it wouldn't be."

"She's got rheumatism in her hands, Grodie. She wouldn't have been able to pull the trigger."

Sick of all the speculation regarding the robbery, Sunny turned away and saw Bar standing in the hallway, smoothing his shirt at the waistband.

Howard spied Bar first. Grodie lunged to draw him into their conversation. "What do you think of a woman seen dancing on a man's grave, Landry?

Don't it sound like murder to you?" Howard poised his pencil, ready to write whatever Bar said.

"McKidrict's grave? When?" Bar asked, obviously interested.

"Last night," Grodie said. "In the moonlight, cussing him nine ways to hell in Spanish."

Sunny's heart sank. She had to go outside to breathe. There was no hope of saving Bar Landry from himself.

12

The day that had begun with such frail hopes for Sunny was over. Frank and all the guests had gone back to town. Sunny, Helen, and Bar had repaired to the porch with the four boarders, but now the night air was proving too cold. They gathered in the parlor once again to talk. Inevitably, the subject returned to the robbery.

Sunny made coffee. She didn't know yet if Bar intended to spend another night with them. The morning promised loads of laundry to be scrubbed in the washhouse. In the afternoon she would stand in the cold wind and hang the heavy wet linens on the lines behind the house. Their daily routine of chores had returned, and Sunny was feeling gloomy about it all.

Bar seemed tired and withdrawn. Grodie and Howard jabbered about the robbery while Willis offered useless suppositions. Foote, the only eye-witness, insisted he could recall nothing of note.

Finally Sunny's mother rose from the divan. "Gentlemen, I beg your pardon, but I must retire for the night."

Foote leapt to his feet. "I still have business with you, madam. You can't avoid me any longer."

Helen looked alarmed. "My dear Mr. Foote, I cannot think that I have avoided you in the slightest this evening. Feel free to speak your mind."

"In private," he whispered.

"You'll forgive me, I'm sure," Helen said in a firm tone Sunny had never heard her use with Foote before. "But I'm so very tired I could not possibly do justice to any subject requiring privacy just now. Besides, we're all well acquainted here. I can't imagine anything you would want to discuss with me that could not be shared with your fellow boarders."

Sunny became so intent on hearing what Foote and her mother had to say that she could scarcely bring herself to carry a tray back to the kitchen. She went nonetheless and returned at a run. From the hall she heard Foote's list of complaints.

". . . cost me one dollar for each night I was in that hotel," he was saying, "not to mention the charges for meals."

"I'm sorry you were inconvenienced by Mr. Landry's sudden illness," Helen said.

Sunny entered the parlor in time to watch Foote glance anxiously at Bar, who was observing the scene with narrowed eyes.

Howard Ivery moved to Helen's side. "We're just glad everyone is all right . . . and the famous Mr. Landry, too."

Foote was not deterred. "You owe me one dollar and sixty-one cents for five days' room and board. I was not here to avail myself of your services, and therefore I shall not pay for them."

Sunny was about to intervene on her mother's behalf when Helen waved her back and fixed the banker with a firm eye. "Mr. Foote," Helen began, "while you were away, rather than take my ease as the doctor prescribed that I should do, I thoroughly cleaned and aired your room. The entire time we were under quarantine, your belongings were safe in my care. Only if I had packed up your things and moved them out into the rain would I have considered your room vacant. I would have then assumed that you deserved a refund." Before he could retort, she went on. "As it was, I took in a sick man who was forced to sleep three nights on a cot, and two nights on a bench in the washhouse because I didn't offer your room, or any one of the other rooms, to him. For five days and nights your room was still yours. I have no intention of giving you a refund or credit. You yourself, Mr. Foote, taught me to stand firm on such details as these."

Sunny wanted to clap her hands.

"You'll be sorry about this, woman," Foote said, looking Helen up and down.

Howard began writing on the rumpled note book he jerked from his pocket. Willis Tate's face flushed crimson. Grodie got up and sat down again.

Like a snake slowly uncoiling, Bar rose from his chair.

Foote edged away from him.

"Mr. Foote," Helen went on without missing a beat. "A few things are going to be different around here now that our debt to you is paid. And you will not threaten me, sir. Not ever again." Helen turned to the other boarders. "Gentlemen, I beg to inform you that I shall no longer serve Sunday dinner at Summerlin House. I'm taking a day off every week. The Lord's day."

Scarcely able to contain her surprise and admiration for her mother's sudden fit of courage, Sunny rushed to her mother's side and threw her arms around her. "There you go, Ma!" she cried. "And about time!"

From the corner of her eye, Sunny caught Foote about to say something more. She pinned him with a glare and said, "We may even raise the rent."

Before Foote could make a suitably caustic rejoinder, the shadow of Bar Landry fell across his face. Foote shrank back like a mongrel. His eyes grew dark with fear.

"Pardon me for intruding, but I need to speak to you, too, Mrs. Summerlin, on the matter of my bill." He was looking at Foote as he spoke.

It was then that Ethridge Foote realized Helen had far too many resources to be intimidated by his one dollar and sixty-one cents. Fuming, he turned away.

Sunny felt her mother gather her strength for another bout.

"Yes, Mr. Landry. Will you be staying another night with us? The office is vacant again."

Bar stroked his jaw. Sunny watched his eyes crinkle at the corners as if with a sudden, hidden smile. "One more night, if you please."

"Of course," Helen said.

Sunny's heart leapt with joy. She would have another day in which to convince Bar to give up his hopeless pursuits.

"But in the morning I'll be moving into town," Bar went on. "I'll be looking into the robbery. I'm going after the bounty, gentlemen," he said, turning to make sure Howard wrote that in his book. "You might consider saying in your article about me, Mr. Ivery, that bringing in outlaws dead instead of alive has afforded me no sense of victory. Death is no punishment for the wicked. Only in life, and in living, can we prevail."

He looked at Sunny but with an unreadable expression on his face. Then he glanced at Foote.

"I'll find who killed Luck McKidrict and bring him back to stand trial. If I find the strongbox, it and whatever contents remain in it will be returned to the bank."

"No need to move to town, Mr. Landry," Helen said, obviously uncomfortable beneath Foote's sullen stare. "You can conduct your investigation from here as easily as from the hotel. Why, Sunny was in town the day it all happened. She can tell you about the robbery as well as anyone. Sheriff Brummer just got done telling me this afternoon that there's no two stories alike. Even our Mr. Foote can't recall what happened, can you, Mr. Foote?"

No one said anything, so Helen went on. "Question all you like, Mr. Landry, for as long as you like. The charge will be four bits a night including meals. Should a room become available . . ." She tossed a warning look toward Foote that amazed Sunny. ". . . you'll be welcome to it."

"You're very kind," Bar replied.

Foote tightened his arms across his chest. "Very well, madam, but you will get no sympathy from me the next time you're in a pinch and come begging for even a dollar." He stalked from the parlor and thumped up the staircase as loudly as he could.

Sunny kissed her mother's flushed cheek. "If Frank could only see you."

"Thanks to you and Frank I've found my courage," Helen said. "Good-night, gentlemen. I hope you sleep well."

"Breakfast at the same time, ma'am?" Willis asked, looking worried and hungry already.

Helen's pause had the three remaining boarders holding their breath. "Service as usual," she finally said.

After Helen left the parlor Sunny glanced self-consciously at Bar. "I'll lay the fire in the office as soon as I—"

"I can do that," Bar said, nodding good-night to the boarders as they started out of the parlor. "But before you retire, I need to speak to you, too."

"Oh." She blushed and blinked nervously at the three men, who were turning back with keen interest. "I'll . . . uh . . . let's talk now, Mr. Landry. I'm sure Mr. Tate wouldn't mind carrying this tray into the kitchen for me. It's awfully heavy."

Willis Tate reluctantly nodded and took away the tray full of the last of the cups and saucers.

"Mr. Meahan, would you be so kind as to close the drapes? And Mr. Ivery, did you perhaps bring this week's edition? Mr. Landry might like to read awhile before going to sleep."

Sunny then took a lamp and followed Bar into the cold, dark office. She made a point of leaving the door standing wide so that anyone would be able to see and hear all that transpired within.

"I can see you don't want to be alone with me tonight for some reason," Bar said softly.

"With those gossips about, no," Sunny said, lighting the candlestick on the desk with the flame in the lamp that she carried.

Bar stuffed tinder and kindling beneath the logs Frank had brought in that morning. "You didn't tell me the banker lived here."

"No, I didn't." She offered the candlestick, and he lit the fire.

"And you failed to mention that you were in town on the day of the robbery."

"I've been trying to forget that awful day!" Sunny blurted. "My friend's father was killed. While she and I aren't as close as we once were, I still feel upset about it. Besides, I saw nothing. I was halfway up the street. Mr. Foote is the one you should talk to about . . . Bar, please. Don't keep at this. Look what bounty hunting has done to you. I believe I know the real you. I saw you the morning you woke. This . . . this . . ." She indicated his dark clothes. ". . . you should give up. I can see that your headache is back. I believe what you've done with your life is tearing your soul to pieces. You're a decent man, Bar, not a man hunter."

But every word she spoke seemed useless. She could see that she'd lost Bar to his twisted logic, and what frightened her the most was that she felt so very badly that she had.

He looked down at her, his face cast into harsh shadows by the light from the candlestick. "You mustn't concern yourself so much with me, Sunny. It's not a good idea."

"I can't . . . help myself," she whispered.

"Then you must understand how I feel because I can't stop myself from doing what I must do."

"It's not the same!"

"To me, it is. Come with me tomorrow. Show me the way to the McKidrict ranch," Bar said, stepping closer to her.

She pulled away. She couldn't think. "You mean, *help* you investigate?"

"I want to meet your friend May Sue and her brothers. You can introduce me to them."

"I won't! I won't be a party to your sick pursuit of vengeance."

"Justice," Bar corrected.

"It's not justice, and you know it," Sunny said more loudly than was wise. "This is all some kind of glorious playact for you, the great, the fearsome Bar Landry, bounty hunter. I watched you today. I saw how you savored the admiration of the simple people of this community."

She couldn't believe the things she was saying to him. Now that she had risked speaking her mind, however, she couldn't hold back.

"You hide behind your sad stories about your father and that poor shoeshine man, claiming that giving the survivors the bounty you earned made killing those outlaws all right. But you're just fooling yourself if you truly believe that."

"Am I?"

"We live in this wild place where men do things their own way regardless of the law because they have guns . . ." She waved her hand toward the door. ". . . or money."

Bar's eyes widened. "You think I'm a bully?"

"You didn't use to be." Sunny stopped herself for a moment. She cared about Bar and yet she was lashing out at him with more fury than she had ever done to anyone in her life. But she drove on, determined that she was right.

"You're no better than McKidrict ever was the way he beat up people and drove them away. In fact, you're worse. At least he did it to have his ranch. You don't have anything. You don't even keep the money. Bounty hunting is a travesty of the justice you speak of."

Bar caught her arm and held her, his eyes locked with hers. Sunny plunged on as she had seen her mother do so boldly a few moments before. "You have no home, no family, no regular employment, no friends, no purpose in life but to—" Her eyes suddenly brimmed with tears.

"You're giving me very little credit, Miss Summerlin," Bar said, his grip on her arm burning her to her bones.

She wanted to kiss him. She wanted to seize him close and press the vengeance out of his heart. She wanted him to be her puppet, moved by and changed by her words and her sincerity. But he was Bar Landry. He could kill a man for stepping outside the law. What did he care if she lay awake at night trying to understand what it took to end the life of another human being, regardless of that human being's deeds?

Finally Bar released her.

Seeing plainly that he was angry, she backed up toward the door.

"Perhaps what you say about me is true," Bar said softly, his voice husky. "But maybe you're jumping to conclusions. Maybe you think you know me so well that you can imagine what I think and therefore can tell me what I should do. I assure you, Miss

Summerlin, you do not know me. You can't prescribe what I should do."

Now she felt humiliated. She wanted to flee.

"You think, because you live in this cocoon of a house and cater to four lonely men who have never done much with their lives but eat and sleep, that you understand a man like me. You play at matchmaking with your mother and Frank Tilsy and fancy that you know about grief and love."

She straightened and glared at him.

He could be relentless, too. "You know nothing of grief because you haven't grieved, Sunny. Your father died, too. I haven't seen a trace of it on your face. I haven't heard the sorrow in your voice."

"How dare you!" she wailed.

"Susanna Summerlin, princess of your realm," he announced, advancing ever so slowly. "Let me inform you, m'lady, that you know nothing of men or of life. Your world is so sheltered, you can't possibly know what another should do with his life."

"I know that what you do with yours is wrong."

"That is my choice."

She waited to see if he had heard his own words. When he didn't go on, she knew that he had. "You are a self-appointed judge and jury," she said. "There's nothing wrong with choosing a decent life to honor the memory of your father instead of the one you have chosen so far. Try leaving justice to God."

He stared into her eyes for so long that she wondered if he was going to turn around and leave. Being right sometimes came with a terrible price.

"It's better than hiding from reality," he said.

"I am not hiding, Mr. Landry," she whispered. "I am leading a decent life, something you obviously have forgotten how to do. If my life is sheltered, it's because I don't choose to go among the thieves and killers of this world and become like them."

Now he was driven too far to hold back any longer. "Miss Summerlin, your so-called decent life makes you nothing more than a serving wench. A laundry maid. A great brewer of horse liniment for pin money. You *are* hiding whether you admit it or not. Nothing is a challenge for you. You're doted upon by everyone you know. You're liked, especially by me, for all your innocence and purity of heart. But you're still untested. Don't tell me that what I do is wrong. I *know* that it is. It's for the likes of you and all the other innocents of the world that I hunt outlaws so that you can go to town on a Saturday morning and perhaps never know violence again."

Sunny looked away. "I won't help you do something that I think will make you sick again. You almost *died* of that fever, Bar. Doesn't that tell you anything? Isn't there a part of you that wants to stop? Don't you want to return to that innocence you once enjoyed?"

His eyes were filled with anguish. "It's because I want to stop that I must continue. How do you think I feel, Sunny? All I did was tell you about Cajah and I drew a gun that I wasn't even wearing. I have to tame my rage. I shouldn't have to explain that to you. I consider you my friend. If I ask you to go with me to the McKidrict ranch because I think it will help me put an end to this, won't you please go with me on that basis?"

Her heart plummeted. He considered her his friend. Was that all he had to offer? Was it all she dared to hope for? She was feeling so very much more than that. She was in love with him!

The silence between them grew long.

She wanted so desperately to triumph over him, and get him to see her logic. She wanted so very much to be right. She realized that sometimes triumphing meant she had to concede and wait to do battle another day.

"All right," she said as Willis appeared with an armload of firewood. "I'll show you the way to the McKidrict ranch tomorrow."

"Thank you," Bar said, but he didn't smile.

13

As Helen came into the kitchen at dawn, Bar took his last swallow of cold leftover coffee.

She looked surprised to see him up and fully dressed. "You're up early, Barnabas. How are you feeling?" She smiled a bit shyly as if she was uncertain how people would feel about her after her unusually assertive behavior of the evening before.

Bar marveled at the warm feeling he got whenever Helen was around. "You were quite the wonder last evening, Mrs. Summerlin."

She blushed. "Well, I—"

"I'm going to town this morning to have a look around," he said before they could become entangled in a lengthy conversation. "I've asked Sunny to show me to the McKidrict ranch later today. But I don't want to go out this early and have her think I'd left for good. Will you ask her to be ready around noon?"

Helen looked troubled. "It's a long way. Wouldn't you rather rest?"

Bar shook his head. Then he left, going out into the chill morning with a deliberate stride. He didn't want to dally and risk having to deal with the boarders. He'd take them on later.

In short order Homer had Sundown saddled, and Bar was off. For all the times Bar had isolated himself on a ranch in order to avoid his obsession and guilt, he had never felt as he did this morning, as if he'd been gone for years and was emerging into a new world.

His determination and sense of hope burned strong. He was going to triumph over whatever memories or emotions had made him into a hunter and killer of men. This would be his last bounty.

The valley looked beautiful to him as he walked Sundown along the road into town. The air smelled deliciously clean. He almost felt as if the haphazard collection of pine buildings and rutted streets belonged to him, as if he were responsible for the place.

Few people were about at that early hour. Bar savored the cool, sleepy hush as he rode. The soft thud of Sundown's hoofbeats in the sparkling, rose-colored dust soothed him. The distant call of a meadowlark reminded him of pleasant spring mornings, of going fishing long ago.

The promise of success was as near as Sunny's smile, he thought. He wanted to kiss her smile, but he could only risk that if his heart was free.

As Bar crossed High Street, Frank Tilsy looked up from where he was sweeping the boardwalk in front of his store. He leaned on his broom and polished his spectacles.

"Mornin', Landry."

Bar returned the man's greeting as if they were friends of many years. Bar almost felt accepted as he rode on. But his smile faded as he located the bank, bringing back to mind his reason for coming to town. He dreaded asking Sunny about the robbery later.

She'd cooperate, he was certain, but she'd give him that look from beneath her lovely lashes that would strip away any pretenses he might be clinging to about his motives. Beneath her scrutiny, he would feel less sure of himself than he liked. He wanted to cover himself with her approval, to know that after all he had done he could still be a good man.

Riding a mile up the pass, Bar speculated as to where the robber in the buggy might have fled. Then he rode a mile south of town, trying to determine where the robber had come from.

By the time Bar had the town thoroughly mapped in his mind, the sun had climbed higher. Merchants had their stores open. Bar left his bent silver spoons at the smithy, asking that they be straightened.

Then he stopped at Grodie's barbershop to get a trim. He paid a brief call at the newspaper office where Howard was already at work with his press. After calling hello to Willis, who was painting at the new Skyline Saloon on Gilpin Avenue, Bar went to the bank as Ethridge Foote unlocked the door.

Key still in hand, the little man looked up into Bar's eyes and went white.

"Morning, Mr. Foote," Bar said, removing his black Stetson and studying the little man who had been so rude to Helen the evening before. "Will you be busy with patrons right away or do we have a moment to talk?"

"C-come right in," Foote said, backing away. He stumbled through the gate in the fence which divided the room, and backed into his chair.

Bar skipped all pleasantries. "You were seated there, like that, the morning of the robbery, sir?"

"Y-yes." Reluctantly the banker described what happened.

As Bar listened, he walked through Foote's description of Luck McKidrict's actions. He observed the bank's interior from Foote's vantage point, and then McKidrict's. Like pieces on a chess board, Bar placed the banker and rancher in his mind and tried to visualize what happened.

Then, pretending to be the robber-señora, Bar went to the door and reentered the bank, pointing his finger as if it were a gun.

"Why are you doing this?" Foote asked in agitation. "The sheriff didn't do this. I don't have time for this foolishness."

"Just a moment more," Bar said, pacing off the distance between the door and the gate. "The strongbox was on the desk? Where, exactly?"

"Right here. We were about to open it."

Bar wondered how the robber maintained his drop on the banker and rancher while lifting and carrying the strongbox away.

Saying nothing of this detail to Foote, Bar pointed to a place on the floor scoured nearly white. "McKidrict fell there?"

"I told you," Foote exclaimed, his voice shaking by then. "I was waiting for McKidrict to arrive. He came in, loud, the way he always was. Calling hello to everyone. Disrupting—"

"With the strongbox on his shoulder."

Foote nodded. "Yes. Yes. He kicked the gate open and put the strongbox here." Foote pointed to the scratches on the corner of his desk.

"Then you said that he stepped to the side."

"I had the papers—"

"You paid full price for each merchant's claim against McKidrict, or cents on the dollar?"

Foote gaped up at him. "What does that have to do with being robbed, Landry?"

"Just curious. Please, go on."

Foote went on to remark at length on the debts owed, just as he had been doing the morning of the robbery. "Then *she* walked in. I heard someone gasp. I looked up. McKidrict moved to the side and turned to look, too. We saw her holding the gun, and the patrons ran out."

Nodding, Bar again paced the room, looking all around. "You'd never seen this woman before?"

"Those Mex—she . . . I . . . can't tell one from another."

"Women, or Mexican women? Never mind. But you know everyone who would come into your bank."

"Well no, I don't know everyone, and certainly not every Mexican woman, or every person who would come into . . . Strangers come here all the time. She could have been one of those. . . ."

"Could it have been a man dressed up? Did you notice her hands, boots, anything about her I might use to identify her, or him?"

Foote's breathing became labored. "S-she looked like a black ghost."

Bar sighed. "What did she say, exactly?"

"I—I don't remember . . . exactly," Foote said. "I told the sheriff that, and I'm telling you. I got upset.

I've never been robbed. McKidrict drew and fired first."

"He had no hesitation about shooting at a woman?"

"I was surprised, too. Then she fired back. Boom! Boom! I . . . She took the strongbox and ran out. That's all!"

"And you were thinking . . ." Bar watched the man closely.

Ethridge Foote kept his face down. His hands were in fists. "Must you shame me like this? I'm a small man. I—I . . . feared for my life. McKidrict and his ilk liked to prey upon that. I had forced his hand. If he had not been shot, he might have turned on *me*."

"Surely a banker of your keen sensibilities would keep a pistol at hand. This is the West, after all."

Foote looked at Bar for so long that Bar wondered why it was difficult for the man to recall what happened.

"I couldn't think," Foote admitted softly, opening the drawer to reveal an old pistol. "I was frozen with fear."

Bar plucked the pistol from the drawer and examined it. It seemed to be in very poor condition. "You didn't draw this?"

Foote shook his head.

"What about the one in your vest?" Bar asked.

Foote's jaw dropped.

"Don't look so surprised. It's my job to notice such things."

Visibly trembling, Foote withdrew the small self-cocking pistol from inside his coat. At least it was in better working order, Bar thought, examining the mail-order pistol often bought by younger marksmen. It was loaded.

Still holding Foote's pistol, Bar went back to the

door and advanced back into the bank, aiming the pistol in Foote's general direction. "She came through the gate like this, or leaned over to get the strongbox?"

Eyes wide and fixed on the pistol, Foote appeared beside himself. "I—I don't remember. Now give that back!"

"Did she carry the strongbox out on her shoulder, or in front of her like this?"

Bar held his hands out as if he were holding something in front of his stomach. One hand, however, still held the pistol. It would have been impossible to carry away the strongbox without holstering the weapon or putting it down. He supposed that in the confusion the robber might have slipped his or her weapon into a pocket.

"I was looking at McKidrict. He fell like a . . . you can see where he grabbed the railing and partly pulled it loose from the wall. Landry, are you trying to terrorize me? I'll have the sheriff on you."

"Sorry," Bar said, handing back the weapon. "Did he die at once? Did he say anything? Do you think he knew the robber?"

"He smiled," Foote said without hesitation. He jammed his pistol back inside his coat. "The way he always did, on one side of his face, like a snake."

"Snakes don't smile. You didn't like McKidrict, did you, Mr. Foote?" Bar said, starting for the door.

Foote lowered his voice to a menacing level. "He wasn't *fit* for humankind. We wanted him out of town, and now he's gone, for good."

Bar searched the banker's face for any sign that he might be lying. With his sort, it was difficult to tell, Bar thought. He thanked the man and bade him good morning.

On the boardwalk, Bar realized his vision had become blurred by a fierce, new headache. Feeling dizzy, he found his way to Sundown and stood several minutes thinking about Ol' Foote. How had Sunny and Helen lived with that little vulture under their roof for so long?

Finally he led Sundown to the doctor's office.

"Two bullet wounds," Dr. Hamilton said after Bar was ushered into the man's office and asked his main question. "One in the upper right shoulder, a flesh wound. One in the heart from the front."

Bar rubbed his eyes.

"You aren't feelin' well this morning, are you, Landry?" the doctor said. "I shouldn't have let you out of bed, I reckon, excepting folks were getting hysterical. You brought a heap of trouble with you when you came to this town."

"I'm fine, just worried that Miss Summerlin won't be pleased to know that I've been in town asking questions this morning."

Joshua Hamilton smiled. "Stop askin', then. If ever there was an ailment without a cure, it's a heart with wanderlust caught in the fair trap of a beautiful female's expectations."

Bar chuckled. He could not have said it better.

"You'd best be done with your little investigation soon and move on," the doctor continued. "Susanna Summerlin is a decent young woman, deserving of a quiet home and a law-abiding husband. She's entitled to children, a warm hearth, and a simple life. That's not the life for you and me, is it? That's why I never got married. Too busy to do a good woman justice. You can't be all bad, Landry, but you ain't the one for Sunny."

Bar bade the doctor good morning with the intention of doing just that, moving on as soon as possible, but his heart ached at the thought.

His final stop for the morning was the sheriff's office. By the time the man returned from his morning rounds, Bar was feeling quite gloomy.

"How many shots were fired?" he asked even before the sheriff was inside the office.

"Four or five," Brummer replied, searching for his written report. "Nobody remembers exactly. Why do you ask?"

"Only two bullets are accounted for. You're sure the robber wasn't hit?"

"Don't believe so. No blood. I found two slugs in the wall behind where McKidrict was standing. It was enough to satisfy me."

Bar supposed it would have been. "What exactly was the robber wearing?"

"Black lace over the head, like the older Mexican women wear in church. A black dress. Not silk, just old dyed calico, likely. Nothing fancy. She left town too fast to be noticed much."

"In a quarter-top buggy?" Bar said.

"Ain't been a buggy like that around here in years. Don't know why a robber would want to use one. They ain't very fast. I couldn't even tell you what color the running gear was because it was so muddy that day."

Bar seized upon this point. "Was *she* muddy? If she'd driven long enough to muddy up the whole underside of her buggy, she'd have splatters on her dress, wouldn't you think?"

The sheriff frowned. "You'd have to ask a woman that one, Landry. Though I don't know what difference it'd make."

"I'd know how far she had come."

"All I remember was running to the bank and looking down at McKidrict on the floor. Never thought I'd see the day."

"Where was Foote?"

"At his desk, like always. Looked plum peaked, too, like a kid ready to pee his drawers."

Bar could not understand why the answers left him feeling as if there were something more to the story.

After thanking the man, Bar left and rode up the canyon again far enough to imagine driving an old buggy in mud. If the robber had escaped in that direction, he would have had to endure a hellish climb. The grade was steep, and the way too narrow in most places for any kind of reckless speed.

If the robber hadn't gone in that direction, but turned off the main street before entering the canyon, he might have gone down any one of three narrow side streets. Bar explored each one until the steadily climbing sun and his empty stomach warned him it was almost noon.

Fighting the desire to keep searching, Bar reminded himself that he had a clerk and several patrons yet to question. He would have at least several more days' investigation before solving the case.

And there was the matter of the woman seen dancing on McKidrict's grave. He would have to find and question her. Why would a woman, or anyone else for that matter, take only the strongbox and leave behind the contents of Ethridge Foote's safe?

Bar stopped at the cemetery long enough to study the footprints around McKidrict's grave before going back to the boardinghouse. By the time he reached the Summerlins' place, his mind was churning. The moment he saw the young woman waiting for him in the kitchen doorway, however, his thoughts scattered. Sunny was fussing with the ties of a ruffle-trimmed Sunday bonnet, and wearing a snug yellow dress with a full skirt. When she got the ties as she wanted them, she reached for her brown jacket. "I'm ready when you are," she said as he approached.

Suddenly all tension had drained from his body. He felt distinctly that he was home, and that was when he realized just how dangerous it was for him to remain in that place with her even a day longer.

Sunny tried to remain stiff and reserved as she sat perched on the seat of the buckboard with Bar, but the ride was rough. The hamper tucked behind the seat, containing peace offerings for the bereaved McKidricts, kept bouncing around. Mud had turned the twin tracks that served as the road to the McKidrict ranch into soft, treacherous ruts. She kept losing her balance and lurching against Bar's shoulder.

"Which way?" he asked as they rode through town, enduring the stares of people on the street.

A train was standing at the depot, its steam whistle echoing across the valley. Sunny was distracted by the crowd gathering there.

"Here," she finally said, indicating one of the roads Bar had taken earlier that morning. "I wonder what everyone is doing at the depot."

Bar offered no thoughts on the matter.

For more than a mile they both stared resolutely ahead as the road became lonely and winding, flanked by high, dry weeds. Sunny tried to keep herself distracted, but every moment she was keenly aware of being at Bar's side.

"It's longer this way, but the ride isn't so steep," she remarked, dreading the upcoming encounter with May Sue.

"It's a nice day for a ride," he said.

Sunny forced herself not to respond. After a few moments, however, she pointed to some clouds gathering in the west. "It won't be nice for long. I should have brought a lap robe."

"How long before the storm?" A gust of wind ruffled the hair grazing Bar's forehead.

"It's hard to say." She had to look away. He was looking at her with such tenderness. "We'd best not stay long at the ranch, even if May Sue does ask us in."

"I want to apologize for everything I said last night," Bar said. "I was rude. I can't tell you how sorry I am about it."

Sunny's blood began to race. She was trying so very hard to ignore the fact that she was alone with him again, sitting so close that she could hear him breathing. His hands looked strong but graceful as he held the lines. He seemed relaxed, but she knew that he was not.

Glancing at him, she searched for words. She wanted to be understanding, but that would only reopen between them what she wanted to keep closed.

"We were both tired," she said at last.

She wanted to apologize, too, but if she spoke, she would lose her hold on her resolve.

They rode on for several more miles until she spied several does and bucks grazing in a grassy hollow near the bluffs. "Oh, look!" she cried.

From the corner of her eye she caught his wistful

smile. Why did he have to be so stubborn? Why did they have to do this tiresome chore when all they really wanted to do was be together . . . as friends?

A mile later Bar sighted a porcupine waddling through the dry buffalo grass. Sunny couldn't resist telling him about the time a skunk had got under the porch with the cats. Before too long they were talking, keeping the conversation polite but impersonal. Bar's efforts to be charming and casual wrenched Sunny's heart. Couldn't it always be like that? she wondered.

Gradually their conversation turned to the McKidricts. Sunny told him about how she used to walk to town each morning before school. She'd meet up with the McKidrict boys riding alongside May Sue, who drove her own wagon at the age of twelve.

"I'd climb onto the seat with her. She'd have to race her brothers, of course. They always won. I'd be all mussed by the time we arrived at the schoolhouse, and May Sue would just laugh at me."

They followed the road up between huge boulders and wind-twisted pines until they reached a broad canyon flanked by rocky ridges. The sky was overcast by then, and the wind quite chilling. The McKidricts' ranch house stood a mile away alongside a chain of small lakes.

"There's water on this land?" Bar asked.

"A spring," Sunny said, beginning to worry what May Sue would say about everyone missing her father's funeral.

"That's why McKidrict was willing to do just about anything to hold onto his land," Bar said. "And that's why others are so very willing to take it from him."

"You can't feel sorry for the man!" Sunny cried.

"He was a beast. The few times I saw him he looked at me as if I were something he might want to have for supper, and I was little more than a child!"

Bar glanced at her and then went back to noting every detail of the valley.

"I've learned there's always two sides to a story," he said, looking sad, as if he knew his words would cause her despair. "When it comes to money, land, water rights, or cattle . . . whatever the prize may be . . . some people are willing to compromise everything to get it. Or hold it."

Sunny felt angry but didn't know why. Was he accusing her, and the entire town, of coveting McKidrict's ranch?

"I'm glad to know you're so willing to be fair," she said.

"Tell me more of what you know about the McKidricts," he said, seeming unperturbed by her clipped tone. "What *you* know, not what others have told you."

"Including what my mother has told me?" Sunny shot back with growing irritation.

"In due time I will ask your mother about them myself. Don't you see that it's better this way? A man was murdered for his money. In my book that's serious business. Even if he was disliked, he deserves justice. I learned that in law school, Sunny. Not with a gun in my hand. The only time I lose control is when I see justice slipping away. I'm not a bad man! I care very much— "

He cut himself off, and Sunny watched him struggle to control his passion. She could not stop herself from placing her hand on his arm. That was just the point. He was such a very good man.

"I can see that you do care, Bar," she said softly. "That's why this is all so difficult for me. The truth is, I admire your courage. There's nothing in my life that summons up such fierce convictions as you seem to have."

He didn't reply.

Finally she gave up trying to hold back. When she was with Bar Landry, her defenses proved useless.

"You were right about one thing, Bar. I do live a sheltered life. You have caused me to wonder if I serve much purpose in my mother's house, cleaning and cooking as I do."

"I'm sorry I ever—"

"But isn't that the whole point of friendship, Bar? To challenge one another, to be truthful and forthright? I value that with you. I truly do."

She looked him squarely in the eye. Her feelings were openly displayed on her face and she could tell that he saw what she was trying to show him.

He looked a very long time.

14

As they neared the McKidrict ranch house, which was nestled in an increasingly narrow valley, Sunny blushed under Bar's penetrating stare.

"*Are* we friends, Sunny?" he asked, slowing the buckboard almost to a stop.

Her breath caught. "Yes, we are, I think." She smiled a little. "In spite of ourselves."

He nodded as if reassured. Except for the hint of sadness in his eyes, he almost looked as happy and carefree as he had the morning he woke from his fever. Sunny's hopes lifted.

Tearing her gaze away before she clutched Bar's arm again as she wanted to do, Sunny turned her attention to the sprawling McKidrict house. She had nearly forgotten that she would soon be dealing with May Sue.

When new, the ranch house had been one of the finest log structures Sunny had ever seen. Not only had it been beautiful, with its deep porch hooding six multipaned windows across the front, but it had been as solid as a fort.

Inside it had been as spacious as any eastern mansion with fine furniture and lace curtains. The bedrooms across the back had sported four-posters with deep featherbeds.

Luck McKidrict's dining room had been more like a hunter's gallery with mounted trophies on the walls. A dazzling array of china, crystal, and silverware had always been displayed on the ten-foot-long table.

Now the roof sagged in places and was bare to the beams in others. Parts of the interior were probably in ruin due to leaks, Sunny thought. An assortment of broken dining room chairs lay nearby. Trash and shattered whiskey bottles spread well into the hard-packed yard.

Beyond the house stood a barn and bunkhouse. No smoke curled from either the house's massive stone chimney or the stovepipe jutting from the bunkhouse's roof.

"Is anyone here, do you think?" Bar asked. "Would they have abandoned the place?"

"I don't know. It doesn't look like anyone has been here in years. The first time Ma and I visited, I thought this house was so fine compared to our little cabin. Julia McKidrict had such nice things. Now look at it."

"What was an Alabama belle doing with a man like Luck McKidrict?" Bar asked, looking up at the threatening gray sky.

"I have no answer to that. The first time I saw them I thought Luck McKidrict was a giant. He laughed as he bounced me on his knee, and I can tell you I was well beyond the age to be bounced like that. His tickling always felt improper."

Bar looked at her, and she blushed again.

Then she went on to tell Bar about the night she heard Julia McKidrict at the Summerlin place, crying and carrying on. She told him that the Summerlins had given Julia money to go away.

"So it's been roughly ten years since this place has known a lady's touch." Bar secured the lines and set the brake.

"Except for May Sue and the cook, Maria."

"She's the one some say was dancing on McKidrict's grave the other night."

Sunny nodded. "McKidrict burned the Arquillas out and beat Maria's husband nearly to death for suggesting that Lyford should marry their daughter, Tomasina. Maria agreed to work for McKidrict after he threatened to finish off her husband."

"Sounds like an ex-jayhawker." Bar twisted around to scan the road behind them. Then his gaze shifted and locked with her.

Her breathing quickened.

"I admit, the matter of McKidrict's character complicates my job, Sunny, but as I said, I believe in justice for all."

"Is he worth risking your life for?" Before she knew what she was doing her hand was on his arm.

He smiled. "I told you, Sunflower, I'm very good at what I do." His left hand closed over hers. "You cannot know how very much it means to me to know that you care about what happens to me, though."

For a moment she doubted whether she should let this man use the endearment her father had once used. But she was thrilled that he had.

"If you must seek another bounty, why do it here, Bar?" she asked. "There must be dozens of other people needing your help."

"Social status carries little weight with me. Do you really think I can walk away now, after telling people my plans? I'm not flighty, Sunny, and I'm not a quitter."

"No, I suppose you can't."

He sighed, as if weary of trying to make her understand. "I don't want to have to go away in order to remain your friend, Sunny. I can't *call* myself your friend if I don't test myself. I wouldn't want you to have the wrong kind of friends. I want you to have the best of what . . . of what life has to offer." He paused as if to stop himself from saying more. "I'll have a look around. Stay here."

She didn't know what else to say. She had never known a man with so much misguided honor.

He climbed down and skirted cowpies littering the yard where cattle had apparently crossed close to the house the day before.

Sunny could scarcely think, her heart was thudding so hard. The image of Bar's earnest smile burned into her memory. She was falling more deeply in love with him by the day, she thought. The feeling was as delicious as it was terrifying.

At the sagging porch that Julia McKidrict had once called the veranda, Bar called a cautious hello. When there was no answer, he stepped up, testing the soundness of the boards, and approached the door.

"Anyone home?" With his hand resting lightly on his holstered gun, he eased the front door open. Then he disappeared inside.

Thunder grumbled deep in the mountains. A gust of wind cut through Sunny's jacket and sent shivers through her. Her mother would be appalled to learn that May Sue and her brothers were living like this. How long *had* it been since Sunny had visited? she asked herself. She felt ashamed that she couldn't remember.

Suddenly, the buckboard tilted to the right. Before Sunny could turn to see who had stepped aboard, her view of the house was blocked by a grinning face. A rough hand grabbed her left shoulder, holding her fast.

"Ornery!"

A mouth still sour with the taste of rotgut whiskey mashed against her lips.

Gagging, Sunny used both hands to push away the stubbled face. "Stop!" Finally she threw herself to the left to get free and nearly pitched herself out of the seat.

Cale McKidrict lost his footing and grabbed her jacket, tearing it in several places. He tumbled sidelong against the muddy front wheel and landed flat on his back on the ground, a whiskey bottle still clutched in his hand. He managed to keep the bottle mostly upright, sloshing only a little of the contents onto his shirt.

"Whew!" he exclaimed, laughing. He paused to tip back his head and fill his mouth with a colorless liquid that had to be one-hundred-twenty-proof home brew. "That's what I call a kiss!"

Sunny dragged her sleeve across her lips. "That was *disgusting*. Where did you come from, Cale? Why didn't you answer when we called out? Didn't you hear us ride up?"

"Hell, yes, I heard you. Seen you from a mile off. What is he, an undertaker or a politician? Never mind. Everybody's the same when they're *dead.* Big of you to finally give Sissy-baby and me a minute of your precious time, Ornery." Cale hauled himself to his feet, his eyes glittering. "How about another one of them—"

Just then Bar came out onto the porch. "I don't think so, friend."

Whirling, Cale grabbed the side of his appallingly filthy denims as if reaching for a gun, but realized he wasn't wearing one. His glance shot back to Sunny. "I'll tell you one thing, Ornery—"

"You got manure all over your back," Bar interrupted, stepping to the edge of the porch.

Cale gave a curse under his breath and carefully put his bottle on the ground. He stripped his shirt, the same shirt he'd been wearing the morning of the robbery, over his head and flung it down. "See what you made me do? Who's goin' to wash that now, eh, Sunny? Maria's gone. May Sue ain't worth a lick when it comes to chores."

Cale McKidrict didn't look very threatening, standing there with his ribs rippling beneath his pasty white skin. His bruised belly stuck out from years of drinking whiskey.

Sunny noticed that Cale's knuckles on both hands were half raw, half scabbed. Perhaps it was the dim afternoon light, but just possibly Cale had two slightly blackened eyes. In spite of her long-standing dislike for the young man, Sunny couldn't help but feel sorry for him.

"Don't you look at me like that, Ornery. Ain't *nobody* goin' to take this place from us. Any jackass son of a bitch stupid enough to come here and try had better be ready for lead."

He started for the house. Then, looking up at Bar, he veered off quickly toward the bunkhouse.

"If I see that banker come ridin' in here, I'll fill his tail full o' buckshot," Cale went on. "I'll have his gizzard on a plate for lunch." He snatched his bottle from the ground, gave a long pull, and coughed.

May Sue appeared in the doorway, jerking her wrapper closed. By the way the increasingly cold wind molded the thin fabric of May Sue's wrapper against her legs, Sunny guessed she must be naked beneath.

Sunny's breath caught. What had Bar found when he went into the house? It was nearly three in the afternoon.

"Well, I declare." May Sue sauntered to the edge of the porch next to Bar. "Sunny Summerlin. I never thought you'd have the nerve to show up here after the way you done treated me." May Sue threw back a tangle of blond hair and smiled up at Bar. The neckline of her wrapper drooped open far enough to give him what Sunny feared was a stunning display of ample impropriety. "But I'll forgive you," May Sue went on, pressing against Bar, "if you introduce me to this *fine* figure of a man."

Cale returned from the bunkhouse, buckling a gun belt around his bony hips. He belched as he bent to tie the strings of the holster to his right thigh.

"Excuse my brother's bad manners," May Sue said to Bar, giving her brother a cutting look. "He was born and raised in a pigsty, as my ma used to say. My mother was a very fine lady from Alabama. Did you know that?"

Bar looked down at May Sue but didn't seem interested in her cleavage.

"This is Barnabas Landry," Sunny said, feeling jealous. Her attention shifted from May Sue's shockingly revealing attire to the woman's hand, which was coyly finding its way into the crook of Bar's elbow.

Behind Bar and May Sue a short man emerged from the house into the wind. "Git away from him," he said to May Sue, grabbing her arm and jerking her back.

He had longish blond hair and apparently hadn't shaved in days. He finished buttoning his baggy denims and stamped his right foot to get his boot on straight. The upper portion of his dingy-looking long underwear was open to the waist, revealing a hairy chest and belly.

Pulling free, May Sue gave the young man a look of disgust. "This here's Johnsie," she said to no one in particular. "Johnsie Rawlins. He *worked* for Pa. He don't work for us *heirs.* I done fired him."

"You and yer Aunt Tilly," Johnsie said, snickering, grabbing at her again. "I'm the only one what hasn't cleared out. We're goin' to be married soon as I hogtie and brand her proper," he said to Bar.

May Sue tried to slap him. "I ain't marrying you. Never said I would."

Johnsie laughed, revealing crooked teeth. "That's my gal."

Cale gave no indication that he thought his sister needed defending.

If Sunny hadn't been so surprised by the entire unexpected encounter, she would have laughed at herself for feeling like a prude. She tried to accept the fact that May Sue had considerably more experience with life, and obviously men, than she. The girl always had.

"Let me explain why I wasn't able to come to the funeral," Sunny said, feeling her cheeks beginning to burn.

May Sue's eyes narrowed. "Better be good."

Cale raked back his stringy hair, and drew his gun with alarming speed. He appeared to sober up now as he looked at them with a cocky smile and leveled the gun at Bar's waist. "Who'd you say you was, friend?"

Betraying no sign of concern, Bar stepped down from the porch.

Cale backed off two steps.

Bar approached Cale with his right hand outstretched. "I came to talk about the robbery and the murder of your father. Did you know the bank's offering a two-hundred-dollar reward for the return of your father's strongbox and the capture of the man who killed him?"

May Sue shook free of Johnsie's touch. Her eyes widened. "You're a bounty hunter? And you come to help us?"

"Yes," Bar said, his tone grave.

"Gull-danged about time somebody done *something* around here besides play paw-paw and drink rotgut. It's a wonder you ain't growed hair on your hand by now." She smacked Johnsie's chest with the back of her hand. "Like you and my brothers. You don't think it was a woman did it, do you, Mr. Landry?" In seconds, her words had turned from curses to caresses, seductive and inviting.

"No, Miss McKidrict, I doubt very strongly that it was."

"Told ya, ya dumb jackasses," May Sue snapped at

Johnsie and Cale. "And git yer cold hands offa me, *cowboy.* Cain't you see I got company? Want some coffee, or a nip of something stronger, Mr. Landry? I make a mighty fine stump water."

Sunny found herself wanting to go inside to see how the house looked. "We can't stay long," she found herself saying instead, realizing at once she shouldn't have spoken.

"Oh, fine— " May Sue snapped, giving Sunny a scolding glare. "You can't be bothered to come to Pa's funeral. Had plenty a' time to think up yer excuse why, too. And now that you're here you're goin' to push off an old hamper full of yer leavin's and think that I'll forgive you. Well, I got me a few things to say about that."

Cale holstered his gun and turned back to Sunny. "What you got in that there hamper, Ornery?"

Before Sunny could explain why she'd missed the funeral, Cale had dragged the large wicker basket behind the seat to the ground. He lifted a chokecherry pie from its checkered cloth wrapping and worked a full quarter of it into his mouth. Globs of crust and filling covered his lips and oozed down his chin as he chewed. He grunted in approval.

Torn between anger and hunger, May Sue finally came down from the porch and marched to where Cale stood groping through the rest of the contents of the hamper. "Save some for me!" She grabbed a portion of the pie in his hand and stuffed it into her mouth.

Johnsie stayed in the shadows of the porch.

By the time Cale and May Sue had devoured the entire pie and half a dozen biscuits, an approaching wagon with two men on the seat and a mounted rider alongside were less than a half mile away.

Cale straightened and wiped his mouth on his bare arm. "What now?" he said through a belch.

Snickering, Johnsie slipped inside the house.

Two hundred yards out, the approaching wagon stopped while the rider continued forward to halt at the edge of the yard. It was Sheriff Brummer. "Put your gun on the ground, McKidrict," he said to Cale. "We got legal papers saying you still got to pay the debts your father owed or forfeit the ranch."

Sunny could see that in spite of his threats, Cale wasn't going to shoot the sheriff without serious provocation. The sheriff was too cool-headed a man to risk that. He sat patiently atop his horse while Cale sifted through his options.

"You know we ain't got no money left," Cale finally said. "Something tells me that that was your plan all along. Maybe that runt of a banker hired somebody to rob his own mud-suckin' little bank." He nodded toward the man in the wagon.

Foote straightened on the wagon seat. "I'm no thief. If you have no money, this ranch is mine."

Sunny wondered if it could be true that Foote might have done such a thing. Where would he have found a bank robber between the door to his bank and her mother's house?

May Sue looked as if she wanted to run at the sheriff, claws bared, but she had the decency to remember her state of undress. With a snort of disgust, she stormed back into the house. "Mangy coward . . ." was all that could be heard as she slammed the door.

"I'm sorry about the loss of your money," the sheriff went on. "Me and my deputies are doing what we can to find who did it. And you got Landry there on your side. Meanwhile, Foote's got claim to this place. You'll have to clear off. Where's Lyford at?"

"Who the hell knows? Probably with his little woman and her bastard. I ain't leavin', Brummer. You'll have to kill me dead." Cale took a defiant stance, one boot in a cowpie.

Brummer calmly shook his head. "I don't want to do that, Cale. I'm tired of this aggravation you McKidricts been causing Cassidy County all these years. Now pack up and clear out. You got thirty more days to pay the debts. I say you got a better chance going to California or someplace. Mr. Purvine here means to have a look around. Foote don't want the ranch for himself, you see. He means to sell it to this Texan, though why anybody'd want this eyesore, I can't imagine. I say give it back to the Mexicans." He twisted in his saddle. "It's safe to come closer, Purvine. Cale's behaving himself. He's a heap smarter than his pa ever was."

"Don't you go talking against my pa!" Cale shouted, his voice high and strained.

"He beat the crap outta you more times than I can count," Brummer said. "Don't defend him."

Sunny wondered if there was anything more she didn't know about this unfortunate family. She felt ashamed for May Sue and Cale, having been raised in such misery.

"Help me down, Cale. I'll go inside and help May Sue pack."

"Where we goin' to go without no cash money, Sunny?" Cale demanded. "You tell me that."

Bar looked concerned for the battered young man.

"You might find a back room at a saloon if you offer to sweep up. I used to do it."

"Oh, sure, I'm going to sweep up in a saloon. My pa's the biggest rancher in two counties, and I'm goin' to sweep."

Brummer dismounted and pulled some papers from his vest. "Your pa's dead, son. You got to go, and you got to go 'fore it rains because I'm getting hungry. Don't force me to do something I don't want to do. Keep your gun holstered."

Cale looked ready to cry.

Bar handed Sunny down from the buckboard. She rushed to Cale and put her hand on his arm. "Maybe you can work something out with Foote to pay off the debt like me and Ma did all these years. Now our house is ours, free and clear. It's not so hard once you set your mind to it."

Cale looked down at Sunny as if she were crazy. "I don't work for no other man. I'm a McKidrict."

"You've got to think of May Sue. Where's she going to go? You're her brother. You and Lyford have to keep her safe."

"She's goin' to marry that jackass, Johnsie Rawlins, wherever the hell he disappeared to. You look after her till she does, Sunny. I can't do it. Keep her at your house till I can think."

Sunny's stomach dropped. Her automatic response was to reject his idea, but she heard herself saying, "All right, if that will help." Her mother would have been proud, Sunny thought.

Stiffly she smiled and started for the house. Her mind was whirling. Where would May Sue sleep? *Would* her mother welcome the girl? She glanced at Bar and saw a glow of admiration in his eyes.

Behind her, Cale muttered, "And I suppose that's the Texan who thinks he's going to live in my pa's house and run his cattle. Come on down here, vulture, and let me have a good look at you."

Sunny paused to watch, fearing Cale might shoot the man in order to prevent the eventual sale of the ranch.

A tall, distinguished man, wearing a fringed leather coat and black string tie, climbed down from the wagon. Foote remained seated. Sunny could just imagine how Ol' Fart's eyes must be glittering at the thought of selling off the place. Even in its sorry condition, it was worth a small fortune.

"The name's Charlie Purvine," the Texan said. His southern accent was thick, his face lean and canny. He smiled at Cale, but no trace of warmth softened his eyes. "Can't say, just now, that I'd spend a plug nickel for this place. Too run down." He looked all around, and his keen gaze finally rested on Cale's panic-stricken expression. "You the youngest?"

"There's my sister," Cale said.

May Sue came thumping onto the porch again. She was trying to hook her bodice. Sunny caught her. "You're coming home with me."

May Sue gawked at Sunny. At first she looked furious, then confused and suspicious. "You'd take me in?"

"You shouldn't have to stay in a hotel." Sunny sometimes amazed even herself with her quick thinking.

May Sue appeared mollified until she caught Bar watching them. Her face split with a grin. "Is *he* staying at your place, too?"

"Uh, yes." Sunny's heart squeezed into a knot.

Brushing Sunny aside, May Sue hooked her hand around Bar's elbow. "You'll help me do right by Pa, won't you, bounty hunter? You won't let his killer get away, will you? I knew the minute I laid eyes on you, you was a *real* man."

15

Thunder rumbled and it was nearly dark. Bar urged the horse and buckboard around the bend.

While May Sue sat next to Bar in the middle, chattering like an irritating child, Sunny fought her rising impatience and jealousy. She must have been out of her head to invite May Sue home. As they pulled into the Summerlins' dooryard at long last, Sunny prayed that May Sue's visit wouldn't drive her to madness.

The moment Bar reined in at the kitchen door, Sunny scrambled down. She caught a glimpse of May Sue's envious expression as the girl looked around, comparing the place to the one she had just left.

Before May Sue could comment, Helen appeared in the doorway with Frank standing behind her. "You're back!" she said with relief. "I was beginning to worry."

Sunny hurried to her mother. The woman smiled uncertainly as Bar climbed over May Sue and then helped her to the ground. He began wrestling her trunk down from the back.

"Why . . . May Sue. H-how are you, dear?" Helen's tone of voice betrayed her surprise.

"Goin' to be soaked here in a minute if we don't get inside. Howdy, Miz Summerlin. Ain't seen you in ages." May Sue strode past Sunny into the kitchen and looked around. "What you folks got to eat around here?" Not waiting to be invited, or even seated, May Sue took a thick slice of bread from a napkin-lined basket on the table and went to sniff a pot simmering on the cookstove.

In a whisper, Sunny explained to her mother all that had happened at the McKidrict ranch that afternoon. Outside, rain began falling. Frank hurried out to help Bar and Homer get the horse and buckboard put away.

"She can stay, can't she, Ma?" Sunny asked in a whisper.

"Of course, honey." Helen went over to May Sue. "Poor dear. I'm so sorry that you lost your pa." Helen bustled about the kitchen, fussing over the girl. No one would ever have guessed her true feelings about May Sue's unexpected arrival.

Determined to be as much help to her mother as possible, Sunny pulled off her jacket, washed her hands, and laid the table. "Have you and Frank eaten?"

"Yes, but there's plenty left."

"That's good," May Sue chimed in, gouging out a finger of apple butter from a crock and spreading it across her tongue. "'Cause I'm starved."

With simple chatter, they bridged the awkwardness of having May Sue prowling about the kitchen.

The girl had no compunction about sticking her nose in every cupboard and drawer, going off to peek into rooms uninvited, and leaving a trail of her discarded belongings everywhere she went.

"You'd better show her to your room before she finds her way upstairs and gets us into deep trouble. Get the trundle bed made up for her. Do you think she should wash up? She smells a bit ripe."

"I didn't know what else to do, Ma. She had nowhere else to go."

"We'll manage. Maybe she can lend a hand."

Bar and Frank came in drenched.

"That's quite a storm they just outran," Frank said, stripping off his coat.

"Then you must stay the night again," Helen said as she abandoned the leftovers she'd been assembling to hand Frank a towel for his dripping hair. "I don't want you slipping down the road in the mud. Do you feel up to another night in the washhouse, Barnabas?"

Without waiting to hear how her mother would arrange everything for the evening, Sunny hurried to her bedroom, calling May Sue's name. "We need to clean up before we eat."

Looking recalcitrant, May Sue followed her. She stopped in the doorway of Sunny's simply furnished bedroom. "This is quite some house you got here now, Sunny. I forgot you had that two-story addition. I keep thinking of you living in a cabin. That's how *long* it's been since I had an in-vite up this way."

"I'll bring more water in a minute," Sunny said, scrubbing her face at the washstand. She wanted to avoid further recriminations.

Drying off, Sunny wished she had time to put away anything in her room that May Sue might like too much. Then she chastised herself for thinking her old friend might think to take something that wasn't hers.

May Sue watched Sunny strip to her drawers and camisole. "You're downright skinny these days," May Sue said.

May Sue peeled back her jacket and thrust out her chest. All Sunny saw was how tight and spotted her friend's bodice was.

"I filled out right nice, don't you think? Johnsie sure thinks so, the varmint. Them don't look like socks in yer camisole either." May Sue lowered her voice. "You ever let anybody . . . you know . . . touch 'em?"

Sunny tried not to gasp out some old-maidish retort. "Uh, no," she said blushing. There was only one man she'd ever thought about having do such a thing, and he was in the kitchen acting as if she'd suddenly disappeared from the face of the earth.

"I hope you don't think I'm loose, leading Johnsie on like I been doin'. He thinks I should marry him, but Pa said he wasn't good enough for me. Told me I was supposed to stay away from the hands . . . cowhands, he meant." May Sue giggled, spreading her hands against her breasts and plumping them. "Ain't easy when I get that itch, you know what I mean? Darn *hard* to wait for marriage, don't you think?"

Sunny's thoughts began to whirl. "Have you . . . uh . . . ." She couldn't think of a way to ask May Sue what she wanted to know without sounding like a fool.

May Sue's eyes flashed unexpectedly. "If you're askin' if I've ever given myself to anybody, no, I ain't. If you're asking if I've had relations . . . "

Helen stuck her head in the doorway. "Supper's on, girls."

Sunny hadn't thought of herself as a girl in years, but around May Sue she found herself feeling and behaving like one.

"I—I was just worried about your safety at the ranch there by yourself," Sunny said. "Cale didn't seem to care *what* was happening to you."

"That's for gull-danged certain. I was awfully darn lucky when you and your Mr. Landry showed up this afternoon," May Sue said, sashaying around the room, casting distrustful glances at Sunny from time to time. "Johnsie had me down, ready to ravish my virtue . . . and I didn't have a chance against him.

"I been mighty alone these past couple weeks. With Pa dead and buried, and not a gosh-derned soul coming to his funeral . . . and him the biggest rancher in two counties, too. Then Maria cleared out, spittin' in my face and callin' me names in Spanish like I had any say on how Pa treated her all these years. I wasn't hard on her. I kind of liked her, truth be known.

"Lyford, he went off with his little señorita. Didn't care a lick what happened to me. Cale's been drinkin' like he ain't never goin' to stop. He's just as bad as Pa ever was. I tell you, Sunny, I had to take comfort someplace. You can understand, can't you? You ain't thinkin' I'm a hussy now, are you?"

"No. I really am sorry that you lost your pa, and that I missed his funeral. Like Ma said, Bar fell into the mud, unconscious. We didn't know if he was going to die or what. We couldn't leave him."

Before Sunny could bring more warm water from the kitchen, May Sue splashed her face with some that Sunny had used in the basin on the washstand. "Mighty glad that man didn't die," May Sue said, wiping one cheek with her sleeve.

"Here," Sunny said, offering her a hand towel.

May Sue dusted herself off and tossed the towel onto the floor behind the washstand. "I feel like I got me a chance now," she went on. "Mr. Landry liked me, don't you think? I seen how he was lookin' at me. You ain't interested in him, are you, Sunny? Didn't think so. You don't go after men like I always done. You got high moral character."

Sunny felt stricken with dread. "H-he's just a friend."

Examining herself in the mirror over the washstand, May Sue noted a smudge on her bosom and retrieved the towel from the floor to scrub it away. Adjusting her neckline to reveal as much cleavage as possible, she cocked her disheveled head and fixed Sunny with a calculating smile. "Where'd you say he sleeps? Lordy, if I'd a' known *he* was around, I wouldn't have let Johnsie paw at me. You seen how fast him and my brother cleared out after ol' Foote put his notice on our door? There's a little bastard I'd like to fix but proper."

"Who? Cale, or Johnsie?"

"Why, the banker, you ninny. I *know* his kind. You ever look close at them eyes? If I lived in the same house with that ol' goat, I'd be for dang certain there weren't no peepholes in my walls."

With that May Sue waltzed out to dinner. Peepholes? Sunny thought. May Sue's imagination was almost as dirty as her hands.

Sunny could barely taste her food as she sat across from Bar at the kitchen table, listening to May Sue's attempts to charm him. She forced herself to accept the inevitable, that Bar would find the buxom May Sue more to his liking than her. Every word May Sue spoke surely fueled the fires of Bar's vengeful emotions. He talked of nothing but the robbery now. All hope that he'd abandon bounty hunting was gone. Sunny wished he was out of her life forever. To think she'd fancied herself falling in love with him!

She pushed aside her plate and sighed. Bar caught her eye, but she looked away.

Her mother combined serving the late meal with tidying up while Frank went to talk to Howard, Willis, and Grodie on the porch until the men retired. The big news of the evening was the arrival of the rich Texan on the afternoon train.

When Foote hadn't returned at nine, Bar wondered aloud if he shouldn't go looking for the man. "Even though the rain's let up, he might have met with an accident. He isn't usually this late, is he, Mrs. Summerlin?"

"No, but he doesn't often ride out so far, either."

"Hope he fell off that gull-danged wagon, broke his scrawny neck, and drowned," May Sue muttered.

"He had Mr. Purvine with him," Sunny put in. "Do you suppose they're having dinner in town and staying the night at the hotel because of the rain?"

Helen began to clear the table. "He said nothing to me about being absent this evening. Shall we clear out his room and refund him a night's rent?" Helen's expression was joking but her words carried a bite. "I'm sorry," she said after a moment. "That wasn't very nice of me."

"Only what we're all thinking, Ma," Sunny said.

Bar turned from where he'd opened the door to peer out into the lessening rain. "I think you're right, Sunny. He's tending to his client in town. If you ladies will forgive me, I'm going to turn in. I have a lot to do tomorrow."

"Another night with us, Barnabas?" Helen's tone betrayed genuine liking for the man now. She turned warm eyes on him.

"You know how comfortable I feel here," he said. "It's the closest I've come to feeling at home since I can remember. I should do something more for you, Mrs. Summerlin, besides pay room and board."

"Oh, call me Helen, please. You can clear out your things so Frank can get some sleep, too. I'm sorry I haven't a decent room for you."

Bar bade them good-night, avoiding Sunny's cool glance as he strode down the hall.

"Where's he goin'?" May Sue cried in alarm.

"When Frank's here, the only space left for Bar is the washhouse. There's a bench in there. He likes being alone." Helen patted May Sue's shoulder. "Don't worry. You're safe here. We won't let Ol' Foote say a word to you when he comes back. How can the man abide himself? That's what I've always wondered."

May Sue folded her arms on the table and settled her chin on them. "A man's got to do something to make himself feel important when all he's got in his drawers is a little pink worm of a—"

She broke off when Sunny's eyes popped open and Helen's face turned purple.

Once Sunny and May Sue retired, Sunny lay a long while in the darkness of her bedroom, listening to how different the house sounded during this rainstorm than the last.

Scarcely two weeks before she'd been worrying about the stranger they'd just taken in. He was a stranger no more and the house was bursting with more people than it had seen in years. When Sunny finally dozed off, with May Sue lying tense and dirty on the trundle bed nearby, Sunny felt defeated. She was losing Bar and didn't know what to do about it.

In the next room, Helen sat on the edge of her bed until she heard Sunny and May Sue stop whispering. The boarders were already snoring. There was no sign of Foote arriving in the storm, and Helen was glad.

Tugging on her wrapper, Helen slipped out of her bedroom and tiptoed through the lower rooms, making sure everything was secure and in place. From a rear window she could see a light burning in the washhouse, but she didn't worry. Barnabas was probably reading.

The man had a peculiar distracted look, however, Helen thought. She knew he was in the throes of his new investigation, and he'd have to get the bounty-hunting business out of his system. She wondered what would happen after he did.

For that matter, Sunny had looked beside herself, too. Helen understood perfectly. She felt the same way. The man she wanted was only a few doors away, and she didn't intend to wait any longer. If Frank was afraid to make his move, unsure after all these years of how fast he dared approach, Helen intended to show him just what it meant when a Summerlin woman made up her mind.

Helen found Frank seated at the desk in the office, thumbing through a book from the shelf. When she slipped into the room and quietly closed the door, he turned and closed the book.

"Can't sleep, Frank?"

She watched his gaze move over her. His face was soft with surprise as he stood and scooped her into his arms. His lips came down warm and giving over her mouth.

"Marry me, Helen. Please." He drew back long enough to tug a small package from his pocket.

Helen's heart melted at the sight of the ring inside the box. With his big awkward-looking fingers, Frank placed the ring on her left hand.

"Does this mean you will?" he asked.

"I will," she whispered.

"Soon?"

She kissed first his left cheek and then his right. "It means tonight, my dear, sweet man."

The ties of Helen's wrapper came loose as his big, gentle hands moved over her. Helen didn't have to think, and she didn't have to try to remember how to show a man the love she felt. It came as naturally as breathing.

And there was no fear, no haunting memories or lingering sadness to spoil the moment. Like the spring, Helen and Frank bloomed anew, their kisses as fresh and sweet as the morning.

Bar wondered what he had done to make Sunny so angry. The slats of the bench cut into his shoulder blades, but the discomfort was nothing compared to the torment in his mind.

He had seen Sunny angry before and had always known why. This time was different. This time she was not holding back, hoping he'd talk to her or coax her opinions into the open. This time she was gone, her face impassive, as cold as a stormy day.

He wanted to talk to her. He wanted to hear her opinions. He wanted to explain . . . explain what? he asked himself irritably. They'd gone to the ranch. In spite of Sunny's reluctance, she'd warmed to him along the way. They'd determined the fact that they were friends. He'd nearly kissed her! What had happened?

Cale had kissed her.

Bar had wanted to thrash the scrawny young man, but it was his skinny, battered appearance and the fact that he was drunk that had kept Bar at bay.

Did she like Cale more than she let on? Bar had thought her expression clearly one of disgust.

Bar rolled onto his side again, found the bench as ungiving toward his shoulder as his spine, and flopped back onto his back. That May Sue was a practiced little hussy if ever he'd seen one, Bar thought. The way she . . .

A wave of cool night air swept into the washhouse as the door was tugged open. Lifting his head, Bar watched a woman slip into the darkness that was relieved only by the light coming from the stove grate. She was a blur, almost an apparition. For a hope-filled moment, Bar thought it was Sunny.

But along with the apparition came the faint odor of that one-hundred-twenty-proof McKidrict home brew and cheap eau de cologne. Bar was about to ask May Sue in a mildly sarcastic tone if she'd mistaken the washhouse for the privy when she let whatever sort of soft-looking garment she'd been wearing slip back from her shoulders. Her breasts were deep and full.

"Howdy," she whispered, stepping free of the fabric that pooled around her ankles. "Thought you might be gettin' cold all by your lonesome out here."

Bar was just realizing the girl was naked save for her boots when she walked right up to him and threw her leg over him, mounting his lap and straddling him and the bench.

Before he could say a word, she bent close and spread her mouth wetly over his lips. She'd had quite a lot to drink, Bar noted, deciding that the only way to handle this girl was to give no response.

"No," he whispered softly, somewhat surprised to find his self-imposed celibacy unperturbed by this poor creature. Some men might have called her low names and abused her ignorance, but Bar knew May Sue was just a lost, frightened child. She saw in him a savior, but strangely, he realized that when he brought in her father's murderer, it would mean nothing for *her* future. Bar understood at last that he was bounty hunting for his own needs and no one else's. All that high-minded talk about helping the victims of crimes was just so much smoke.

"It's all right, Landry," May Sue purred, trying to make him put his hands on her breasts. "Don't you want me?"

"I came to your ranch today to help you, Miss McKidrict," Bar whispered gently, keeping his eyes on her face. "This won't help you. I have too much respect for you to take advantage."

May Sue sat up, still straddling his body. If he had looked, he would have seen all she had to offer. He felt so sad that she thought so little of herself that she would offer herself to a stranger uninvited.

That cowhand, Johnsie, hadn't turned her into this, Bar knew. He wondered who had, and how long ago.

"Get off now, May Sue," he said, taking hold of her upper arms and trying to pry her from his lap. She brought no life to his loins whatsoever, so unappealing was her disrespectful display of herself. "Do you need to talk to me? Did something upset you?"

"Don't you like girls?" she cried, dismounting and snatching up her wrapper from the floor.

Catching her wrist, he saw hope flare in her eyes and wink out just as quickly when he smiled but not in the way she wanted. "I'm your friend, May Sue. I intend to help you."

Even as he spoke, Bar knew he was a fake. He was going after the bounty because he couldn't resist the challenge. He wanted to feel that vicious sense of satisfaction one more time.

Ice flooded his veins. It was true. He wanted to kill. He needed to. . . .

"I suppose you're my friend just like you're Sunny's friend?" May Sue went on. "Thanks just the same, Landry, but I don't need no kind of friend. I need a *real* man to take care of me, and I can see . . ." She glanced at his lap where there was no telltale bulge to reassure her, ". . . that you ain't no kind of man at all. What makes you think you can find my pa's killer or my pa's money? You ain't got no kinda *gun* that's any use to anybody."

Bar swung off the bench and stood over the girl. May Sue's expression reflected sudden fear and uncertainty. "I'm the kind of man who will never hurt you, Miss McKidrict. If you want to talk, we'll talk. But we're not going to muddy the waters with intimacy."

She mouthed his words as if trying to understand what he had just said. Unable to fathom his meaning, her face darkened like a thundercloud. She grabbed her wrapper and put it on.

When she pushed the door open, he tried to hold her back, but she wouldn't look at him. Bar felt so sorry for her. "May Sue," he whispered. "Don't be insulted. I'm just not the kind of man you're used to."

She stepped outside. "You sure ain't. You call yourself a bounty hunter, but you ain't nothin'."

He had never felt more incapable of explaining himself. Then he wondered why it should even be necessary to explain anything to a girl who would never be able to understand him.

Worried that someone might wake and hear them, or see them together, Bar released May Sue's arm. Her face was twisted with anguish, poor thing. Without a decent start, she'd be working in a saloon in less than a month, he thought.

May Sue jerked her wrapper closed. "I'm gettin' tired of men talkin' with their guns anyhow instead of makin' a woman feel like a woman. I thought you could do the job proper, Landry, but I guess I was pretty gull-danged wrong about that."

Looking toward the back of the house, Bar saw the door to the kitchen open. In the darkness he couldn't tell if it was Sunny or Helen standing in the doorway. He gave an exasperated sigh. He knew how this looked— him in the doorway of the washhouse with May Sue just leaving, her wrapper twisted and half closed. Anyone with an ounce of imagination would think . . .

It was Sunny standing there, staring across the darkness, boring holes through him. She came marching out into the night.

While May Sue fluttered and fussed, unable to decide what to do, Bar waited. He was ready for whatever Sunny had to say. May Sue's words didn't trouble him. He knew he was a man. He just wasn't certain if he was the kind of man he could live with any longer.

"When I woke and found you gone, I got worried," Sunny whispered to May Sue.

"I'll just bet you were worried," May Sue snapped. Then she flounced back to the house.

Sunny looked up into Bar's eyes. Her gaze swept over him, from his bare chest to his partially unbuttoned trousers. She began to shake her head. When he didn't leap to defend himself, she said, "You're just going to stand there?"

"I already know what you're thinking, Sunny."

"Oh, you do?"

He couldn't think of a way to soothe her. "You're right. I don't know what you're thinking. I was asleep when May Sue came in."

Sunny's chestnut hair was down, tumbling around her shoulders in waves of silky shadows. Her expression was as anguished as May Sue's had been. Bar peered through the darkness, wondering if the girl was watching them now from the kitchen window.

"You don't need to explain anything to me, Bar Landry," Sunny said almost loud enough to make her voice echo across the canyon.

"Then I won't, although I think it would help if I did."

"Help what?" Her eyes locked with his.

He couldn't prevent himself from reaching for her. She was stiff and tried to twist away, but he knew somehow that she was begging him to hold her. He caught her arm firmly and kept his eyes locked with hers, although everything in him wanted to drink in her body the way May Sue had yearned for him to drink in hers.

This was the woman he wanted in his arms, Bar thought, drawing Sunny relentlessly closer. He tipped back his head and closed his eyes, willing her to move close to him. She did. At long last she was against him, trembling and perhaps beginning to weep a bit.

He wrapped one arm and then the other around her, enfolding her against him, wishing she could read his feelings so that he wouldn't have to find words for them.

"I don't want that girl," Bar whispered into Sunny's hair. "I want you."

She melded with him. He felt her hands move uncertainly around his cold, naked back to hold him. Then she was holding him harder and more fiercely. She lifted her face. He opened his eyes to look down and see what she was feeling. Her cheeks were wet.

Drawing her just inside the doorway so that anyone who might be watching would not see this precious moment, Bar lowered his lips to Sunny's soft, giving mouth.

Skyrockets shot through Bar's body. He was instantly on fire. He deepened his kiss to savor the life force surging through his veins. Could he ever want anything more than this?

16

How could a man who kissed like that also be capable of drawing a gun and shooting another human being? Sunny wondered as she clung to Bar.

Suddenly she didn't care to know, or even to wonder. She just wanted him. *Don't stop kissing me,* she thought, *don't stop!* But she dared not speak those words. To speak was to shatter the delicious spell between them. Some unknown part of her knew this moment wouldn't last. She had to savor it.

"Sunny, Sunny," Bar whispered into her hair.

Shivers of desire passed through Sunny's body, centering deep inside where she had never felt such intensity before. Hungrily, she sought his mouth. She hadn't known passion could blot out reason so completely like this.

"After all this is over," he breathed, "I promise—"

Concentrating on the way his arms felt holding her, Sunny shut her eyes tightly and held her breath.

She wasn't going to let herself listen to any promises from this man.

Outside, rain lashed suddenly against the mountain side, making the washhouse quake. A few drops dribbled down the stovepipe and hissed into the fire. Sunny pressed her face to Bar's chest, trying to memorize the fragrance of his warm skin. There was no "after." There was only now.

"Oh, Bar. Don't think about it anymore."

Feeling him stiffen, she stopped herself. How could she have spoken. The delicious sensation of surrender ebbed, leaving her feeling weak and defenseless. But she didn't draw away. If she didn't open her eyes, maybe she could get the feeling back.

"We can't keep arguing about the same thing over and over again, Sunny," Bar said. "I've made a commitment, if to no one else but myself."

She looked up at him.

His eyes appeared tortured in the darkness. "Please try to understand what I'm trying to do."

"Don't you see, Bar?" she said, easing free of the hands she longed to have touch her everywhere. "*Can't* you see that a woman . . . that *I* can't let myself feel what I'm feeling for a man who . . . who can . . . No, no, I'm not going to say it again."

She twisted away, her heart hammering. What was she doing? She wanted to weep for the delicious feelings that were gone now.

"I understand what you're saying," he said.

"If we argue again, I'll tell you that I can't let myself care," she went on as if he hadn't spoken. "You'll ask me to understand why you have to go after this bounty. I won't be able to. We can't . . . we can't do this. You're going to do whatever it is you came to this town to do. I'm going to go on being who I am."

"That's what I've been trying to tell you."

"I shouldn't have come out here. I shouldn't have interfered. I'm sorry, Bar. The one you should be kissing is May Sue. I . . . I . . ."

Tears welled in her eyes. She felt as if a thousand impossible knots had just been tied in her heart. When she saw Bar's anguished face she knew she had to flee. How could he hold vengeance in his heart and kiss her as if he truly meant it?

How could she kiss him when she knew what he was bound to do? Oh, she thought, as her arms reached for him of their own free will, oh dear Lord, she wanted to be kissing him forever!

He held her off now. "I'd better go to town, Sunny. I can't keep putting you through this. We're at an impasse."

"Why do you have to be so stubborn? I don't think you want a normal life." She was appalled to hear her angry tone when her heart lay open and bleeding before him. "You like being lonely and miserable. It fits some kind of twisted idea of—"

Sunny managed to stop herself. She didn't want to shout at him. She couldn't bear to hurt him. Why would Bar want to punish himself by living alone, outside society, with no family and no one to love him?

There was a part of him she didn't understand. She feared she never would understand him. What upset her the most was that because of those unknown parts that she couldn't understand, she might never be able to give herself over to Bar completely, or to any man for that matter. Men were far too imperfect to be borne, she thought. She might be alone forever.

Bar reached for his shirt. "I'm going now. Tonight." His tone was flat. "If I don't, May Sue will keep coming around. That will cause more hard feelings between you and me." He thrust his arms into the sleeves. "I want to know that we parted friends."

He really was going, Sunny thought. Moving toward the door, she held herself more tightly. Moments before they had been kissing. They could have been kissing still if she hadn't spoken.

"I'm sorry," she whispered. "I won't say anything more. I promise. Don't go like this. Please. It'll worry Ma."

"I can't ask *you* to be anything but who you are, Sunny," Bar said, rolling his blankets, tying them with vicious jerks. "That's how it is when you—" Abruptly he stopped. He looked at her, and then away.

He jammed his feet into his boots. He had to sit down to get them on.

"Please. *Stay,*" she whispered.

"Tell your mother . . ." He stopped long enough to fish a twenty-dollar gold piece from his saddlebags. "Give this to her."

When Sunny refused the coin, Bar grabbed her hand and coldly slapped it into her palm, forcing her fingers to close around it.

"Thank you for saving my life, Sunny. Thank you for thinking so much of me. Thank you for trying."

"You don't have to go," she pleaded, knowing that this time she'd gone too far. She'd asked too much.

"I know you're only trying to help me. You're try-ing to keep me from making another mistake that I'll surely regret. But I've realized, Sunny, it's too late. I made my choice years ago. I can't bring back the outlaws I killed. The truth is, I wouldn't want to."

She wanted to stamp her foot. "You could just stop!"

He was shaking his head. "I can't be the man you dream of, Sunny. I can't make myself worthy of anyone else no matter how much I might want to do that. I have to be worthy of myself first."

"Bar, you're not making any sense! You are what you are, you say, but you want to be worthy? Listen to yourself!" she cried.

"If I stay another minute, Sunny, I'll just hurt you more." He stood and glared down at her, not so much angry as defiant. "Right or wrong, I must be true to myself."

"Noble words," Sunny muttered, looking away.

She couldn't believe she was saying such things when all she really wanted to do was understand, just *understand* and accept what drove him.

"Yes, the very thing you want me to be, noble. But you would make me your puppet, Sunny Summerlin, and I am not that. I am a man, and I am very . . . I have this pain inside. It doesn't go away. No matter what I do, no matter where I go. As much as I admire you, Sunny, you only make it worse. Good-bye."

He went out, and he didn't look back.

He wouldn't really go, she told herself as she listened to him splash down to the barn in the rain. He'd get soaked. He'd miss the road in the dark and decide to come back.

She covered her face with her cold, trembling hands. That outlaw who robbed the bank had killed McKidrict. If Bar was successful in finding him, Bar might get killed, too.

Come back. Come back! Come back! she wanted to scream.

He wasn't coming.

Why was it so wrong to ask him to stop doing something that had nearly killed him already with tortured dreams and a savage fever? Why wasn't it making him sick now?

Because he wasn't struggling anymore, she realized in panic.

Slamming the washhouse door, Sunny hurried down to the kitchen and threw that door closed, too. She didn't care how late in the night it was. She didn't care if she woke the world. Nothing blotted out the fact that she'd driven Bar away.

He hadn't been fighting some deep battle of the soul when he first came to them, she tried to tell herself. It had just been a fever, an ordinary fever. He wasn't special. In those first few moments when he awoke she'd fancied he was something other than he was, just as her mother had done. But he was still just a stranger. He was a bounty hunter.

He might get killed.

She began stoking the low fire in the huge kitchen fireplace with angry jabs of the iron poker. He was too smart to get killed. He'd find that outlaw. He'd kill the outlaw, prop him up in front of the sheriff's office and get his likeness made. He'd collect his bounty and be gone. Good riddance.

With her throat aching with unshed tears, Sunny realized she couldn't even shut herself in her own bedroom and cry all night into her pillow. May Sue was there. Pathetic, shabby little May Sue. Sunny wanted to scream until her throat was sore.

Running to the front window when she heard quiet

hoofbeats in the rain, Sunny watched a shadowy rider on a black horse disappear into the darkness. "Be safe, Bar Landry," she whispered, closing her eyes. "I love you."

She'd get over him, she told herself. In a few weeks life would be back to normal. Like some mysterious fever, she'd suffer and then weep Bar out of her system. Afterward, she'd be as good as new. She raised her head. No one need ever know how much she had wanted Bar Landry to teach her about love.

Sunny was frying bacon and had biscuits baking in the oven when her mother came into the kitchen just after dawn a few hours later.

"May Sue's still sleeping," Sunny said, hoping she sounded normal.

When her mother didn't say anything, Sunny peeked at her, unwilling to have her mother see her swollen eyes.

Helen stood beside the pie table, a distracted look on her face as she tied her apron strings behind her back.

"Are you all right, Ma?" Sunny asked in alarm.

Seconds later, Frank thumped into the kitchen, smelling of shaving soap. He gave Sunny a huge grin. "Mornin', Sunflower!"

Before Sunny could venture a guess as to what was going on, Frank swept Helen into his arms and kissed her soundly on the mouth. "Sleep good, dear?"

Helen ducked her head and blushed. "Y-you know I couldn't sleep a wink."

Giving Sunny a shy smile, Helen held out her left hand. A gold ring sparkled on her fourth finger.

"Ma!" Sunny cried, abandoning her griddle. She searched their faces and then laughed. She grabbed them both and hugged them. "Finally! I'm so happy. When?"

"Next month. That should give the boarders time enough to make other arrangements," Helen said, looking pleased but a little worried, too.

Sunny backed toward the cookstove, and then concentrated on turning the overly browned bacon. A month. Her thoughts began to whirl.

"There'll be so much to do," Sunny said breathlessly. "You'll want a new dress, won't you, Ma? Make her say yes, Frank. She hasn't had a new dress in a year. And you'll need a going-away dress, too. You're going on a wedding trip, aren't you?"

"To Denver," Frank said, his eyes shining as he watched Helen check the biscuits and begin laying the table.

"I heard Ol' Foote come in during the night," Helen said. "Looks like he tracked mud all the way up the stairs."

Sunny glanced at the small footprints crisscrossing the kitchen floor. To Sunny, it looked as if Foote had stood at the rear window a long while.

Her mother and Frank looked so happy, Sunny thought. Her heart was so full, she scarcely knew what to do. She couldn't think about the footprints.

"I'm in such a tizzy, I'm liable to burn the rest of breakfast. I need some air."

Sunny handed her mother the cooking fork and hurried to the back door. Outside, the rain had stopped. Her only escape was the privy. She fled up the flagstone walk into the sweet morning mists.

When she came out, she found her mother waiting

in the kitchen doorway. Sunny didn't know how to avoid her. Though the morning sky was overcast, there was no hiding the fact that Sunny had been crying most of the night.

Looking worried, Helen searched Sunny's face. "You're upset, honey. Tell me the truth. You're happy about me and Frank?"

"You know I am, Ma." But Sunny couldn't stop her expression from falling. "I don't know why I'm crying. I'm so happy for you. I seem to be all mixed up inside. I've worked so long for this. All the liniment, and the wallpaper. Now it's finally happened."

Helen gathered Sunny into her arms. "There, there."

Sunny sobbed in her mother's arms. She couldn't stop the words from spilling out. "He's gone, Mama. I tried to change him, and now he's gone."

Her mother patted her back. For a moment Sunny relished feeling like a little girl again. Then finally she straightened and scrubbed away her tears.

Helen looked at her closely. "Maybe it's for the best."

"How can you say that? You liked Bar. I could tell that you did."

"Yes, I did. Come on, now. We have a meal to cook and boarders to do for. Weeping won't get you anywhere. Thinking won't either. You work, and you wait and see."

Sunny wanted to run off and spend the day feeling sorry for herself at the Indian cave.

"I need your help, honey," her mother said. "I must tell the boarders that they have to move at the end of the month. I'm going to tell them this morning. Feeling obligated to them has kept me from living,

Sunny. It's time I started doing for myself, and Frank, and you."

Sunny felt as if someone had jerked the world from beneath her feet.

"I want a big wedding," Helen went on, "with everyone here to share our happiness. I'll invite every eligible man in the state. You won't have time to cry over a man whose heart is trapped in the past. Yes, I liked Bar, honey, but you can't hold a man back, even if what he wants to do is bad for him. That's not how love works."

"I don't love him, Ma," Sunny lied.

"Of course you don't. You've only known him a few short weeks. Come inside now, and tell Frank how happy you are. He's a bit worried."

"Will I ever find a man as sweet and gentle as Frank?" Sunny asked, her heart sore.

Helen nodded as she steered Sunny back into the kitchen. "I believe you will."

Sunny could tell that her mother was more worried about Bar than she was letting on because a few moments later Helen went to the front window and looked out. After a few minutes, she said, "Homer's getting surprisingly good with those spoons."

After Bar left the Summerlin place he rode Sundown into a silent town that was still closed up and dark. Unable to locate the night clerk at the hotel, he spent the remaining hours before dawn slumped in a lobby chair.

He was glad to be away from Sunny, as his way was clear now. No more confusion. No more distractions. No more foolish thoughts of love.

The clerk who came on duty at seven had obvious misgivings about renting to the drenched black-clad stranger in the lobby, but Bar got his room on the third floor in the rear. He hoped he would find peace there.

Frank Tilsy paid a call late in the afternoon with Helen's change from Bar's twenty-dollar gold piece and an invitation to supper, which Bar declined. Bar had little to say to the man regarding his sudden departure during the night. Frank suggested that Bar attend the next town meeting, and then left, bidding him luck with his manhunt.

Bar paid for a week at the hotel, and for a week at the nearby livery for Sundown. Then he slept for what seemed like days. Nothing he did, however, soothed the dull ache that filled his head and heart. He thought about Sunny. He dreamed of her. When he finally went out to prowl the town and pursue his investigation, he watched for her in the streets.

Before he knew it, Bar was sleeping away most of his days and wandering Crystal Springs's streets at night. He explored every saloon, talked to anyone with an opinion regarding the robbery, and when he ran low on funds he stopped at the bank. He asked Ethridge Foote to oversee personally a transfer from his account in St. Louis. Foote was suitably wary but impressed.

There Bar learned that Charlie Purvine was still in town but undecided about buying the McKidrict ranch. Bar had dinner with the man one night.

"All those McKidricts need to do is come up with a few hundred dollars and the ranch is theirs again," Purvine told Bar over venison. "'Course, if those boys want to piss away their rights, drinkin' and whorin' instead of tendin' to the debt, who am I to argue? That land's worth a fortune."

Bar listened, but in the back of his mind was the picture of Sunny on the buckboard, getting kissed by Cale McKidrict.

"What I can't figure," Purvine went on, "is why Foote ain't *askin'* a fortune for that land. There's a legal hitch somewhere. Foote might not have the right to seize the place like he said he did."

Bar's interest flared. "Didn't McKidrict have legal title?"

Purvine had leaned back in his chair and lit a cheroot. "He wasn't what I would call a top-of-the-deck man. I hear tell he beat his wife. He ran roughshod over his children. He chased women on both sides of the street, if you get my meaning. And his hate of Mexicans was well known. Nobody seems to know for certain where he came from; in my neck of the woods that means he didn't want nobody to know."

"How do you know he beat his wife?" Bar asked. He had thought Sunny and her mother the only ones privy to that information.

Purvine paused to study his thin brown cigar. "I don't come five hundred miles without checkin' into things a bit. Truth is, I doubt that man was born with the name McKidrict.

"I think he borrowed the name from a man killed during the war. I think he 'helped' the man die and 'inherited' the fine things that are now turning to rot out in that ranch house."

"You're saying he killed someone, took his name, came west, and pretended to own the land? That everything in that ranch house is stolen and this whole mess is based on a lie?"

Purvine's gaze was startlingly cold. A perfect ring of smoke drifted from his lips. "I wouldn't swear to it. All I know is, I wouldn't have made my daughter marry a no-account thieving grave-robber like that just because she . . . I'd have shot him for seduction and had his oysters for breakfast."

Bar was curious as to how Purvine knew so much about the McKidricts. "Is this your way of telling me, Mr. Purvine, that the bounty on McKidrict isn't worth my time?"

"Hell, it won't do no harm to collect it if you give it away like you claim you always do. Question is, who you plannin' to give it to?"

"Don't know yet."

"Frankly, I don't think the bank got robbed. McKidrict may have had the biggest ranch in two counties, but he didn't drive enough beef to market to earn the price of a decent night in a sportin' house. I know, Landry, because my business is cattle. I'd bet my boots he couldn't pay. If his sons hadn't been out on the street that day, I would've bet one of my ranches that one of *them* staged the robbery."

"That had crossed my mind," Bar said.

"No, sir. You go right on ahead and find the man who killed McKidrict. Don't kill him, though. I want to shake his hand. Then I'll hire him the best lawyer south of Denver to make sure he don't hang. I hear you were reading law at one time, Landry. Why'd you turn from it?"

Bar didn't have time to answer.

Purvine laughed suddenly. "Why, you could bring the fool in. Then you could defend the son of a bitch!"

*　　　*　　　*

In a small saloon at the south end of Fremont Street a few nights later, Bar sat hunched over a shot of whiskey. He never found solace in liquor, but those who might be willing to talk to him didn't trust a man who didn't drink. So he turned the filled shot glass in circles, waiting for someone to come along.

After all the questioning and searching that Bar had done since leaving Sunny in the rain, he was no closer to finding the bank robber. No two stories told to him were alike. No one really cared if McKidrict's killer was brought in anyway. Folks were just infuriatingly curious about the event.

Just stop, Sunny had told him. *Give up the hunt.*

Bar closed his eyes and tried to imagine doing that.

He did want to stop, with all his heart.

Purvine believed there hadn't even been a robbery, just a staged playact that had gone awry. To continue investigating made Bar out to be a greedy fool.

For the first time, Bar had no idea in which direction to ride. This time he might not find his quarry. It might be divine Providence's way of telling Bar that his man hunting days were over.

Yet he didn't leave town, as many had suggested that he do. By day, women crossed the street when he passed. Children peeked at him from corners and doorways. By night he sat in one saloon or another, thinking, watching, listening. Men began wondering if Bar Landry was really so tough after all.

He pondered his big black Stetson, placed on the table before him. Big bad bounty hunter, he chided himself. His trousers and coat looked like something a gambler might wear. Maybe it was time to go shop-

ping. He'd heard that Frank had given the ring to
Helen. It might be nice to stop by and visit.

But, Bar thought, chuckling, he wouldn't buy new
boots. He liked the black snakeskin ones. And Sundown was a great horse. As for the gun . . .

"You laughin' at me, Landry?" came a voice to the
side of the murky saloon that caught Bar unaware.

Bar turned toward two men slouched at the bar.
Cale McKidrict. Johnsie Rawlins. Scruffy, dirty, no-
account men, ripe for a fight.

"No, friend," Bar said with a casual air that surprised even himself. "I'm not."

Before the men could think of something to argue
with him about, Bar snapped a coin onto the table
and left. But instead of heading back to the hotel, Bar
stepped into the shadowed space between the saloon
and the closed-up, darkened store next door.

He hadn't even had time to get comfortable lean-
ing against the wall to wait for them when the two
men thumped out onto the boardwalk. Bar could
smell them; whiskey, tobacco, and sweat.

"Maybe she'll feed us," Johnsie said, belching
loudly. "I ain't had a decent meal since yesterday
morning. Now I've lost all my money. Ain't you hungry? Ain't you interested to know how your sister's
gettin' on out there?"

"Only thing I'm interested in," Cale grumbled, his
words slurred, "is teaching prissy Miss Sunny a long
hard lesson."

Bar straightened as the two untied their horses
from the hitching rail.

"Call my kiss disgusting, will she? I'll give her disgusting." Cale threw himself atop the horse and
nearly pitched headlong over to the far side.

Johnsie snickered. "She ain't never goin' to give you the time o' day. Let's go to Annie's. I know a gal there who'll—"

"You want my sister or not?" Cale snapped, weaving on the saddle. "I'm givin' her to you. Goddamn females. I'll show Sunny how it's done. She'll come beggin' for more. May Sue ain't beggin' you no more, I see. She's done got her head turned around by that bounty hunter. Probably gettin' it regular from him now."

As Johnsie scrambled into his saddle, Cale started out of town at a full gallop. Johnsie was quick to follow. By their whoops and shouts, Bar wondered if they'd fall off into a ditch somewhere. He hoped so.

17

Sunny had just blown out the lamp and crawled into bed when she and May Sue, who was lying on the trundle bed nearby, heard the shouts outside.

"Oh, Lord," May Sue grumbled in the darkness. "I'd know that sound anywheres. It's Cale and Johnsie. Drunker'n hoot owls. I wonder if they know about Lyford yet."

May Sue was out of bed and hurrying from the bedroom wearing Sunny's extra nightgown before Sunny could ask what the girl meant. What had May Sue found out about her oldest brother that afternoon when she rode off without a word of explanation?

Scrambling out of bed, Sunny grabbed her wrapper and hurried after the girl. Helen had left a low-burning lantern on the kitchen table in case anyone needed to use the privy in the night.

"Sh-h-h," Sunny whispered when she found May Sue standing in the open kitchen doorway. "You'll wake Ma. What do they want?"

May Sue gave Sunny an impatient look. "What the hell do you think they want, Sunny? Are you really as dumb-innocent as you let on? It's wearin' on me, it surely is. They want *us.* Johnsie's probably got an itch about six inches long about now. And Cale, all he ever used to talk about was marrying up with you, except that Pa didn't like such talk. Pa would tell the boys, 'Don't you never saddle yourself with a woman. Look what I got for my trouble.' And he'd look at us young'uns like we was a curse on his head."

May Sue waltzed out the door into the chilly darkness.

"You don't have a wrapper on!" Sunny called.

May Sue ignored her.

Sunny shivered with irritation. Each day in such close proximity with May Sue was proving harder than the one before. Sunny felt ready to throw her old friend out into the cold and damn the consequences.

"Who-ee, May Sue!" Johnsie bellowed, throwing his leg over his saddle horn and sliding to the ground. "By the light comin' from that there door, darlin', I can see clean through yer gown. Come 'ere." He swaggered up and put his arms around her. While smothering her face with a kiss, both of his hands groped at her backside.

Nothing May Sue said or did shocked Sunny now, but even so, Sunny edged back inside. She feared Cale would want to do the same thing if she let him get too close.

How could May Sue let a man handle her like that when she wasn't even married to him? Didn't the girl have any self-respect?

Cale dismounted, fell to his knees, climbed back to his feet again, and steadied himself against his shying horse. "Come on out here, Ornery. Have ya missed me?" he called loud enough to be heard across the valley. "Got somethin' for you. Make you feel real good inside."

Sunny stiffened.

Johnsie was close enough to cuff Cale's arm. "You got no manners. Go on over and kiss her. She'll warm to you."

Panicking, Sunny wanted to slam the door and throw the bolt, but she couldn't let them carry on, waking up the whole house. So she stepped outside and pulled the kitchen door closed behind her. "Quiet! You'll wake the men."

"You call them leather-brained old peckerwoods *men*?" Cale waltzed toward Sunny.

"Don't you touch me," Sunny said as Cale began to reach for her. "Get off our place. We don't allow drunks here."

"Oh, no? Let's see who around here can make me leave." He seized her arm and jerked her close.

Sunny recoiled at the vile smell of alcohol coming from his mouth.

"Le'see now," Cale went on. "You got one old fart, three useless younger ones, a crazy handyman, and a few dogs I can shoot. Do I look scared, Ornery? No, I don't. So don't threaten me." His grip on her arm stung her to the bone.

Sunny glared into Cale's face but inside she was quaking with fear.

"Now, Ornery, gimme a little taste of your lovin'."
His free hand slid up her side. "Hell, I might even
propose to you. I been waitin' long enough to hold
you like this. Bet you didn't know you had been practically engaged to me all these years." His hand closed
on her breast.

She felt nothing but revulsion.

Then, from the darkness, came the sound of a gun
cocking.

Pushing Sunny away, Cale whirled and drew his
own gun.

"Who's out there?" Cale stumbled and looked
ridiculous.

"It can't be your conscience, McKidrict," came a
low voice. "But don't worry. I didn't come here to kill
you. Clear out, and we'll forget this happened."

Sunny felt like weeping for joy. It was Bar!

"Show yourself, coward!" Cale shouted again,
staggering. He cocked his gun, too.

Johnsie quickly ducked into the blackness between
the house and barn.

Sunny motioned May Sue to escape back into the
house, but May Sue sashayed farther from the faint
light cast across the yard by the lantern-lit window.

"Is that the famous bounty hunter I hear out
there?" she called in a singsong. "Show yourself, big
fella. Let a girl have a good look at you."

"Are you all right, Miss McKidrict?"

Bar's voice sent delicious shivers of relief through
Sunny. She hadn't realized how much she had missed
him until that moment. What was he doing there?
How could he know they were in danger? And why
was he asking if May Sue was all right when it had
been she who had been fondled against her will?

Johnsie crept into the light falling across the yard. He gave May Sue a wounded look and threw himself atop his horse. "I'm done with you, May Sue. I truly am."

"You'll have to pay the next time you touch me, Johnsie Rawlins," May Sue said.

"Already have. You comin', Cale, or are you goin' to let the bounty hunter shoot you just for touchin' her?"

Cale looked confused, as if the question were too much for him. "What the hell would he care for?"

Behind Sunny, the kitchen door quietly opened. "What's wrong, honey?" Helen whispered, tying her wrapper at the waist.

"It's Cale McKidrict and the cowhand, Johnsie."

Johnsie galloped out of the yard and disappeared around the bend in the road. Cale hesitated but finally climbed with great effort onto his horse and followed, weaving in his saddle and swearing as he left.

After a moment, Bar emerged from the shadows. He looked like a devil dressed in black and riding his black horse. The two of them were nearly invisible in the darkness.

Helen fetched the lantern from the table and turned up the wick. "Is everything all right, Barnabas?"

Bar walked Sundown closer. He paused to slide his long dark pistol into his holster. "I heard them talking in town and followed them to make sure they didn't cause any trouble."

"They were just drunk," May Sue muttered from the yard, giving Bar a strange look before pushing past Sunny and her mother and stomping inside. "Just havin' a little fun." May Sue paused long enough to add privately to Sunny, "That bounty hunter of yours is mighty handsome, but he ain't no fun a-tall."

"Mine?" Sunny repeated, edging back into the kitchen. She couldn't bear to see Bar looking so sinister.

"Well, ain't he? Didn't you send him away the minute I tried my luck with him? Oh, don't look so gull-danged innocent. Your face is red. I know what's goin' on between the two of you. Don't think I don't. And I ain't stayin' here a minute longer than I have to. It's boring. I can't stand it."

Helen glanced back at May Sue and then started across the yard. Sunny longed to hear what her mother had to say to Bar.

"Are you all right, Barnabas? You're looking thin."

He looked as if he missed being there with them. "There's no telling what those two will think up to do now that they're on the loose. McKidrict was the only one who could control them, so I'm told."

"I'm not worried about two pups. Won't you come in? We could talk. Willis will be moved out tomorrow. You could stay in his room for a few days. We're all interested to know what you've learned about the robbery. There's been so much idle speculation lately."

Sunny thought that Bar looked tempted by her mother's invitation, but finally he tipped his black Stetson and turned his horse.

"Thanks, but no. Take care, Mrs. Summerlin, Sunny. Sorry for the intrusion."

He disappeared into the night so quickly it almost felt to Sunny as if he had never been there. The entire episode seemed like a bad dream.

"Don't look so worried, honey," Helen said,

returning to the kitchen and hugging Sunny's shoulders. "It's hard for Barnabas to stay away from you. I'd say, given time, he'll put that gun away for good."

Sunny searched her mother's face. "I'm half afraid he's right about needing to prove to himself that he can control his rage. I felt it just now, Ma. I was waiting for him to kill Cale and Johnsie."

"Whatever would make him do that? They hadn't committed a crime. Like May Sue said, they were just drunk."

Sunny threw back her head and closed her eyes. "How can I care so much about him when I know what he's done?"

"It's in the past, Sunny," her mother whispered. "And besides, if he means nothing to you—well, isn't that what you've been telling me? What does it matter what he's done if he means nothing to you?"

Sunny forced herself to take a deep breath. "Oh, Ma, sometimes I don't understand you. One minute you're for Bar. The next minute you're against him. Now you sound like you're for him again. You tell me to wait. Forgive. Forget. Not to judge. What am I supposed to do when just seeing him like this makes me feel as if I'm losing my mind?"

"Where is it written I have all the answers, honey?" her mother asked.

Sunny lowered her voice to a whisper. "And May Sue is driving me straight over the edge! Did you see how she let Johnsie . . ."

In a blinding flash of insight, Sunny realized she was jealous of May Sue's freedom from restraint. Sunny wanted to kiss Bar without reservation. She wanted to hold him. She wanted to feel his hands on her body. And she didn't much care if she was married to him or not when it happened. She just wanted it to happen.

"Does it help, honey, to say such things against May Sue?" her mother asked.

"I'm sorry, Ma, I don't know what's got into me. I think I'm afraid of what the future holds. Everything's changing so fast."

"I know exactly how you feel, honey. I've been in torment ever since I decided to marry Frank. I've led an empty life rather than face up to a full one that I might lose again. You're learning to live, dear. It's not easy. You're learning to love."

"Ma, do I really love Bar?"

Helen paused to consider the question. "Sunny, you can love someone and never be with him. You can be with someone and never love him. You can love and it won't change a thing. Or you can keep yourself from loving, and everything will fall into your lap anyway. I think the question is, what are you willing to do for love?"

Sunny didn't understand what her mother was getting at. "I think May Sue loves him, too," she said.

Helen giggled. "Oh, dear me. What that girl feels isn't love, Sunflower. I feel so sorry for May Sue. Her ma's been gone ten years, yet May Sue's just like her. She's a child, Sunny. You're a woman grown. Start acting like one."

An hour later, Bar stood in front of the mirror in his hotel room, staring at his reflection. He took off his hat and threw his gun belt across the bed. Next he stripped off the black coat and dull gray shirt and stepped up to the cold, impartial glass. He almost expected to see that his eyes had turned black, too.

But his eyes were blue. He couldn't forget how Sunny had looked up at him from the doorway a while ago, so fearfully. He wished he hadn't seen it.

He couldn't remember the last time she'd smiled when he was near. He remembered that first day he'd seen her, when she was pulling her wagonload of liniment across the muddy street. She'd been smiling then. He'd started to fall in love with her that very moment.

When he woke from his feverish dreams and laughed with Sunny, he'd felt reborn. He'd been happy there at her mother's house. It made no sense to keep pursuing something paltry like this bounty, which was bringing him such pain, when to turn from it might bring back that smile of Sunny's. It had to be worth a try.

After disassembling his gun and placing the pieces in the case, Bar lay down on the creaking bed and stared at the ceiling. Wanting Sunny overpowered his desire to prove to himself that he hadn't become a killer. He wanted to be holding Sunny. He was so lonely suddenly, he didn't know if he could go on without her. What would be the harm in trying to do things her way for just a while?

In moments he was sleeping, dreaming of a piece of land he'd seen up the canyon a few days before.

When he woke he heard birds twittering outside his hotel room window. He could smell the fresh, delicious morning air moving the pine branches against the hotel's outside wall. He could see a patch of turquoise sky beckoning beyond the muslin fluttering against the sill.

He was hungry. It was nearly ten o'clock in the morning and his misery had vanished with the night.

Summer arrived the following week, leaving the Summerlin house overwarm and confining.

"I've got to get out for a while, Ma," Sunny said, coming into the kitchen and throwing down her apron. "We've been scrubbing for weeks. Every curtain is washed and starched. The floors shine like new. And May Sue's driving me absolutely crazy. I don't think she knows the first thing about house cleaning."

"Her ma's been gone a long while, and she had Maria to do for her."

"She works for a minute or two and then she starts snooping in drawers. Or she flops down across the bed we just made and claims she needs a rest."

Helen tasted the stock simmering on the stove. "A little air might do you good."

"Is Frank coming for supper again tonight?"

Her mother nodded.

"I think I'll go to town. I could get some calico for a new sunbonnet."

"All right, go!" her mother said, laughing. "You're driving *me* to distraction."

Sunny yanked on her boots and fled. If she was becoming as irritating as May Sue, she'd never be able to live with herself.

It was such a warm day Sunny didn't need her jacket or shawl. She marched down the road, noting how the clouds looked like wisps of white hair in the turquoise sky.

She hadn't been out walking since the day she

and Bar had gone up to the Indian cave for the picnic. Weeks had passed since then. Now her mother
was planning her own wedding and a trip to Denver.
Sunny found herself staring at the blank pages in a
book that was the rest of her life. As she entered
town Sunny considered all sorts of possibilities,
from becoming a schoolteacher to going back east to
college.

It seemed perfectly natural that her first stop
should be Frank's store. The bell jangled as she went
in. In spite of herself, Sunny remembered that morning when the bank was robbed. Today Frank was in
the back, where his best hats were stacked, and a tall
man in a blue plaid shirt was trying on a wide gray
Stetson.

"Morning, Frank," she called. "I need two yards of
calico. I'm in the mood for blue flowers."

"What do you think?" the other customer said,
turning from the mirror.

The man was smiling. His blue eyes were enhanced
by the color of his new shirt. When he lifted the light
gray Stetson, Sunny's breath caught.

"Bar? I hardly recognized you! What's the occasion?" Her heart leapt into her throat. She had been
trying very hard not to think about him.

Bar gave Frank a warning look, as if there were
something he didn't want Sunny to know about.
When Bar approached, Sunny saw that he had also
traded his black trousers for a stiff pair of indigo blue
jeans. All that was left of his original outfit were the
snakeskin boots, and they were dusty.

"You look like a cowhand," Sunny said, but she
wasn't laughing. If she had thought that Bar looked
handsome before, he looked devastatingly so now.

"That's better than being mistaken for an undertaker or card shark. I tore my coat last week, and the seat of my pants split this morning. You're looking well, Sunny, considering your scare the night when Cale and Johnsie were drunk at your place. There's been no more trouble since, I take it."

"You came along just in time, Bar," Sunny said. "Ma's wondering how you are."

Actually, her mother hadn't said a word; the wondering was all inside Sunny's own head.

She wanted to say more, too, to ask if Bar's change of clothes signified a change of heart, but she had learned a painful lesson. She would let Bar tell her what he was doing and thinking about when he was good and ready. No more badgering with questions. They were friends, after all. She would never have interfered in a friend's personal business as she had in Bar's.

"I'm fine," Bar said, his eyes glowing as he looked at her.

"Have you . . . uh, enjoyed your stay at the hotel?" She supposed it was all right to ask that.

"Nothing compares to your mother's hospitality," he replied. "Do you have time to walk with me a ways? I've been thinking about you."

"I guess if I've waited this long for a new bonnet, I can wait a few hours more," Sunny said, tucking her hand in the crook of Bar's elbow. Her heart danced as she let him escort her outside to the boardwalk.

"How's everything going now that your boarders are moving out?"

"Howard's better off in town, he tells us," Sunny said. "He missed a lot of news at the house with us. But he's starving, he claims." Sunny laughed and blushed all over. "There's another boardinghouse just a few streets over. I think he's all right there. Grodie's talking of moving to Durango. Business has been slow, he says."

"And the banker?" Bar asked.

They crossed to the newly built pavilion and took a seat in the shade. Sunny noticed how many townspeople were bidding Bar hello as they passed. They didn't seem afraid of him now.

"Ol' Foote isn't himself these days," she said, her mood darkening. "Ever since the—" She paused, aggravated to think how every conversation led back to the robbery. "Ever since the robbery, Foote's been jumpy and irritable. He's complaining about every little thing. He's late for meals. Nobody knows where he goes off to. Everyone's hoping . . ." Sunny lowered her voice. ". . . that he's planning to move away, too. I mean, I can't imagine him living at the hotel, or with Willis or Howard at the other boardinghouse."

"Or buying a place of his own," Bar put in.

Sunny laughed. "He could sleep in the bank."

He laughed, too.

Sunny looked at Bar and her heart fluttered. "I've missed you," she said softly. "I've worried, too. Come to dinner tonight. Ma would love to have you."

His smile was so delightful, it was all Sunny could do to keep from kissing him. He looked as if he were having a difficult time keeping his hand from stealing around her shoulder, too. She longed for him to touch her.

If she could only keep herself from asking the questions flooding her mind, Sunny thought, she might get him to kiss her again. As it was, she was content to sit near him, with him so handsome in his new clothes, smiling, looking at her as if he were memorizing her, and having folks pause and whisper about them as they passed by. If two people could kiss without touching each other, Sunny thought, she and Bar were doing it right there in broad daylight.

18

"*I'm afraid I can't* come to dinner tonight, Sunny," Bar said, his expression falling as he remembered his previous commitment. "I promised to show up at the meeting of the town council."

Sunny's heart sank. "Well, it was just an idea. Perhaps another night."

"Do you have to go now?" he asked.

"I'm afraid so," she said, not wanting to leave him after such an enjoyable conversation.

"Take care then, Sunny," Bar said, smiling. "Perhaps I'll see you at Lyford's wedding. May Sue invited me out to meet her brother the other day, and I met Tomasina and her family, too. The little boy is smart as a whip. I hope everything goes well for them now."

"I—I hadn't heard about another wedding," Sunny said. "I've been so involved with helping Ma make her dress for hers. It's possible May Sue doesn't intend to invite us. She and I haven't been getting along terribly well in the last few days. I've been short with her."

"Then I've spoken out of turn," Bar said. "It hadn't occurred to me that you and your mother wouldn't be invited. Maybe May Sue forgot."

"It's probably her way of getting back at us. We didn't go to her father's funeral." Sunny shook off the uncomfortable sting of being left out, and smiled awkwardly. "Let's forget it. Stop by for supper anytime. Ma and I are still in the habit of cooking for six."

For the tenth time, Helen went to the kitchen door and looked out. The hour was growing late, but still Sunny hadn't returned from town.

"She's going on twenty-three years," Helen muttered aloud to herself. "You'll be leaving her here alone while you traipse off to Denver for a week with Frank. Then . . . who knows what will happen? You've got to let her go."

But Helen's heart ached over all the changes yet to come. Stepping back in order to let Sunny forge her own future would prove difficult.

She was about to turn from the doorway when she saw a figure at the bend in the road by the spruce. Thinking it was Sunny at last, her heart eased.

Then she realized it was her last, reluctant-to-depart boarder, the sour, the irritating, the most disagreeable Mr. Ethridge Foote. Glancing at the clock, Helen went to busy herself at the cookstove. Why was he coming along earlier than the bank's usual closing time? she wondered.

He entered the kitchen and slammed the door. "I'll

close the bank to every depositor and move back to Cincinnati before I give that incompetent whelp a raise. Thinks he can insist . . ."

Foote's voice was so high with fury, Helen had to force herself not to chuckle.

"I beg your pardon," she said. "You're early today, Mr. Foote."

"Mind your own business, woman." He stormed down the hall.

Instantly angry, Helen listened to Foote stomp up the stairs. She couldn't wait to have him move out of her house. Without the support of her daughter and the other boarders who had all moved out by then, Helen wasn't certain she could withstand Foote's temper.

She was very nearly quivering with the dread of some further confrontation when she realized she hadn't seen May Sue in a while. She couldn't recall if the girl had gone off somewhere outdoors or was cleaning up as she had been asked to do hours before.

"I'll never get used to having that girl here," Helen said. "She's got me talking to myself." But then Helen supposed the girl might prove adequate company for Sunny after the wedding when she and Frank were honeymooning in Denver.

An indignant shriek interrupted Helen's brooding.

"I ain't touched nothin' in your gull-danged box, you ol' fart!"

Helen heard tumbling footsteps coming down the stairs. Before she could dry her hands, May Sue burst into the kitchen.

"That old fool's crazy!" May Sue screeched. "I wish he'd move out. Can't you make him go? How'd you stand him livin' here all these years? I don't think he's right in his head. I mean, my pa had his vices, and one helluva temper when he'd had too much to drink, but this ol' buzzard, he's . . ."

Helen's heart was in her throat by the time Foote came marching into the kitchen. He looked as ferocious as a fighting cock.

He pointed a bony finger at May Sue. "I come home early and find this young trollop in my room, going through my things."

Helen's mouth dropped open. "Remember yourself, Mr. Foote. May Sue is a guest in my house." She shot a look at May Sue.

"What's he got to hide that's so important, that's what I asked myself." May Sue folded her arms and glared at Foote. "So I went in and . . ."

Helen could hardly squeeze out the words. "You *never* look in someone's personal belongings, May Sue McKidrict. You dust, you mop, you change the linens, but you never—"

"I ain't emptying no more piss jars, either. I don't care how grateful I have to be to you for takin' me in, that ain't no human job. If he's so gull-danged important that I got to tolerate him starin' at my bosoms all the time and watching me like I'm goin' around naked, then he can just take his own chamber pot out to the privy. Ain't you got no pride, Helen? It's plumb disgustin', if you ask me."

Foote's face turned purple. "She was going through my . . . my . . . cash box."

"That's a lie! He's got French pictures in there." May Sue whirled on Foote. "Don't you go denyin' it, you ol' peckerwood. I don't need your ol' money, and Lord knows, you got plenty of it stashed up there. I'm talkin' about them pictures. Naked ladies with big bosoms and men with great big peckers . . . I'll swear on a Bible."

Helen was shocked. She couldn't seem to bring Ethridge Foote's face into focus as it drained to a ghastly white.

"They was laying out in plain sight," May Sue went on. "They *was!* Right out in the open where God and anybody might see 'em. I swear on my pa's grave this old coot is trying to corrupt me. I think he's trying to find out if I'd . . . well, you know what I'm gettin' at, Helen. He thinks I'm that kind, but I'm *not!* Not with him, leastwise."

Helen longed to sit down to collect herself, but she dared not. She went immediately to May Sue's side and drew the girl firmly into the circle of her arms.

"Mr. Foote, am I to understand that you have made improper advances toward this young woman?"

He looked at Helen as if he couldn't comprehend what she had just asked. May Sue's eyes widened, too.

Helen began to wonder if she was taking the right stand, and yet she knew she couldn't back down now. She'd had enough of the little man.

He took a step forward.

"Go on up and take a look for yourself," May Sue said to Helen. "He couldn't have had time to put 'em all away. I wasn't snoopin', honest. He left 'em for me to see. You and Sunny ain't safe with him hereabouts."

Foote bared his teeth. "You . . . you young harlot! I wouldn't dirty myself with you. And you, madam." He pinned his fearsome gaze on Helen, sending shivers down her back. "I've had to tolerate the intolerable while living here. This house of iniquity should be burned to its foundation. I once had pity for you. I once thought to call on you and help you in your hour of need, and indeed, I did help you. But it was a fool's errand."

Helen was beyond shock by then. Foote had just stripped away his mask, and she wanted to know exactly who and what he really was underneath.

"The one to help you should have been your lover," Foote went on to say, "the very foul Mr. Luck McKidrict." Foote gave an approximation of a triumphant smile and stood waiting eagerly for Helen's response.

She was beginning to feel faint with disbelief.

"Oh, yes," he went on. "I knew about him, sniffing around your door long before your husband had even gone to his grave. You disgusting woman. He tried his luck with you, and found you willing. And you, going to church, holding your head up. I watched you. Yes, I did. I watched you dally with every man who boarded here. Well, I'm tired of playing the gentleman."

Helen's head whirled. "You, a gentleman?" she whispered as if she'd never before heard the word.

"I'm here to claim what I'm entitled to, what I've been waiting for all these years." He started toward her with his hands out and seized her by the arm.

Helen recoiled at his touch. Her voice came out deep and forceful. "Get out of this house and don't ever come back."

Unaware that she was making a horrible, inhuman sound that was something between a roar and a growl, Helen rained her fists on Foote.

"You took the others to your bed!" he cried, dodging her blows. "Now you're going to—"

Helen slapped him so soundly she lost her footing

and fell back against the table. Seeing her opportunity, she kicked, found her mark, and doubled the little man over.

Coughing and gasping, he fell onto his side. Suddenly his reason seemed to return, and he stared at her. She could almost see his thoughts moving in repugnant circles behind his eyes.

She dragged him to his feet. "Don't you ever repeat what you said here today. I was *never* unfaithful to my husband. I hated Luck McKidrict with all my heart. He came around here, bothering me and scaring me when I was alone. He was a vile, disgusting bully of a man. I would never . . . *never* . . ."

Helen paused long enough to meet May Sue's eyes. Then she plunged on.

"I have never once had any sort of personal relation with any of the men who were my boarders. I have lived an upright, lonely existence here, thanks to you and your constant threats to foreclose. You have a sick and perverted imagination if you think I have ever done anything such as you suggest."

"What about the other night with your precious Frank?" he asked with a sneer.

"Oh!" She literally flung him from her kitchen.

He lost his footing and stumbled out the door into the yard.

"Wait right there, Mr. Foote."

Helen stormed up the stairs to his room. She opened the window and looked out to see Foote climbing unsteadily to his feet. He dusted his clothes. The knees of his trousers were torn open and bloody.

She grabbed his clothes off the hangers in the wardrobe and flung them out the window. Then she jerked a drawer from the bureau and emptied its contents over the sill, watching socks and neatly folded handkerchiefs flutter down.

The strongbox lay open on the bed, and among the dollars and gold coins inside were the French pictures May Sue had claimed to have seen.

Helen stared at the assortment and then with a cry of indignation gathered everything into her apron and ran back down the stairs. By the time she reached the yard, Foote was looking disoriented and pathetic.

Sunny was just rounding the bend in the road. Her broad smile vanished as she drew nearer. "Ma?" she said as Helen dumped the contents of her apron at Foote's feet.

A small picture of a naked woman blew into the bushes.

"Ride for the sheriff," Helen said to Sunny while glaring at Foote.

Struggling for composure, Foote glared back, looking as if he were going to march away and leave the pictures and money lying in the dirt. Then he remembered himself, hastily gathered everything, and stuffed it all inside his vest.

Feeling sick to her stomach, Helen went back into the house and up the stairs, where she stripped Foote's bed and pitched the linens out the window. By then she knew she had lost all self-control. In moments she'd collapse in a heap of shame, embarrassment, and tears, but for as long as it was going to last, she reveled in her anger. She was free at last. No loathsome little man was ever going to enslave her with fear again.

Overturning the mattress, dragging the bureau from the wall, rolling up the rug, Helen made certain no remnant of Ethridge Foote remained hidden in the room to soil her house.

When she looked out the window next, Sunny and May Sue were gathering up the scattered linens; Foote was disappearing around the bend with his armload of clothes. Helen sank to a chair.

Strangely, no tears came. She was not ashamed of the night she'd given to her betrothed the week before. And she was not ashamed of her angry indignation now.

When Sunny appeared in the doorway a few moments later, Helen was standing at the window on the chair, pulling down the curtains.

"Ma? Are you all right?"

"I want this room scoured with lye soap from top to bottom. Every corner, every crack. If Homer won't come inside to dismantle the bed, I'll get Frank to do it."

Sunny laid a soothing hand on her mother's arm. "We couldn't have known about him, Ma, although May Sue guessed his true nature the very first night she was here. We're a little naive, Ma, living here away from the rest of the world."

Helen paused to look around the room. "I feel like there's a tornado inside me."

"Calm down, Ma. He's gone, and we're all glad."

Helen let Sunny guide her down the stairs to the wholesome warmth of her kitchen, where Sunny poured her some strong coffee. She was grateful for her daughter and tried to smile.

May Sue stood by the door looking small and contrite. "Helen . . ." the girl began.

"Come and sit down, May Sue. Please forgive my outburst. I don't think I've ever been so angry in all my born days."

May Sue crept closer.

"And please excuse what I said about your father, too, dear. I'm sorry you had to hear that. I wouldn't have damaged your memories of your father for anything in this world."

May Sue's eyes filled with tears. "You was just speakin' the truth. My pa was a mean man, and I ain't sorry he's gone. I'm just scared to be so alone. I ain't got nobody but a no-account brother who can't do nothing but drink. And Lyford, all he cares about is marrying that girl because she's got his son. I mean, I don't have nothing against Mexicans, and I don't blame him if he loves her, but what about me? What am I going to do?"

"You're safe here," Helen said, though she was not sure at all what would become of the poor unfortunate girl.

May Sue finally sat down next to Helen. "Would you and Sunny do me the honor of coming to Lyford's wedding on Sunday? I wasn't goin' to invite you, but sometimes I'm just as stupid as my pa and I don't appreciate who my friends are."

Helen saw surprise register on Sunny's face.

"Ain't nobody ever stood up for me like that," May Sue added.

"We'd be honored to attend," Helen said, heaving a sigh that left her feeling weak.

With Frank attending the town council meeting that night, and all the boarders gone, the Summerlin house seemed quiet and lonely that evening.

Helen went to lie down for a rest while Sunny finished preparing supper. May Sue chattered about riding out to the Mexican village all by herself earlier in the week. She talked of the fun she'd had daring to do something on her own for the first time in a long while.

"A girl never knows when some varmint might come out from behind a rock and . . . You know, Sunny, your ma's some kind of woman. I don't recall my ma ever doin' anything so brave as what Helen done today. I can't hardly recall my ma, except that she was always crying. I used to wish she'd up and give Pa a wallop, but she never did. Nobody ever would. You should've seen Cale and Lyford creep around like mangy dogs when Pa got in a temper."

Sunny wished she had some place to ride off to by herself. She had no intention of inadvertently showing May Sue the way to her Indian cave or gold mine, but she needed some time alone.

"Did your pa ever hurt you?" she suddenly asked.

May Sue stared at the table. "Sometimes, but I had my hidin' places," she said softly, after a thoughtful pause. Brightening, she went on. "The only thing I ever did that worried Pa was if he got too ornery, I'd run off. There was this cabin in the canyon. I could hide there a long time before he'd sober up enough to find me. I was up there yesterday, and come to find out that ol' bounty hunter's trying to put a new roof on the place. I practically ran him off till he explained that it's his place now."

"His place?" Sunny asked, her attention instantly aroused.

"Bought it, he told me. He's fixin' to settle down here. Ain't that a surprise, what with you and me both likin' him? I guess he done gave up lookin' for the one who killed my pa." May Sue sighed.

Sunny was too surprised to be elated. She concentrated on remaining calm.

"I ain't sorry my pa's gone," May Sue went on, "but somehow it don't seem right that somebody gets to shoot him down and take all his money—our money—and get away clean, too. We ain't even got our land or our cattle 'cause that ol' bastard Foote is holdin' it to sell to that Texan. Pa's probably rollin' over in his grave. I went lookin' for that peckerwood, what's-his-name Purvine, to ask him how come he wants our land so bad, and turns out he's gone back to Texas . . . to consult his investors, they tell me. Feels like somebody's tryin' to run us McKidricts clean out of this county."

Sunny scarcely heard a word the girl was saying. All she could think about was the fact that Bar had bought land. She'd just spent the better part of the afternoon talking to him, and he hadn't said a word about it.

But his manner had seemed a little different. He had been smiling. And now, to find out he'd bought land! Sunny wanted to jump up and cheer. He'd given up bounty hunting for good!

Bar had most of the interior dirt floor of the old abandoned cabin cleared of debris from the roof that had long ago collapsed. The sky was pure turquoise over his head. The flagstone fireplace seemed sound, and the chimney still drew. In town he'd been told that the cabin dated back as much as twenty years, to trapper days before Crystal Springs had even existed.

Now it was his, a place to call his own. True, it was

just a slice of canyon, more vertical than horizontal, but that was all right. To him the place was beautiful.

He paused to survey his efforts. His back and shoulder muscles were sore, his hands were covered with calluses. His new jeans were dirty, and his face sunburned, but he felt good. He felt very good. He was alive, happy, and well. In fact, he felt as well as he had the morning he woke to Sunny Summerlin's beautiful brown eyes.

Wind rustled in the tops of the surrounding pines. The sun beat down, burning his cheeks and nose to a smooth, shiny red. He had sawdust in his hair, and that night he would eat some atrocious beans warmed over a campfire while critters watched from the darkness. He almost laughed.

For the first time in years he had found a sense of satisfaction that didn't come from stalking a man with his gun. He was falling asleep at night exhausted and waking refreshed with no dreams to haunt him. He had Sunny to thank for challenging him, prodding him, and expecting more of him than he'd expected from himself since that long-ago day when his father had died and the world had turned black.

Sitting down on a boulder next to the canvas tent pitched near the roofless cabin, Bar drank from a canteen bought at Tilsy's Mercantile and thought of the day before when May Sue had unexpectedly appeared at the cabin.

"What the hell'r you doin' here?" she'd demanded, instantly softening her tone when she recognized him. "Well, well, if it ain't the famous bounty hunter. Found my pa's killer yet, you peckerless excuse for a man?" She'd been baiting him to see what he'd do, and he'd done what infuriated the girl most: nothing.

Letting the hot sun pour down on him, Bar leaned back. Peckerless, she'd called him. Not exactly. He was more of a man than she would ever understand.

Regardless of what May Sue said Bar could tell she was interested in him. He knew he could have that girl, but he wanted something more than physical satisfaction with a woman. When he was younger, that would have been enough, but he had come to want more. He wanted satisfaction for his mind and heart. He wanted Sunny Summerlin. He wanted to marry her.

The realization washed through Bar like sunlight, hot and quick and sparkling, flowing through his blood and leaving him energized and yet weak at the same time.

She'd never settle for this cabin, he thought, opening his eyes and gazing at the fragile structure. He wondered what she'd think when he told her he was trying with all his might to begin his life here anew. Would she gloat over her victory? No, May Sue might, but not Sunny. Would she distrust his efforts? Perhaps.

He closed his eyes. Just stop, she'd told him. Stop bounty hunting. He hadn't thought it possible. But, strangely enough, he had been able to do it.

It had required the laying down of some weighty pride. It had required that he admit the possibility that he'd done wrong in his efforts to do right.

What amazed him most was that stopping had been so easy. The piece of the canyon had been cheap to buy. He was learning how to build a roof that eventually would keep the rain off his head. And he was coming to realize that he belonged to the present, not the past. He could build a new life from the remnants of the old and be a better man for it, a man he could feel proud to be. Sunny had offered him the way to self-respect, and he had had the sense and courage, at the very least, to give it a chance.

"It's true, then," said the voice of his dreams.

Bar's eyes sprang open. There stood Sunny at the rim of the outcropping where the cabin was perched. He felt her smile shining down on him more brightly than the sun in the sky.

Her chestnut hair was coming loose and falling about her flushed face. She approached, her skirts dusty from climbing up the narrow road along the creek below.

Without a conscious thought, Bar jumped off the boulder like a circus performer shot from a cannon. Joy exploded within him, and he caught her in his arms, swinging her around as if she were his playmate as well as his friend. He found himself laughing. He couldn't remember when he had last laughed.

"I was just thinking of you," he said, finally setting her on her feet.

She looked dazed. "Well, I expected you'd be surprised to see me, but . . ."

He scarcely heard her as he drank in her delighted smile. He couldn't resist. He lowered his face, sensed her shrinking back from him, and kissed her anyway.

She was stiff with shock at first, and then he felt her give way, becoming completely soft and willing in his arms. Suddenly he was aflame with desire for her. He wanted to be a part of her so badly it was all he could do to keep from making her his own right then and there.

Her mouth felt wonderfully sweet and giving against his. Her body molded against him, her arms gripped firmly around his back. Suddenly he buried his face in her neck. It was her arms he craved, her embrace he longed for. He felt foolish for perhaps an instant, needing her so desperately.

And then he pulled back and looked into her eyes. She was so beautiful, those brown eyes full of wonder, that smile so pink and tender.

When he kissed her again, softly, tentatively, she responded so completely, so unquestioningly that he felt his throat tighten. He had to go on kissing her to keep the words from tumbling out, the words he knew he mustn't say, the words that might change things too fast and court disaster in some way.

Finally he just held her, hugging her to him, surrounded by a moment that he wished could last forever. "I'm so glad to see you."

She laughed softly and held her head back so that she could look into his eyes. Questioningly now, she searched his face. "When I heard you'd bought land, a little cabin, I had to come. I brought a present." She pulled a brown paper packet of seeds from her skirt pocket and smiled like a shy young girl. "My favorite flower."

19

Sunny could hardly catch her breath as she stared at Bar in wonder. He had kissed her again, and it had felt even more wonderful than the first time. He looked as if all his inner torment had vanished. She wanted to kiss him some more and never stop.

"Sunflower seeds," he said, emptying the brown paper packet of seeds she'd given him into his palm. "Where's the best place to plant them?"

"In the sun," she said, smiling. "Like over here where the sun won't be blocked by the mountain every afternoon."

He followed her to the edge of the outcropping and flung a few of the seeds into the air. "Like that?"

"No, they have to be planted," she said, laughing, taking a few of the seeds from him and burying them in the soil along the edge of a large boulder. "To protect them from the wind," she said.

"Good idea." The way he looked at her made Sunny think he had a lot more in mind than planting sunflower seeds.

Her chest became so tight she couldn't think of what to say next. "What made you decide to buy this place?" she finally asked, fearing that her questions would eventually spoil the mood. She would have to be very careful.

"I've been all over, looking for a place where . . . where that robber might have hidden the buggy." He shrugged as if to say he couldn't avoid the subject. "It wasn't logical for him to have driven it very far, not when he was being chased."

"*Did* anyone chase him?"

"Eventually. While looking for a gulch or a barn or . . . I don't know . . . any place where someone might conceivably hide something as large as a buggy, I saw this place. Suddenly I knew it was mine. What do you think?"

"It's wonderful," Sunny said. "It captures my imagination. I don't think I've ever been up this particular canyon. My explorations have been limited to the other side of the valley. This is spectacular, Bar. You must be so happy."

She ducked into the roofless cabin to have a look around. All she really wondered about was whether or not Bar would kiss her again.

"It shouldn't be too hard to make this livable," she said. The cabin was just big enough for a bed, a table, and a trunk or two.

Bar came inside and stood next to her, looking up at the sky. "I'll put on a new ridgepole. A couple of people have offered to show me how to attach the beams. Then the shingles . . . and a door."

She looked at him thoughtfully. "You really mean to live here, then? Even in winter?"

"Maybe it'll be my summer place. I don't know, it's hard to figure how things will turn out. In the past I would have had the matter of the bank robbery solved and my bounty in hand by now. This time things aren't working out as I expected. I felt perhaps that was a sign that I should . . . stop." And then he smiled. "I've attempted to take your advice, friend."

"You've given up seeking the bounty, then? For good?" She could hardly dare to believe it.

"I've stopped," he said simply. "I wasn't sleeping well. My headache was back. I couldn't eat. So I stopped, as an experiment. Then I felt better. It's not easy for me to thank you for suggesting it. I suppose my stubborn pride has led me to do things I've regretted in part. To me this is a sign of hope that I can at least try to forget about bounty hunting. Don't expect miracles, Sunny. I'm just a man."

She moved closer, studying his eyes. He looked a little sad, perhaps even uncertain of himself. His dark hair was tousled, his face wondrously rosy from the sun, his mouth curved in a faint, vulnerable smile.

She couldn't stop herself. She went on tiptoe to kiss him. "It takes a man to try to change, to admit to confusion. I apologize for all the harsh words I've spoken about it before." And she touched his cheek with her lips.

He laughed softly. "Those harsh words made me take a look at myself. Oh, Sunny, what you do to me."

His mouth joined with hers. She felt weak, straining up to meet him. Then his arms went around her. Her body was tight against his, warming to his fire, wanting more and more and more.

Drawing back abruptly, he chuckled. "I've dropped some of the seeds," he said, looking at the few remaining ones in his palm. Some of them were on the ground now under his feet.

She stumbled, feeling dizzy with desire. She couldn't think of seeds. When she looked into Bar's eyes she saw that he felt as dazed as she did.

"I'm going to forget myself here in a minute," he said, pulling her out from the relative privacy of the roofless, doorless cabin. "I want to show you what I've found. Are you up to a short hike?"

She nodded, but she was lying. She would rather stay there and kiss him. She would rather know what it felt like to be one with him. Her cheeks went hot.

Bar led her away from the cabin. The outcropping eventually led them into a steep gulch. After only a few hundred feet at a slightly upward grade, the gulch broadened abruptly, revealing a wide expanse of smooth granite rocks sloping down from the rocky crag above.

Aspens grew all around, their leaves rustling softly in the breeze. The creek snaked across the broad flat rocks to a little fall that dropped about three feet into some rocks beside a shallow pool. Off to the side, massive granite boulders were piled together, forming a kind of shelter where the sun couldn't reach. There it was cool and private.

"Look here," Bar said, leading the way across the rocks and to the shelter. He pointed to initials carved there that were dated more than forty years before.

"It doesn't bother you to be enclosed like this?" Sunny asked, remembering his reaction to the old gold mine. She stared at him.

"It doesn't seem to."

He looked so pleased with himself, Sunny imagined that this was what he had been like before his father died.

She ducked out of the shelter and scrambled up the smooth rocks to a place where the soil around the aspen stand looked rich and deep. "How about scattering some of the seeds up here?" He followed and dutifully planted them with more care this time.

"Only a few left," he said then, looking down on her with an expectant smile.

Suddenly he flung the seeds high into the air. The breeze carried them among the grasses, and he looked happy at the idea that some might sprout without much care.

"For luck," he said.

"Is this your land, too?"

"I'm not sure. If it isn't, I'll just have to buy it. I know that I own about ten semivertical acres right now. It sounds like a lot, but when it's the side of a mountain, it doesn't amount to much."

"You're not going to go off someday and let the bank have it back, are you?" she asked, realizing it was a leading question. She might as well have asked if he was planning to stay forever.

"Do you think that little weasel would lend anybody any money these days in his present frame of mind? No, I own the cabin and the ten acres free and clear. If something was to happen to me, it would go to my sisters."

"I'd forgotten you had sisters," Sunny said.

"I've written them to say that I'm making an attempt to give up bounty hunting for good. I can't tell them that I have quit permanently, because I might let them down later. What my sisters will think,

I don't know. But I thought perhaps they'd be a bit less worried about me if they knew."

Sunny chose her next words with care. "But I thought you told me you gave your bounties away. How were you able to buy ten acres with no money?"

"I *have* money, in an account in St. Louis. I've had many jobs between bounties. Don't you remember me telling you that I was working for a rancher in New Mexico Territory? I've tried before to stop doing what I seem compelled to do. Only this is the first time I've tried land as a cure."

The more he spoke of this new development the less delighted Sunny felt, and the less certain she was that any cure would work.

"Part of me wants very much to know who killed Luck McKidrict, and why," Bar went on. "So far it still looks as if his death was an accident. He died in the cross fire. Another part of me wants to feel right with the world, and to make you smile, Sunny. I want to have a normal life like other men."

"You're . . . not doing all this for me, I hope." She knew at once she couldn't carry that burden of responsibility for his future.

"No, my dear Sunflower. In fact, I wasn't even certain you'd like my little shack on the mountain. I'm here for the peace, solitude, and sense of . . . I don't know what. I needed a place to call my own. I needed a home. Despite how it looks right now, I needed some place I could come to when my thoughts are black, a place where I can feel like myself again. Does that make sense?"

Sunny nodded. She had to press her lips tightly together to keep from blurting out how she felt about understanding. It was bad enough to know that her feelings were visible in her eyes. She was quite certain that Bar could see that she loved him. She loved his changing moods, he hopes, his fears. She loved his pain and his courage.

Darting across the rocks suddenly, she called back, "Got any water at the cabin? I'm thirsty."

"Try the waterfall," he said, coming up suddenly behind her as she faltered.

"Oh, I hadn't thought of that."

She made her way across the rough spot to where the water tumbled down from above.

Bar followed, steadying himself on the rocks beside her. Then he stuck his face into the pure clear water and opened his mouth.

As he drew back, water dripped from his chin onto his shirt.

Sunny couldn't hide what she was feeling when she saw his eyes softly darken and his lips curve into a sensuous smile. She forced herself to dip her head and take the icy mountain water into her mouth, too.

It was so cold it made her teeth ache, but she drank and drank, eyes closed, knowing he was watching her and feeling that they were already one.

When she'd had enough, she straightened and looked at Bar. His eyes were a clear midnight blue. He touched her wet cheek. Then he kissed her as lightly as the breeze that was tickling her hair. His lips moved across hers, warming them until a deeper thirst was welling inside them both.

His hand trailed down the side of her neck to the wet spots on her bodice where the water had dribbled. He touched the curve of her breast and then slid his hand around her back, pulling her against him.

He kissed her mouth deeply, gently, and then her face and her neck. His breathing grew quick and urgent in her ear.

Her heart was pounding. She didn't know where she was, only that she wanted with all her being to lie down somewhere with him.

He caught her as she sagged, then stared intently into her eyes. Finally he drew back and pulled her away from the slippery place where they stood.

Without saying anything more, he took her back to the cabin. What was going to happen there was clear to Sunny. She was going to give herself to Bar without hesitation.

But when they emerged from the narrowed ledge that led to the cabin, May Sue was standing there, drinking from Bar's canteen.

"There you are . . ." May Sue wiped her mouth with her forearm. ". . . Bar. Oh, how-do . . . Sunny. Didn't expect to find *you* here."

Sunny couldn't get out a word because the jolt of seeing May Sue was so painful. Damn May Sue, she thought, trying to get her mouth to smile. Damn her scruffy little hide.

She felt Bar's hand tighten around hers and then release it. She'd been so dazed, so intent upon reaching the cabin with him that she hadn't even realized he was touching her.

Sunny had never been sorrier to see anyone in her life. May Sue wasn't stupid. Sunny knew her old school chum could easily see what she and Bar were feeling.

"Where have you two been?" May Sue asked, raking Sunny with a keen gaze.

Sunny refused to answer.

"So you're back," Bar said, not sounding interested.

"Yep, and none too soon, I reckon. I'm surprised Sunny didn't come hightailin' it up here last night when I forgot myself and mentioned to her that you'd bought yourself some land hereabouts. Could have bit off my own tongue." May Sue's expression was pert, but her eyes looked startlingly hard. "Me and you have had some mighty fine times together, haven't we, Bar? Remember the washhouse back at Sunny's place?" She smiled up into Bar's impassive face.

Sunny's mind reeled. Had more happened in that washhouse than she'd let herself believe? Had more happened at the *canyon* between Bar and May Sue than she wanted to think about?

May Sue brushed seductively against Bar as she strolled around the campsite and came to a saucy pause at the small canvas tent pitched ten feet from the roofless cabin. Smiling ever so slyly at Sunny, May Sue ducked inside.

Sunny looked at Bar and he looked back at her, as if daring her to believe May Sue's insinuations. Was May Sue an outright fabricator, or was there some small grain of truth to what she was implying?

"Oh, my, do we have a new book to read?" May Sue came out of the tent carrying a brown leather-bound volume that probably weighed five pounds. She squinted at the title stamped in gold on the spine. "L-l-l-lay-wuh. Lay-wuh?" she said, making a face. "Is this Greek or somethin' like that, Bar?"

"You can read better than that," Sunny blurted, aggravated by May Sue's theatrics.

"Why the hell should I? What's readin' ever goin' to do for me in my life?"

Bar moved swiftly to May Sue, took the book from her, and tossed it back into the tent. "It might keep you out of a saloon, which is where you're headed if you keep acting like this."

May Sue's eyes flashed. "Oh, you're feelin ornery today, Bar Landry. Sunny, you'd better run along 'cause I'm goin' to cuss this boy out proper."

"Thank you for coming out here, Sunny," Bar said. He looked as if he were about to say more and then thought better of it.

Sunny understood what she and Bar had been feeling before May Sue appeared. It had been powerful and real. She had her doubts about what might have happened between Bar and May Sue before, but she couldn't let those doubts spoil things further. Sunny knew she'd already come very close to losing Bar's friendship. She wasn't going to make that mistake again.

She could go off now in a terrible huff, playing May Sue's childish game and acting jealous. Or she could act like a woman grown, as her mother had instructed her to do.

Sunny found the grace to smile warmly at Bar. "You have a place here to be proud of, Bar. Thanks for showing me around. Remember, my invitation to supper stands. Ma and I will look forward to seeing you again."

She felt wonderful giving Bar a little wave and starting down the steep path to the creek and road below. Not only was she acting like a woman grown, she was feeling like one.

Her cheeks went hot, and deep inside it pained her to leave Bar and May Sue alone together, but she had no other choice. It was that or hang around, acting as if they were all still taunting one another in a schoolyard.

To mask his anger, Bar ducked into the cabin as if he had something to do inside that needed urgent attention. He hated to see Sunny leave. He wanted to be holding her, he wanted to make her his.

"She don't waste no time, does she?" May Sue said, coming to the doorway and trapping him inside. "Had you goin', did she? Well, Bar, like you said, I'm probably bound for a saloon, unless some fine gentleman like yourself sees what I got to offer."

He didn't reply.

"You ain't gettin' anything from a girl like Sunny, you know. She'll come around makin' eyes at you and gettin' your lather up, but she won't never deliver the goods." May Sue winked and gave Bar a coy smile.

"Excuse me, May Sue. I have a lot of work to do." Bar had to take hold of May Sue's shoulders and move her aside in order to get outside the cabin.

He went to the sawhorses set up behind the cabin where he'd been stripping the bark from a pine which he had cut for the ridgepole.

Several minutes later he realized that he hadn't heard May Sue leave. He dreaded seeing what she was doing in her continued efforts to seduce him. He couldn't figure out why she would want to except that she was the sort to want the man another woman wanted. Sunny wanted him, Bar knew, and therefore May Sue wanted him, too. He didn't believe, however, that she truly cared anything about him. He was simply a male to be seduced and used in order to save her from a frightful future.

"Oh, Ba-a-a-ar," came May Sue's sultry twang. "Come see what I can do for you that you ain't never dreamed about before."

Bar clenched his jaw until his teeth ached. He should have guessed she was still around. Marching to the tent, he found May Sue inside, reclining on his bedroll, naked. For a man who had wanted lovemaking so very much only a short while before, Bar found May Sue's display roughly equivalent to watching a female cat in heat, somewhat humorous.

May Sue had a lovely body, to be sure, as delectable and plump as any man could want to enjoy, but the fact was, Bar loved Sunny. She was the only woman he wanted sprawled and willing on his bedroll.

"You can leave now, May Sue."

She pouted with incredible expertise.

He smiled a little. "Yes, you're beautiful. You know you are, but I'm not interested. Go before you force me to carry you down the mountain and deposit you on the road."

"Oh, Bar, you're no fun."

He caught her wrists and pulled her to her feet. "Then leave . . . or I will."

She threw her arms around his neck. "I love you!"

"No, you don't."

He didn't like being driven from his own land, but it seemed to be the best alternative. He wondered if Sunny had come on foot or by horse. Perhaps he could catch up to her.

Expecting to hear curses flung after him, Bar started down the slope to the road. May Sue was strangely silent. A half mile later he was approaching town. He could use a bath and a good meal, he thought, forgetting about May Sue's pathetic

attempts to lure him into an assignation. Sunday was
Lyford's wedding. While at the mission, he might find
time to speak with the priest.

Smiling, he entered the bathhouse on Gilpin
Avenue and paid his quarter for a stall with a tub full
of hot water, a clean towel, and cake of soap. The
memory of Sunny drinking from the waterfall was
going to serve him well in his dreams, he thought,
stripping to the skin and stepping into the big
wooden tub for a long hard scrub.

20

Sunny observed the Mexican village from the back seat of a rented surrey. It looked more like a deserted collection of crumbling adobe houses scattered along the narrow dirt road than the organized community with a market square that she had expected. In the lengthening afternoon shadows, the poverty of the residents was evident at every humble doorstep.

Escalera, as it was called, faced the rail bed outside Crystal Springs some three miles, but for all the commerce between its quiet residents and the rest of Cassidy County, the village might as well have been fifty miles away.

Luck McKidrict had made certain that no Mexican felt welcome in Crystal Springs. Conversely, no white person felt welcome here. As Frank parked the surrey near the pink stucco walls of the mission, Sunny realized how vulnerable she felt.

"Is anyone else from Crystal Springs coming to the wedding?" Helen asked, twisting around to address May Sue, who was sitting stiffly in the rear seat with Sunny.

"That's Bar Landry's horse tied up over there," May Sue said. "I didn't invite anyone else."

For all May Sue's recent visits to see her brother Lyford in Escalera, Sunny thought she looked none too comfortable as she climbed down from the surrey. An old Mexican man with a burro walked by, staring at May Sue. May Sue looked relieved to spot the priest emerging from the high gate beneath the mission bell at that moment. The passerby, who had looked as if he had been about to spit on May Sue, hurried on.

Sunny hoped there would be no trouble. "Will Cale be coming?" she asked, following May Sue down from the surrey, clutching her new calico bonnet ties firmly beneath her chin.

"He said he'd sooner shoot Lyford than see him married to a Mexican. Guess that means no."

"But you don't feel that way about Lyford marrying Tomasina, do you?" Sunny asked.

"Lyford can marry the devil's sister for all I care. If he settles down, maybe he can get the ranch back. Then maybe I'll have a place to live again. You know I can't stay at your house forever, Sunny. We'd wind up killin' each other. And I ain't marryin' Johnsie, that's for damn certain. Let's get inside. Gull-danged wind."

The priest was a tall, grave-looking Spaniard in his late forties with a rugged-looking, angular face and a shock of gray hair. With the utmost courtesy he came forward and shook May Sue's hand. The wind billowed his black robes just as it did May Sue's and Sunny's full skirts.

"So good of you to come, Señorita McKidrict. And this must be your dear friend, Susanna," he said, releasing May Sue's hand and clasping Sunny's. "How very honored I am to meet you, Señorita Summerlin. Please come inside. We are about to begin." Then he addressed Helen and Frank. "Oh, Señora Summerlin, and Señor Tilsy. Welcome. So very kind of you to join us this afternoon."

Sunny had never been inside the mission before. The small, enclosed compound had been the first settlement in the valley, the only sanctuary at one time for a hundred miles.

Within the walls, she found the display of bright spring flowers already blooming in pots and boxes breathtaking. The mission chapel was a one-room adobe structure in the rear of the yard. The chapel had foot-thick walls and a door of weathered planks banded in black iron.

As they filed inside, Sunny was struck by the dim coolness of the interior. Outside, the mission bell began tolling with measured dignity. She found the entire place mysteriously appealing.

Except for what light could enter the chapel through narrow slots in the adobe the interior was hushed and shadowed. The Arquillas were already seated in front on the left.

Sunny recognized Juan, the bride's brother. He was a railroad brakeman, one of very few Mexicans allowed to work a job ordinarily reserved for an Anglo.

Juan's middle-aged mother Maria, who had been Luck McKidrict's cook, sat as rigidly as a statue beside him. Her head was completely covered with a black mantilla. Sunny thought she looked just like the bank robber.

Beside the señora sat a gray-haired man unable to remain upright, so severe had been his beating at Luck McKidrict's hand four years before. The gifted carpenter could work no more. Sunny marveled to think that the family was now willing to allow their daughter, Tomasina, to marry the son of that man they so hated.

A string of stair-step dark-haired children filled the pews behind the Arquillas. Assorted other relatives who, by the size of the village, might have constituted the entire Escalera population, filled the remainder of the left-hand side of the chapel.

The pews on the right side of the chapel were empty.

"Why didn't your father want Lyford to marry Tomasina?" Sunny whispered to May Sue. "Lyford must love her. He came straight here after the funeral."

"Pa wasn't one for explainin'," May Sue snapped. "I wasn't one for askin', especially if he was goin' to smack me if I did."

"Your father would strike you for asking a question?" Sunny asked, appalled.

"Honestly, Sunny, you ain't had a normal upbringin'. You and your ma, alone out at your place all these years . . . Hell, yes, Pa whaled the tar outta me more'n . . . excuse my language."

May Sue cast a worried glance around the murky shadows of the chapel and noticed a number of painted wooden statues gazing benevolently down at her from the niches in the walls. She seemed to shrink beneath her bonnet, subdued and penitent.

"Ma was Catholic," May Sue added in a whisper, "but Pa hated this mumbo-jumbo, as he called it. I ain't so fond of it myself."

"I thought your mother was from Alabama."

"They have Catholics in Alabama, too. But truth be known, I don't think Ma always lived in Alabama. She used to talk about New Orleans a lot, about how fine it was to go there. On and on. Pa once said he could . . ." May Sue stopped herself and frowned. "I guess some Mexican cheated him at poker one time. Pa had to set him straight. Mexicans was too proud, he used to say. Catholics was too holy. 'Thought they was better'n me. I showed 'em who was trash.'"

Helen shushed the whispering young woman, took Frank's arm and went up the narrow center aisle to the fourth row. She nodded to the people who turned to look at her as she took her seat.

The priest came to escort May Sue to the front, where he paused to genuflect and cross himself as he passed the altar. Then he indicated the first pew on the left for May Sue. She lowered herself stiffly onto the seat and glowered as she looked around the humble sanctuary.

Left standing in the rear of the church alone, Sunny nearly jumped out of her skin when she noticed movement nearby. Like one of the saintly statues coming to life, Bar emerged from the shadowed corner where he had been standing all the while.

"Would you care to sit with me?" he whispered, smiling down at her and offering his arm.

Before Sunny could reply, May Sue twisted around in her seat. By the expression on her face, it was clear she had expected Bar to sit with her.

As Bar escorted Sunny to the row behind her mother and Frank, he gave May Sue a formal nod. His expression betrayed no trace of their encounter at his cabin earlier in the week and no hint of warmth.

To Sunny's shock, she realized that Bar was not wearing his long-barreled pistol, but he was wearing his black clothes again, mended, brushed, and looking utterly severe. As the bell stopped tolling, and a man began playing a guitar in the rear, Sunny wondered if Bar actually would have need of a weapon. She had never before felt so much tension as in this place.

Then the ceremony began, after a brief procession of the mission's priest, two brothers, and an altar boy carrying candles to the altar. Lyford arrived. He wasn't wearing a gun, either. His Mexican-style brown suit looked borrowed and snug.

In a somber dress that looked no different from everyday wear, Tomasina proceeded up the aisle alone, unsmiling. After much standing, kneeling, and Latin responses from those who understood the ceremony, Lyford looked soberly at his dark-eyed bride and they were pronounced man and wife. Their four-year-old son squirmed free from his grandmother's arms and joined the newlyweds at the altar. "Can we go now, Mama?" he asked softly in Spanish.

The couple and their son exited the chapel into the soft reds and golds of the sunset. Outside, the man with the guitar began playing again, gaily this time. Quickly people strung colorful lanterns around the mission courtyard and lit the little candles inside them. Long tables were carried in and set up along the perimeter. Covered with mended lace cloths, they were quickly laden with heaping platters of spicy food. In a matter of minutes the mood had changed from wariness to rejoicing.

The thick adobe outer walls protected them from the worst of the wind and advancing chill of the evening. Overhead, the sky turned slowly from lavender to black. Stars appeared and winked between the clouds. The ceremony that joined two people for a lifetime seemed over so quickly, Sunny thought.

"I'll introduce you to the bride," May Sue said, dragging Sunny by the elbow to where the newlyweds stood at the chapel door.

May Sue's efforts were awkward but sincere. Sunny shook hands with Lyford and smiled at Tomasina, looking into the girl's eyes to see if she was happy. Tomasina looked more embarrassed than anything.

Grinning nervously, Lyford seemed to anticipate his father's ghost would appear at any moment to drag him down to hell for marrying the Mexican girl.

"I hope you'll be happy," Sunny said to them both.

Tomasina gave a slight curtsy. Lyford shrugged.

Crouching in front of the little boy, Sunny smiled. "I am pleased to meet you, Miguel."

Frail-looking and thin, the boy had enormous brown eyes and silky dark hair. Even at his tender age he seemed wary of his father and the guests who were standing about, watching.

A few moments later Cale burst through the gate, obviously drunk. He staggered into the courtyard, waving a gun in one hand and a nearly empty bottle of whiskey in the other.

Everyone backed away.

"My brother has finally done the forbidden," Cale shouted. "I salute you, ol' buddy."

Looking around, Sunny saw no trace of May Sue.

Bar had disappeared, too. Frank and Helen were sampling tortillas and beans at one of the tables. At the sight of Cale, their faces fell. Miguel shrank behind his mother's skirts.

Unsure what she could do to prevent trouble, Sunny quickly stepped forward. "Would you dance with me, Cale?" she asked, touching his arm. "Please? He'll play something we Anglos know." She gave the man with the guitar a pleading look.

Cale gazed down at her, his eyes slow to focus, his mind slower still to comprehend. "Why, Ornery, I didn't know you'd be here tonight. Don't you look fine. Good enough for Sunday dinner. Hell, yes, I'll dance with you." Shoving his gun into his holster, he looked around for a place to put his bottle. Lyford rescued it for him.

As Sunny was swept into Cale's arms, she saw Lyford draining the bottle. Bar was still nowhere to be seen. She was in Cale's arms now, and judging by the look in Cale's eyes, he would be kissing her in less time than it would take to say no.

"I don't know what good it might do to give my confession to you, Father," Bar said quietly to the priest. "I'm not a Catholic, but it occurred to me the other night that I might begin a new life with more confidence if I could be certain that God had forgiven me."

"I'll do what I can, Señor Landry," the priest said, guiding Bar to his office just behind the sanctuary. "I think you will be more comfortable speaking to me in here than inside the confessional."

Bar took a chair beside the desk. Now that he was there, he didn't know exactly what to say. Faint strains of music drifted in through the open window in the rear of the chapel office. The smell of incense and candles was strong. Somewhere out there was the woman he loved, and Bar wanted to be worthy of her. He knew that he had to be worthy of himself first.

"My father was killed," he began. "I haven't been able to forget. I haven't been able to accept it."

"I am sorry to hear that, my son."

"I've been angry at God for letting my father die as he did," Bar said in a hushed voice. After a lengthy pause, he went on. "I'm impatient with God's justice. Criminals run free while decent men die. I can't seem to trust that God will make things right. In a rage, I have gone after the criminals myself and . . . I have taken the lives of eight men." Silence closed in around Bar. He felt engulfed in remorse. "I'm dying inside, Father, but I want to live. I want to love. Yet I want justice too. All I have found is grief, shame, and sorrow."

The priest was long in answering. "You're not one of the Catholic faith, so I cannot counsel you as I would one of my own flock," the man said. "You have broken a commandment, and for that you suffer as God said you would."

Bar nodded.

"You have learned, my son, that to kill a killer makes you one with him, a killer yourself. You must now separate yourself from the killer. Give him back his wickedness. Trust that God will make all things right even if you never see that He has done so. These are the words I have spoken to my children in this village when the rancher McKidrict treated them badly. These words have prevented much vengeful thinking. Perhaps today we will find peace in the joining of Lyford and Tomasina."

"You believe McKidrict's death was God's justice at work?" Bar asked.

"I would not presume to know such a thing," the priest said softly. "But I do know that God forgives those who seek him."

Sunny felt embarrassed as she struggled in front of everyone to avoid Cale's lips and hands while they danced. When she saw Bar's shadow fall suddenly across Cale's drunken smile, she was so glad to see him she almost cried.

"May I cut in, friend?" Bar asked, smiling.

Cale looked him over. "What if I say no, *friend?*"

"This is your brother's wedding," Bar said. "Would you spoil it with a fight?"

"I ain't plannin' to fight you, bounty hunter. I'm plannin' to beat the piss'n shit outta you."

But just when Sunny felt sure Cale would throw the first punch, he looked into Bar's eyes and slunk away. She realized Cale felt ashamed, despite his bravado.

Even so, she couldn't spend too much time feeling sorry for him when Bar was enfolding her in his arms. His touch was more gentle than ever. She looked up into his eyes and what she saw made desire explode inside her. How she wished they could disappear into the shadows for a kiss.

"You look so . . . Where have you been, Bar? I was afraid you'd gone."

"I was making a contribution," Bar said, smiling.

Sunny couldn't tell if he was joking or not. She simply let the music carry her around and around the lantern-lit courtyard in the arms of the man she loved.

She wasn't going to let anything spoil this evening with him.

When Frank cut in, Bar reluctantly let Sunny go. He moved to the perimeter to watch the celebration. Everything seemed to be going remarkably well. He should have known, however, that May Sue would seize the opportunity.

"Well, well, well, bounty hunter. Ain't you goin' to ask *me* to dance?" May Sue attached herself to Bar's arm. Until that moment she'd been standing near the gate with Cale, sulking. "Ain't nobody else here I'd touch. I can't see how Lyford could . . ."

Bar couldn't allow May Sue to make any disparaging remarks that might be overheard. Besides, he was tired of her derisive attitude. "You must think your father was right to deprive that little boy of his father," Bar said. "You must wonder how you'll choose a husband of your own someday without your father's opinion to guide you."

She frowned. "What'd you say?"

Bar's good intentions to remain patient and unperturbed by the girl vanished. "You let your father think for you. He beat your mother and drove her away—"

"Ma ran off with somebody," May Sue snapped, rising to the challenge in Bar's tone.

"So your father said. Your father beat and cowed your brothers. Did he beat you, too? He let his house fall into ruin. He wouldn't pay his debts. He crippled that man over there and refused to recognize that innocent little boy as his grandson. This is the man you take up for, May Sue, the man you revere."

She couldn't think of a retort, but Bar could see her mind turning in slow circles behind her slitted eyes. She struggled with the truth that he was throwing in her face and finally said, "He's the man you came to avenge, bounty hunter."

Bar was surprised that she was so shrewd. "I'm sorry for you, May Sue," he went on, his tone more firm with her than ever. "I understand that you're afraid and feeling alone since your father died, but you have to face up to something. I'm not going to fall prey to your seductions."

"Oh, oh, oh, you're so very stuck up, bounty hunter. Too good for the likes of ol' May Sue."

"I've already told you not to throw yourself at me. Maybe that works with other men, but not me. Close up your dress now and keep yourself for a man who truly loves you."

Her eyes glossed with sudden tears. "Like that varmint, Johnsie?"

"I don't know. Does Johnsie truly love you? Do *you* love anybody, May Sue?"

Her chin dropped. "I love you," she said in a small voice.

Bar forced himself to soften his tone. He'd managed to be gentle with Cale. Maybe he was being too harsh with May Sue, when all she had was childish words with which to provoke him.

"You flatter me, May Sue. You just have to stop—"

"Flatterin' ain't what I had in mind for us, bounty hunter." She pressed against him. Other men would have leapt at her offer, but Bar could only feel angry.

"I'm not going to sleep with you," he said flatly.

She looked as if she were searching for something more to say. Bar realized that to argue with her would prove futile. He would have to risk her retaliation. He walked away, leaving her agape and alone.

*   *   *

Because driving the surrey back to Crystal Springs in the dark would have been dangerous, the wedding celebration lasted all night. By dawn, Sunny felt more tired than she'd ever been. She could scarcely think as she thanked the Arquillas for a wonderful time and bade them farewell. She climbed into the surrey with the full intention of sleeping all the way home.

May Sue sprawled in the rear seat. Bar and Lyford loaded Cale's limp body into the back of a dilapidated mule-drawn cart. Cale had passed out drunk hours before.

"Lyford's going back to the ranch with Tomasina and the boy," Bar told Frank, who was in the front of the surrey, as he checked Sundown and adjusted his saddle before mounting up. "They've asked to go along with us."

"That's not much of a wedding trip, laying siege to a ranch taken by the bank," Frank said.

Sunny leaned across May Sue. "Will they be safe there?"

Bar looked worried, too. "It's all he has to offer Tomasina. If he can't take back the ranch, he'll have to go to work for someone else. He's too proud to do that."

Bar led the procession out of Escalera. Bull Valley looked beautiful in the morning mist. The scent of pine was strong, and the meadowlarks sang their lilting call from the creek to the ridges.

Lyford followed Bar in the cart. His bride sat stiffly on his right, with the boy asleep in her arms. Cale's body jostled from side to side in the back as Lyford seemed unable to avoid any of the holes and ruts in the track leading back to town.

Frank brought up the rear, with Helen slumped against his shoulder. He held back to avoid as much dust as possible. May Sue snored and nearly lost her hat. Sunny rescued it for her and snuggled deeper into the lap robe. "Is Ma asleep?" she asked.

Frank nodded.

"You're next to tie the knot," Sunny teased.

"Two weeks," he said, his fleshy face creasing into a grin. "All on account of you and that wallpaper."

Sunny's thoughts returned to the morning of the robbery as a shot rang out. It came from such a distance that its echo reverberated all across the valley. She bolted upright.

"What was that?" May Sue cried, waking with a start.

Helen woke, too.

Reining hard, Frank pointed to the left where the dense growth along the creek could have easily hidden a sniper.

Tomasina's scream split the air.

21

Sunny's blood ran cold. Someone had just taken a shot at them from the high boulders along the creek.

Frank leapt out of the surrey. "Can you see anybody over there?" He ducked down, defenseless, motioning Helen to do the same. He didn't ordinarily wear a gun and that morning was no exception.

Helen flattened herself across the seat. "Let Bar handle this, please, Frank. Don't risk yourself."

Terrified, Sunny scrambled from the surrey on the far side. Peeking around, she couldn't see Bar through the dust their procession had stirred on the road. She was frantic, not knowing if he was all right.

May Sue looked around wildly. She jumped down after Sunny and ran along the right-hand track of the road toward the cart. When she got close enough to see what had happened, she shrieked, "Not Lyford, too!"

Sunny's stomach rolled over. Poor May Sue, she thought, while a small corner of her mind was relieved that Bar hadn't been injured.

May Sue collapsed in a heap, wailing, "I can't take no more! I can't take no more!"

Tomasina's cries rang across the valley, too, and Miguel began wailing. Sunny wanted to shut it all out. How could such a thing happen on a beautiful morning like this?

At the head of the procession, in front of the cart, Bar rode Sundown in circles. Squinting toward the creek, he tried to determine where the shot had come from.

"See anything?" Frank called out to him.

Bar didn't answer. He wasn't wearing his gun either. It would be foolhardy to ride after the sniper, but Sunny feared he would anyway.

Bar brought Sundown around to the rear of the cart where Cale lay in the back, unconscious. Reeking of alcohol, Cale still wore the gun he'd been brandishing when he swaggered into the wedding celebration the evening before.

Sunny could just imagine what was going through Bar's mind now as he looked down on Tomasina and the boy with Lyford's body sprawled across them. If he had Cale's gun, he would be able to ride out and seek revenge.

Sunny started toward him. "Bar," she cried. "Don't!"

Jumping down from his horse, Bar tore the gun from Cale's holster and made sure it was loaded.

Looking up from where she sat in the dust, May Sue scrubbed tears from her face. "What'r you waitin' for, you jackass? Go after 'em."

As Bar struggled with his decision, May Sue scrambled to her feet. Seeing Cale lying in a drunken sprawl, she began slapping his legs. "Wake up, gull-dangit! Somebody's killed Lyford." She grabbed Bar's wrist. "Gimme that gun. I'll catch 'em myself."

"Ride for the *doctor,* Bar. Frank could go, but you can ride harder and faster."

Bar looked at her as if she'd lost her mind, and May Sue tried to hit her.

Throwing up her arm to ward off May Sue's slap, Sunny repeated, "Ride for the doctor, Bar."

Bar threw himself back into the saddle. Fighting Sundown's desire to rear and buck, he looked from Sunny to May Sue. Then he glanced toward the creek.

She was losing him, Sunny thought in despair, but she could hardly blame Bar for wanting to catch the sniper. She wanted to do something, too.

Bar galloped around to the front of the cart. The horse reared, and Bar fought to remain in the saddle. He looked down at Lyford's motionless form. Tomasina was shaking the body, chattering in anguished Spanish. Then Bar looked back at Sunny. She sent him a pleading look. Bar turned the horse and galloped down the road toward town.

Sunny couldn't believe her eyes.

May Sue struck her hard on her shoulder blade. "Bitch! Lyford's *dead.* What the hell good is the *doctor* going to do?"

"I didn't want Bar to get shot, too!"

Lips twisted and fresh sobs heaving from her chest, May Sue marched toward Cale's horse tied up at the rear of the surrey. Frank threw his arms around May Sue and wrestled her to a stop.

"It's too dangerous to ride out there, girl. Chances are, they've got away by now anyhow."

"Ain't *seen* nobody runnin'," May Sue snapped. "Ain't *heard* nothin'. Why aren't you goin' after them?"

Helen caught Frank's arm. "Stay with me, Frank." Her voice was so firm, Frank was taken aback.

"This is the sheriff's job. *Please*, Frank."

He pulled Helen close and kissed the top of her head. "You're right, dear. I'm sorry, May Sue. I can't risk getting myself shot up two weeks before my own wedding. Come around to the far side where we'll be safe. Tomasina, do you need help down?"

May Sue gave Frank and Helen scathing looks. "You stinkin' ol' coward. You selfish ol' bitch. To hell with you both."

Sunny wrapped her arms around herself. How could they ever forget this day? Realizing how vulnerable they all were, standing exposed on the road, Sunny helped Tomasina extract the boy from beneath Lyford's limp, heavy body. What a complete tragedy, Sunny thought as she took the frail, trembling boy into her arms and held him tightly. "It'll be all right," she whispered, though she didn't feel so certain that it would be.

Heedless of the danger, Tomasina climbed out of the cart. She looked as if she were daring the sniper to shoot her, too. The front of her wedding clothes ran red with her bridegroom's blood. Reaching back, she tried to arrange Lyford's body in a more seemly position.

Finally, with all of them huddled against the far side of the surrey, Sunny watched May Sue glance now and again at Cale's horse. At length, she dropped to the ground and doubled over. Rocking back and forth, she wept helpless tears. Sunny had never seen anything more pitiful.

*   *   *

In less than an hour they heard the thunder of returning hoofbeats. The sheriff veered his mount into the
tall grasses along the creek while Doc Hamilton
reined at the cart.

Bar had traded his exhausted Sundown for a fresh
horse, and somewhere along the way he'd lost his
black hat. Sweat rolled down his face as he dropped
to the ground to pull Sunny and Helen close. "You're
both all right?"

Sunny nodded.

"Thank you, Bar," Helen said.

Refusing to look up at him, May Sue stayed on the
ground beside the rear wheel.

"She's angry because I didn't go looking for whoever was up there," Frank said.

Bar clasped Frank's shoulder. "Your place was
here with the women. Lyford's dead?"

Frank, who had checked to be certain and then
covered the dead man's face with his coat, nodded
gravely. "Never seen shootin' like that. Must be at
least two hundred yards."

The doctor confirmed that Lyford had died from a
single shot.

Soon Sheriff Brummer returned. "He musta stayed
near the rocks. I can't find a single sign. You folks
can go now."

Bar's expression was dark with thought.

Sunny caught his arm. "There's nothing more to be
done," she said, but he didn't seem to notice her.

"Mrs. McKidrict?" the sheriff said to Tomasina.
"I'm more sorry than I can say. What do you want to
do?"

"We must go back for a funeral," she said in heavily accented English. "But Lyford would want to be buried beside his father. I am very thankful for your help, señor."

Nodding, the sheriff rode back for another, more thorough, search of the area.

"Your family will be so sorry to hear about this," Helen said, offering the young widow a hug.

"No, Señora Summerlin," Tomasina said, her face somber. "They will not. No one wanted me to marry the man who . . . who dishonored me . . . by force. He said he loved me, but what he did was to defy his father." She paused to gather her strength. "I only married the father of my son so that Miguel could claim his birthright. Now Miguel will get nothing. This is not an easy thing to understand."

Still lying in the back of the cart, Cale finally stirred. "What the hell is all this talk? I can't sleep." He struggled upright, clutched his head and groaned. His face had gotten sunburned.

When he realized he was on a cart, halted on the valley road to Crystal Springs with Frank and the Summerlins all staring at him, and with Tomasina gazing at him and the boy clinging to her skirts, he made a pained face. "What'd I do now?"

Then he noticed the doctor coming around to lash his instrument bag to the rear of his saddle, and saw the mounted sheriff scanning one side of the valley and then the other.

May Sue got to her feet. She slapped dust from her skirts and adjusted her stubborn bonnet until it made her so furious that she tore it from her head. After tossing it out across the grasses, she brushed past Bar and stopped at the cart. Hands on hips, voice husky, she choked out, "They done shot Lyford while you was passed out, you good-for-nothin', addle-brained excuse for a brother!"

The doctor tried to calm her, but she jerked free of the man's solicitous touch.

May Sue flung her hand in Bar's direction. "You goin' to sit there lookin' like some kind of idiot all the day long, or are you goin' to find who did this? That gull-danged excuse for a bounty hunter ain't helped a whit."

Sunny could see how difficult it was for Bar not to take charge and go riding off half-cocked. The sniper had an hour on them. Finding him after so long would be quite hopeless.

"Do you think the shot was meant for Lyford?" Sunny asked, suddenly considering other possibilities.

Bar looked down at her. "I was wondering, too, if he was aiming at me."

While Lyford McKidrict was laid to rest alongside his father the following morning, Crystal Springs buzzed with the news of the latest shooting. Tomasina and her boy retreated to Escalera, their future uncertain.

After the funeral, Cale disappeared. Worried, Sheriff Brummer swore in two extra deputies and rode out to make certain the McKidrict place was secure. They reported that someone had removed a number of valuables from the ranch house recently.

A few hours later, Julia McKidrict's silver chest and silver turned up at the second-hand shop on Gilpin Avenue along with Luck McKidrict's extensive knife collection. The shopkeeper admitted buying the silver and knives piecemeal over the past few weeks.

Rather than work for pay at the saloon where he spent most of his time, Cale had been living off the proceeds of his parents' valuables.

For all her fiery complaints, May Sue stayed close to the Summerlin place, spending silent hours on the porch chewing her nails. Pitying the girl in her grief, Helen cautioned Sunny to leave May Sue to her thoughts. "She has a lot to consider, honey."

"You'd think Cale would be here, making plans to care for her," Sunny said, secretly glad that Cale *wasn't* underfoot.

"Cale can't take care of himself, much less that poor girl," was Helen's reply.

Sunny and Helen put the finishing touches on Helen's gray linen wedding dress, which would, with a fitted jacket, double as a traveling suit. As the afternoon waned, both women became lost in their own thoughts.

When Sunny finished the last of the hem stitching, she realized that she couldn't go on without knowing how Bar was faring as a result of the latest shooting.

"The way Bar stared down at that grave, Ma, you would think he had been looking down at his own father being buried," she said, hanging up the wedding skirt and smoothing the folds. "I'm worried about him. I mean, I'm *really* worried."

Helen tugged at the matching jacket that she was working on to make sure the twenty covered buttons were straight. "What can you do to help Bar through this? He'll do what he must, regardless."

Sunny was wondering that herself. In her room, she changed into a riding skirt and then went back to where her mother sat in the parlor, pondering the contents of her sewing box.

"I've got to go to him, Ma."

Helen shook her head. "It's not safe, honey. Frank doesn't think an outlaw did this. He thinks somebody is after the McKidricts. Any one of a hundred different people could be seeking revenge. What if you were mistaken for May Sue and shot?"

"I don't look anything like May Sue," Sunny retorted. "Besides, *you* don't think anyone in our valley would really do such a thing, do you?"

Helen's expression remained grave. "That's how it's beginning to look. Cale's probably hiding under a rock somewhere cowering in fear."

"Well, Ma, I can't just sit around not knowing what Bar's decided to do." Feeling her mother's eyes boring into her, Sunny nevertheless started for the door.

"I couldn't hold back your pa, honey. I nearly came to ruin trying." Helen's tone was soft with warning.

Unsure what her mother referred to, Sunny stepped out into the long afternoon shadows. "I know what I'm doing. Don't wait up. I'll be late."

Hearing Homer playing the spoons in the barn, and playing them quite well by that time, Sunny hurried and knocked, asking the handyman to saddle her horse. Homer had him ready in moments.

Hoping not to rouse May Sue's curiosity, Sunny took a circuitous route down through the pines to the road. Only when she was certain May Sue wasn't following did she gallop across the valley, headed for the narrow, secluded canyon where she expected to find Bar. Strangely, she felt watched and wondered if it could be true that someone was trying to wipe out all the McKidricts as payment for their past wrongs.

At dusk Sunny found Bar sitting on the ground

near his cabin, his back against a boulder, staring into nothingness. His campfire had burned low, and his campsite looked as if someone had deliberately laid it to waste.

Noting that he hadn't even changed his clothes since Lyford's funeral that morning, Sunny tied up her horse. When he didn't greet her, or even acknowledge her presence, she resolved to ride out his mood. Silently, she gathered dead wood from the surrounding area and built up the fire. By then it was dark and too late to fetch fresh water. On a moonless night, the landscape looked as black and sinister as in a frightening dream.

Bar gave off an air so forbidding, Sunny couldn't think what to say to comfort him. At length she sat down beside him and, gathering her skirts around her legs, settling in for a long silence. It was enough just to be with him, she told herself, worrying that her plans to soothe him would come to nothing.

"Are you here to make sure I'm not on the trail of another killer?" Bar asked at last, his tone bitter.

She felt stung and thought suddenly of leaving. "I was worried that you might be blaming yourself," she said softly, reaching instinctively for his hand.

Glancing at her in astonishment, he winced and drew up his legs. He crossed his arms over them and dropped his face into the folds of his coat sleeves. "If I'd kept on looking, Sunny, I would've found the bank robber weeks ago. He'd be in jail now—I would *not* have killed him in a fit of rage—and Lyford would be still alive. Now Miguel has nothing because Foote will sell the ranch to that Texan when he gets back. None of this would've happened if I'd done my job."

"Your self-appointed job, Bar. I can't imagine that Lyford would've turned out to be a better father than his own was. He might even have hurt Tomasina and Miguel one day."

Bar straightened and took a deep breath. "No, I shouldn't have stopped looking. Now that I have, I can't start up again without alienating you. But I saw those faces at the funeral today. They were wondering why I wasn't doing something."

Sunny had to admit she'd seen the looks, too. "Why would anyone think you responsible?" she asked in spite of her own misgivings. "Lyford McKidrict wasn't exactly some fine, upstanding—"

"Since when does one's character have anything to do with the rightness or wrongness of being shot to death? Sunny, sometimes I don't understand you. You're a fine woman, but you seem to think some people don't deserve justice. It's everyone's right. That's how we civilize the world."

"I was only trying to make you feel better," she said in a small voice. "But you're right. I didn't like Lyford. He was capable of being as mean as his father was, but I suppose he was trying to make things right. He must have cared about Tomasina. Even if he did force himself on her. . . ."

Bar flashed her a look.

"That's what she said he did! Bar, whether shootings are right or wrong, deserved or undeserved, *you* are not responsible for them all. I can't understand why you think that you are."

Bar had nothing to say to that.

Sunny started to get up. "I did *not* come here to argue with you. I swore to myself that I was done trying to influence your thinking. When we stopped

arguing about justice, we were all right together.
More than all right."

He looked at her with a mixture of emotions
behind his eyes that she found irresistibly fascinating.
He obviously wanted her to go, and yet she could see
that he also longed for her to stay.

"I'm just afraid that if we can't talk about certain
things, we'll have nothing," she said. "Not even
friendship. I don't know what to do about the outlaws of the world, or the McKidricts, for that matter.
All I know is that you want to do something about it,
and it's killing you."

"Only if I let it get out of hand. That's not going to
happen ever again."

She looked at him a long time. "And I'm saying
that I can't love you if you make your living as a
bounty hunter. It's as simple as that."

He closed his eyes.

Her heart sank. "Good-night, Bar," she said, not
wanting to go at all. "Y-you seem able to think more
clearly when I'm not around. I'll just . . ."

Opening his eyes, he caught her hand. Even as she
tried to pull away, she thrilled to his touch. He drew
her back to his side. She lost her balance and lurched
against him. In seconds his mouth was on hers, passionate and searching. Her body flooded with desire
so intense that every coherent thought vanished from
her mind.

"Don't leave me, Sunny," he said between kisses.
"You're all that keeps me sane."

She clutched his shoulders, savoring the warmth
and power of his lips on her mouth. His kisses were
all that she could think about. His kisses were the reason she had come. As he pressed himself against her,

running his hand down her side and then around to her back in order to draw her in closer, she felt her body warming with desire for him.

The power of that desire this time grew more fierce than anything she had ever known. Wanting him erased a lifetime of teachings about waiting for marriage or the risks of bearing a child conceived out of wedlock. She knew only that he was holding her and her body craved complete union.

This was her one and only chance to make him part of her, to give him her love, her courage, and convictions. She would hold him with the only power she possessed. In the morning he would propose. They'd forget about the McKidricts and begin a new life of their own together.

Struggling free of his mouth, seeing the hungry look in his eyes, she got up and pulled him to his feet. Then she gathered him into her arms, realizing that sometimes a woman had more strength than a man when it came to matters of the heart.

Kissing him with every ounce of her being, and then kissing him more softly, more tenderly, she led him into the tent. The interior was still warm from its hours in the afternoon sun. The rumpled bedroll was warm, too, as she lay down and pulled him across her body.

Bar looked into her eyes, but he wasn't asking why. And he wasn't resisting. He was looking at her, looking into her. She could see that he wasn't thinking. He was drinking her in, first her face, then her hair, which he loosened and spread all around her head on the pillow where he'd spent so many cold and lonely nights.

He looked down the length of her body, setting off

fireworks inside of her. Suddenly his hand was following his eye and moved to the hem of her skirt and her ankle. Sunny's breath caught. She could not pretend they were only sparking, she thought, sinking into an oblivion that made her yield with pleasure to the warm pressure of his hand on the parts of her that had never been touched before. They were going to be together in perfect union.

He buried his face in her neck, kissing her where her pulse beat so strong. He trailed his lips to her throat and then pressed his face between her breasts. She felt as if she were swelling to his touch, her nipples contracting to exquisitely sensitive points that connected mysteriously to the depth of her womanhood. The desire to merge intensified. She felt a swelling begin there, too, making her arch against a gentle palm holding her warmth with such possessive assurance.

Her entire body came alive with desire. Wanting him closer to her, she tore at the buttons of her bodice. In what seemed like an eternity of fumbling, his hot breath was teasing her soft skin, lingering over her breasts.

She smoothed her hands around his shoulders to his neck where she felt his veins pulsing. Then her hands were seeking the warmth of his skin, too, remembering the muscled back, exploring with increasing daring the chest with its silky hair, and finding that his shirt had come undone almost by itself.

22

Holding Bar's shoulders tightly, Sunny let herself get swept away into a realm of pleasure she could never have imagined. His body was so warm, so powerful. No thoughts from the outside world intruded. She knew only the feel of the man she loved gently moving against her.

Then abruptly, unexpectedly, she was caught by waves of pleasure that sent her gyrating into space. The experience was so explosive, she wasn't sure what was happening.

Bar clutched her too. He groaned against her neck and then smothered her with kisses so passionate she wanted to laugh and cry at the same time.

"Did I hurt you?" he whispered, holding himself up with his elbows, trying to keep his weight from crushing her.

She could scarcely think. "No," she lied, breathlessly, remembering by then only a brief period of dis-

comfort before the incredible pleasure began. "I—I
didn't know I would feel so . . . so much."

It was so dark inside the tent, Sunny could barely
make out Bar's expression as he looked down at
her. He pulled away and snuggled down beside her
beneath the rough blankets of his bedroll. She
pressed herself securely against him. His heart was
beating hard and fast. His skin tasted slightly of
salt.

"I love you, Sunny," he said, tipping her face up
for another kiss. He almost sounded apologetic. "I'm
not sure we should have done this."

She shushed him. They lay together quietly, each
drifting in thought, reveling in the other's warmth
until the idle explorations of Sunny's hands roused
Bar once again.

She was more bold this time, exploring the contours
of his chest, slipping her hands down the sensitive,
almost ticklish tautness of his belly to the magnifi-
cence of his arousal. She explored it with her fingers
until he leaned against her, gasping, and smothered
her with a kiss that caused her to blossom with desire
again.

His eager hands were all over her from the
smoothness of her throat to the curves of her waist
and rounded hips. He stroked her legs, drawing them
up, opening the cradle and cupping her backside to
lift her once again and join her.

This time he lay poised, staring into her eyes,
drawing in measured breaths and then moving with
precision until she could no longer focus on him.

She clamped her legs around him, taking him full
and deep, sucking in her breath at the miraculous
sensations such a movement produced. When he

kissed her intensely, she began to move against him, harder and faster, until this time the tumult drove her over a breathless cliff of tension into a tumbling spiral of satisfaction so overwhelming she could not imagine ever returning to the world they had left behind outside the tent.

When she opened her eyes and gave a ragged sigh, he was still looking down at her, his face only kisses away, his breathing controlled, his body a coil of desire still impaling her.

He stroked her cheek with utter tenderness, looked down at the curve of her shoulder, the round, soft peak of her breast and let go with a burst of pleasure that sent his head arching back. Eyes closed, he strained against her with every ounce of his strength. His expression almost resembled pain.

Then he smiled ever so sweetly and dipped his head to kiss her nose.

"My treasure. My sunflower," he whispered, gazing at her in a kind of wondrous disbelief.

She curled against him, shaken by the power of her emotions. She felt safe in her assurance that after such a union nothing could ever go wrong again.

Even when she woke in the night to the pressure of him wanting her again, urgently, she didn't think about how late the hour was. She didn't worry about any consequences. She wasn't even much concerned by the rasp of his faintly stubbled chin as he explored her with the passion of a long deprived and insatiable man. She took him in, enfolded him and gave herself up to the strength of her love for him. She did not look back.

*   *   *

Bar opened his eyes. Gentle morning sunlight, playing down through the dense pine boughs, made shifting patterns of light and shade on the sagging canvas overhead. Beside him, Sunny's body lay warm with sleep.

She smelled delicious. Her skin was silky against his, her face relaxed and free of care. He had never noticed before just how high and lovely her cheekbones were, or how fragile the slope of her brows.

Keeping still in hopes of preserving this one perfect morning, he memorized every detail. He traced the silhouette of her cheek, treasured the cool tangle of her chestnut waves spilling across his arm and the gentle brush of her breath against his chest.

He wanted the moment to last forevermore. Her complete trust, her love and concern, her passion, this was all he needed, he told himself. She was right. He didn't need to prove . . .

He closed his eyes.

His emotions tumbled. Within seconds of waking, the world was intruding.

He slipped from the bedroll without waking her and ducked out into the chilled hush of morning.

A delicate haze hung among the pines. The meadowlarks were calling their cheerful trill, along with the far-off cries of a circling hawk. Even though he had felt the earth literally move beneath him the night before, the towering rocks and massive boulders were still standing in their places. The babble of the narrow creek rushed by alongside the road below. The sky was clear. The mountain air had never smelled so sweet. He was strong and naked and proud to be a man in love with a very wonderful woman.

Hoping to escape his intruding thoughts, he pulled his denims from the tangle of clothes protruding from the tent flap, and put them on. Then he went to tend Sundown, who was tethered nearby. The gelding had suffered a slight sprain during their wild ride into town the morning Lyford died.

Trying to keep his mind off that, Bar applied a poultice of Summerlin Salts purchased at Tilsy's Mercantile. The smell reminded him of that first day, when he had seen Sunny delivering a wagonload of the liniment to the store. If he had known she would eventually come to him like this . . .

Briefly, he thought to wake Sunny and make love to her again. Then he would propose on bended knee. It seemed so natural.

Then he thought of Lyford and Tomasina and Miguel. Grief crashed in around his desire, withering all thoughts of love. He recalled all the other victims from his past. And finally, reluctantly, he thought of his father lying in the weeds. His joy in the morning shriveled. He had no right to be happy.

Why think of this now? he asked himself, unable to stop wallowing in the past once he had started the memories rolling. Did he seek this pain? Did he want torment, loneliness, and remorse? He had Sunny. What more could he need?

What right did he have to give up his search for the justice he insisted was so important simply because he wanted to make love to Sunny for the rest of his life?

His confusion returned full force, and with it, his old headache. He should have sent her home last night. He should never have let himself taste that which he craved. To love Sunny as he wanted to love her, fully and without reservation, was the answer to a prayer. He had asked for and received forgiveness. Why then, *why,* had Lyford died?

He sank to a boulder and clutched his head. Sunny would think him a fool and a cad if he continued his search for the robber and also the sniper after all he had shared with her. She'd never forgive him. To lose her after that would cap the misery he'd lived with for the past twelve years.

A scene began to roll in his mind. He couldn't stop it. He saw a time in the future when he would be happy with Sunny, and another outlaw would come to town. Some poor soul would die, leaving helpless ones behind, and Bar would want to help. How desperately he would want that. Trying to understand, Sunny might send him off to right the wrongs that so pained him, and Bar would go.

She'd trust him and he would try to trust himself. But he might kill again. The rage might overtake him as it had before. He couldn't even trust himself to act as a gentleman, to welcome a young woman's love but not take advantage of it. He had wanted her. She had offered herself. He had taken her virginity. He hadn't even thought to wait until the proper time.

Her gift of herself astonished and sobered him. For him it was a treasure beyond imagining, but if he had made her pregnant it could turn out to be the greatest of dishonors for her.

He had to finish what he had started, and bring in the bank robber. First he had to figure out if the man was still nearby, perhaps picking off the remaining McKidricts, one by one. While he lay in Sunny's loving arms, Cale and May Sue might be walking in mortal danger.

He dressed hurriedly in his black clothes, his heart feeling sore and heavy once again. A part of him held back, wondering why he could not stop himself from leaving the one good thing in his life.

Was it possible that he was solely responsible for his own happiness or misery? And through some twisted thinking he managed to choose the latter every time? What Sunny had said before was too simple for him. Just stop. He didn't stop until the gun case was lashed to the back of his saddle and he was mounting, a prisoner of his own logic and the silence that always came over him when he was bound to do what he felt he had to.

He started down through the trees.

At least say good-bye to her.

He slowed and looked back.

The tent flap moved to the side and Sunny stuck her head out. He could see her bare shoulder and part of her breast. He felt as if the sight of her shocked, disbelieving expression was burning into his brain.

The craving to act, to satisfy that which love and lovemaking could not, overtook him. He hoped his expression conveyed enough sadness that Sunny would understand.

But even as he turned away and made his way down to the creek, he knew she would not understand. And she would not forgive. That was how he would protect her from loving him.

He had to put an end to this confusion. He had to do it or die. He couldn't propose, much less marry Sunny, when he felt to the very pit of his soul that Lyford McKidrict's death was his fault.

*   *   *

He was leaving her! Sunny thought in disbelief. She shrank back into the tent, stunned. Clutching part of her discarded skirt to her bosom, she stared at the rumpled bedroll and wondered why.

She knew he wasn't the kind of man to use her. He hadn't seemed upset or troubled when they fell asleep just before dawn.

Tears threatened, but she held everything tightly inside. She wouldn't cry. She would keep control. She was a woman now, in every respect.

She tried to rationalize his sudden departure. Perhaps he was only going for something to eat. But no, he was wearing those black clothes and had strapped that damnable gun case onto the back of his saddle. She should have thrown all of that into the fire when she had the chance weeks before.

She tried frantically to think what she should do. Hastily she dressed lest someone come along and find her naked in Bar's tent. The memories of the delicious pleasures of the night before washed over her, tearing at her, tormenting her. He loved her, she reminded herself. But he was gone.

Suddenly her fury erupted, and she plunged out of the tent, wanting to shout with rage. How could he be so foolish, so thoughtless? If he could not even pause long enough to explain himself to her, she had no intention of seeing him ever again. After angrily pacing the campsite for a while, she finally forced herself to return to the tent and tidy up. Then she set out for home, trying not to think how her mother would look at her when she arrived after an entire night away.

When she plodded in the kitchen door more than an hour later, Sunny felt years older. Her mother was seated at the table, staring at her folded hands. She looked as if she had been sitting there all night.

When Helen looked up, relief evident in her expression, Sunny saw worry, too.

"He's gone back to bounty hunting," Sunny said, hearing a hopeless tone in her voice. "I couldn't hold him back."

She didn't wait for her mother's reply but went straight to her room.

Looking sleepy and none too well herself, May Sue was in the process of dressing when Sunny entered the bedroom. Startled, then laughing a little, May Sue muttered, "Ain't very good, is he? I've had better."

Sunny straightened her back and glared at May Sue. Swiftly, she crossed the room and slapped the girl full-handed on the cheek. The sound seemed to echo through the house.

As May Sue's cheek flamed with the scarlet imprint of Sunny's hand, her expression mirrored absolute shock.

Sunny managed to hold back every horrible thing she wanted to say to the girl who so delighted in soiling everything. As May Sue raised her hand to retaliate, Sunny caught her wrist. Staring May Sue down in formidable silence, Sunny was tempted to order May Sue from the house.

But in spite of her malicious expression, the girl looked pale and haggard. Frustrated by her own sudden compassion, Sunny abruptly released her and marched as fast as she could out of the room and up the stairs to the deserted upper floor where the boarders had once lived. The floorboards resounded with her determined footsteps. She threw herself into Grodie's old room and fell across the bed, her chest a knot of heartache and grief.

She had done the unforgivable, Sunny admitted at last. She had tried to hold and control the man she loved with her body. She had expected something in return for last night. That made her no different from the scheming, conniving May Sue McKidrict.

She was hurting, Sunny realized, because Bar had not submitted to her wiles. She loved him, but she had gone to him not so much out of true love for him as out of her own selfish needs. She cried tears of despair, certain she would never see him again.

The sun sizzled through Bar's shirt, searing his shoulders. Without his hat, he felt his nose and cheeks burning in the hot afternoon glare, but the physical pain was a distraction from his heartache.

He wanted to go back to Sunny and explain, but he had made his choice. The damage was done. His chance for wondrous love and a normal life was over.

He sat among the boulders, casually watching the road to Crystal Springs. Two hours before he had stuck a branch upright in the road where Lyford had died. From where he sat, he could gauge the trajectory of the fatal shot. By Bar's best calculations, his current position had to be the very spot where the sniper had been hiding, waiting for the procession to come along.

Bar had talked with the sheriff. He had also stopped by Frank's store to see if Frank had recalled anything more about the incident. Frank only reminded Bar that he was still expected to come to his wedding the following Sunday.

Now Bar tried to put himself into the mind of a

man bent on killing in cold blood. It was not so very difficult to do, Bar thought, disgusted with himself for having taken so long to do what was surely a simple job of reasoning and deduction. He was a killer himself. Who knew better than he what it felt like to hunt down a man?

How had the sniper known they would be passing that way? Why had there been only one shot? Could it have been an accident? And how had the sniper managed to climb to this particular place? From which direction would he have come, from Escalera or Crystal Springs?

Only a mountain goat could have reached this place from Escalera. That left the simple route Bar had taken up from the creek. Simple or not, someone had been clever enough to hide his tracks by traveling upstream from Crystal Springs. Bar was willing to bet the sniper was still in town, waiting for his next target to move into view.

When Bar was certain of his conclusions, he untied Sundown and mounted, walking the horse back toward town through the creek. He moved cautiously, pretending that several people were watching from the road. With nearly an hour's delay in pursuit, the sniper could have returned to town undetected.

Helen gazed at herself in the mirror and smoothed the folds of her wedding skirt. Ivy Tuttle, the dressmaker who had made the matching hat, positioned the concoction of linen roses and tulle on Helen's neatly coiled graying hair.

"Perfect," Ivy whispered, smiling.

Sunny, who looked thin and wan after days of

brooding over Bar, brought Helen's gloves. "You look so lovely, Ma," Sunny said, making an effort to appear happy.

Helen's heart was breaking for her daughter. She wanted to reassure her on this special day, for Sunny was not her usual, confident self. But Helen could think of nothing to say.

Sunny and May Sue weren't speaking. Helen suspected that May Sue would be leaving the house as soon as she and Frank were gone on their wedding trip. Then Sunny would be left alone, with Homer her only protector.

Sunny appeared to read Helen's thoughts. She forced a smile. "I'm going to be just fine, Ma. Everyone is waiting. It's time to go down."

Helen noticed for the first time the sounds of the guests gathered in the yard. Because so many people had been invited, and because the day had turned out to be so lovely, she had elected at the last minute to be married outside on the steps of the porch.

As she descended the stairs and crossed through the dining room to present herself at the kitchen doorway, Helen said a silent good-bye to the house and her years there. When she and Frank returned they would tell Sunny of their plans to live over the store. Both of them wanted a fresh start. They were even thinking of building a new house closer to town. Naturally, Sunny could join them if she chose, but Helen suspected that her daughter would never want to leave the house her father had built.

Helen hoped Sunny would be pleased with their decision. Believing Sunny would thrive on her own, free at last to seek a stable man to marry, Helen felt certain that Sunny wouldn't take long to make her selection from among the many young men interested in her.

A clumsy rendition of "Greensleeves" played on the piano in the parlor by the dressmaker's mother signaled the beginning of the wedding ceremony. Helen scarcely heard the music as she followed Sunny out into the brilliant afternoon sunlight.

All their friends were lined up along a makeshift aisle, and at the end, standing on one of the porch steps was Frank Tilsy, bedecked in his finest mail-order suit. He looked like a proudly puffed, starched, and buttoned mannequin with a huge grin.

When Helen reached the steps, she felt too giddy to balance on the narrow porch step, so Frank stepped down to join her on one of the pink flag-stones that was partly buried in the reddish dust of the yard.

Behind them, the guests closed in. Helen relinquished her bouquet of wildflowers to Sunny, who was looking odd indeed. Helen noticed then for the first time that Frank had two men standing up for him instead of the usual one: his oldest friend, Orrin Colstern, and the somber-looking, very sunburned Barnabas Landry.

Helen smiled uncertainly, and Bar bowed to her gravely. Then he managed a smile so wistful, Helen couldn't think what to do for him. More than anything she admired Frank for trying to draw Bar back into the gentle world of the simple, God-fearing people from Crystal Springs. Secretly, Helen hoped Bar would soon live there as Sunny's husband. He was the one, she was certain now.

Helen looked up at Frank's face and felt all her cares suddenly melt away. Everything was going to be all right. A sense of peace settled over her anxious thoughts. She had never before felt quite so serene as at this moment.

When it came time for the usual exchange of vows, the Reverend Walters closed his prayer book, folded his hands over it, and nodded to Frank.

Frank's voice, deepened by emotion and hushed with sincerity, spun a web of magic around Helen's long-empty heart. "I, Frank Tilsy, take you, Helen, for my beloved wife. I've loved you a long time, dear. As your husband and friend, there isn't anything I won't do for you in the years to come. I'll include you in all my plans. Everything I've got will be yours. I'll take care of you no matter what, and I'll always be true. In God's name, I promise."

Helen's eyes filled with tears. "Frank, we've waited a long time for this day," she said, surprised by the fragile smallness of her voice. "I welcome you gladly as my beloved husband. I'll be with you always, helping you, caring for you. Our days will be beautiful and safe together." She looked deeply into his eyes and smiled. "Wherever you go, I'll be with you. Whatever you do, I'll support you. I offer all that I am to you because I love you, and I'll hold nothing back. In God's name, I promise."

Sunny's face hurt with the effort to hold back tears. Those words, so tenderly spoken, threatened to send her weeping into the house.

But she kept her eyes averted from Bar's sunburned face. He stood only two feet from her but might as well have been on the far side of the earth. He didn't matter to her anymore, she told herself. He couldn't.

Pronounced husband and wife, Sunny's mother

and Frank turned toward the guests, who cheered and clapped. In moments everyone was swarming inside to sample the food on display in the dining room. The celebrating would go on all day. Sunny rushed off to be of service.

It wasn't until it was time for Helen to don her traveling jacket that Sunny realized Bar had long ago disappeared from the scene. He hadn't even spoken to her. Homer brought around the buckboard, which Frank would drive to the depot with his bride at his side. Sunny rode with several others in the rented surrey, and the procession that wound its way into town late that afternoon for the send-off at the train reminded her horribly of that morning only two weeks before when Lyford McKidrict had been killed.

All too soon Sunny's mother was kissing her cheek, holding Sunny's face in her gloved hands, and reminding her to keep the doors barred. Sunny felt as if she were caught in a dream. This was what she had wanted for her mother, marriage to Frank and a happy future. Why, then, did she feel like a small child being abandoned? She could have stayed in town with friends if she had wanted to, but she had insisted she would be fine at home.

"Have a wonderful trip, Ma," Sunny said, sending her mother off with a confident wave. "Don't worry about me."

Frank hugged her, and for just an extra second, Sunny clung to him. She was grateful to have a man like him acting as her new father.

"I'll take good care of her," he said.

"I know you will. Be safe."

And then she was waving and waving, watching the train carry her mother and Frank away. Everyone congratulated her and then went away, too. Someone took the rented surrey back to the livery stable. She drove home in the buckboard. Alone.

Momentarily, the future yawned before Sunny, overwhelming and just a little frightening, but she had so much to do to prepare for her parents' home-coming the following week, she didn't have time to fret. She wanted the house perfect, ready to receive them. By the looks of things, May Sue was gone, Sunny noticed when she went into the silent house. May Sue had packed her things early that morning. Sunny didn't expect to see her again for some time.

The first order of business was to put that paper with the yellow roses on her mother's walls. Sunny intended to transform the room, where she expected her mother and Frank would sleep, into a lovely, happy new haven. It would be as Sunny had always wished it would be, her house with a family living in it.

The feeling that she had been abandoned, how-ever, persisted into the night. Sunny kept a number of lamps burning and prowled the echoing rooms in search of herself. She fell asleep exhausted at dawn, dreaming of Bar's hands on her, and awoke with a start to hear spoons outside, tapping out a jaunty rhythm.

Pulling the covers over her face, Sunny wept until there was nothing left to do but get up and mix the wallpaper paste.

23

Her ma was going to be so surprised, Sunny thought, struggling to drag her mother's huge old bed away from the wall. She had all the lengths of wallpaper cut. The stepladder was in place and the paste was ready. All she had to do was—

A small dusty book fell from a niche behind the headboard. Surprised, and instantly curious, Sunny abandoned moving the bed and picked it up. It was a diary. Although she had no intention of reading something meant to be private, she saw no harm in opening the cover.

In a childish hand, "Helen Elizabeth Johnston," her mother's maiden name, was neatly lettered on the first page. The date was 1851, when her mother would have been about ten years old.

Sinking onto the bed in the middle of the chaotic, sheet-draped room, Sunny couldn't stop herself from beginning to read what she assumed was a quaint

journal from her mother's girlhood. The first few
entries were snippets from her mother's early years as
an orphaned maid of all work on the farmstead of a
veterinarian with a small rural practice. Helen had
been worked hard and was often lonely.

Following a gap of several years, Helen had
resumed writing in a more mature hand. By then she
had married Abel Summerlin and was expecting her
first child. Sunny found the account of her own birth
so fascinating that she couldn't put the diary down
even after it was clear that her mother's remarks,
written during Abel's service in the Union army, were
personal.

Helen suffered the miscarriage of her second child
while he was gone but continued working without
pause. Abel's return from the war and his long recovery from dysentery filled several pages of less than
happy entries in which Helen was consumed with
conflicting emotions regarding her marriage.

Expecting to read of Helen's mixed feelings about
coming west, Sunny was alarmed to discover further
that Abel and Helen had parted on a troubled note
when he was well enough to try his luck in the west.
Only after her employer's older son showed an
unwelcome interest in Helen had she packed up and
followed Abel into the wilds of southern Colorado.

Sunny paused to ponder these details of her
mother's past. How strange it was to imagine her
mother as an attractive young wife, compelled to follow her husband to a strange and lonely land, particularly while her mother and Frank were enjoying their
wedding trip in Denver.

When she read on, Sunny found another long gap
in time. Her mother took up writing in the diary again

when "a rowdy rancher named Luck McKidrict" started calling on Abel to tend his stock. The man had acquired the habit of stopping by whenever Abel was on call elsewhere. Sunny's blood ran cold as she read the entry in which Helen recounted the afternoon Luck had tried to take advantage.

Luck handled me in a way that was frightening. He cared nothing for my heart. He thought of me as a mere body with breasts and treated me as such. He laughed when I resisted. The fact that I could drive off such a large man told me that he was only toying with me. He promised to return, and I fear he will. Luck could have easily dishonored me had it not been for Sunny coming home from her play at the cave and making a good deal of noise in her arrival. Heavenly Father, preserve me from this horrible man.

By then nothing could have stopped Sunny from reading to the end. There were accounts of visits with Julia, and Helen's thoughts on her friend's plight as the wife of such a man.

One entry, written without breaks, took up several pages. It concluded with,

I cannot tell for certain if Abel goes to the McKidrict ranch as often as he does because Luck calls him there, as Abel claims, or because he feels such pity for Julia. But that remark overheard in church this Sunday past has set my mind whirling, and I worry still. Is my Abel taken with Julia McKidrict? Does Abel know that Luck comes by here and laughs at my fear of him?

What am I to do here, alone, with Sunny near enough to stumble upon scandal at any turning?

The following entry calmed Sunny's stunned reaction to the suggestion that her father might have been unfaithful and that her mother had been stalked by a rapist.

The moment we let Julia inside, she wept piteously and threw herself on Abel. I could see that he plainly did not welcome Julia's touch and that all my fears had been unfounded. But Julia looked so battered, her lips and eyes swollen, her nails broken and bleeding. Luck had beaten and raped her again, his own sad wife, and she told us that he had held a gun to her head for hours until he passed out from drink. In the end I agreed that Abel should give her our savings. Julia is gone now. I know not where. I worry that Luck will find and kill her, and then come for us. What courage my Abel has shown throughout this. How could I have ever doubted him?

The next entry was written a week after Abel's funeral a few months later.

Sunny sits so quietly at Abel's gravesite. My heart breaks for my dear child. All I can do is pray, for her, for myself. Keep this vengeance from my heart, Lord, but I do not believe Abel's death was an accident. If he had died from a kick to the head, the mark on his skull would have looked different. Luck McKidrict murdered my husband for helping Julia escape, and I have no

proof that anyone will listen to. We are prisoners
of the monster McKidrict, and God forgive me, I
pray for the man's resting place in hell.

Horrified, Sunny flung the diary to the floor. The
spine split, leaving the book in ruin.

She stared at it a long moment. Then she retrieved
it from the floor and read the last entry again. Finally
she closed her eyes, unable to think. She dared not let
herself think about what she had just read.

Luck McKidrict had . . . Luck McKidrict had . . .

Sunny stood. She felt an ugly emotion fill her
chest. "Papa!" she cried, hearing her voice echo
throughout the empty house. "Papa. Oh, no, Papa!"

She looked around in a panic, wanting to run to
the office for comfort, to scream for the injustice of it,
to ride all the way to town and demand vengeance for
her father.

But the events were long over, forgotten, con-
signed to a dusty diary hidden behind her mother's
bed. There was nothing to be done. Luck McKidrict
was already dead.

She couldn't imagine how her mother had lived
with such a terrible secret all these years. Yet suddenly an appalling understanding washed over Sunny.
Her mother had no proof, and surely she blamed herself, if only in part.

Sunny recalled the years and years when she and
her mother had catered to the boarders. Did her
mother need the boarders around to shield her from
the McKidrict monster? In all those long, arduous
hours, had she been doing penance for the kiss Luck
McKidrict had stolen from her? Or for doubting
Abel?

"Ma, I wish you were here," Sunny whispered.

Sunny wanted to hug and comfort her mother. She wanted to be hugged and comforted herself. And she wanted satisfaction. She wanted someone like Bar Landry to right a most regrettable wrong. She would have paid every last dollar she had.

Knowing Bar couldn't help her in this, she nevertheless wanted to go to him. She wanted his strong, capable arms around her. She wanted to know why he had left her without so much as a word after making such beautiful love to her.

Finally she understood why Bar had left her. He was trying to spare her his infectious desire for revenge. That first night when he was in their house, Sunny had feared catching his fever. She had caught his rage instead.

When Sunny emerged from her mother's bedroom an hour later, she felt as if she had aged several years. She saw life in harsh new colors. She was filled with biting questions and a restless impatience to hear the whole story from her mother's own lips. The diary was only a fragment of those tragic events, she knew. Helen herself would have to fill in the myriad of details which Sunny could only guess at.

Making her way outside, Sunny went to her father's grave and knelt beside it. "Papa," she whispered, beginning to weep. "I didn't know. I never guessed. I'm so sorry."

She understood only too well what had been driving Bar to hunt his bounties. He could ease his rage with a simple act of primitive violence to which she had thought herself immune.

Vengeance is mine, saith the Lord. How naive she must have sounded, spouting that. If Luck McKidrict had still been alive, she thought, digging her nails into her palms, she would have gladly shot him down.

In any case, she was glad he was dead. She was glad Maria Arquilla had danced on his grave. For that matter, she was not very sorry that poor Tomasina and her little son had been spared having a McKidrict man as a husband and father.

There remained Cale and May Sue, and for them, Sunny was able to summon no pity. She had been robbed of a loving father. Nothing would ever make that right. She hadn't allowed herself to grieve when he died so abruptly, but she was grieving now. It felt as if she was going to drown in it.

Bar walked his horse up the pass, looking for wheel tracks which had probably long since been obliterated by wind and rain but which he still hoped to find, nevertheless. He imagined driving the buggy through the mud with the horse struggling for footing. The bank robber might have paused there, or there, he thought. He might have doubled back, or . . .

Bar paused to again consider the fact that the robber was a slight man, small enough to wear the disguise of a woman without drawing attention to himself. In Bar's imaginative reconstruction of the eventful morning, the disguised man had just shot McKidrict at the bank and fled with his strongbox. Bar was about to follow the road he and Sunny had taken out of town to the McKidrict ranch weeks before when it occurred to him that driving the buggy into the grasses might have been a possibility that morning, even in a heavy rain.

Mounting Sundown, Bar turned the horse off the

road and made his way away from town through the tall grasses, imagining the buggy avoiding the pass and side streets altogether.

Within a mile, Bar knew by the county map that he had studied at the City Hall office weeks before, that the McKidrict acres started somewhere in the vicinity. Before McKidrict, the land had belonged to a Spanish nobleman.

Reining suddenly, Bar saw the faint marks of an old wagon road almost completely grown over, skirting the bluffs. Deep wheel marks, dried and turning to dust by then, cut a distinct path for several hundred yards before disappearing straight into a dense clump of scrub oak growing against the weathered bluff.

Dismounting, Bar tore away the branches to find the crudely fashioned log doors of an old trapper's dugout. "Eureka!" he whispered, yanking the doors wide. "McKidrict, you ol' son of a bitch!"

Inside was a buggy covered with dried mud jammed against the earthen back wall. Tracks around the buggy remained undisturbed, revealing a distinctive bootprint which Bar recognized. He'd done it! The hunt was virtually over. He almost laughed aloud.

After memorizing every detail of the scene, he climbed into the buggy to look at the torn black dress and lace mantilla which were lying on the seat. These were the exact items worn by the robber and described by a score of witnesses.

On the far side of the buggy Bar found the strongbox lying on the ground, smashed open, its contents almost undisturbed because the dozen or so coin bags were filled with rocks and the bundles of money were nothing but paper. Luck McKidrict had had no intention of paying his debts that Saturday morning he was shot to death, Bar thought.

If McKidrict hadn't intended to pay . . .

Bar's mind leapt upon the only remaining possibility, that Luck himself had hired someone to rob the bank. Luck had expected to leave the bank with Foote's note signed, but without paying a penny. Bar chuckled. Somewhere out there was a sorely disappointed hireling, Bar thought, and he knew who it was.

"You want to tell us how you got into this mess, son?" The sheriff pinned Johnsie Rawlins with a sharp eye and spat quietly into the cuspidor beside his desk. "Take your time. You ain't goin' no place." He took Johnsie's boots and studied the pattern of holes on the soles that had made the impressions that Bar recognized.

"I didn't mean to kill him, Sheriff! I don't even remember aiming at him. I don't want to hang."

"Just tell us what your part was."

Johnsie closed his eyes. "I worked for McKidrict for two years. He beat me bloody once just for talking to May Sue. Said I wasn't never to get near her. Said the same thing to all the hands. She'd come around poutin', sayin' things like, 'Don't you boys like me none?' and we'd have to swallow it down.

"One day McKidrict comes to me and says, 'Rawlins, you still got a hankerin' for my May Sue?' And I says, 'Sir, I got strong feelings for your daughter.' He looks me over like he's goin' to kill me, maybe. Then he says, throwing his arm around my shoulder like I'm one of his own boys, 'Rawlins, how'd you like to marry my girl?' I says, 'Sir, I'd be honored.'"

"He asked if you wanted to *marry* May Sue? After tellin' you to stay clear of her?"

Bar watched the sheriff's eyes pop. He could hardly sit through the confession. He wanted to be on his way to Sunny's place to tell her how blessedly easy it had been for him to bring in Johnsie . . . alive!

"I was plenty damned surprised, too, Sheriff," Johnsie went on. "He grabs my shirtfront and smiles nasty into my eyes. 'You help me, I'll help you.' He goes on to say he's got a score to settle with the banker, says he plans to fix the piss-ant for good. He takes me to the dugout to see his wife's old buggy."

To move things along, Bar interrupted. "McKidrict said this after Foote served him the papers, about how much he owed."

Johnsie nodded. "So he tells me we're goin' to rob the bank. Says it works every time." Johnsie shrugged. "I'm supposed to put on the duds McKidrict took from Maria and walk into the bank. I'm supposed to shoot up the place so McKidrict can kill Foote. I'm supposed to take back the strongbox and hide in the dugout till McKidrict comes for me."

"What went wrong?" the sheriff asked.

"As I'm waitin' outside, along comes McKidrict and into the bank he goes. I'm supposed to wait till he gets his papers signed. Only I start to wonder how long does it take to sign 'em. I get out of the buggy and stand a minute at the door, watchin'. McKidrict's leanin' over Foote's desk, so I think they're finished. I walk in with my gun drawn.

"McKidrict turns and gives me a crazy look. I don't

know what the hell to think. I can't hardly see with
that black thing over my face. Suddenly I wonder if
maybe McKidrict is fixin' to kill me, too."

"This is the first time you've considered that possibility?" the sheriff asked.

Johnsie nodded. "The banker, he looks shocked
like he can't believe somebody's robbin' *his* bank. I
feel like laughing except suddenly I can't remember
nothin' McKidrict told me to do. All I want to do is
run. May Sue ain't worth this, I'm thinking.

"I m-motion for Foote and McKidrict to put their
hands in the air. I get up close and look in the strongbox quick-like. There's a couple coin bags and some
paper money bundled up."

"You didn't stop to count it?" the sheriff asked.

"Hell, no! I point at the safe and say *por favor* in
my best Spanish. Foote gives me this look like I'd
asked him to drop his drawers. I cock my gun. I can't
see what McKidrict's doin', but I sense movement,
like he's reaching for his gun. I'm so scared, I start to
pee my drawers!"

Bar couldn't help but chuckle.

Johnsie swallowed hard.

"Foote's movin' so slow I'm thinkin' the teller's
had time to bring an army. Finally Foote opens the
safe, but he won't move aside. I go like this. . . ."
Johnsie motioned with his hand. "Behind me,
McKidrict takes something offa the desk."

"The unsigned legal notice we found clutched in
McKidrict's hand," the sheriff said.

"'Don't touch that paper, we're not done yet,'
Foote says, bold as brass. McKidrict draws his gun,
but he looks at *me!* The safe is open. I'm supposed to
clean it out. Suddenly I hear a shot. Or maybe it's

Foote slamming the safe door. I don't know which, I'm so scared. I can't think. McKidrict gets a wild look. I remember I'm supposed to shoot up the place. I squeeze off a couple shots. McKidrict is stumbling backward, firin' all over creation. Then he goes down. I've killed him, I think."

"What's Foote doing?"

"Hell if I know. I try to pick up the strongbox, but it's heavy. I chuck my gun inside and clear out. Suddenly I'm in the buggy and it's raining like crazy and the horse can't run. Then I'm in the dugout finally, tearing into the strongbox, remindin' myself I've just shot May Sue's pa so she ain't likely to want to marry me much. Then I see the bags is full of rocks, not coins. Not gold. Four dollars in old Texas bank notes. The bastard didn't have hardly any money in that damned strongbox, and I don't know what to do next."

"So you went back to the ranch," Bar said, ever more impatient.

"I had to act like I hadn't done nothing, right? I remembered him tellin' me that much. When nobody came after me—you questioned Maria, just like McKidrict said you would—I decided I'd marry May Sue after all, but shit, you come along, bounty hunter, and she ain't given me the time of day since. I'm a dead man, ain't I?"

Bar started for the door. "Hold tight, Johnsie. Don't give up yet. I'll be back, and we'll talk."

A half hour later at the bank, Ethridge Foote counted out two hundred dollars and reluctantly turned it all over to Bar.

"Much obliged," Bar said, striding from the bank, feeling as happy as he had since waking from his fever. His future lay before him clear as crystal.

Grinning all the way out to Escalera, Bar's satisfaction dimmed only slightly when he remembered he hadn't stayed at the sheriff's office long enough to find out why Johnsie had shot Lyford. He'd have to deal with that later.

When Bar placed the entire two hundred dollars into Tomasina's hands, Bar felt so certain that his dark days were behind him that he spent the next hour by the side of the road carefully dismantling his gun and placing all the pieces into the case. He never intended to assemble it again.

He rode back to his cabin to find it in perfect order except that dirt and debris had sifted over everything while he'd been gone. The tent was sagging and about to fall in on itself. He tidied everything and when he was done, he lit a fire, warmed some water, washed, shaved, and changed into his plaid shirt and denims. He couldn't wait another minute. He had to go see Sunny.

It wasn't going to be easy, reconciling with her, Bar reminded himself as he crossed the valley and started up Pine Ridge Road. He couldn't have known he'd find the robber so quickly or easily, but now that he had, he would simply have to make Sunny understand why he had left her.

He paused at the spruce, seeing the house as it had looked that first time. The dooryard seemed quiet and deserted. The dogs were slow to respond to his arrival as he urged Sundown forward and came to a stop at the hitching rail in front of the kitchen door.

Helen and Frank would be back from their wedding trip in another day or so, he thought. He looked forward to seeing them. As he dismounted, Bar felt uneasy at the silence pervading the place. When he knocked and no one answered, he began wondering if Sunny might be in town, or spending a few days with friends.

Homer emerged from the barn. Bar shook his hand and smiled. "Where's Sunny, ol' buddy?"

Homer looked toward the back of the house where the small graveyard stood among the pines. Bar patted him on the shoulder and then started up the path.

He found Sunny seated next to her father's grave. She glanced up at him and her cheeks flamed.

"Are you all right, Sunny?" Bar asked.

"No," she said flatly.

"I've come to apologize."

"It won't do you any good. I can't listen to anything you have to say."

"Can't or won't?"

"Can't. Won't. Same thing." She flashed him a look that he had never seen on her before, and it troubled him deeply. "Go away, Bar."

"I'm ready to explain," he said, keeping his voice even. He felt to his bones that she wasn't going to forgive him. He had chosen the most exquisitely vulnerable time to abandon her; their friendship was over.

"I brought in the bank robber alive today, Sunny. A few hours ago."

She leveled her hot, gaze at him. "I'm so very happy for you, Barnabas. But it's too late. You can't turn back what's happened any more than I can."

"Won't you let me explain?"

"There's nothing to explain. I've recently learned that Luck McKidrict murdered my father. I have to sit here and wait until my mother gets home to explain why she never told me. I have to sit here feeling this . . . this . . . awful thing inside me churning and burning. Now I *understand* to the pit of my soul what has driven *you* all these years. A person can't have love and hate in their heart at the same time."

"Sunny—"

"I don't know myself anymore. I'm not the same naive person you knew even a few days ago."

He looked at her, and the only thing he could think about was how very desperately he loved her. Nothing she could say would ever change that. He forgave her her anger. He loved her for it. Believing he could do nothing for her, Bar turned on his heel and left. He would contribute no more to the torment of her soul.

24

Helen's greatest concern throughout the wedding trip had been just how to tell Sunny that they'd be moving into town where Helen would be free of old memories to begin a new life. Now Helen stood in the kitchen of what had been her boarding-house, looking down at the old book lying on the table. Her mind went blank. Sunny had found her diary.

Sunny sat on the bench, looking up at her with the anguished eyes of a child betrayed. Frank didn't know what was in the diary, but he could see that Sunny wasn't herself and that Helen knew why.

He patted Helen's shoulder. "I'll go help Homer with the chores. You two look as if you need to talk."

Helen caught his sleeve. "I think you'd better stay to hear this, dear. We're a family now."

Looking concerned, Frank stepped back and waited.

Helen pulled the long pins from her hat and lifted it from her hair. "How did you find the diary?" she asked Sunny, stalling for time, trying to think.

Sunny's eyes filled with tears. "I was getting ready to paper the walls. I know I shouldn't have read it, Ma, but . . ."

Helen sank to the bench beside her daughter. She drew Sunny close and waited for the girl—for she was a girl at that moment—to finish explaining about moving the furniture. Helen watched Frank, her beloved new husband, hang his coat on a peg by the door.

When Sunny was finished, Helen began her story, at the beginning when she first met Abel. She left nothing out as she recounted all that Sunny had read about in the diary, concluding with the day Abel Summerlin was brought home to die.

"We had a sheriff in those days who feared Luck McKidrict, but I went to him and tried to impress upon him that Abel was too good around horses to have been kicked by one. I told him I thought Luck must have hit Abel for helping Julia run away, and I begged him to look for a weapon, a horseshoe nailed to a board or something like that. I begged him to consider the possibility at least, but he wouldn't go out there."

Helen felt calm revealing the tragic events she had once feared would go with her to the grave. Frank was rubbing his eyes. She got up abruptly and put on water to boil for coffee. Then she hugged him and kissed his cheek.

"That's all there is, honey," Helen said when Sunny didn't move or give any sign that she was satisfied with the story. "How could I burden a child with truth that I could scarcely bear myself?"

"Would you have *ever* told me, Ma?" Sunny cried.

Helen shrugged. "We do our best not to hurt the ones we love. What good does it do for you to know, honey? Your pa's gone. Luck McKidrict's gone."

Sunny looked so strange, Helen thought. Had she been mistaken not to tell her sooner? She couldn't believe that she had been. There were times when she had to take a firm stand with her daughter. Oddly enough, this appeared to be one of those times.

"Frank and I are planning to live in town now that we're back," Helen said, speaking of their plans a bit more bluntly than she had intended. "You worked so hard to pay off the loan, and I know how dearly you love this house. I feel you should be sole owner. We'll see to the title in the next few days, when you feel up to it."

Sunny stared at her, dumbfounded. "I thought you loved this house, too."

"It was Abel's. Now it's yours. You'll be able to fix the place up just the way you like. When you marry—"

"And just who am I supposed to marry?" Sunny spat out, jumping up and glaring at Helen.

"You're free to think about that now," Helen said calmly, no stranger to Sunny's abrupt passions. "You don't have to take care of me anymore."

In the past, Helen would have submerged her own desires in favor of her daughter's, but just as she had found the strength to stand up to Foote and the boarders, Helen found herself able to withstand Sunny's reaction to these unexpected intentions, too.

"You're playing mighty fast and loose with my future, Ma. Do you think I enjoyed the past week alone, wondering what more I didn't know about you and Pa?"

"That's the whole story, honey. I'm sorry you're upset by the idea of me moving to town. Do you want to sell the house and come along?"

"No, Ma!" Sunny cried. "This is my home. Am I in the way now? Is that it?"

Helen gathered her close. "Of course not!"

"Ma, I've just learned that Pa was murdered. I can't sleep. I can't think. I'm heartsick. How will I ever get over this? I need you both close to me for a while."

"Of course. Of course," Helen whispered, fighting sudden tears. "We don't have to go today." She'd been so happy with Frank, she thought, she hadn't realized what so many changes would mean for Sunny. "Have you eaten today, honey?"

Sunny gave a cry of frustration and stormed off. "Mother, what ails me can't be cured by eating. I'm afraid it can't be cured at all."

Shaken, Helen watched her daughter disappear into her bedroom and then went quickly into Frank's arms. "My solution to everything. Food." Her voice caught.

"Will she be all right?" Frank asked.

Taking his dear face in her hands, Helen smiled sadly and nodded. "Of course she will. She's our Sunny. I just hate to see her suffer so over something long past."

Bull Valley wasn't known for summer heat, but for the next several weeks the temperature defied the norm and rose to unpleasant highs.

Sunny worked cheerlessly, papering the walls of the room that wasn't going to be her mother's and

Frank's after all. They were sleeping in Grodie's old room.

She matched the pattern of yellow roses perfectly, recalling her many fantasies about her mother's birthday and how she had hoped things would go. Those days seemed long ago indeed.

In time, however, the pain regarding the truth of her father's death lessened. She sought out May Sue, who was wearing out her welcome at one of the boardinghouses across town. May Sue had no money and her rent was long overdue. She had become peevish and was inclined to complain, so after a brief visit, Sunny left. Some time would have to pass before she and May Sue might meet again as friends.

As the days wore on, Sunny turned her thoughts to Cassidy County's much anticipated Independence Day celebration, hoping it would prove an enjoyable diversion. She found that her heart had grown weary of grief. That terrible rage which she had expected to follow her forever, eased. Unlike Bar, who had fought his rage for twelve years, Sunny's emotion was not so uncontrollable. She mourned her father and then was done. Acceptance soothed her sore heart. Once again she began looking forward to the future.

By the end of the month she was happy to see her mother move into Frank's apartment over the store. She apologized for her behavior following their wedding trip and, of course, was forgiven.

Alone on Pine Ridge Road, Sunny took to sitting on the porch of her house in the evening when the breeze was cool, relishing the peace and solitude. She liked to recall how Bar looked that first day in town, dressed in black, the unhappiest man she had ever seen in her life, and then compare that to the way he

looked the day she visited him at the cabin. He had
been smiling. In some small part, she felt she helped
him achieve that.

She didn't regret giving herself to him, either. She
didn't brood over his reasons for leaving her. It
seemed to make sense now. She still loved Bar.
Sometimes she fantasized that he would come riding
up and sweep her into his arms again for a kiss.
Sometimes she even tried to will him back, but he
didn't appear and she supposed he never would.

She lay awake at night, letting herself remember
their lovemaking, and wished she could be with him
again, if only for a little while. But that was not to be,
she reminded herself. Somehow she had to forget that
she had ever known passion with Bar Landry.

A barbecue pit had been set up south of the town
square, and its fires had been burning since early
morning. The savory aroma of roasting beef, venison,
and chicken pervaded the air.

On the new pavilion, which was draped with red,
white, and blue bunting, Sheriff Brummer was concluding the introduction of the governor who had
come down from Denver for the occasion. Hundreds
of people had gathered in the sweltering sun to hear
his speech.

Sunny's chocolate cake was entered in the baking
contest. Winning that would surely attract a dozen
new suitors. Her mother had bread loaves, fruit preserves, and several pies covered in the shade near the
tables where everyone would be eating.

Sunny ate, too, at noon when all the speechifying
was over, but she found herself constantly looking for

Bar. He was nowhere to be seen. She assumed he had left town.

May Sue and Cale weren't there. Sunny had expected May Sue to make great show as she had in the past, but this year there was no money for a new dress. Ordinarily Cale would have been hanging around, calling her Ornery and making lewd remarks that Sunny would denounce. Without the McKidricts, Crystal Springs seemed downright dull. She almost missed the pesky pair.

The afternoon wore on, with a parade and a horse race and a raffle. The next day the rodeo events at the stock pens west of town would take place. Everywhere children ran wild. The older men pitched horseshoes while the younger ones threw knives or performed amazing feats of target practice with their pistols. Everyone cheered when Ol' Foote, who was inept at everything, was made to take part in the sharpshooting contest and won the final round with his vest pocket self-cocker.

By evening, Sunny longed for a nap, but she changed into her dancing dress at the store's apartment which her mother had already decorated in blues and whites. She marveled at how pretty the place looked after only a few weeks.

"You wouldn't have liked those yellow roses, would you have, Ma?" Sunny asked, brushing back her hair and tying it with a yellow ribbon.

"Yellow is your color, honey," her mother said, grinning.

The dance that night was the first of three to be held during the weekend celebration. So many people were expected to come to town, and the town hall could only accommodate a fraction of them at a time,

that two years before the town council had decided
more than one dance was needed.

This first one was likely to be the most subdued,
for hard-working ranchers weren't used to much
relaxation. It would take them time to unwind. Once
the music started, however, several young men asked
Sunny to dance. She declined, preferring to watch
from the sidelines.

Helen and Frank became the center of attention
when they led one of the marches. Sunny laughed, her
throat oddly tight, and marveled to see her mother
looking so happy and beautiful.

Then the fiddle player and the banjo player, and
the big girl with the guitar, welcomed a new addition
to their rustic orchestra. A tall, dark-haired man in
gray trousers, red suspenders, and a fine white linen
shirt stepped up onto the stage. He grinned as he
crouched down and began a lively spoon accompani-
ment to their rendition of "Turkey in the Straw." Now
and then he looked across the sea of swirling dancers
to grin at everyone.

Sunny couldn't take her eyes off Bar's face. How
good it was to see him happy. At least she could take
comfort in that, but how was she going to get through
life, having him living only a few miles away, remembering what it felt like to make love with him . . . and
yet not to be part of his life?

Not being a part of his life was her choice, Sunny
reminded herself. Perhaps it was time to change that.
Surely Bar hadn't forgotten what they had shared.

Making her way closer to the stage, Sunny decided
to brave her uncertainty. When Bar saw her, she
noticed a slight tensing in his body, but his expression
betrayed nothing but congenial regard for her. She

managed to keep a smile on her otherwise wooden face. He nodded and played on. Only after several songs did he beg off and dismount the stage.

"You're looking well, Sunny," he said, gazing down at her with about as much visible feeling as any casual acquaintance might.

"I thought you'd left town," she said.

"After I brought Johnsie in, he asked me to defend him at his trial next month, but I can't do that, of course. I left my studies six years ago and was never admitted to the bar. Lately I've been thinking about going back east to finish up. I think my father would have wanted that."

She wanted to say something light and pleasant, but couldn't think of anything but the fact that he seemed cured of his desire to hunt bounties. And that was the last subject she wanted to bring up.

Bar went on. "I assumed that whoever robbed the bank and killed McKidrict also shot Lyford, but we've since learned that Johnsie was asleep in his room at the saloon that morning, so we're still trying to figure who would have wanted Lyford dead. At least Johnsie won't hang for that. He's got a lawyer just in from Durango. Have you met him?"

Sunny shook her head. She didn't care about Johnsie or the lawyer or anything. She couldn't when her heart was breaking. There was not a flicker of warmth left in Bar's eyes for her.

She wanted to draw him out of the hall into the cool night air, to take his hand and have a real talk with him, but it was too late. He obviously didn't love her anymore.

He smiled and seemed about to say something when he thought better of it. "Take care of yourself,

Sunny, and thanks for everything. You saved my life, you know."

Her heart plunged as he turned away, but she couldn't bring herself to grab his sleeve. She watched him approach one of the matrons and ask her to dance.

During the following song, he danced with Helen, and then with another lady. A while later Ivy Tuttle blushed and giggled in his arms. Sunny could scarcely breathe for watching him move farther and farther across the room.

If she could just get outside, she thought, perhaps she'd be able to make her way home. She'd have to forget him, she told herself. As she started through the crowd, which had gathered around the dancers, she heard a commotion toward the back of the hall where the doors stood open to the night's cool air.

The way ahead of Sunny parted. Cale was standing in the doorway, a gun and gun belt strapped to his hips, and a shotgun in his hands. He looked sloppy and unshaven, more drunk than Sunny had ever seen him. He advanced into the room with a look of belligerence on his face that made her blood run cold.

Behind him, May Sue looked as if she was trying to make herself invisible. She cast fearful glances at those gawking at her and her shabby satin dress. Sunny saw deep purple circles beneath May Sue's eyes, and the smudges on her cheeks that were dried tears—apparently the trademark of the McKidrict women—like the bruises. Had Cale struck her? Sunny would have a word with him about that!

Cale didn't see Sunny as he stumbled into the crowd, his gaze sweeping every face until he saw the one he was seeking. Spying Bar on the dance floor, whirling a laughing twelve-year-old girl a foot off the floor, Cale's eyes narrowed to murderous slits. He planted his feet, made a move to level the shotgun at Bar, but a dozen men caught the barrel and tore the weapon from his hands.

"Get hold of yourself, son," one of them cried. "There's women and children present. What's ailin' you?"

Cale's molten glare slid to the man and then back to Bar. As the music died, Bar stopped dancing. Everyone backed away, watching breathlessly for Bar to respond to the challenge of the McKidrict facing him.

Taking in Cale's appearance, Bar let the girl he was dancing with go and stepped forward. "Are you looking for me, McKidrict?"

Sunny felt her mother and Frank close in behind her. She backed into their welcome protection.

"What's wrong?" Helen whispered. "That's how Luck used to look when . . ."

Frank shushed her.

"I reckon you've been expecting this, Landry," Cale said. "You got anything to say to my sister?" He jerked May Sue closer.

The hall went so quiet Sunny could hear her heart drumming.

Bar looked confused. "I'm sorry that I had to bring in Johnsie, May Sue, if that's what you're upset about, but he robbed the bank and—"

"Not that, you damned jackass." Cale looked around, his face turning red. "I mean, about the wedding we're goin' to have here tonight."

"I don't think I know what you're talking about," Bar said, his tone growing wary.

May Sue stifled a cry, and Cale shot her a blazing look.

"Just hush up, girl! Okay, Landry, since you're goin' to stand there and play dumb, I'll refresh your memory. You done had relations with my sister up at that boardinghouse where you was staying when me and her got evicted from our place."

May Sue winced.

Sunny's heart shivered to a stop.

Helen gasped as folks drew up all around to look at her askance. Frank stared them down.

"You done welcomed her up at that cabin, too, but then you threw her off when you was done with your dalliance. She's expecting a little stranger now, and I'm here to see that you do the right thing."

25

Sunny couldn't believe what she'd just heard. May Sue pregnant? Was it possible? May Sue and Johnsie, perhaps, but not May Sue and Bar.

"You're mistaken, Cale," Sunny said, stepping forward, her voice sounding strong.

Cale whirled on her and snarled, "This ain't none of your affair, Sunny." He drew his gun.

Women began herding children out the back. The hall, which had been suffocatingly crowded moments before, thinned to an assortment of steadfast townsmen and ranchers.

Howard Ivery came closer, scribbling on his little notebook. Sunny noticed Ol' Foote on the fringes of the crowd, watching Cale with a terrible gleam in his eye.

The sheriff pushed his way past the fleeing women and children. "What's going on here?" he bellowed.

"Holster that gun, McKidrict, 'fore I take it from you. You're in a public assembly, for pity's sake."

"He's got my sister in a pickle, Sheriff!" Cale cried, as he reluctantly holstered the gun. "It ain't right he should get away with it."

"Look, Ma," Sunny whispered to her mother. "Do you think Ol' Fart's been—I mean, Ol' Foote's been drinking? He looks so odd."

Helen and Frank noticed Foote's peculiar expression. Frank motioned for his fellow merchants to watch the man.

Another man emerged from the crowd which was closing in around Cale. Sunny recognized him as the Texan who had been interested in buying the McKidrict ranch. She hadn't heard that he was back.

"Excuse me, Sheriff," the man said in his mellow southern accent. When the sheriff frowned, the distinguished looking rancher refreshed his memory. "Purvine."

"When'd you get back in town, Texas? It's all your fault, this business with the McKidricts. If it wasn't for you going after the ranch, Foote never would have tried buying up McKidrict's debts, McKidrict never woulda got shot in that holdup, and we'd all be havin' a good time right about now."

"I can see that hard feelings have arisen because of my efforts to assist a very dear friend." Purvine surveyed the men around him. "Would you allow me to explain, gentlemen?"

"This ain't none of your affair, either," Cale grumbled.

"But perhaps it is." Seeing that Cale was too confused to protest further, Purvine continued.

"Friends," he said, turning to address the crowd, "I

wrote the banker, Ethridge Foote, some months past, asking if the bank held any land that might be available for sale. I have acquired ranches in this manner numerous times in the past."

Bar moved in closer. "It's not necessary to distract Cale, Mr. Purvine. I'm not the father of May Sue's child. Cale will soon see that his sister has made a slight miscalculation."

Purvine smiled. "I'm sure it is unnerving to be the accused for once, Mr. Landry, but do let me continue. You see, I didn't really intend to buy McKidrict's ranch."

A murmur of surprise rippled through the crowd.

"I came to see how the McKidrict children had fared in the ten years since their mother's disappearance. I was alarmed to discover that their father had just died in the holdup, yet for my purposes, it was a blessing."

"You're glad our pa's dead?" May Sue cried.

Purvine turned to her and a look of pity came over his face. "My dear Miss May Sue, yes, I most certainly am glad. There is someone who wishes to see you again, but for years she has been afraid to return and risk her husband's wrath."

Purvine paused to survey the rapt faces all around.

"With Luck McKidrict dead, your dear mother is free to reveal herself at last. Julia asks that you forgive her for leaving and listen to her story. Those of you here tonight may or may not know that Julia was regularly subjected to the cruelest of abuses at her husband's hand. The night she fled this town she had been beaten nearly to death. This kind lady," he said, indicating Helen, "and her late husband, were Julia's only friends. They provided the money necessary for

Julia to escape her fate, for surely Luck McKidrict would have eventually killed her."

"You're a dirty liar!" Cale shouted.

May Sue just stared in disbelief.

"How come you know so much about Julia McKidrict?" the sheriff asked.

"I've been her closest friend for years. She has recovered her physical wounds, but her heart is still broken. I haven't a hope of marrying her until she has seen her children again, and sadly, when I returned to Texas I had to tell her that Lyford had met his death as well."

Cale pulled his gun again. "I don't believe a word of it. My ma's dead. She has to be, or else she never would have stayed away so long."

"I beg to disabuse your mind, son—"

"I ain't no man's son now," Cale yelled. He brandished his weapon. Whirling, he grabbed May Sue's arm and jerked her forward. "I came here to get my sister married up to the man who—"

"Cale," Bar said firmly, and calmly, "I have never laid a hand on May Sue. Tell your brother, May Sue. Johnsie is the father of your child."

"But Johnsie's in jail!" May Sue wailed.

Cale glared at May Sue. "You tryin' to make a fool out'a me?"

"Are you goin' to make Bar marry me?" she shot back.

His jaw clenched, Cale twisted around, causing everyone nearby to rear back. He marched up to Bar and glared up into his eyes. "She says you dallied with her. I say you marry her or else I shoot you down right here."

Sunny caught Bar's arm, reassuring herself by the

firm muscled warmth of it, that the world wasn't spinning out of control. She recognized the woman approaching behind Mr. Purvine as Julia McKidrict.

"May Sue, sugar? Don't you remember me?"

"Ma?" May Sue whispered, beginning to weep.

Cale just kept glaring, shaking his head, looking around as if trying to make sense of everything.

Then Ethridge Foote stepped forward. The men standing next to him looked ready to grab him.

Foote whipped his pistol from his vest and pointed it at Cale and May Sue. "If she's carryin', it's likely an incestuous idiot like all the rest of the McKidricts. Mongrels, the lot of them. They shouldn't be allowed to live, and I'm here to see that they don't, same as I saw to their pa. When I saw my chance I took it. Same as now."

And he fired before anyone realized he meant what he said.

Cale went down wounded, firing his own gun as he fell.

Cries of alarm went up everywhere, filling the hall with a din of terror and confusion.

Cale shot again and again toward the ceiling.

Somewhere, Julia's cry rang out. Purvine gave a shout to take cover. The sheriff was yelling, too. All Sunny could see was Foote's hate-filled eyes, and the pistol turning toward her, toward Bar, toward May Sue.

As another shot rang out, Sunny had no time to react. All she saw was Bar throwing himself forward. May Sue stood frozen, staring at the pistol aimed directly at her belly.

Struggling to get up, Cale fired again. The bullet struck Foote in the center of his chest as he was firing and threw him back. His pistol went flying, discharging again as it went.

Sunny covered her ears. May Sue was still standing. Cale doubled over and commenced to groan. Foote lay flat on his back, dead.

Sunny turned to where Bar had been standing seconds before. He wasn't there.

Woodenly, she looked to the place where he had lunged, the place between Foote's pistol and May Sue's belly. Then she looked down. She saw a white linen shirt spattered with blood.

Bar was lying face down on the floor.

Everything stopped.

If the hall was in complete confusion, Sunny didn't notice. Almost instantly she fell to her knees beside Bar. Someone touched her. Someone else spoke. She didn't notice or hear. All she could see was spatters of red. Her mind refused to take it in.

As someone rolled Bar onto his back, she quickly cradled his head. "Bar," she whispered.

Someone pushed the onlookers back and crouched on the other side of Bar. It was the doctor. He tore Bar's shirt open to find the wound. Sunny found blood on her hand as she reached to smoothe back Bar's hair.

"Bar," she whispered more loudly.

"It could be bad," the doctor whispered.

Sunny shook her head. She leaned close. "Bar! You are going to be just fine." She pressed her lips to his soft mouth. She could almost feel the life force draining from him.

His eyes fluttered open a little, and he looked around, at the faces so near, at the open beams overhead, at Sunny. He smiled. It was a soft smile, dimming quickly. His eyes went out of focus and drooped. "He . . . shot Lyford."

"Foote?" Sunny said.

"And McKidrict, too," someone said. "Crazy ol' coot."

"My pa," Bar said softly.

Sunny grabbed his shoulders. "What about your pa? Stay with us, Bar!"

"Get back, Sunny," the doctor said. "I've got to get him to my office. That bullet's got to come out right now."

She didn't release her hold on him. "Bar! Don't leave me!"

Bar's faint smile returned. His eyes rolled, then settled on Sunny's face.

"Sun . . . flower," he breathed. "He . . . took the bullet . . . meant for me."

For just an instant Sunny was confused. "Your father?" she said, understanding then. "Your father died to save you from being shot?"

He looked into her eyes and she felt him touch her soul.

"Bar, you'll be just fine."

"Don't cry, Sunflower. I've made it . . . right. I've taken the bullet . . . meant for her."

Sunny could scarcely muffle the cry of anguish that erupted from her throat. She didn't hear anything else going on around her, the people tending to Cale's wounded arm, the men carrying Foote's body out the side door, or Julia McKidrict, with Purvine's help, comforting the wailing, hysterical May Sue.

She saw only Bar.

At last she truly understood what had happened to him. His father had given his life to save him. Now

Bar had sacrificed himself to save May Sue and her baby.

As if by holding him she could keep him from dying, Sunny grabbed Bar's shirt and never let go even after four men lifted Bar from the floor and carried him quickly across town to the doctor's office.

"You've got to get out of the way now, Sunny," the doctor said, trying to pry her fingers loose of their hold on Bar's shirt once Bar was lying on the surgery table.

"I'll help," she said. "I'm not leaving him."

"Wash up, then."

Sunny's back ached. Her eyes burned from lack of sleep, but she kept her vigil at Bar's bedside. She couldn't remember the last few days. She knew only that she was sitting in the rocker in her father's office again. Bar was on the cot, looking much as he had that first night with his fever.

Even though it was the middle of summer, a fire was burning in the hearth, and it was raining. The doctor came and went at regular intervals. "There's nothing more we can do," he said each time. Helen and Frank had come back to assist Sunny in her ministrations. Sunny felt as if she was struggling in a fog.

Bar didn't wake. Some whispered he might be like that for the rest of his natural life. Sunny wouldn't listen.

She didn't accept the invitation to May Sue's and Johnsie's wedding that was held in the jail because she wanted to be at Bar's side when he came around. Julia and Charles Purvine returned to Texas to be married, too. Sunny had heard that Cale was all right. Tomasina and her boy had visited him and remarked that he seemed different. Sober.

When Homer crept into the office to see Bar, his misshapen face contorted with anguish, Sunny had felt certain that Bar would wake for him. Homer even sang for his friend, "Come nigh, lil' Johnny, forty telliue a stowwee . . ." but Bar didn't wake.

All Sunny could do was sit and wait and pray.

Bar struggled a long time to find his way through the dreams that held him in the murky fog that existed between life and death. When he was finally able to open his eyes, he found himself lying in Abel Summerlin's office. He wondered for a moment if all he remembered happening between himself and Sunny Summerlin had been just a dream.

Then he saw her, seated on the chair, asleep. Moaning, Sunny slumped forward to lean against his side, hold his arm, and place her head on his shoulder. Her cool chestnut waves rippled across his arm. It took all his strength to whisper her name.

Waking, Sunny straightened and rubbed her eyes. She looked so very tired, Bar thought. Suddenly her expression brightened. "Bar," she said. "Are you back?" Her smile looked like the sun.

"I'm . . ." No sound came from his throat. "I love you," was all he could say.

Tears welled in her eyes as she laid her hands against his cheek and kissed him ever so softly. "Heavenly Father, thank you."

*   *   *

With the approach of autumn, the aspens in the narrow canyon had turned to gold. Sunny found a place to stop the buckboard and gave a satisfied nod of her head. "Here we are."

Bar drank in the beauty of the fall day. "I've missed this place."

She set the brake and climbed down to assist Bar to the ground. Still weak from his lengthy recovery, Bar gently pulled Sunny into his embrace. He looked a long while into her eyes and then pressed a kiss to her lips that kindled all the fires of her soul. "Have I told you yet today how much I love you?" he asked.

"A thousand times, in a thousand ways."

"I'd like to tell you in one particularly special way."

"Sh-h-h! You're a sick man." She tossed him a flirtatious little smile.

"Not so sick that I can't want you with all my heart."

She pretended to be stern. "In time, my darling. In time."

They made their way across the creek and slowly up the steep path to the campsite abandoned so long ago.

"Are you all right?" she asked, noting his strained expression.

He nodded.

The cabin looked the same as Bar had left it, but the tent had long since fallen in. Amid the ashes of the campfire was the gun case and custom-made gun, a lump of metal and char now, never to be used again.

"When did you do that?" Sunny asked.

"Just before the dance."

She was more glad than she would admit.

Everywhere they looked, from every place a seed had fallen, a tall plant with big waving leaves and large yellow blooms nodded in the breeze.

"Oh, look!" Sunny cried, going to the cabin door and pointing.

Bar joined her and laughed to see sunflowers blooming inside as if the place were their own secret garden.

"I feel as if I've been gone so long," he said. "What would have become of me if I hadn't stumbled upon you that first day?"

"What would have become of me," she said, gazing up at him.

"Will you marry me, Sunny?" Bar asked softly, caressing her with his eyes.

"Yes, I will."

"We'll go back east for our wedding trip, and I'll see about my law degree."

She nodded. "And then we'll come home and fill those empty bedrooms with lots of laughing children?"

"And Homer will work for us," he said.

"He'll like that. When May Sue gets back from her visit to Texas, I'll piece a quilt for her baby."

"We'll take supper at your mother's new restaurant."

Sunny laughed. "I swear, that mother of mine will never stop working."

Bar grinned. "And Johnsie will run errands for Frank after he gets out of jail. Who would have thought in all that confusion over the bank robbery that Foote shot and killed McKidrict."

She shook her head. "I still hate to think about it. At least Cale's got the ranch back."

"And Johnsie won't hang." Bar hugged her.

"Don't ever leave me again, Bar. Please," she whispered.

"Sunflower," he said, "you're stuck with me. After Doc gives me a clean bill of health, we're going to have the biggest wedding and rowdiest reception Cassidy County has ever seen."

Sunny molded her body against his and marveled at the power of love.

CIRCLE IN THE WATER by Susan Wiggs

When a beautiful gypsy thief crossed the path of King Henry VIII, the king saw a way to exact revenge against his enemy, Stephen de Lacey, by forcing the insolvent nobleman to marry the girl. Stephen wanted nothing to do with his gypsy bride, even when he realized Juliana was a princess from a far-off land. But when Juliana's past returned to threaten her, he realized he would risk everything to protect his wife. "Susan Wiggs creates fresh, unique and exciting tales that will win her a legion of fans."—Jayne Ann Krentz

DESTINED TO LOVE by Suzanne Elizabeth

In the tradition of her first time travel romance, *When Destiny Calls*, comes another humorous adventure. Josie Reed was a smart, gutsy, twentieth-century doctor who was tired of the futile quest for a husband before she reached thirty. Then she went on the strangest blind date of all—back to the Wild West of 1881 with a fearless, half-Apache, outlaw.

A TOUCH OF CAMELOT by Donna Grove

The winner of the 1993 Golden Heart Award for best historical romance. Guinevere Pierce had always dreamed that one day her own Sir Lancelot would rescue her from a life of medicine shows and phony tent revivals. But she never thought he would come in the guise of Cole Shepherd.

SUNFLOWER SKY by Samantha Harte

A poignant historical romance between an innocent small town girl and a wounded man bent on vengeance. Sunny Summerlin had no idea what she was getting into when she rented a room to an ill stranger named Bar Landry. But as she nursed him back to health, she discovered that he was a bounty hunter with an unquenchable thirst for justice, and also the man with whom she was falling in love.

TOO MANY COOKS by Joanne Pence

Somebody is spoiling the broth in this second delightful adventure featuring the spicy romantic duo from *Something's Cooking*. Homicide detective Paavo Smith must find who is killing the owners of popular San Francisco restaurants and, at the same time, come to terms with his feelings for Angelina Amalfi, the gorgeous but infuriating woman who loves to dabble in sleuthing.

JUST ONE OF THOSE THINGS by Leigh Riker

Sara Reid, having left her race car driver husband and their glamorous but stormy marriage, returns to Rhode Island in the hope of protecting her five-year-old daughter from further emotional harm. Then Colin McAllister arrives—bringing with him the shameful memory of their one night together six years ago and a life-shattering secret.

COMING NEXT MONTH

COMANCHE MAGIC by Catherine Anderson
The latest addition to the bestselling Comanche series. When Chase Wolf first met Fanny Graham, he was immediately attracted to her, despite her unsavory reputation. Long ago Fanny had lost her belief in miracles, but when Chase Wolf came into her life he taught her that the greatest miracle of all was true love.

SEPARATING by Susan Bowden
The triumphant story of a woman's comeback from a shattering divorce to a fulfilling, newfound love. After twenty-five years of marriage, Riona Jarvin's husband leaves her for a younger woman. Riona is in shock—until she meets a new man and finds that life indeed has something wonderful to offer her.

HEARTS OF GOLD by Martha Longshore
A sizzling romantic adventure set in 1860s Sacramento. For years Kora Hunter had worked for the family newspaper, but now everyone around her was insisting that she give it up for marriage to a long-time suitor and family friend. Meanwhile, Mason Fielding had come to Sacramento to escape from the demons in his past. Neither he nor Kora expected a romantic entanglement, considering the odds stacked against them.

IN MY DREAMS by Susan Sizemore
Award-winning author Susan Sizemore returns to time travel in this witty, romantic romp. In ninth-century Ireland, during the time of the Viking raids, a beautiful young druid named Brianna inadvertently cast a spell that brought a rebel from 20th-century Los Angeles roaring back through time on his Harley-Davidson. Sammy Bergen was so handsome that at first she mistook him for a god—but he was all too real.

SURRENDER THE NIGHT by Susan P. Teklits
Lovely Vanessa Davis had lent her talents to the patriotic cause by seducing British soldiers to learn their battle secrets. She had never allowed herself to actually give up her virtue to any man until she met Gabriel St. Claire, a fellow Rebel spy and passionate lover.

SUNRISE by Chassie West
Sunrise, North Carolina, is such a small town that everyone knows everyone else's business—or so they think. After a long absence, Leigh Ann Warren, a burned out Washington, D.C., police officer, returns home to Sunrise. Once there, she begins to investigate crimes both old and new. Only after a dangerous search for the truth can Leigh help lay the town's ghosts to rest and start her own life anew with the one man meant for her.

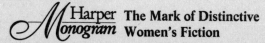